Atramentum et Telum Pulvis

ALINA COMSA

BOOK 3 OF THE LOST HOPE SERIES

First Published in Great Britain in 2024 by

Malum Canticus Books in collaboration with In Somnis Publishing

Edited by: Aneta Easton (LiteraFix)

Cover design by: Malum Canticus Books

Cover elements by: Siiri Becker (Ultrasonic Assets)

Character Art by: Oleelaw DigiARTPH,

Formatting: Malum Canticus Books

Proofreading: Aneta Easton, In Somnis Publishing, Malum Canticus Books

E-book ISBN: 978-1-7385278-4-7

Print ISBN: 978-1-7385278-5-4

Contents

Dedication

This is for the misunderstood. It's not for anyone to judge what hides under the cover. They don't get to judge the presentation either. You're strong. You're worthy. Fight!

Mr. Right, thank you for supporting me even though you absolutely cannot understand WHY I'm writing. <3 You rock my cotton socks. I love you more than coffee and chocolate during the monthly descension of dragons.

Blurb

My entire life I've been blinded by distrust, forever damaged by the selfish choices of those meant to choose me first. Finding my father at the bottom of a bottle while my mother sneaked around with another man obliterated all my foolish hopes for a happy family.
It's only fitting that I stay in Lost Hope. Twenty years later, my mother's betrayal still smarts against my skin. The steel walls around my heart are reinforced when my son is abandoned at birth by his own mother; and my distrust in women cements.
Until an unexpected Thanksgiving dinner ends with HER in the close-confines of my car.
Quiet, reserved, and impossibly beautiful, she puts a spell on me.
Between my deep-rooted obsession and her innocent curiosity, we strike a deal. A one-night deal that ends with the sunrise.
Except... one taste is not enough. My instincts to run away fade into nothingness with every stolen glance and possessive touch. Her lips are forbidden to me, yet all I think about.
I may wear a badge, but I'm no wallflower's knight in shining armor.
So what does it say about me when all I want is to destroy the wallflower of Lost Hope with my love?

This book has been an absolute blast to write. Well, just under half of it. The other was pure emotional angst and rage. Welcome back to Lost Hope, the small town surrounded by mountains, where wandering souls come to find a place to hide, and instead, find a place to heal.

I hope you enjoy the laughs and the groveling. But mostly the groveling. Maddox's story is full of up-and-downs, much like the man himself. He's a self-declared asshole, and everyone in town supports the theory. Let's see if you agree by the end.

For the best reading experience, it is recommended to start with *Lege et Lacrima* and continue with the order the books are released in. Each novel has the spotlight on a different couple, but the main story continues in subsequent books.

Latin words and their meaning in Atramentum et Telum Pulvis:

- **Atramentum et Telum Pulvis:** Ink and Gunpowder.

- **Lege et Lacrima:** Read It and Weep.

Because my main characters have gone and made friends with a burly, surly Irishman, expect to find some very creative Irish swearing. It's the accent, I'm telling ya'. I can't help myself.

We also have a mini-main character who absolutely refuses to roll his Rs. But he's the cutest four-year-old with a massive crush on grapes, so he's forgiven. Expect to find some Ryker-isms throughout the book.

Radio-calls used throughout the book:

10-67 - Person calling for help

11-71 - Fire

10-97 - Arrived at the scene

10-8 - In service/Available for assignment

Trigger Warnings:

I take mental health issues with the utmost seriousness. I don't speak in the name of anyone but myself. The issues portrayed in *Atramentum et Telum Pulvis* are issues portrayed not as textbook and not generalized, but based on my opinions, views, or reactions. Not two experiences are identical, and not two individuals survive through them in the same manner.

If you ever find yourself in any of the situations depicted, please find help. You are not alone.

The following sensitive subjects are touched in the book, either by mention or graphic depiction, and I've done my absolute best to treat them with the sensibility and care these subjects deserve. Please note, this is not a dark romance, even though the MMC has occasionally been... off-white morally. As such, any touch on an unhealthy relationship does not describe the relationship between the main characters.

Atramentum et Telum Pulvis has the following trigger warnings:

Mentions:

- cheating

- alcohol abuse

- death

- bullying

- sexual assault

- emotional abuse

- abusive relationship

- child abandonment

Graphic:

- Assault

- Attempted murder

- CPR

- Degradation Kink

- Dub-con

- Fire

- Hospitalization

- Infertility

- Profanity

- Sexually explicit scenes

Your mental health is a priority.

Atramentum et Telum Pulvis **is the third book in the Lost Hope series of interconnected standalone novels. It's a single dad romance with a pinch of suspense, complete with HEA, and a cliff-hanger introducing book four of the series. This book is intended for readers 18+, with explicit scenes, mature language, touching on sensitive topics, and more.**

Playlist

♡Eminem - Mockingbird♡
♡Julia Michaels - Heaven♡
♡Austin Giorgio - You put a spell on me♡
♡BRKN Heart - River (cover)♡
♡EMO -Promises♡
♡Antonia - Marionette♡
♡SIA - Fire Meet Gasoline♡
♡The Script - Breakeven♡
♡Rag'n'Bone Man - Human♡
♡Kat Leon & Sam Tinnesz - I'll make you love me♡
♡Maneskin - Beggin'♡
♡Nana Mouskouri - Over and Over♡

Prologue

I've never been in love. Not a day in my life. Never saw myself tied up to one woman. I like women just fine, but only trust them as far as I can throw them. Unless I'm tossing them on a bed to have my wicked way with them, there's no throwing of any kind. No trust either.

We can all thank my momma for that. Everyone sees the beautiful, kindhearted Lucy. The whisperer of vegetables, master of fruits. No one sees the heartless cheater who nearly destroyed me and my father twenty years ago.

I've learned my lesson the hard way with every trip up the stairs, carrying a drunk-out-of-his-mind Peter Lawson to sleep; with every trash bag full of bottles I emptied; with every suitcase full of my mother's clothes I packed and moved to the middle of our living room when I've had enough of his alcohol and her wandering ways.

It took me the better part of two decades to come to terms with my father's decision to forgive her. No one wishes for their parents to divorce. But teenager Maddox desperately wanted Dad to let her go. Adult Maddox forgave her—I've just never forgotten.

Sure, they're happy now. They've been happy for a while. If I were a better man, I could've tossed my coin and hoped it landed on my own happily ever after. But I value my sanity more. I trust fate just about as much as I trust women. And if the price I have to pay to keep my sanity and pride intact is loneliness with the occasional meaningless fuck, I'll gladly pay it. Nothing is ever what it seems. Least of all my own family.

So it makes no sense why, after thirty-four years of life, I fell obsessively and desperately in love with *her*.

The one who hates me.

The one who can't stand the goddamned sight of me.

My son's laughter startles me from the doom and gloom gutter my mind took a direct dive in. I blink against the last rays of sun as it sets behind the mountains. Ryker runs in circles around the swing set in my parents' backyard, unconcerned with the bite of chill lingering in the air. He's chasing imaginary foes and mighty dragons, poking at nothing with a stick that's about as sharp as a yoga mat.

My beliefs of staying away from any relationship were reinforced when he was born. My son came with a blue blanket, a binky, and a shiny piece of paper stating his mother ended her parental rights. And he's been the love of my life ever since. When the midwife placed him in my arms, all chubby cheeks and upturned nose, wrinkled like he was pushing a hundred instead of mere minutes, I swore I'd always protect him.

Was I prepared to be a father? Fuck no. Was I prepared to leave the hospital with a newborn in my arms and absolutely zero fucking knowledge of what to do with him? Definitely not. But I ground my teeth and pushed forward, just like I always do. I learned how to change a filthy diaper, how to soothe his cries, how to be a good enough dad so that he never feels unwanted and abandoned.

"Daddy, look. Are you looking? DADDY!" Ryker shrieks as he battles mercilessly with the trunk of a weathered cherry tree.

I slap my palms on my knees and force myself to stand. Every fucking joint in my body creaks and protests, a tired sigh rushing out of me. I force a smile onto my face. My son doesn't need to suffer my foul mood.

"What are you fighting there, partner?"

"Daddy, you gots to save me," he cries out as he throws himself backward onto the dried-out grass. "S-save me, D-Daddy."

I roll my eyes at his theatrics, but jog to his side anyway, falling dramatically to my knees. Warmth rushes through my chest at the wide smile on his face. His blue eyes watch my every move, so much trust shining back at me that for a second my breath stalls in my lungs.

He's my carbon copy, my mini-me, from his light brown hair down to his second toe—just a touch longer than his big toe.

"Daddy, you gots to save the fairy. The dragon snatched her up. Take my sword." He hurriedly throws the stick at me, and I scramble to catch it midair before it pokes my eye out. If my stomach churns and flutters at the object of my brave rescue, well, that's nothing a swift jab of the toothpick I have for a weapon won't fix.

I jump to my feet and do my best impersonation of a world-class fencer, jabbing and withdrawing, dancing quickly and nimbly from one side to the other of the tree trunk. Groaning and grunting, I duck and attack. For a wounded knight, Ryker has entirely too much fun, giggling away behind me, being no help whatsoever in my brave fight against the mighty dragon.

"Boys, dinner is ready," my mom shouts from the porch.

I drop the stick and pat the rough bark. "You put up quite the fight, but you're no match for me," I say in my most menacing voice. "You have until after dinner to return the fai-princess to us. If not, I shall make me an armor from your scales."

A soft breeze rustles the few yellowed leaves still braving the start of the fall.

"Yeeees, Daddy, you did it. Look, he's shaking in fear," Ryker squeals.

I narrow my eyes and point two fingers at the tree, then at my face. "He'd better. He knows I'm watching." I bend and scoop Ryker up, hoisting him onto my hip. He lays his head on my chest, patting my abdomen with his small palm.

I dread going home tonight. He's staying with my parents for the weekend, their monthly tradition—a grandson-spoiling-fest. In the past, I welcomed the break. As much as I love being his father, having a couple of days for myself every month was a godsend. Until now.

Now all that's waiting for me are four cold walls and silence. I would've drunk myself stupid tonight, give my liver a reason to exist, if I wasn't on patrol duty tomorrow. As it is, I'll lay in my bed, staring at the ceiling, contemplating all my fucking choices from the past seven months that led me to this point.

The point of no return.

The point where my ribcage caves in, constricting my heart. Longing floods my veins, and I hug Ryker tighter to me. With the heel of my palm, I rub the center of my chest in a futile attempt to plug the hole that opened up inside of me when I let her go. I swallow down the lump of devastation in my throat.

I made the right decision.

My mind screams at me that I'm a goddamn liar. I can't be right when every fucking cell inside my body feels tethered to her, and the distance I forced between us hurts worse than any pain I've ever experienced in my life. Cutting one of my limbs off with a rusty saw would've felt less torturous than the past twenty-four hours since I've turned my back on her and run away like a coward. Just like my father. The apple doesn't fall far from the tree.

The haze from earlier settles over my shoulders, pressing heavy against me, dulling the colors around. I go through the motions of washing Ryker's hands, then mine, before dropping him in his booster chair next to my place at the table. I cut his portion of grilled chicken breast with the precision of a neurosurgeon.

My parents are chattering away, seemingly distracted, going over the numbers at Lucy's Market, but I know if I dare to lift my head and look at either of them, they'll see right through me. So I cut away at Ryker's dinner and count the peas I dropped onto his plate, one round green blob at the time. It's for his sake that I'm sat at this godforsaken table in the first place. My son deserves to have people in his life who love him.

I have no reason to feel so empty, so bereft of everything that's good and pure in life. My son is happy and healthy. If anything, I should feel proud. I have a roof over my head. I'm surrounded by family. Absolutely nothing is wrong in my life.

Except…

My phone vibrates in the pocket of my jeans. I throw a cautious look at my mom, knowing she'll rip me a new one if I answer it at the table, but being Chief Deputy and in charge of the Lost Hope Police Department doesn't leave me much choice. I might be doing shifts like all the deputies working under me, but some things require either my presence or the sheriff's. I don't see Richards coming all the way from Forrest Falls because answering the phone at the dinner table offends Lucy Lawson's sensibilities.

A peek at my screen has me biting my tongue. I hesitate to answer for a heartbeat or two. Nothing good can come out of this, I know that for a fact. But I also know I don't have it in me to just hit *ignore*. I push back from the table and hurry to the kitchen before accepting the call. My phone is plastered to my ear, my heart hammering in my chest in its desperate attempt to escape my ribcage and jump through the device straight into her soft palms.

"Hey…" I whisper, my voice soft and soothing, but the rest of my words die on my tongue as the scuffle on the other end of the call intensifies. My blood turns to ice in my veins. A shiver runs up my spine and nausea churns in my stomach, the few bites of dinner I managed to choke down earlier sitting like lead in my gut. "Stay on the phone if you can," I bark, although I have no hope that she heard me.

A few taps of my finger against the screen bring up the map. The red dot blinks at me, mocking me with the distance between us. I have to get to her.

In three long strides, I'm back in the dining room. Three pairs of eyes fixate on me, my father lifting a questioning, bushy eyebrow. I shake my head, but I'm sure he can see in the pallor of my cheeks that something's not quite right.

Not quite right is a goddamn understatement. A fucking catastrophe is more accurate.

I kiss Ryker's forehead and bolt out the door as fast as my legs can take me. My limbs grow numb by the time I jump into my truck, turning the key so fast, for a second, I fear I broke it.

Fumbling with my phone, I somehow manage to keep my eyes on the road as I move the call on speaker and mute my microphone. My teeth sink into my bottom lip to keep the curses at bay; to keep the rage contained. I grip the wheel so hard, my knuckles turn white. With a flick of my finger, I turn the warning lights on, but keep the siren silent.

This is all my fucking fault. What have I done?

My truck eats up the miles between us. When I finally reach her neighborhood on the outskirts of Lost Hope, the blue dot showing my location nearly overlaps the red one, and I brake hard. My tires squeal on the gravel as I park my car on the side of the road and jump out, leaving the engine running.

Her whimpers reach my ears, and all I see is red. I'll fucking kill him. I'll rip him apart limb from limb. A high-pitched ringing sounds in my ears, drowning out any other noises as I tackle the motherfucker to the ground and start pummeling his fucking face. He tries to fight back, but I'm fueled by pure madness. His feeble attempts to shield his head are no match for the inferno raging up inside of me. When I'm done with him, there won't be a goddamned cell left for DNA match.

He shifts his arm, a silvery flash penetrating the veil of red settled over my eyes. I freeze. My heart stops. The ringing in my ears ceases abruptly. The world fucking stills with that one flash of the streetlight hitting the bloodied knife he's fisting.

No.

NO.

Fuck. *NO.*

He cries out when I twist his wrist until I hear a snap, and the knife drops to the ground. I kick it with my boot away from him in my haste to get to her. My hands shake, desperate to stop the relentless crimson river spilling through my fingers and onto the dirty, dusty pavement.

I've never been in love. Not a day in my life. Not until I fell obsessively and desperately in love with *her*.

The one who hates me.

The one who can't stand the goddamned sight of me.

The one currently bleeding out on the filthy ground of a darkened, cold side-street.

PART ONE

A season for change.

"Because there's nothing more painful than
existing with no meaning;
My days hold no light, my nights bereft of stars.
Your eyes too cold, your touch too hot,
my soul is singed.
I bear your mark."

SAWYER CARTER

Chapter One

Sawyer

I discreetly cover my yawn with the back of my hand. If the pint-size masters of torture see even the smallest sign of weakness, they'll pounce. When working with children aged two-to-five, the witching hour is 2 p.m. The crankiness is dialed up to maximum. It's when they become restless and unsettled, waiting for their parents to pick them up. If even one of them singles me out, wanting a bit of extra special attention, they all descend.

I peek through my lashes at the twenty-three kids in my care, all sprawled out on their colorful mats, listening intently to Andrew as he reads *Beauty and the Beast* to them. It's been completely heaven-sent having the teenager here. What started as community service—courtesy of his mother as punishment for him slashing Lalah's tires last summer—has now turned into a full-blown volunteering service for him.

The sixteen-year-old comes in three times a week to read stories and play with the kids in the afternoon hours. Once everyone has gone home, he stays and helps tidy up the classroom. It has definitely made my life a lot easier. The daycare center is severely understaffed—an issue I plan to fix as soon as the building for Happy Bumblebees is finished being renovated.

I've known since childhood that I was going to work with children. Growing up in a house where my father was mostly absent—first during deployments, then pouring all his efforts into building up Tate's Shop—and my mother, as strong willed as she is, struggling to keep three rambunctious children in line, has stoked this fire inside of me to be a helping hand for overworked, overly-tired parents.

My childhood was beautiful. I never lacked attention, affection, or love. But being the youngest of three meant I was either overlooked or treated like I was breakable. Between the force-of-nature that is my sister Selena and the protective beast that is my brother Tatum, my voice was not always heard or was simply dismissed. I saw my mother struggling, being pulled in ten different directions at the same time; raising her children, cleaning the house, putting food on the table, and working full-time as a kindergarten teacher, all of it took a toll on her.

Her job is what inspired my love for children. Her struggles inspired my ambitions of opening a private daycare center, where parents could trust leaving their offspring while they went to work, or simply wanted a few hours for themselves to just... breathe. It all felt like a pipe dream since I knew I could never source the funds needed to open and maintain a business of this magnitude. Mrs. Mayor did her very best to allocate some funds to the community daycare center, but money was thin everywhere and better used somewhere else.

That is until Lalah moved to Lost Hope last spring. A recluse, always keeping to herself, she assessed all the businesses in town and invested a lot of money to help us keep going. She made fast friends with Tatum and, through him, brought me into their circle as well. It was probably my brother, the one who spilled the beans to Lalah about my dreams of opening Happy Bumblebees.

Using a sneaky invitation to the Thanksgiving dinner she and her group of friends organized, she cornered me and made me tell her all about my plans for the private daycare center. Next thing I knew, we were partnered—with her being a silent investor—and my business plan was fast-tracked. She brought in the architect who designed her house, roped Matt Anderson—who has a construction company—to renovate the building as soon as the plans were ready, and used the mayor's guilt for how her daughter tried to wreck Lalah's life to have all the permits and licenses done with the highest priority.

And now I am mere months away from seeing my dream made into a reality. All I must do is finish the projections spreadsheets and start interviewing to fill in the necessary positions. We're going to start with three full-time teachers, some paid volunteer positions, outsource a cleaning company and a full-time cook to prepare snacks and lunches for the children in our care. Easy-peasy.

My phone buzzes on my desk, and I sneak a glance at the screen.

> *Don't forget about the TBRC book club meeting tomorrow. Choose: sunglasses, flames, snakes, or clairvoyant charms. 11 a.m. Don't be late. It'll be only the base-six.*

Emma

I scrunch my nose at the message one of my best friends sent. Emma Denvers is a new friend to me but managed in three short months to climb to best friend status. Apart from Selena, I didn't have many friends. Between Tatum scaring away anyone who dared look in my direction and my inherent wallflower status, I was never prime friendship material. But Emma and I have an unfortunate thing in common—our bullies.

Trauma-based friendship is a real thing, right?

Emma lived all her life thinking Maddison Brown and Amanda Straton were her friends, only to realize the maliciousness they showed everyone else was also directed at her, just in more subtle ways. After Maddison roofied a drink meant for Lalah that Emma ended up drinking, she cut off all contact with them. And it's all for the best, considering both are awaiting trial for different criminal charges, with Maddison detained and Amanda roaming free on bail.

I shake my head, trying to dispel the sadness and rage flooding my blood whenever I think about those rotten... women. Their evil knows no bounds. While I'd never wish ill on anyone, the world would be a safer place with them locked in a prison and left there to wilt away.

> *I'm excited. I'll be there. Snakes, please.*

Me

> *Of course that's what you chose. Wear a black hoodie; make sure you drown in it. You're lucky I know you and love you.*

> *You should have a bracelet delivered when you get home. That's mandatory, too.*

**Emma

Yes, ma'am. Any other orders I need to comply with or that'd be all for now?

Me

Just get your cute butt here on time.

Emma

I roll my eyes and bite my cheek to stifle a smile as I slide the phone into the hidden pocket of my dress. I'm beyond curious what everyone else has chosen and how it relates to the book. We've only had one book club meeting so far since the To Be Read Café opened its doors just before Lalah's wedding in February. We also have firm rules in place—monthly meetings, locking ourselves inside TBRC, reading the book together, and dressing up in something related to the book. The only one in the know about what we're reading is the person choosing the book of the month, and this month Emma has the honor.

"Miss Sawy?" A sweet voice sounds next to me as the skirt of my dress twists around my thighs. I turn carefully in my seat to see Clara's blonde curls bouncing as she jumps in place, trying to reach for my arm.

"Yes, sweetheart. Are you okay?"

She pulls harder at the pale pink plaids of my dress, so I have no choice but to lift her in my arms.

"Ryker is sad. He has a funny tummy." Clara gasps and giggles when my stomach gurgles. "You have a funny tummy, too."

I give her a smile and stand with her still in my arms. Pretty sure my stomach is funny because of the lunch I skipped to finish going over the dreadful expenses' spreadsheet Blake, Lalah's brother-in-law, put together for me.

"Okay, you little caregiver. Let's see if we can help Ryker," I say and stride to where he's lying curled up in a tight ball on his mat. Clara crawls out of my arms as I crouch at his side and feel his forehead with the back of my hand. The poor thing feels clammy, cold sweat coating my skin as soon as I touch him.

Swallowing down the lump in my throat at seeing his tiny face contorted in pain, I smooth my palm over his damp, soft hair and get Andrew's attention. "Please, could you get Miss Violet here? She should be in the staff kitchen." I'm lucky that today of all days, Violet has afternoon tutoring sessions scheduled.

Andy blinks big green eyes at me, worry creasing his forehead. A chorus of protests sounds as soon as he closes the book and sets it back on the bookshelf.

"Everyone, please settle down. Andrew will return in a minute and continue to read to you, I promise. In the meantime, how about we start tidying up our toys and surprise him with a clean classroom?" I make my voice as cheery as I can, considering the worry weighing down my insides.

"Yes, Miss Sawy," Clara whispers, and I don't miss the concern in her tone. She might only be just shy of her third birthday, but her empathy knows no bounds. And it's her best friend suffering next to us.

Ryker's chubby cheeks are pale, his brow creased, pain etched all over his face. I pick him up carefully, cradling his tiny body in the crook of my arm. He whimpers a sad, pitiful sound, and my heart lurches in my chest. I know I'm not supposed to have favorites, but he is one of mine. Ryker is normally a bundle of joy and smiles—always happy, always full of life, curious beyond belief, with an overactive imagination.

"I'm here, I'm here." Violet rushes through the door, her curly mahogany hair bouncing around her head. "What happened?"

I hoist Ryker higher in my arms, making sure he's comfortable with his head on my shoulder. "We're going to the Infirmary. Could you keep an eye on my class until I return? If I'm not back by the time the parents or your kids start to arrive, just have Jessy at the reception watch over them, please."

"You got it, doll." She turns her back to me and claps her hands once, dismissing me. "Now, let's have some fun, sweet darlings. The fastest helper gets a special golden star from me."

The response from the children in my care is drowned out by the classroom door closing behind me as I hurry up the stairs to the Infirmary room on the second floor of the building.

A sharp antiseptic smell permeates the landing as soon as I clear the narrow hallway. I don't waste time knocking, but stride through the open door, startling Beth—Matt's wife and another volunteer at the daycare center, courtesy of Lalah.

"Sorry, sorry," I rush out. "Ryker is unwell and obviously in pain. One of the kids mentioned his 'tummy is funny'. I'm not sure if that means his stomach hurts or something around his abdomen."

"No worries, Sawyer. Lay him down on the bed, and I'll take a look at what we're dealing with here." She smiles kindly, pointing to an examination bed covered in a large blue paper sheet.

I make sure Ryker is as comfortable as possible and smooth my hand over his head before taking a step back to allow Beth to work her magic on him. My chest constricts, and all my instincts drive me to hover over him, to check for myself that he is doing well. I'm insanely vigilant with all the children in my care, but the urge riding me to pick him up and protect him is unnatural.

So I force myself to turn around and step out into the hallway. I slide my phone out of my hidden pocket and dial Maddox's number. It rings a couple of times before his voicemail kicks in. I sigh and leave a voice message, letting him know of his son's condition, and inform him I will be calling his parents next since they are listed as next of kin and approved for pickup.

I'm sure whatever's ailing Ryker right now, he would feel more comfortable resting and recuperating in his own home, rather than the ratty examination bed he's currently in. Another pained whimper coming from him has me jogging to his side, all my self-doubts pushed aside. I stand by the head of the bed and hold his tiny hand in mine, squeezing it reassuringly.

"I'm here, sweetheart, don't worry," I tell him in as calm of a tone as I can muster, throwing a look at Beth who continues to palpate his abdomen under his green T-shirt.

"My tummy's a big ouch, Miss Sawy," he whines, the pain in his voice pulling at my heartstrings.

"I know, sweetheart. But Mrs. Beth here is going to do her very best to make you feel better soon, okay?"

He nods minutely. Tears brim in his icy-blue eyes, open wide as he stares at me with so much trust, I'm just about to melt in a gooey puddle on the linoleum floor.

"Well, young Lawson," Beth says, and both Ryker and I swivel our heads in her direction, "your tummy looks just fine to me. Which tells me that you most likely ate something a bit too heavy for your stomach. Luckily for you, I have just the magic fix." She winks at him, then spins on her orange crocs and makes her way to a cabinet on the far wall of the room.

I give him a cheerful smile, my entire body relaxing under the relief coursing through my veins. "You'll be just fine, little troublemaker. Can you tell me what you ate today?"

His eyes widen even more and quickly dart to the door before returning to me. His expression turns entirely too innocent for my liking. "Gwapes," Ryker whispers.

I playfully narrow my eyes at him, biting back the laugh threatening to spill past my lips. "How many grapes?"

"All the gwapes," he tells me, awe and wonder in his voice. Oh dear, no wonder his stomach is hurting so much. If Ryker has one weakness, it's grapes—the bigger, the better. We're extra vigilant during lunch hour to ensure he doesn't eat all his snacks, but somehow, he always manages to sneak in more than his allotted portion.

Beth returns with a plastic glass and has him drink a pink concoction, the taste making Ryker grimace adorably. "This should settle his stomach, but I'd recommend he goes home for now. Should be right as rain by dinner time. Is anyone coming to pick him up?"

"I tried calling his father, but he didn't answer. I meant to call his grandparents, but..."

"Don't worry," Beth cuts me off. "How about I let you guys stay here and I'll go give Lucy a call myself?"

"Thank you," I tell her. I don't know what she sees on my face, but I'd be hard pressed to move from his side while he's unwell. "It's you and me, buddy," I murmur to the little boy curled up in my arms.

Chapter Two

Maddox

"**S**hit," I hiss, running a hand through my hair while shoving my phone in the pocket of my jeans with the other.

"What's up, boss man?" Carson, one of my deputies, asks from where he's perched against the reception desk.

"Ryker's teacher called. He's unwell, and she thinks I need to pick him up, but I missed her call. Just finished listening to her voice message."

"Go take care of the little man. We'll hold the fort here and let you know if there's anything urgent."

I give him a salute as thanks and jog outside to my truck. Sawyer said she'd call my parents next, so I quickly send a text in the family group chat to let them know I'm on my way to the daycare and there's no need for them to go.

Worry swirls in the pit of my stomach. No one fucking tells you how much you worry once you become a parent. Everything is a worry; every small thing is a potential danger to your child's life. I'd never forgive myself if I overlooked something, and Ryker would get hurt because of my oversight. I run through our morning routine in my mind, but he seemed fine when I dropped him off.

It's not much of a drive, considering the daycare center is just on the other side of the Town Hall, but if my son is unwell, it's for the best to have the truck close. I push through the doors of the old two-story building. Brook waves at me from behind the desk.

"Afternoon, Chief. Ryker's up in the Infirmary."

"Thanks, Brookie," I reply over my shoulder as I take the stairs three at the time in my haste to reach my son, only to stop dead in my tracks when I clear the landing as if I hit an invisible wall at the sight greeting me.

Sawyer, sitting cross-legged on an examination chair, pink dress covering her legs entirely, sings softly to my son, who's nestled in her lap with his head on her chest. His eyes are closed, but a smile tugs at the corners of his mouth.

I'd be fucking smiling too if I were sitting in her lap with my head on her gorgeous tits.

I clear my throat to draw her attention. It's no business of mine what Sawyer Carter looks like. For fuck's sake, she's my son's teacher. And even if she weren't, she's as off limits to me as a church is to Lucifer. Not only is she younger than me by at least eight years, she's also Tatum's sister. The man already hates my fucking guts. I don't need to give him a reason to murder me in cold blood.

"Oh, hey Maddox, I didn't see you there."

"Just got here," I reply sharply and school my face in an indifferent mask. The goddamn woman just smiles at me. Unwanted warmth surges in my chest at the sparkle in her beautiful navy-blue eyes. "How's Ryker?"

Get a fucking grip, man. Your son is sick. This is not the time to think with your dick, not unless you wanna part with it.

"Better now. His love for grapes is bigger than what his stomach can tolerate. Beth gave him some medicine to help with the bloating and indigestion. He'll be okay by tonight, but she recommended he rest at home."

I can't help the chuckle escaping my throat. Of course, he stuffed himself full of grapes. I don't know where his love for the damn fruits came from. If it were up to him, that's all he'd eat all day, every day.

Three long strides are all it takes for me to get to their side. Bending at the waist, I pick up Ryker from Sawyer's lap, the back of my hand accidentally touching the softness of her breast as I cradle his head in the crook of my arm. Shivers run up my spine. I bite my tongue to stop myself from moaning like a fucking teenager as electricity courses over my skin at the slight touch.

I ignore her gasp. I have to. *Off limits, off limits, off limits.* I might be a bastard only looking to get his cock wet, then part ways with any woman who might warm the sheets of whatever hotel is closest to the bars I frequent, but I made it a fucking rule to never get involved with anyone in Lost Hope.

Even if Tatum wouldn't chop me up and feed me to Lalah's dog, she's not the type of woman I could take to bed for a night and then resume whatever non-relationship we have now. And I've already had a crazy woman on my hands. I don't need a second one sniffing around me.

"Thanks for looking after Ryker. Have a good one," I bark and, turning my back to her, practically run out of the room without giving her a chance to reply.

Fuck me.

I swallow down the embarrassment and guilt swarming my gut. Better she thinks I'm an asshole. Almost everyone in her circle thinks it, anyway. So what if she does, too?

Sawyer Carter means nothing to me.

She's Ryker's teacher, and that's all she'll ever be.

I TOSS AND TURN IN MY BED. Sleep is eluding me, my body keyed up, my cock throbbing in my boxers. Fuck, I will not rub one thinking of how soft and full her breast felt against the back of my hand. I'm not a damn teenager. Rolling over, I press my face into the pillow and groan. This is getting fucking ridiculous.

What I need is to go out and get laid as soon as possible. I haven't had a woman under me for far too long. That's all this is. It's been too damn long since I had a good fuck. My cock is all confused by the lack of action, getting hard at a brief contact with the underside of a breast. But what a goddamn breast... I bet she's packing more than a handful under those prim and proper dresses she always wears.

If I were to cup those gorgeous tits of hers, they'd spill out of my hands so beau- *Bad Maddox.* What I need is an icy cold shower. That would tame the unruly steel pipe in my boxers. No more thinking of Sawyer, or Sawyer's tits, or any enticing body part belonging to her.

I swear the woman is a goddamn witch. If I'm honest with myself, tonight is not the first time I can't sleep because she's living rent-free in my head. One time in my life I've tried to be a gentleman, and, of course, it came back to knee me in the balls.

We grew up in the same town. I've known her since she was a pigtailed toddler, always chasing after her older siblings. I've never paid her any mind. She was just Sawyer, the wallflower of Lost Hope—always in the background, just... there.

Until that fucking Thanksgiving dinner last November.

My first mistake was offering to drive her home. My second mistake was touching her. An innocent brush of my palm against her lower back, an innocent hold of her soft hand as I helped her into my truck. My third mistake was daring to breathe in the close confines of the cab. I swear her perfume has permanently embedded in the leather of my seats... and deep inside my damn lungs. Bergamot, freesia, pear, and the filthiest of my fantasies—that's what she smells like.

Ever since that night, I can't get her out of my head. I'm sure that knowing she is off limits is what makes her so alluring to me. She's not even my goddamn type. I don't get it up for the damsel in distress, and she looks absolutely breakable. The women I fuck are all bold, owning their sexuality and appeal. Sawyer looks like she'd become one with the wallpaper if a man ever winked in her direction.

She's nothing like what I usually go for.

And yet, I can't stop thinking about her.

I go out of my way every single day just to get the smallest glimpse of her. I'm going crazy.

A rustle of sheets and muffled cry comes from the baby monitor on my nightstand. I quickly jump out of bed and make my way to Ryker's bedroom. It's not the first time he ate himself into a nightmare. While it pains my very soul to see my son hurting, I can't help but smile at the cute gluttony he has for grapes. I push the door to his room open, taking in his small form hidden by the covers on his *Lightning McQueen* bed.

"Daddy," he whimpers.

"I'm here, partner," I soothe, scooping him up in my arms and carrying him back to my bedroom. I don't make a habit out of letting him sleep in my bed with me. But, during the nights when bad dreams plague his rest, it's him and me against the world. My son is the love of my fucking life. If it's within my power to make things easier, better, and safer for him, then I'll bend over backward for him. Only ever for him.

Ryker must really be suffering right now because, as soon as his head hits the pillow, his thumb finds the way to his mouth, and he starts suckling on his finger. I settle his weight against my chest, rubbing circles over his stomach, hoping it'll settle his pain and the terrors chasing him as he slumbers away. His rhythmic breathing lulls me to a restless sleep, and my eyelids slide shut.

After what feels like only minutes later, my phone buzzes on my night-stand. Ryker squirms against me, scrambling to his knees. A pained grunt escapes my chest when his knee connects to my groin. *Fuuuuuuuuuuuu-uuck.* My eyes spring open, squinting when sunlight filters through the gap in the curtains.

I swallow down the nausea churning in my stomach as the pain coils and ebbs, radiating from my bruised jewels down to my goddamn toes.

"Daddy," Ryker shrieks, and I wince.

I need coffee. Scratch that. I need an icepack and an IV drip with caffeine. He is entirely too energetic for... I fumble my palm on the cold wooden surface of the nightstand until I find my phone. Unlocking it blindly, I mentally curse when I see 8 a.m. shining back at me from the screen and a missed call from my parents.

"Morning, buddy," I rasp, patting his back. "How's your tummy feeling, huh?"

His smiling face moves in my field of view, way too close for comfort, and I press my head further into the pillow. All I need right now is for my nose to take a turn against his forehead. Been there, done that, have the hospital bill as a souvenir for my trouble.

"It's all better, Daddy. Wakey, wakey," he squeals before his small hands land on my cheeks, squishing my lips together. A laugh bubbles up in my chest, chased away immediately by warmth and the all-encompassing love I feel for this small human when his nose brushes against mine in a butterfly kiss.

I might be damaged goods and sentenced by my own hand to spend my life alone, but Ryker makes everything better. Every day I get to live and see him grow, every day I get to experience through his innocent eyes, every moment I am by his side, it's all worth it.

Down the road, we'll have our struggles. He's too young now, but soon enough, I'll have to deal with questions about his mother. That's the one hurt I cannot save him from. But I'm determined as fuck to make this life a good one for him. I'm determined to love him fiercely enough so he'll always know that he *is* wanted. If I'm lucky, maybe the sting of abandonment won't be too harsh on him.

"All right, grape-monster. Let's get out of bed and have some breakfast. Your granny is waiting for you. I heard you'll have a full day of running around in the orchard with Clara and Eliza."

The snort testing the strength of my nostrils is physically painful at the love-hearts in his eyes when I mention Lalah and Cole's adoptive daughters. Go figure, like father like son. Maybe I should be worried he's a bit too young to have a crush. I'd say I'm a bit too fucking old for one too, yet here we both are.

I take my mini-me to the bathroom and help wash his face and hands. In the mirror, my smile is blinding when Ryker takes off his pajamas and dumps them into the laundry basket, then climbs up onto the stepping stool I put in front of the sink just for him. He imitates my posture, now that he's in the same state of undress as I am. He scrubs vigorously at his teeth with a soft brush, smiling back at me, his lips white and covered in minty foam.

I might occasionally feel guilty that I could give Ryker a mother and refuse to entertain the idea. But I know it in my gut, a mother has the potential to hurt him worse than never knowing what it's like to have one. We're better off just the two of us.

Whatever faint fantasies poisoned my mind in the midnight hours of a silver-blonde fairy and happy families go down the drain with the foamy water as I rinse my toothbrush.

I'll drop Ryker off for his weekend with my parents after breakfast, and tonight I'm getting over my dry spell. I have no need for idealistic dreams of white-picket fences and generous tits attached to one spellbinding wallflower of a woman.

Chapter Three

Sawyer

I fan myself with the book, stretching my legs as I sprawl over one of the many beanbags. They're all scattered around the coffee shop section of To Be Read Café.

"That Cain is something else." Lalah laughs. "It's funny, though. I've never thought I'd like a *why-choose* romance. I'm far too possessive to share or to want to be shared."

My cheeks flame. I understand the theory of sex—take slot A and insert in slot B, or, as I've just read, C and D at the same time—but I've never put the theory to the test. Yeah, yeah, gasp, shock, and horror, I'm a twenty-six-year-old virgin. And I'm not ashamed of my virginity.

I'm not holding onto it until marriage or anything of the sort; sex was simply never a priority for me. During high school, I was far too shy to even contemplate kissing a boy, never mind actually getting... frisky in the back seat of a car or the cliched bleachers. Plus, I was terrified that Tatum would find out and hang anyone who dared touch me by their testicles on the football field's scoreboard.

I only had one relationship. Rob and I were together for two years in college. The inexperienced, sheltered me swooned all over the place over his preppy haircut and mild mannerisms. He held my hand, cuddled with me on the twin bed of my dorm room, and kissed my lips with exactly zero passion. Rob liked my purity and my shyness. Instead of supporting me and allowing me to grow at his side, he kept me locked in a box—fragile Sawyer.

Oh, the plans.

He'd go to law school, and I'd be the dutiful fiancée, planning our June wedding, impressing all his lawyer-to-be golf buddies. I'd be a princess-in-training, helping his mom run her thousand-and-one charities. And then we'd get married. I'd pop out exactly two-point-five perfectly mannered children, living the rest of my life as a trophy wife.

The prospect of such a bleak life terrified me. While I am all about helping the community, I grew up with a hardworking Sarah Carter. I had my own hopes and dreams for the future. And I made the grave mistake of voicing them.

"I'd definitely let Wyatt take away all my hurts." Violet laughs, her own cheeks beet-red, the sound of her giggles taking me out of my head.

"I wouldn't mind my own harem of overprotective growly men," Emma whispers, her coppery eyes sparkling with mischief. My lips tip up in a smile. I love seeing her true personality emerging, her playfulness, and thirst for life. She calls herself shy; I call her stifled. Her spark was doused by the evilness of her bullies. Now she's allowing herself to shine.

"Of course you wouldn't. That's why you chose this book." Annalise, the owner of TBRC, wiggles her eyebrows. "I personally love a good *why-choose* story. But the ones I usually read are mostly focused on the individual relationship between the FMC and each of her MMCs. This book, though? The connection between all five of them... dayum. I felt it deep in my soul."

"The longing," I murmur. "That deep craving for acceptance. To be seen as you are and loved for your flaws, not despite them. This was an amazing choice, Emma." I give her a grateful smile.

Yeah, I might have blushed all the way to the last page as we read *Black Widow's Bite* by Bella Reves, but I can't help but feel a deep kinship to Austin. I chose correctly when I went with the snakes. We share the same need and crave, Austin and me. I too want to belong, want to be seen and desired.

"Cain's my main man," Maevis, my *hopefully* future sister-in-law, declares. She is pregnant, her hands protectively cradling the smallest baby bump in existence. My brother is absolutely crazy about her, but their road to happily ever after... they're not there yet. I hope beyond hope they'll find a middle ground and end up together. Even a blind person can see how much love there is between them. They deserve to be happy, and more than anything else, they deserve each other.

Lalah throws a handful of buttery popcorn at her, a couple of stray kernels landing on my lap. I pluck them both and shove them in my mouth. There's no reason to waste perfectly good snacks.

"Don't make me hurt you," she threatens. "Didn't I just say I don't share?"

"You wouldn't hurt a pregnant woman, would you?" Maevis flutters her dark eyelashes, pure innocence plastered on her face. "It's not my fault my Vanilla Bean makes me crave."

"Then have Tatum stuff your cravings. What is he, a Picasso painting? He has a dick, and since you're already pregnant, I'm quite certain he knows how to use it," Lalah retorts, and I swallow down the bile pooling in my mouth.

"STOP!" I shout. "For the love of all smutty books, please, don't."

She shrugs, her dark hair shifting away from the black hoodie she's wearing. A pair of smoking eyes is drawn across her chest, '*Who thinks I'm a demon?*' written in flaming cursive below her breasts.

"You cheated," I accuse, pointing a finger at her. How did I not see it for the past five hours?

"Sue me. I needed to know what I was getting myself into." Her face turns serious, and she leans over Annalise, patting my knee. "Reverse harems in general hit too close to cheating for me. So I locked myself in my library to make sure I'm able to read it without being triggered."

"Oh shit, I didn't even think of that," Emma hisses.

"It didn't, though, did it?" I ask. "The book was all about connection, openness, and accepting that happiness comes in many different ways. Five people starved for affection prove their love for one another by being selfless, allowing themselves to be happy together rather than taking what they want and keeping it for themselves."

"I begrudgingly have to admit Bella Reves might have changed my stance on *why-chooses*." Lalah grins, no grudge whatsoever in her hazel eyes.

Emma stands, stretching her back. "There better be a second book coming soon, otherwise I'm not responsible for my actions."

"It can't be too expensive to rent a private jet and kidnap a certain author. I'm sure I can have Matt build a writing-cave annex to my house and lock Bella there until she finishes the second book, no?"

"Jesus Christ, Lalah. I can't tell if you're serious or joking." Maevis laughs, but there's plenty of unease in her tone. "Let the poor woman be. Just tell me where we stand with Cain."

I tune them out as they debate the merits of an alpha man versus those of a cinnamon roll. As far as I'm concerned, I'm all for the cinnamon roll. My father is a dominant man; my brother is his carbon copy. I have incredible love and respect for them both, but I'm too soft to fall for a man with the same levels of dominance as them. He'd walk all over me. I might be a wallflower, but I refuse to allow myself to be a pushover, too.

Although, I admit, being in the presence of a commanding man brings a certain thrill. All that power and strength entirely focused on me. A shiver runs up my spine at the memory of a large, warm hand brushing against my breast. My nipples pebbled and my panties dampened. All from a barely-there touch that lasted for less than a second.

I bite my cheek and will the pain radiating from my smarting flesh to wash away any and all thoughts of him. He's not relationship material, even if I'm not necessarily looking for one right now. I may be inexperienced, but I'm not stupid. I learn from both my mistakes and the mistakes of others.

He's off limits for more than one reason.

Maddox Lawson is the father of one of my students. Lalah and Maddox had a full-on drama going on before Cole, her husband, came into the picture. He's the Casanova of Lost Hope and callous to a fault. He'd chew me up and spit me out before I'd even blink my eyes open. And if all that isn't enough for me to keep my distance, Tatum cannot stand the sight of him.

Any man willing to share his life with me needs to be soft, not take up all the air in a room with his ego until I'm so small I can't even look at myself in the mirror. I've been there once. I let myself be fooled by the wolf in preppy clothes and mild manners. Never again.

"I'm going to Lockwood tonight. There's a new club that opened just last week, and I thought I'd check it out," Violet tells me. "Wanna come?"

My eyebrows hit the middle of my forehead. "Wouldn't that get you in trouble with your parents?"

Violet might be an adult, but she was raised in a religious community in Forrest Falls, and her father is the pastor. Her family is incredibly strict when it comes to what Violet can or cannot do. Transferring from Forrest Falls Elementary to Lost Hope Elementary was her one act of defiance, a desperate attempt to put some distance between her and their controlling ways.

"What they don't know doesn't hurt them. I told them I'm spending the night at your place since I'm helping you finish up the Happy Bumblebee project. It's not technically a lie. Also, it helps that they like you."

I don't know what their approval of our friendship says about me. There's not one rebelling bone in my body, but, for a while now, I've felt...

uncomfortable in my skin. Being shy is not a crime, but I want to spread my wings. I want experiences and to just... live more. While I love my work and I'm beyond excited about what the future will bring, now that Happy Bumblebees is not just a dream, but a reality, I realize my personal life is severely lacking.

Yes, I now have friends and have book club meetings.

A night out at a club, dancing and having fun with a friend doesn't sound like the worst idea.

Plus... clubs are excellent grounds to hunt for a one-night stand. I might not be ashamed of being a virgin, but I'm sick and tired of feeling like I'm missing out. Worst-case scenario, he's a selfish lover and I'm left feeling meh. Surely that's better than not knowing what it feels like to have a man fill me up and move above me.

At the very least, I won't have to evade all the sex conversations in a feeble attempt to avoid having to justify my choices.

"I'm in."

Chapter Four

Maddox

My knee bounces up and down as I spin the glass of whiskey on the tabletop. The club is full to the brim. It's always the same with new openings; everyone and their mother rushes to be part of the hype. Fucking perfect for me.

The pickings have gotten slim since I keep frequenting the same bars and clubs. That must be the reason for my dry spell. I've not taken anyone to bed lately simply because I don't do seconds. My eyes dart toward the dance floor, where women of all ages, clad in the skimpiest of outfits, move to the sensual beat, dropping and gyrating, shaking their asses up and down like it's a fucking twerk competition.

I don't give a fuck what they're wearing. Once I've chosen my partner for the night, her clothes will lie in a pile on the floor of my hotel room.

"See anything you like?" Joshua asks from the barstool next to mine. He smirks like a goddamn wolf. Well, he can shove that know-it-all smile right up his ass. He's here for the same thing I am—to get his rocks off and get out.

"Not yet," I murmur.

"Aren't you a picky one?" He outright laughs in my face.

Sometimes I wonder *why* we're friends. He's a new transplant to the area, from New York City, where he was a big shot prosecutor. Now, he's here in the middle of the goddamn mountains, prosecuting petty theft and... Well, I'd like to say nothing bad ever happens in the middle-of-nowhere, Montana, but that's not exactly true.

Not with the trial against Maddison Brown and Amanda Straton looming over our small town like a thunderstorm.

Bitterness and guilt rise in my chest. I can't fucking help but blame myself for all that went down last year. One simple decision would've changed the outcome of Maddison's delusions and spared many people a lot of pain. Instead, I walked around like a fucking peacock, thinking I knew better.

My overinflated ego had Lalah nearly dying after I believed Maddison when she told me my one-night-stand was stalking me. In turn, I convinced Drake, my best friend, not to believe a word coming from Lalah's mouth. My poor judgment led to Lalah almost not being rescued on time, after she'd been run off the road and her car flipped.

I was well aware of the crush Maddison harbored on me, but I stupidly thought she'd get over it eventually. Couldn't have been more wrong. Even when I didn't give her the time of the day, she continued to pop up wherever I was.

And then she took it a step further, attempting to roofie Lalah and God-knows what else, which led to Emma OD-ing and Tatum falling victim to Amanda.

If I had stopped her sooner... none of that would have happened.

I wasn't the most liked person in Lost Hope even before all that, but at least I liked myself. Now, I can't even look in the fucking mirror without wanting to punch myself in the face.

"Honestly, man, if you're not feeling it, we can just drink ourselves stupid and call it a night," Joshua comments casually, none of his usual arrogance on display.

Like calls to like, since the prosecutor's ego is just about as big as mine. Maybe that's the reason we became fast friends when we met for the first time shortly after he moved here, six months ago. I don't have many of those, except for Drake. He's the only one who's put up with my difficult ass, ever since childhood. But now that he's a married man, I see him less and less. I don't hold it against him, but fuck if it doesn't sting to be left behind while everyone around me moves forward with their lives.

"Nah, I'm alright. Night's still young." I give him a perfunctory smirk. A flash of white at the corner of my eye draws my attention, and I swivel in my chair to turn toward the bar. If this were a cartoon, my tongue would roll out of my fucking mouth like a red carpet, and I'd howl at the moon. As it is, I just about have a goddamn heart attack as I take in the woman in front of me. My fingers grip the glass so hard, I'm surprised it doesn't shatter in my palm.

What the fuck is she doing here?

Her white dress looks painted on her body, hugging those gorgeous tits of hers. Christ, is that what she has hidden under her prim and proper clothes? My gaze travels down from her chest to the cinch of her small waist, lingering on the sensual flare of her hips. I just about fall out of my damn chair when my eyes snag onto that high slit in the skirt of her dress. I force myself to continue taking her in, goosebumps sprouting on my arms under my button-down when I notice the length of her dress. The non-fucking-existent length. One inch higher, and her goddamn ass would hang out of the flimsy material she calls a dress, revealing her mile-long legs and toned thighs.

My throat dries and my heart sputters in my chest. She's a goddamn wet dream, an ethereal being plucked straight from the filthiest of fairytales. I have *got* to leave, and I've got to leave fast, before I do something I'll regret for the rest of my life. My cock springs to life under my fly, going from nothing to ready to explode in less than five seconds.

"I'm out of here," I bark at Joshua and jump to my feet, determined to put as much distance between me and the sinful temptation that is Sawyer Carter. I have no death wish, and she's a sure ticket straight to hell.

How goes the saying? The road to hell is paved with good intentions.

And mine crumbles under the soles of my Italian dress shoes the second a slick fucker crowds her from behind and grips her hip with his filthy paw.

I don't breathe.

I don't think.

My eyes zero in on his fingers toying with the opening of the way-too-fucking-high slit.

I can't even blame the alcohol for my out-of-body experience, since I barely had two sips of that top shelf whiskey. I swear, one second I'm at my table, saying goodbye to Joshua, and the next I'm all up in her business. My fingers coil around her forearm, pulling her to my chest and away from the pouty, slimy cocksucker. All it takes is a silent glare over her shoulder for the nutless cunt to scurry away like the coward he is.

I bend my neck and hiss in her ear, "What the fuck are you doing here, Sawyer?"

Her pretty blue-navy eyes narrow at me. Fire spills out of her mesmerizing irises, taking me aback. The little wallflower has some backbone. And why do I find that so fucking sexy?

"What's it to you, Lawson? Let go of me."

The laugh spilling out of my chest is manic, if not slightly unhinged. The minute I saw him touch her, all my sanity flew out the fucking window, all semblance of control evaporating.

"Don't make me repeat myself. What are you doing here, Sawyer?"

Her soft palm reaches my chest, trying to push me away from her. I'm undeterred. If I'm leaving, she's coming with me. That doesn't stop me from pushing back against her hand, desperate to feel the heat of her skin against mine.

"Good god, I can't get away from overbearing men even here. Seriously, Maddox, what's gotten into you? Let me go."

I swear I hear the words spilling out of her beautiful mouth, but I can't make sense of them. Not when I have her this close to me, her sweet perfume surrounding me like a cloak of madness and desire.

"We're leaving," I bark and let go of her forearm, only to entwine my fingers to hers and pull her toward the exit.

She digs her heels in and stops dead in her tracks, forcing me to stop too unless I want to drag her behind me.

"Are you on drugs? Is that what this is? Maddox, I'm not leaving. I came here with my friends. I haven't even gotten the chance to dance. What is going on?" she shrieks.

My feet have a mind of their own, and instead of continuing to carry me to the exit, change direction and move toward the dance floor. I spin her around and hook an arm around her waist, plastering her front to mine, just as the song changes, and Austin Giorgio starts crooning about love spells and the floors swallowing his lover's clothes.

Fitting. She's definitely put a spell on me.

She's as stiff as a statue in my arms until I start swaying, my hips grinding against her lower belly. My free arm coils around her shoulders, fingers gripping her nape. No escaping my hold now. I lower my forehead to hers, and I feel the moment she gives in. Her body sags in my embrace. A deep sigh pushes her soft breasts against my chest, her minty breath washing over my face.

"There, you're dancing now, little fairy," I murmur, my lips brushing against the bridge of her nose.

Her fingers tighten where she clutches the material of my shirt, before her palms smooth over my chest until her own hands grip around my neck. *That's a good girl.*

I close my eyes and let the sensual beat of the song course through my body as I hold her against me like she's precious. I have no fucking plan here. The only thing that's crystal clear, as my adrenaline levels lower and the need to break that asshole's hand slowly leaves my body, is that I needed Sawyer away from him.

She's in my arms right now; she's safe and with me. That's all that matters.

"Oh, hey, there you are," a feminine voice shouts over the loud bass, breaking the spell I'm under. Sawyer startles and pushes away from me. My arms fall from around her, and a trickle of sanity has me taking a step back. "I thought I lost you there for a second. So, what did you think of Mark? James assured me you'd be safe with him."

She'd be safe with him?

I'm rooted to the spot. My brain short-circuits. I'm tempted to poke a finger in my ear, sure I didn't hear her friend right. Over my dead fucking body is she going anywhere with the slick asshole. No way, no how, no sir.

Before I have a chance to make my presence known and inform her friend that the only man Sawyer goes anywhere with is me, my silver-haired fairy bends and whispers something in the woman's ear, then with a wave over her shoulder, makes her way back to me.

"Not a word out of your mouth, Lawson," she threatens, pushing past me. And for the second time this evening, I grab her forearm and pull her back into my arms.

"Where do you think you're going?"

Her eyes close, defeat written all over her gorgeous face, her bow-shaped pink lips tipping down. "I'm going home, Maddox. Are you happy now?"

I tighten my hold on her, stepping into her body until there's not even room for air between us. I trace her high cheekbones with the tip of my nose, following the delicate curve of her jaw, and whisper in her ear, "Is that why you came here? To pick up a random fucker and let him bend you over the sink in a dirty bathroom like a common whore?"

Regret drowns me the minute those words leave my mouth. I can't take them back now. The sting on my scalp as she grips my hair and pulls my head back with all her might is well fucking deserved. I wouldn't blame her, not one bit, if she removed one of those sharp-looking heels she's wearing and stabbed me in the neck with it.

She bares her pearly-white teeth at me, sneering with all the derision she finds inside. "That's rich coming from you. Isn't this your hunting grounds? Or are you a misogynistic low-life of a man who holds women to a double standard? You're allowed to sleep with them and think less of them when the sun rises, no?"

I shift on my feet, that new asshole she just tore me feeling mighty uncomfortable. But she's entitled to think the worst of me. I certainly didn't give her any reasons to think otherwise. Still, she hasn't stepped on my foot and run away cursing my name, so maybe there's time to salvage *something* out of this wreckage.

"I'm sorry," I murmur in her ear.

"Oh, that's mighty of you, apologizing to a common whore." Sawyer scoffs in my face. I might have deep mental problems because my cock throbs and lengthens as her plush lips curve around the word *whore*. "You need to let go and stay away from me. For my part, I'll forget this night ever happened." *Now* she starts pushing away from me.

Terror grips my stomach, climbing up my spine. My hands tremble and sweat peppers my hairline. I need to fix this, and I need to fix it fast.

"Please, Sawyer. I admit, I'm an asshole. Those words should have never left my fucking mouth. Please..."

She lifts her head and looks straight into my eyes. My knees weaken. I swear I could lose myself in those navy-blue eyes of hers. "What do you want from me? I don't understand what is wrong with you tonight."

Bending my neck, I bring my nose close to hers, my lips almost feathering over her mouth. "I don't know," I grit, my jaw clenching so hard, I hear my teeth grinding. "Just... tell me what you're doing here."

"I don't owe you any explanation. Maddox, we're not even friends." Her eyes roll, widening with disbelief.

Welcome to the club. I'm fucking lost. I have not a shred of an idea why the hell can't I just let go of her and go on my merry way.

"I know..."

"Fine," she sighs. "If I tell you, do you promise to let me go?" Clearly, she understands there's no negotiating with a madman. I have enough sanity left to know that I might not live to see tomorrow once she gets home and sics her brother on me. What I don't have is any sense of self-preservation left, but I tip my chin, lying to her face with a silent promise I have no intention of keeping.

Sawyer's reason for being here is the goddamn hill I choose to die on. And she just about kills me herself when her next words leave that pretty mouth of hers.

"I wanted to know what it feels like to have an orgasm that didn't come from my own hands."

Yeah. I'm dead.

Chapter Five

Sawyer

*H*oly ink, what have I done?

I feel the blush starting on my chest, burning through the skin of my neck, and pooling in my cheeks. He's completely unhinged. Surely, he's lost his ever-loving mind. My own is working furiously, trying to make sense of how I ended up here, in the middle of Everlasting's dance floor, caged in the steel arms of Maddox Lawson out of all the men in this club.

His mouth opens and closes. His warm breath, tinged with the spicy aroma of whiskey, washes over me. My tongue darts out, swiping over my bottom lip. All the courage I felt a minute ago crashed out of me as soon as those words spilled past my lips. A reckless thrill fights for dominance with a tendril of fear curled up at the bottom of my stomach.

Maddox both scares me and entices me.

My clit throbs and butterflies take flight in my belly when the anguished look on his face is replaced by wickedness and determination. His icy-blue irises sparkle. All traces of repentance vanish, giving way to the predator he so cleverly masks in the body of an all-American man.

"That so, little fairy? You want to have an orgasm at the hands of a man? Maybe you'd prefer his tongue or his cock instead? All the above?"

The grit in his voice makes my insides flutter and quiver. That dainty piece of lace covering the most intimate parts of me dampens further. "What are you saying?"

I gasp when I feel his fingers trailing down my hip bone, the roughness of his fingertips scraping against the bare skin of my thigh. My knees buckle and my grip on his hair falters. BRKN Love's cover of "River" thumps through my chest, in rhythm with my speeding heart, and I dare peek between us, where our hips touch everywhere.

His hand has completely disappeared under the skirt of my dress, his knuckles brushing against my panties.

"Look at me," he orders, and I tip my chin up, gazing at him from under hooded lids. "This is your chance to tell me no. Choose, little fairy," he grunts in my ear, and I jolt when the pad of his thumb presses against my clit.

Apart from an easy sway as he keeps us dancing in the same spot on the dance floor, he's otherwise still. Not breathing, not blinking, not applying any more delicious pressure.

The gamble is simple.

I say *no,* and I go home no worse than how I was when I left; no better either.

I say *yes,* and I'll finally get to feel what it's like to have a man desire me.

That was the whole purpose of this little trip Violet and I took. I'm safer with Maddox than I'll ever be with a stranger. I'm also well aware of what I'm getting into with him.

One night. And then business as usual.

I look dead into those icy-blue eyes of his resembling Alaskan glaciers. My lips part on a silent word, "Yes."

Maddox buries his face in the crook of my neck, the stubble on his cheeks scratching against my soft skin as his mouth peppers feather-like kisses on my shoulder. He continues swaying gently from left to right, right to left. My body follows his every command, his every move.

A breathless moan escapes my throat when he brushes my panties aside and trails his fingers against my slit; the hardness of his nails, the heat of his calloused skin sends electric shocks through my body. *More, I want more. I need more.*

I buck against his hand, seeking the pressure of his touch and the promise of bliss that I know will soon follow. His fingers part my pussy with infinite gentleness, seeking my entrance, the heel of his palm pressing against my throbbing bundle of nerves.

I rock against him, silently begging for more. He grounds his palm against me at the same time he thrusts a finger inside my channel. There's nothing silent about the moan escaping me then, nothing soft about the clench of my walls around him.

"Patience, greedy girl," he admonishes me. I feel the vibrations of his words against the shell of my ear more than I hear them.

His finger moves in and out of me leisurely. His movements are controlled, precise, while I'm anything but. I feel everything at once. The pulse of the bass, the commanding lyrics of the song, his overwhelming presence surrounding me, burrowing into me. I'm spinning and flying and free-falling.

It's never been like this.

"Please," I beg him, not an ounce of shyness in me, not a drop of shame.

"Grip my hair," Maddox barks, and I obey immediately, my fingers tightening on the silky strands at his nape. "If your eyes leave mine for even a second, I stop. Do you understand?"

"Y-yes."

The word is barely out of my mouth before a second finger finds its way inside of me, filling me up, stretching me out. A tinge of pain shoots through the unused muscles of my pelvis when his leisure thrusts speed up. His thick fingers crook and scissor. My knees tremble in time with his in-and-out movements. Pressure builds and builds inside my lower belly, and my nipples pebble painfully. I plaster my chest to his, rubbing my breasts against the soft material of his shirt, desperate for the tempest building inside of me to find relief.

My skin is too tight for my body. I'm burning from the inside out, the need for him all-consuming and all-encompassing.

I'm hypnotized by the pure predator peering back at me from behind those cold irises, mesmerized by the tortured look on his face and the hard set of his plump lips. His one and only focus is me. To be the object of his undivided attention is an experience unlike any other.

I'm empowered, alive, enthralled.

The pressure in my belly grows and expands until all that's left is me and him and the sparks feeding the fire threatening to consume me.

"Come for me, little fairy. Come on my fingers like the good girl you are. Fucking soak my hand with your need."

And then he twists his wrist, his thumb thrums against my clit, and I'm gone. My pussy flutters and quivers, clamping around his fingers like he's never allowed to remove them from me ever again. Pure lightning courses through my veins as the orgasm detonates through me like a category five hurricane. His name on my lips is a blessing and a curse, a beg for more and a plea for mercy. His grip around my nape tightens, his forehead lowering to mine. Ragged breaths wash over my skin, and I taste on my lips the spiciness of the whiskey still clinging to him.

"You're so goddamn beautiful when you come for me, I struggle for breath."

Maddox lowers his mouth to mine and, at the very last second, I turn my head, offering him my cheek instead.

If he is offended by my refusal to kiss him, as he slowly withdraws his fingers from inside of me, he doesn't show it. Instead, he brings his glistening fingers to his mouth, tips my chin up with the knuckles of his free hand, and forces me to watch as he licks clean every single drop of me from his skin.

I swallow down the lump in my throat. How is it possible to want him even more after he made me come on a dance floor full of people? My core is still clenching over nothing after he just gifted me the best orgasm of my life, and all I want is more. More of his fingers, more of his tongue, more of his...

"We need to talk," he whispers in my ear. All my desire vanishes as if he dropped a bucket of ice over my head.

Maddox doesn't wait for me to agree but clutches my wrist and leads me to the bar. Pushing me in front of him, his hulking form cages me from behind against the sleek black bar top. He signals the bartender and leans over me to place his order.

And I just... stand there, my mind still spinning, my words trapped on the tip of my tongue.

"Drink this." He pushes a sealed bottle in front of me, unscrewing the lid with a flick of his wrist. I don't have enough energy left in me to argue, so I just do as he commands. Turns out, I'm thirstier than I realized, greedily gulping at the cool, fruity liquid.

Maddox watches me with a pleased look on his face, like he is proud of himself for caring for me, proud I accepted his care. His hand settles on my shoulder, his thumb rubbing soothing circles on the bare skin below my collarbone. When he's satisfied I've had enough, he plucks the bottle from my hand and throws his arm around me, plastering me to his side. He leads me through the sea of bodies writhing and jumping around on the dance floor, then through a set of sliding doors.

The cool midnight air bites at my skin, goosebumps peppering my arms and legs. He guides me to a table tucked away in a corner of the open-air terrace, the closest one to an electric heater. Pulling out my chair for me, he helps me get settled before dragging another chair next to mine and taking a seat himself, caging my legs between his thick thighs.

I reach for the bottle and take another swig of the fruity drink, fidgeting with the lid as I wait him out. He wants to talk; he better get started. I'm not going to open my mouth and make a fool of myself. I've done enough of that for one night.

Maddox gives me a boyish grin, a dimple popping under the scruff on his jaw and cheeks, but his eyes are dead serious.

"I want you."

That's it. That's all he says.

My own cheeks are burning, but I went this far tonight, I can make it a bit further. I square my shoulders and arch a questioning eyebrow.

"Okay..." I prompt him, hoping he'll say more. I'm so out of my depth here; I brought a kiddie pool to an Olympic swimming competition.

"Was I unclear?" He chuckles, and the sound of that raspy laugh, so deep, so rough, travels through me, sending distress signals to my clit.

"Not in terms of your feelings. I don't know what you want me to say, Maddox." I lift my shoulder in a barely-there shrug. Despite the heat radiating from behind me, I can't suppress the shiver running through my spine as those unsettling eyes of his rack over my entire body. His teeth sink into his bottom lip, leaving tiny indents in the plump flesh.

"That you're mine for tonight to do with as I please."

My heart hammers in my chest. We're still gambling. *I'm* still gambling. Back in the darkness of the club, it was easy to be brave. It was easy not to be a wallflower, but the strong woman who got her very first orgasm on a busy dance floor in a newly opened club.

But under the yellowish hue of the nightlights, I'm on display in front of him. Out here, reality sets in. On Monday morning, I'll have to see him dropping Ryker off and picking him up. A week from now, I'll accidentally bump into him on the street, as we've done many times before. He is friends with my friends. We'll always be in each other's lives one way or another. Would he still look through me like I'm there but don't matter, or will there be a knowing twinkle in his eyes, the ghost of tonight's memory?

"We need rules," I state, proud of myself when my voice comes out strong and assured, instead of meek and breakable like I feel inside.

"Okay. I agree. Name yours."

If I cursed, now would've been the perfect moment to spit about a thousand expletives. The ball was supposed to stay firmly in his court. I have no experience to speak off, apart from some cuddles here and there and kisses with Rob's fish lips against mine.

"I'd like you to name yours first."

He leans back in his chair, crossing his arms over his broad chest. My eyes roam over the dips and valleys of his torso, visible even through the material of his shirt, then further down, widening when they stop on the bulge of his dress pants. *Holy poetry.*

Maybe sleeping with Maddox isn't such a good idea. How's all that supposed to fit inside of me? I struggled to take two of his fingers. That baseball bat he carries around in his trousers looks just a smidge thicker and longer than two fingers, regardless of how talented they are.

My eyes spring back up to his, and the cocky man winks at me. *Busted.* Well, he ogled me all night long. I won't be shamed for returning the favor despite the whispered prayer I sent out in the Universe for the Earth to part and swallow me whole.

"One night only."

"That's a given," I retort.

"It can't be more. You're my son's teacher," he continues explaining as if I haven't said a word.

"You don't need to justify yourself, Maddox. I agree that whatever this is, it ends with the sunrise."

I expect him to smile and agree, but the light blue of his eyes darkens and his forehead creases on a frown.

"What happens between us, stays between us."

I flick my wrist and roll my eyes. "Clearly. Violet didn't see who I was dancing with. Anything else?" I ask, hopeful that maybe he'll get into the nitty gritty of the actual… act itself.

"Nope," he says, popping the p. "Your turn. Likes, dislikes, hard limits."

"Uhm… about that," I stammer and busy myself with another drink. I better get through this conversation fast because the bottle is nearly empty, and I'll have no more excuses to stall. "I don't know what my limits are. As it is right now, I'm willing to try everything once. Uhm… I'll let you know if I don't like something as it happens?"

That predatory look flashes again in his eyes, and despite my squared shoulders and the false bravado I've plastered on my face, I instinctively lean back, away from the danger rubbing against all my self-preservation instincts.

"What are you saying, Sawyer?"

"Don't play the clueless-man card with me, Maddox. If you have a problem with my lack of experience, this is where we part ways," I tell him, pushing up on my feet as I stand. Regret settles in the pit of my stomach.

Not for anything we've done, but for missing out on what this night could have been.

He's on his feet in a flash, his large palm gripping my hip, the other cradling my cheek. He grinds his erection against my lower belly, making his intentions crystal clear without words. His jaw ticks, his entire body coiled and ready to strike.

"Are you sure? There must be a reason you've waited so far. I don't want you to wake up in the morning and regret us. If we leave this club together, there's no going back."

"Here's a rule—we don't talk about anything personal. It's none of your business why you could be my first, and it's none of my business what you do once we part ways in the morning."

Maddox looks like he wants to protest, his eyes narrowing at me, searching my face. What for? As I said, none of my concern.

"Okay," he says slowly, testing every vowel and sound on his tongue. "Any other rules?"

Here goes nothing.

"Yes. No kissing. You can put your lips anywhere you want on my body, except my mouth. The same goes for me."

A breath hisses through his teeth. Now he really looks ready to fight me for this. Butterflies explode in my chest. Yeah, I want to know what he tastes like, or if his lips feel as soft and demanding as they look.

But kissing means affection, connection.

While I hold the hope that tonight will be unforgettable—by all means, Maddox looks very much capable of rocking my world and my body—I need tonight to also be mechanical.

Insert slot A in slot B, potentially C and D, and make fireworks explode on the ceiling.

What I don't need is a connection.

Not with the biggest asshole in all of Lost Hope.

Chapter Six

Maddox

I push through the hotel room door, uncaring as it slams against the wall. If I don't get inside of her soon, I'll keel over and die. The last half an hour was an exercise in restraint, ever since she dropped that little bomb on me.

A virgin. Sawyer is a fucking virgin.

I know I'm going straight to hell. I made my peace with spending my eternity boiling away in the hottest cauldron the devil may muster just for me. See if I have any fucks left to give. Heaven means nothing compared to the feel of her tight walls choking my cock as I bury myself to the hilt inside her sweet pussy.

My tongue darts over my bottom lip, where I can still taste traces of her. That will have to be enough for now. I'll have the rest of the night to taste her, but first...

"Lose the dress," I order. Impatience floods my blood. My desire for her nearly blinds me.

She looks at me over her shoulder, from where she's posed in front of the window. The silver flow of the moonlight frames her slender body, making Sawyer look ethereal in the darkness of the night.

If she were any other woman, by now I would've turned the lights on, ripped her clothes off, and chased my pleasure.

With Sawyer, I enjoy the darkness. I revel in the tension coiling and ebbing between the two of us, like there's an invisible cord connecting her to me. The low light and the silence of the night only heighten my pleasure, pushing my desire for her to the point of madness. She looks... angelic, pristine even. Every cell in me vibrates with the need to sully her, dirty her up with my tongue, my fingers, my cock.

She hesitates for a second, and I can't help but move closer to her, losing my shoes with each step in her direction. Her palms smooth over the sensual cinch of her waist before she crosses her arms over her chest. I drop my jacket to the floor and plaster my front to her back. I nuzzle my nose in her hair, just below the braid crowning her head, and inhale her sweet, flowery scent.

"You're not undressed," I murmur in her ear.

She tilts her head, resting her cheek against mine. "You're going to have to help me. The zipper is at the back."

I kiss her shoulder, trailing my hand from the small of her back to the upper hem of her dress, feeling for the hidden slider, and pulling it down in slow motion. My stomach flips, tingles exploding at the base of my spine. I'm torturing myself, but if I'm only having Sawyer for one night and one night only, then I need to savor every moment I get with her.

The lapels of her white dress part, revealing creamy skin and the edges of a tattoo, shocking the hell out of me. My little wallflower has a wild streak. My cock jolts and thickens further. He's on board with me testing exactly how wide that wild streak of hers is.

When the zipper stops just above the plump curve of her heart-shaped ass, I take a step back, admiring the view. Her dress hangs open; the lapels draped aside like wings ready to take flight. She uncrosses her arms, and without preamble, the silky material cladding her body slides down, pooling at her feet.

Without any conscious thought, I bring my fist to my mouth and bite my knuckles. HARD. *Fuck me, if I'm not the luckiest son of a bitch alive.* Sawyer Carter is a work of art. Every line of her body is gracious and elegant. I groan when my eyes skim over the dark swirls and curly cursive writing making up her tattoo, spreading around her ribcage like a corset. My knees just about give up when I notice the twin dimples at the small of her back, above the lacy scrap of material disappearing between her ass cheeks.

I might die tomorrow at the hands of her brother; but fucked if I'm not about to die a very happy man.

"Turn around," I rasp. Even to my own ears, my voice is deep and growly, the beast inside of me rising to the surface. I bite on the inside of my cheek. I've got to leash myself, calm down the frenzy. At least, until I've had her for the very first time.

She spins on her heel and faces me, and I just about swallow my tongue. *Holy fuck.*

Just the sight of those teardrop tits has me nearly coming in my pants. My balls draw up, heavy and full. My eyes latch onto those full, heavy tits, with pale pink nipples just begging to be sucked on, bitten, and teased. My fucking teeth ache with the bolt of desire hitting me. The throbbing behind my fly intensifies to the point of pain, and I lower my hand, gripping my dick through my dress pants, squeezing forcefully.

"Get on the bed," I grit out.

It takes every last bit of self-control I have left inside of me not to push Sawyer against the window and fuck her like a rabid animal. We might not be involved in any romantic sense, but she deserves to be handled with tenderness. For the first time, at least.

She walks past me, her hand brushing against the back of mine where I'm still gripping my impatient cock, testing the very limits of my sanity. Gingerly, she sits at the foot of the bed, then scoots backward until her head rests on the pillows. Her back arches, pushing her tits up, and her long legs spread wide as she bends her knees.

Sawyer looks like the most decadent of treats, all laid out just for me.

My eyes roam over her smooth calves, her creamy thighs, zeroing in on the damp, stretched out lace between her legs. Her belly quivers, hollowing out, as if feeling my gaze like an invisible touch.

I take a step closer, and then another one, until my thighs hit the foot of the bed. My eyes latch onto hers, serious, demanding, urging. With unhurried moves, I unfasten the cuffs of my shirt, one at a time. A glint of defiance shines in the dark pools of navy-blue staring back at me.

The button restricting my neck at the collar loosens under my fingers; one more follows, then two. My hands hook onto the material and pull. A rain of pearly circles falls onto the carpet along with my ruined shirt. I make quick work of shoving my dress pants and boxers down, my cock granite-hard bobbing against my abdomen.

She takes her sweet time perusing my naked body. Her tongue slicks across her lips as her gaze roams over my pecs and down to the valleys and ridges of my abs. Her eyes widen once they swipe down to my dick.

I climb onto the bed, crawling between her legs. Hooking my fingers around the fragile lace of her thong, I slowly drag it down her legs and throw the useless fabric somewhere behind me. My shoulders bear her welcoming weight as the soft skin of her calves brushes against my back. Burying my face in her pussy with no warning, I give her slit a long lick with the flat of my tongue, tasting her sweetness, breathing in her musky scent. My hunger for her only grows when she rewards my efforts with high-pitched mewls of pleasure and surprise. Her hand shoots to my hair, gripping tight, her hips bucking against my mouth.

"Settle down, little fairy. I need to get you ready for me," I growl, pressing my forearm across her belly, pinning her to the bed before diving back in. I thrust two fingers into her channel, sucking in a breath when her heat envelops me. I grind my hips against the cool sheets of the bed, needing to put some pressure on my cock before I come prematurely like a fucking teenager at the sight of her pretty pink pussy and swollen clit.

I suck hard at her bundle of nerves and chuckle against her sensitive flesh when she cries out my name. "Maddox, please," she keens, breathy and needy, exactly how I want her.

I want Sawyer as desperate and wanton for me as I am for her.

My mouth is relentless, biting, sucking, and licking. I'm eating my fill of her, savoring her taste, reveling in every quiver, tremor, and flutter she gifts me with.

I scissor my fingers inside of her, stretching her out, pressing and rubbing against her tight walls. Sawyer stiffens in my arms, her thighs smothering my head against her greedy pussy as she grinds against me in earnest, fucking my face with abandon. I reward her greed with a hard suck on her clit, grazing her throbbing flesh with my teeth before soothing the sting with quick flicks of my tongue.

And she lets go. For me, only for me.

Pride and satisfaction surge in my veins, knowing I am the only one to have ever seen her like this. I am the only man who's ever made her fall apart on his tongue.

Sawyer is mine.

I lick my lips and nuzzle my cheek against her trembling thighs, waiting for her to come down from her orgasm. My palm flattens over her belly, and all that silky smooth skin flushes under my touch.

I push up on my knees, looming over her. Sawyer watches me from under hooded lids, that pretty, pink blush covering her from belly button to her cheeks.

"Last chance to change your mind," I tell her, my voice gravelly and rough, as I back away from her and climb out of bed.

Her head shakes against the pillow, her pretty braid messy, tendrils of platinum blonde hair hallowing the crown of her head. "I'm not changing my mind."

I pick up my trousers and slide a condom out of my wallet, ripping the foil with my teeth and making quick work of rolling it down my length. Cuffing her ankles with my fingers, I drag her down on the mattress until her lower body hangs off the tall bed, circling my waist with her long legs.

"You ready to take me, then?" I ask, my eyes laser-focused on the dark pink of her pussy, her arousal glistening in the silvery moonlight seeping through the windows.

"Yes, please. Fuck me, Maddox," she begs oh so prettily.

My dick jolts at the profanity spilling past those beautiful lips of her. My hips push forward, notching the head of my cock to her entrance. I shift back and forth, gently, slowly, barely half an inch in before retreating, playing a twisted game of hide and seek until she relaxes enough for me to slide in with ease. Her tight walls soften, and my knees nearly give out when all her delicious wet heat clamps down around the tip of my dick.

"Fuck, you're so tight, little fairy. You grip me so well," I choke out, the muscles in my neck corded and tense. It takes every ounce of control in me not to snap my hips forward and drive myself into her until my balls slap her ass.

"More, please, give me more. I can take it. I can take you, I promise," Sawyer whimpers, her chest heaving. The sound of her begging is my goddamn undoing.

My hands anchor on the curve of her hips, my fingers pressing against her hip bones. I tenderly thrust forward, her walls fluttering around my length as she takes me inch by agonizing inch. Every back and forth of my cock, in and out of her dripping pussy, sends bolts of electricity down my spine, pure molten lava flooding my veins.

A sharp gasp spills from her lips when I push past the point of no return. I can't help it; I look down at where we're joined as I retreat until only the very tip of me remains inside of her. My mouth nearly fucking drools at the sight of her blood smearing my condom.

Every cell inside of me itches with the absolute irrational desire to rip the latex sheath away and have her blood on me, to feel the flutters of her swollen pussy around my bare cock. So I drive forward in one smooth thrust until I'm buried so deep inside her tight heat, I don't know where I end and she begins.

Sawyer's pussy is my fucking Nirvana.

Stars burst behind my eyelids once I'm fully sheathed inside of her. Her quivering soft walls are a perfect match to all my wild, unwavering hardness, as they relax and contract around me.

She cries out again, more pain than pleasure in the mewling sound ripping out of her throat. A pang of guilt stabs through my chest. I shake my head against the foreign feeling curling around my heart that demands I treat her with care and tenderness.

I give her my weight, hooking one arm under her lower back and tilting her pelvis so that she can take me better, deeper. My other arm sneaks under her upper back, my fingers gripping her delicate nape, until we're nose to nose, my eyes boring into the blue-navy depths of hers.

I grind my hips against hers, slowly withdrawing before ramming back in, making sure that on each drive forward, my pelvic bone grazes against her clit. Her pained mewls give way to breathy moans. Her back arches, plastering her gorgeous tits to me. Pebbled nipples rub against the coarseness of my chest as I start fucking her in earnest.

Tingles explode at the base of my spine, my balls draw up tight, heavy and aching. Nothing has ever felt better than Sawyer in my arms, losing herself to me, me losing myself in her. She's a goddamn drug, and I'm putty in her hands.

A wildfire burns bright under my skin, incinerating me from the inside out, and I fuck her harder and faster. My heart beats so fast, I fear at any moment it'll break out of my chest and jump into hers. Her heaving breaths wash over my overheated jaw, and I sink my teeth into my bottom lip to stop from spilling my seed inside her; to stop myself from taking her mouth with mine, fucking her sweet lips with my tongue the same way I'm fucking her pussy.

What I don't do is stop looking into her eyes. There's only one way she's coming right now, and that's with my name on her lips and her eyes boring into mine.

Her hands roam the expanse of my back. Sharp nails dig into my skin, enticing me, spurring me forward. I move faster against her, inside of her. The bed creaks, her moans echo in the room, my grunts accompany her pleasured sounds in the silence of the night. I have no words; I need no dirty talk. Every pulse of her pussy, every quiver of her belly, it's all too much as it is.

And not nearly fucking enough.

Her mouth parts on a silent scream. Her dark irises widen as her back arches completely off the bed. And then she's coming on my cock like a goddess of sin and filthy dreams. Her pussy clamps down on me so hard, I can't move, I can't breathe, even my damned heart stops and stalls.

For one brief moment, I'm suspended in space and time.

Like a bolt of lightning, my orgasm detonates out of me. My cock throbs and jolts inside of her as her greedy channel milks me of everything I have, her quivers and flutters around me prolonging my pleasure. Her name rips out of my chest on an inhuman roar, and I sag against her, depleted and sated to the very marrow of my bones.

When I feel strong enough to blink my eyes open, we're in the center of the bed. Sawyer's naked body is draped over my chest. My exhausted arms are wrapped tightly around her. My hands roam over her back, her skin slick and soft under the pad of my fingers.

And we're still connected.

Fuck me, I came so hard I blacked out for a second. Now *that* has never happened before.

Chapter Seven

Maddox

A faint buzzing on my nightstand stirs me awake from the best sleep of my life. I stretch my sore muscles. With my hand, I pat around the tangled sheets, seeking Sawyer's sleeping form and coming up empty.

My eyes spring open. All traces of sleep leave me as if I've been doused in ice-cold water, and I sit up abruptly. The hotel room is empty and cold like last night never happened. My stomach flips, a feeling of complete and utter helplessness washing over me.

She left.

Sawyer fucking left.

I cover my face with my palms, rubbing at my scruffed cheeks as I'm trying to make sense of... the morning after the best sex of my life. And I woke up alone and deserted.

If it weren't for the soreness in my muscles and the coil of pain and pleasure in my gut, I'd have thought I hallucinated last night. I hallucinated taking Sawyer's virginity, then fucking her on every available surface of this hotel room. If it weren't for the sting on my back, where her nails scratched my skin, I would've thought the hours I spent buried deep inside her magnificent pussy were a simple product of my imagination—the culmination of the months I've spent obsessing over the wallflower of Lost Hope.

My phone buzzes again from where it's charging on the wireless pad on the nightstand. I push to my feet, unceremoniously swinging the covers bunched on my lap off, and check the flashing screen, hoping beyond hope to see a message from Sawyer, an explanation as to why she sneaked out on me.

Disappointment sits heavy at the bottom of my stomach when I see a couple of missed calls from Joshua. Whatever he wants can wait until I've had a shower and checked out of this damn room. I can't be here without her.

I groan as I walk into the bathroom, images of a naked Sawyer bent over the sink counter as I ate her out from behind playing around in my head. This fucking obsession needs to stop.

It's unsettling.

I fucked her. It's the morning after. I should be over Sawyer right now.

This is what I wanted. A good fuck, and then to part ways.

So then, why do I feel like my heart was ripped out of my chest and my insides are all twisted in a knot over waking up alone?

I prop my hands against the cold marble of the sink and take a deep breath. I will allow myself a man-wallow for exactly thirty minutes as I shower and check out. As soon as I reach my car and head back to Lost Hope, I'll vanquish all thoughts and any drop of need I have for Sawyer Carter.

Luckily, I woke up early enough that the traffic home isn't too bad. Billings is tediously busy during the weekends, with everyone and their mother being out and about. I crank up the radio, drumming my fingers against the steering wheel, my windows rolled down halfway, allowing the end-of-March chill in the air to sting at my skin.

I drop by my house for a quick change of clothes, donning my work uniform, and make my way to Suga'High. Since Ryker is with my parents until later this afternoon, I can at least pop by the police station and catch up on the never-ending paperwork collecting dust on my desk.

No one likes the Sunday shift, even though it's generally quiet. I decide to reward Charlie, our police dispatcher, and Theresa and Roman, the two deputies assigned to work today, with some baked treats. Maevis smiles at me from behind the counter, her whiskey-colored eyes sparkling with happiness.

"Morning, Madd. Your usual?"

"Morning, Mae-Rae. Yeah, but throw in a dozen chocolate croissants. Theresa will hit me over the head with her service gun if I show up without 'em."

"You got it." She laughs and sets about getting my order ready. Warmth surges in my chest as I hear her humming to herself while working quickly and efficiently on packing up everything for me.

Maevis is the twin sister of my best friend. The three of us grew up together, and I've come to love her like a sister myself. She's had a rough time lately. My stomach churns and heaves, while guilt floods my bloodstream.

My passiveness with Maddison contributed plenty to robbing Maevis of her happiness.

I shove a twenty-dollar bill in her tip jar. Sure, I'm buying my redemption. Even if she doesn't blame me for what happened with Tatum and the way their relationship imploded, I know what I've done. And that's something I have to live with for the rest of my life.

She passes me the box of croissants, a paper bag with a printed vanilla flower resting atop the cardboard lid. "Thanks, Mae-Rae. Same time tomorrow?" I wink. Fake it 'till you make it. No one believes I have an ounce of common sense in me, not even Maevis, and she sees the best in everyone.

I push through the door, squinting against the early morning sun, and freeze when I find myself face to face with Tatum. *For fuck's sake.* His jaw is ticking, blue eyes narrowing in my direction. *Shit, does he know?* I feel the color leeching from my face. Images of Sawyer spread-eagle on the hotel room bed, begging me to fuck her harder and faster, play in my head, and I swallow thickly, hoping to dislodge the lump settled in the back of my throat.

"You doin' okay there, man?" he barks, watching me like at any moment I could keel over. He wouldn't be wrong. I will my legs to move and my heartbeat to calm the fuck down. He can't know, otherwise I would've been chewing on my teeth as soon as I bumped into him.

I clear my throat, looking at the Dine&Dash sign above his shoulder. I'm pretty fucking sure that if I look into his eyes, he'll read every filthy fantasy I've fulfilled with his sister last night. "Morning, Carter. I'll live," I mumble as I walk past him, adding under my breath when I feel I'm at a safe enough distance, "unless you know and you're here to kill me."

I breathe a sigh of relief when I hear the chime of Suga'High's door. It looks like I get to live another day. I'm not one to look a gift horse in the mouth, so I hightail it to the precinct. Sliding the box of croissants across the reception desk to Charlie, with a wave over my shoulder, I lock myself inside my office.

Exhausted already, I plop onto the chair and prop my elbows over the hardwood surface of the desk, dropping my head into my palms.

Hindsight is twenty-twenty. What the fuck was I thinking sleeping with Sawyer? I'm not a teenager anymore. My dick doesn't control me. So what if at thirty-four I've developed a crush on my son's teacher? I'm a goddamn man, I'll get over it. I've had crushes before. Not a one has lasted for more than a few weeks, and never once have I acted on them.

What is it about this fucking woman that has me all twisted up inside? What is it about Sawyer Carter that made me lose my godforsaken mind last night?

My locked office door bursts open, and for a second my blood freezes in my veins. I lift my head slowly, expecting to see a fire-breathing Tatum looming over me. Instead, I'm greeted by the shit-eating grin and mocking face of Joshua Craig as he pockets whatever he used to break into my office.

"Well, you look well and truly fucked." The bastard laughs, shoving a coffee in my direction. I take it from him gratefully and down half of it in two long gulps.

"Fuck off, man. What are you doing here?" I ask once my tongue stops smarting. I'm pretty sure I burned off about half my taste buds, but at this point, there's not much I have to lose, anyway.

He loses the smirk, his features sharpening. "Since you can't be bothered to answer your phone, I thought I'd come and deliver the news in person. Maddison Brown changed her plea. Word around the courtroom is that she requested a meeting with Alana Hayes and Tatum Carter before she's whisked away to spend the next twenty, potentially thirty-five years in prison. So that leaves us only with the trial for Amanda Straton in less than two weeks."

I whistle long and hard, my body sagging on my chair. "Shit. She must've pissed off the judge something fierce." Both relief and guilt swarm me at the news.

"The judge?" Joshua scoffs, his eyes hard and unfeeling. "The judge was lenient, giving her the possibility of parole in twenty. If it were up to me, that vile woman and her predator of a friend wouldn't see the light of day anymore, except from behind the bars of their cell rooms."

"Charges?"

"Second degree attempted murder."

Well, ain't that a kick to the balls. A woman I've known practically my whole life just got locked away because of a stupid crush she had on me. Nearly one year ago, I made the mistake of dancing with a stranger and taking her to my hotel room. That stranger turned out to be Lalah McAdams—now Hayes—the newest resident of Lost Hope. The lunatic blamed Lalah for my lack of interest and set out to make her life as miserable as possible, going as far as running Lalah's car off the road and roofying her drink.

Maddison is... *was* a childhood friend. It makes me question my ability to judge someone's character. How the fuck have I been so blind to her insanity? If only I'd acted sooner, none of this would've happened.

This is just one more reason my behavior last night makes absolutely no fucking sense.

If I keep going down this slippery slope, soon I'll smuggle cigarettes behind bars with Maddison Brown.

THIS TRIAL CANNOT FINISH SOON ENOUGH. The amount of lies pouring out of Amanda's mouth is ridiculous. Every single person in this courtroom who has ever met Tatum knows for a fact that he hates the very sight of her and wouldn't have touched her with a ten-foot pole if she was dying in the middle of the street. Never mind asking her to meet him at the hotel across the road from JC's Pour, a local bar, for a romp in the sheets.

I don't even know what I'm doing here. The investigation is concluded. I got Amanda arrested. My part here was done months ago. I might be on amicable terms with Tatum, but I'm not part of his circle. There's too much bad blood between us after how I treated Lalah, despite her insistence on calling me a friend.

He couldn't care less about my wanting to support him, to be another person in his corner.

My presence might be considered a futile means to assuage my guilt. It brings no relief to see Amanda punished. Sure, she's paying for her brand of evilness. But nothing can bring back those months Tatum lost with Maevis. Nothing will erase from his mind the damage his ex-wife inflicted on him.

Yet here I am. Glued to the wooden bench, in the last row of the courtroom, where I have an excellent view of the witness stand, and the ethereal beauty answering Craig's prodding questions.

Scratch that. I know exactly what I'm doing here, and it has nothing to do with having Tatum's back. He's not even in the courtroom and hasn't been, except for the first day of the trial. I'm here because I felt like I was going to die if one more day passed, and I didn't see her.

I've been good for two weeks. My parents dropped Ryker off to the daycare center and picked him up every day. Like a coward, I claimed I was busy at the precinct just to avoid seeing her. Well, seeing her was not the problem. The problem was not knowing if I'd be able to stop myself from touching her.

That still *is* the problem.

But since yesterday, the walls started to close in on me, my lungs constricting under the tightness of this fucking tether anchored in my chest, pulling me to her. Like an addict, going cold turkey got me into withdrawal. So, I'm indulging myself, drinking in the sight of her from a safe distance.

If the safe distance is for my benefit or hers... that remains to be seen.

My heart squeezes painfully in my chest as she gently wipes a tear from her blotchy cheeks. Joshua is relentless. I grip the bench under me until my fingers grow numb in a futile attempt to calm myself down.

Sawyer is not the fucking defendant, yet he's going at her as if she dragged her brother by the hair into that hotel room. She wasn't even there that horrible night back in December. But he's determined to put Amanda behind bars, and he's leaving no stones unturned and no feathers unruffled.

The fucking prosecutor might be my friend, but he's about to get extra close and personal with my fists if he keeps harassing Sawyer.

After what feels like a torturous eternity, Sawyer is dismissed from the witness stand. With her head held down and eyes firmly focused on the floor, she is escorted by the bailiff to her seat behind the prosecution table.

My knee is bouncing up and down, my blood rushing through my body like overly-shaken champagne on New Year's Eve. Everything inside of me is screaming to go to her. To hold her in my arms and protect her from anyone or anything that poses even the smallest inconvenience to her well-being.

And that's just fucking insane.

I don't do relationships. I don't do seconds. My life consists of Ryker and my job. There's no space for a woman in my mind, nor in my heart. These feelings that twist my insides and make it hard to breathe are as unwelcome as a colonoscopy. I'd rather volunteer to have a root canal done on all my teeth with no anesthesia than crush on this woman for one more second.

I came. I saw. I despaired.

Lost Hope *is* a small town, but it's not *that* small. I can and will put as much distance between me and Sawyer as I need to get over myself. Midlife crisis at thirty-four is rare, but not unheard of. Instead of running off and buying myself a red Porsche, my subconscious simply decided to shoot me in the dick and take a sledgehammer to the reinforced steel walls I've built around myself. For fucks and giggles.

Decision made, I push to my feet, determined to slip out of the courtroom and be on my merry way, just as the judge calls for recess. Sawyer runs past me like the hounds of hell are chasing her. The muffled anguish of her sobs hits the bullseye in the center of my chest.

Just like that, all thoughts of distance evaporate into thin air.

I'm out in the hallway a second later, close on her heels. I reach her as she pushes through the bathroom door and crowd her with my body. I guide her to the closest stall, locking it behind me. Giving her absolutely no chance to have a go at me, I spin her around and hug her trembling form to my chest. Warmth surges inside of me when she nestles her head in the crook of my neck. Her hands come around my waist, dainty fingers clutching my shirt.

"It's okay, little fairy," I murmur in her ear. "I've got you." There's conviction bleeding through each of my words. I don't have a future to offer her, but I can hold her right now. For five minutes, in the dirty bathroom of the courtroom, I can be her rock. I can be the man she deserves before I become nothing once more.

Five minutes.

Chapter Eight

Sawyer

This month has been... a lot. The highs were higher than the mountain peaks my eyes are currently focusing on. The lows dipped lower than the valley the sun seems to rise from. With my hands around my mug, I sip the piping-hot black coffee. Yes, I'm a psycho that way. I like my coffee strong and dark, apparently the same way I like my men.

I haven't seen Maddox in exactly twelve days, eighteen hours, and fifty-three minutes, give or take. Not that I'm counting or anything.

I know true and well what I signed up for when I left Everlasting with him that night a month ago. Same as I know I had to get out of there post-haste when I woke up the next morning with the heat of his skin singeing my back, his strong body protectively curled up around mine.

In those ten seconds, when my mind was blissfully suspended between awareness and dream state, he nuzzled his face against the back of my neck and sighed contently. Butterflies exploded inside of me. His large palm, possessively splayed across my belly, sent electric shocks through my veins.

I *knew* I was in trouble.

And trouble wasn't part of the deal we made. I gave him one night and my virginity; he gave me countless orgasms and made me soar with his hunger for my body. Fair trade.

Well, the deal also included returning to standard operation, which we both failed at. Spectacularly so.

I was doing well. I was happy about our amazing encounter and moving on with my life.

Until he followed me to that bathroom and held me like I was precious to him as I cried my eyes out. He held me as if he couldn't bear the weight of my grief, but he'd fight it for me anyway.

Amidst all the pain I felt for my brother and the misery choking all of us with each of Amanda's dirty lies exposed, something latched onto my heart.

I didn't realize what had happened right away. A red flag slowly rose at the back of my mind when my eyes sought him in the courtroom the next day. The red flag flew higher when disappointment sat like a lead ball in the pit of my stomach as it dawned on me that he wasn't there. A full tornado alarm rang when, after I congratulated Tatum for finally being rid of Amanda, the only person I wanted to celebrate justice being served with was Maddox.

So, I guess it's a good thing he's avoiding me, because crushing on Maddox Lawson is the gravest mistake I've ever made. I don't want a relationship right now, but I'll want one, eventually; and the white-picket fence; and the minivan with the two-point-oh-five children.

Most of all, I'll eventually want my loving, doting husband—my partner in crime and poetry. The man who'll be happy to wake up next to me each morning; the one I'll share my glass of wine and weird poems with; the one I'll be excited to fall asleep next to every night.

My future husband would be the nicest, tastiest, softest cinnamon roll to complement my black coffee.

And Maddox Lawson ain't that.

I gulp the last of my bitter coffee, sloshing the hot liquid around my mouth, coating my tongue with the rich and earthy taste of the dark roast before swallowing. Quickly rinsing my mug, I drop it in the dishwasher and make my way to the bathroom. I shed my PJs and throw them in the laundry basket, then turn on the shower and wait for the water to heat.

I love my little one-bedroom cottage, but the house is old. It could have used major updates about the time I was born, including a newer heating system. However, beggars can't be choosers. Running the day-care doesn't come with the fanciest paycheck, so it was either renting the cottage or moving back in with my parents after college.

Stepping in front of the mirror, I take my hair out of the protective braid I had it in for sleep. My eyes scan over my naked body, the same way they did every time I took a shower this past month.

The deep reddish-purple love marks on my breasts and collarbone have completely vanished. The dark finger-shaped bruises on my hips are gone, too. There's no trace of him or the night we shared left on my skin.

A deep twinge of loss washes over me with that observation.

There are zero physical changes to my body to bear the evidence of the night I finally took the plunge and lost my virginity. My only keepsakes remain the memories of the few hours I've shed the wallflower persona and embraced a dose of courage.

I shake my head, quietly admonishing myself. The tips of my nearly silver hair brush against the top of my shoulders as I step under the hot stream of water. My eyes stare at the drain as the shower pouring down on me washes away the pointless longing and despair bubbling in my chest.

Going through my routine of shampooing and then conditioning my hair before scrubbing every inch of my skin, I let my mind wander to my Happy Bumblebees and how beautifully everything is coming together. In fact, I'm headed there right now, so Matt can give me an update and unofficial tour before the TBRC meeting today.

I don a pair of leggings that I'll have to ditch for book club in favor of high-knee socks, and a large, gray T-shirt with a purple cursive script across my chest stating *Blake's first choice*. My wet hair is piled atop my head in a messy bun. I'll have to untie it when I get to TBRC since Violet always ends up playing with it after two-three glasses of wine. There's no good reason to waste a blow dry.

A swipe of mascara over my lashes, pear scented lip gloss, and a dab of perfume complete my ensemble.

I grab my backpack and shove in the tin container of cheese puffs I baked last night for the book club get-together, followed by an eggplant dip and spicy salsa. Last, I add the simple fruit salad I made—a laughable attempt at pretending there's something healthy in the midst of all the sugar.

The doorbell rings, and I shout over my shoulder, "Coming," then tie up the backpack and secure it over my back. I make my way to the door, unlocking it, only to be greeted by the blinding smile of one Blake Hayes. He leans down and kisses my cheek, and I can't help the blush heating up my face.

Here's the thing. When Blake moved to Lost Hope a short six months ago, I developed the biggest crush on him. Which is silly. I've known Blake since he was five years old.

Tatum, my older brother, enlisted with the Marines when I was eight. He met his best friend, Cole Hayes, during basic training. Cole is also Blake's older brother and now Lalah's husband. When Tate got hurt and medically discharged from the Marine Corps, their friendship continued as strong as it was during the time they were deployed together. When they lost their mom and Blake, Eliza, and Clara's father in a tragic car accident last year, Cole found himself the sole guardian of his younger stepsisters.

He decided to move his little family to Lost Hope, to give all of them a fresh start, closer to the only other people he considered family—Tatum and Jackson.

Cole met Lalah, and she ended up rescuing all of them from a snowstorm, and the rest, as they say, is a fairytale. They fell quickly and irrevocably in love, and got married just two months ago. Blake, who had just graduated college before his parents died, now works for Lalah's angel-investor company, Lege et Lacrima.

Even with all that history, even with the memories of a tooth-gaped Blake running around their backyard, chasing after Selae and me, I still had a crush on him. I still have the hardest time reconciling the image of the sweet five-year-old with the six-foot-two rock of a man smiling down on me right now.

"Morning, Sawy," he greets me, pushing a to-go coffee cup in my direction. "Ready to see where HeeBee's at?"

I take the coffee from him, narrowing my eyes in his direction. "You didn't make it, did you?"

His gray eyes sparkle in the early morning sunshine, while he splays his free hand across his chest. "You wound me. I'll have you know, I make excellent coffee. Just not in spaceships that require three doctorates in mechanical engineering and one in rocket science."

I only stare him down, eyebrow popped, mean-teacher mask firmly in place.

"Fine," he huffs. "You're safe to drink. Stopped by Dine&Dash and got you the darkest, thickest, and strongest palpitation-inducing coffee they had."

"Thanks, handsome." I give him my brightest smile and hook my hand around his elbow, sipping carefully from the hot-brew goodness as we stroll leisurely toward the Town Hall on our way to Happy Bumblebees.

My infatuation with Blake died a swift death during Thanksgiving dinner last year. Right after I stuffed myself full of Mae, Annalise, and Lalah's cooking, I went outside to call Selae and wish her a happy Thanksgiving. Instead of a phone call, I got to witness Blake holding Jackson against Lalah's garage door, kissing the living life out of him. Can't say I've been too heartbroken to realize Blake's affection lay elsewhere. But on paper, he's my perfect type—laid back, relaxed, textbook golden retriever personality.

"So, I'm your first choice, huh?" He wiggles his eyebrows at me, causing me to laugh, as we round the corner past the precinct.

"Always." I wink, even though I feel my cheeks heating up. In the months since they moved here, and I got over my crush on him, Blake has become a wonderful friend in the most platonic of senses. Despite that, it's difficult not to have a reaction when you're used to living in the background and, suddenly, a drop-dead-gorgeous man flirts with you. Even if it's nothing of substance and just good-natured teasing.

Suddenly, a chill washes over me and the hairs at the back of my neck stand up straight. I turn my head, looking around the street, as the strange feeling of being watched blossoms in my chest, but there's nothing out of the ordinary. Blake is clearly not affected as he chatters away, spewing numbers and projection-charts poetic about the future of my new daycare center.

I shake my head, dispelling the weird sensation. This is what I get for not drying my hair. It may be nearly the end of April, but the month has been more overcast than sunny. Even though the sun shines brightly today, it's early enough in the morning for the air to still have a small bite to it.

We finally reach the street leading to my daycare. I can't help but gasp as I take in the tall, white fences and the cascading white and green flowers covering them. "Wow, this looks... amazing."

"Why, thank you, young lady," Matt says from behind us, startling the bejesus out of me to where I nearly drop my coffee. "Beth's going to be pleased as punch to hear that."

"Good grief, you scared me." I exhale, playfully slapping his biceps with the back of my palm before giving him a side hug.

"My apologies, doll. I thought you saw me. I'm kinda hard to miss," he teases, his booming laugh echoing through the empty street.

He's not wrong.

Matt Anderson *really* is hard to miss. At six-five, he's towering over everyone around. He's also built like a linebacker due to all the manual work he does on construction sites. Despite his hulking presence, he's a teddy bear and our group's unofficial 'adopted' father. Even though he's less than ten years older than Tatum, Cole, and Jackson, who are the oldest of us at thirty-six.

"You're only forgiven if you drop your twins at the daycare center to volunteer," I tease back.

"It's like that, then? Blackmailing free labor out of my demon-spawns?" Matt chuckles.

"Good hands are hard to find," Blake interjects. "Just the other day Rhett held me a half-an-hour lecture on the difference between dystopia and sci-fi books. And Raven..."

Matt groans and drags a large hand over his bearded face. "I don't want to know. When Raven gets all older-by-seventeen-minutes overprotective sister over her brother, unless I have to post bail to get her out of jail, I don't want to know."

I sneak my arm around his waist and squeeze him gently. "You raised good kids, Matty. Smart as a whip, confident, happy kids."

He points a finger at my face and mumbles, "Remember that when you call me to come fix your classroom after Hurricane Raven passes through." His words may be harsh, but the fondness in his warm eyes and the flicker of pride reflecting back at me are unmistakable.

He walks us through the wide-open gates and takes two yellow hardhats from a table nearby, passing them to us.

"Keep to the areas marked with green tape. I don't have any safety shoes for you," he orders as he ushers us through the door. My heart nearly explodes in my chest as I see my dream taking shape right in front of me.

Chapter Nine

Sawyer

My future sister-in-law is kinda terrifying. Which is saying something, considering the top of her head barely reaches my shoulders. I wipe the sweat on my forehead with the back of my hand and move the ballooned ceremony arch *'just slightly to the left'* and then *'no, one step back.'*

One more step back, and I'll take a swim in Lalah's pond.

Planning a surprise engagement-hopefully-wedding in seven days is nothing short of exhausting. During last week's book club meeting, Maevis shared her plans to propose to Tatum. And hoped, if she got really lucky, he'd also be down to marry her the same day. If I cried like a baby while Maevis told us this is her way of making it up to him for keeping their relationship a secret when they started seeing each other, well, that's my prerogative as his baby sister.

All I've ever wanted for Tatum was to find someone who would see what an amazing and selfless man he is, and love him as much as he deserves. I'm convinced he's found his soulmate in Maevis. She's the sunshine to his grumpy, his absolute perfect match. When she's not being a pregnant bridezilla, her calm and nurturing personality is just the balm needed to soothe Tatum's hurts.

So here we are, the lot of us, getting Lalah's huge backyard ready for the celebration of my brother's—and his pregnant soon-to-be wife—happily ever after.

Lalah brings me a glass of homemade lemonade, courtesy of bridezilla, and leans close to me. "Drink it and run for your life. I'll distract the tiny tyrant."

I snicker and down the cool liquid in three gulps, wiping my mouth with the back of my wrist like a lady before passing the empty glass back to Lalah. "Thanks. I do have to leave. I only took a half day off today, thinking we'll set the tables, and I'll be in and out in a couple of hours."

Lalah sighs and pinches the bridge of her nose. "Mae's worried he'll say no. That's why she's riding us so hard. As if the crooked ring on the Saturn balloons would influence his answer."

"A hoard of zombified dragons descending on Lost Hope is more likely than my brother not marrying Mae," I whisper. "He asked my mom for Granny's ring. If she chickens out, Tate's got it handled."

"I'm just happy they seem to have gotten their shit together. Don't put me through the same hell, Sawyer. I beg of you. I'm supposed to enjoy my first year as a newly married woman, not worry about my friends' love lives."

My eyes narrow at her. This is not the first time she's hinted at... knowing. Specifically, about me and Maddox. But that's impossible. None of our friends were with either of us at Everlasting that night, except for Violet. And Violet was too taken with her new boyfriend, James, to notice Maddox.

I cross my arms over my chest and reply haughtily, "Well, I have no love life to speak of, so you're in the clear."

Her eyebrows shoot to the center of her forehead. A wicked grin tips up at the corners of her lips. "Right. Phew, what a relief." She mock-wipes sweat off her brow, then spins on her heel and marches to the back porch.

I release a *true* sigh of relief when she drops the subject and pat the pockets of my hoodie, checking that my car keys are still where I left them, then follow her to get to my car. Just before she disappears through the sliding doors and I'm about to turn the corner around her garage, her head peeks back outside.

"Before I forget, tell your non-existent love life to lock the bathroom door next time, would you? For... privacy reasons." She pokes her tongue in her cheek and spears me with a look so full of warning my feet freeze mid-step.

Oh no. She *knows*.

Maybe not the full story, but she knows enough.

Jealousy curls and twists in the pit of my stomach. Is the warning for me as a friend to tread carefully so I won't get hurt, or is the warning for me to stay away from Maddox because of their very brief past and I broke some sort of unspoken girl code?

I hate, hate, hate that one of my very dear friends, someone I look up to, love, and respect like a sister, knows what Maddox looks like naked. I know I have no claim over him, and I'm fairly certain the ridiculous crush

I've developed for him is now reduced to less than fifty percent potency. After all, I've not seen him in three weeks. In my case, distance does not make my heart grow fonder. Nope, there are no butterflies in my stomach when I think of him. In fact, I don't think of him at all.

Except when I wake up. Or go to sleep. Or see his mini-me almost daily at the daycare center.

I force my feet to move and hurry to my car, turning the ignition with shaky hands and peeling out of Lalah's driveway.

I'm in *so* much trouble.

"Miss Sawy, when do I gets to go home?" Ryker asks me from where he's sprawled out on the carpet in the middle of the classroom.

"I'm not sure, sweetheart," I reply carefully, my eyes darting to my smartwatch. The daycare center closed twenty minutes ago. Normally, we remain open until half six in the evening. Some parents need an hour or two for themselves when they get home from work, either to rest or to complete chores that would otherwise be impossible to complete with rambunctious children running circles around them.

Usually, either Maddox or his parents would pick Ryker up no later than 4 p.m., but it's nearly seven in the evening, and none of them are answering their phones. Everyone else has left, except for me and Ryker. I'm almost tempted to take him home myself, but if his father is not there, I'd be in a world of trouble. And even if he's at home, showing up on his doorstep would be just asking for trouble.

I cannot do anything that would put any licenses I need for Happy Bumblebees in jeopardy.

Ryker crawls across the floor until he reaches me. I'm sitting with my back against the wall as he plops down next to me, burrowing his small body into my side. I hug his shoulders to me and ruffle his hair.

"Let me try to call your daddy again," I tell him and move the phone to my ear. It rings, and rings, and rings, and rings again until the voicemail kicks in. My eyes roll of their own accord, but I listen for the beep and leave a quick message, careful of the words I choose to not make Ryker feel bad or forgotten.

"Hey Maddox, this is Sawyer Carter. Please, call me as soon as you can. Hopefully, I'll hear from you soon. Take care."

I drop my phone back in my pocket and soothe my hand up and down Ryker's arm when his stomach growls furiously. A nervous giggle slips past my lips at the unexpected sound, while ire floods my veins. He's hungry and, most likely, incredibly tired, but none of the adults responsible for him are reachable right now.

Usually, if someone is late to pick up a child, or they'll be delayed past closing time, they'll call or message us to let us know of the situation. But in this case... radio silence.

I'm trying very hard not to jump to conclusions, but my mind runs in circles—from harsh judgements of Maddox's character to worst-case scenarios, conjuring images of a battered and bloodied Chief Deputy, lying lifeless somewhere in a ditch.

When Ryker's stomach growls once more, my decision is made for me. With as much cheerfulness as I can muster, I slap my thighs and push to my feet.

"Alright, buddy. What do you say we ditch this joint and go have some mac'n'cheese at the diner?"

This way, I'll shoot two birds with one arrow; I'll get the kid fed and rope Ruth into tracking down her brother or her nephew.

"Can I get a gawpe milkshake, too?" He blinks up big blue eyes at me, fluttering his eyelashes.

I know when I'm being played, and I totally am right now, but I'll let the little swindler get away with a milkshake. He has been so well behaved all afternoon, despite being bored out of his mind and sad when he saw every one of his friends being picked up, and him left behind.

"Of course you can. Now run and put your shoes on while I lock up." I smile down at him, then collect my backpack from the bottom drawer of my desk and shrug my blazer up my shoulders.

"I'm all weady, Miss Sawy," Ryker squeals, hovering next to the door.

"You're very fast, sweetheart. Well done," I praise and, after giving the classroom a last glance to make sure everything is in order, I take his hand and lead him out. We barely reach the reception when my phone rings in the hidden pocket of my dress. I gently pull on Ryker's hand to get him to stop, then check the screen, only to see Maddox's name flashing back at me.

A tendril of relief surges through my chest. Technically, I knew my worries were irrational, but that doesn't mean my body wasn't all tensed up while the consequences of those imaginary worst-case scenarios were floating around in my head. I connect the call and slide the phone between my ear and my shoulder.

"Hey, thank you for calling. Is everything okay?" I greet him cheerfully. I refrain from saying his name until he tells me for sure he's on his way to pick up Ryker. If something is up or Maddox is delayed, I don't want my little buddy here to be disappointed or upset. He's been smiling ear-to-ear for the past ten minutes since I mentioned us going to the diner, and I'd like him to remain happy for a while longer.

There's a slight pause, then a deep sigh comes from the phone. *"Listen, Sawyer, I can see how my... actions from the courthouse might have been a little confusing, but we had a deal. You blew my phone up in the past half an hour. Sweetheart..."* He stops and chuckles low in his throat. My stomach twists, bile flooding my mouth. *"I don't do seconds."*

I'm struck speechless. What the... what?! Black spots fill my vision before a fiery rage unlike anything else I've ever felt in my life rushes through my veins. The backs of my eyes burn. My lungs heave as an oily feeling of shame and uncleanliness settles over my skin. My limbs grow numb as the cruel realization of how insignificant I am drops like a lead ball to the soles of my feet.

"The daycare center's closing time was nearly one hour ago. I'm taking Ryker to Dine&Dash because he's hungry. You can pick him up from there," I tell him in a monotone, flat tone, each word out of my mouth encased in ice, and end the call.

My heart gives two painful thumps, constricted as it is under the fist he just crushed it with. Sure, my feelings as of late have been firmly in infatuation territory, but I was well aware there would never be anything between us; I understood we wouldn't have a repeat of that night. I've never sought him out and had absolutely zero plans of acting on the urges those silly butterflies rushed through me every time I thought of him.

I knew he wasn't the most considerate man, especially not toward the women he spent time with, but I naively thought he knew me enough to grant me a modicum of respect. That'll teach me my place.

I clear my throat and plaster a fake smile on my face as I look down at Ryker. "That was your daddy, sweetheart. He's coming to pick you up. Let's go fill our bellies while we're waiting for him."

Ryker's smile grows impossibly wider as he cheers to the full volume of his little lungs. "Yeeeees. Let's go, Miss Sawy. The ants in my tummy are hungwy."

Making sure to set the alarm and lock up behind me, I hold tightly onto Ryker's tiny hand and slow my steps to accommodate his smaller ones as we head toward his great-auntie's diner. Dine&Dash is a staple in Lost Hope. Ruth keeps the diner open twenty-four-seven. She claims it's her duty to keep fed all deputies, firefighters, and hospital workers of Lost Hope and the surrounding small towns. If they don't get a night off, neither does the diner.

My phone vibrates incessantly inside my pocket, but I don't have it in me to answer. I'm barely holding it together as it is. I've never felt cheaper or dirtier than I do right now. Not even when Rob and I broke things off, and I had to call Tatum to come and help me move out of the tiny apartment I was renting.

Once the diner entrance comes into view, I let go of Ryker's hand. He runs through the door, a blur of joy and energy. I follow him in, wave a greeting in Renee's direction, and make my way to the tables closest to the children's corner, where my little companion is already waist deep into a box full of toys.

"Hi, Sawyer," Renee says, passing me a laminated menu. "Fancy dinner date?" She grins, her eyes darting to Ryker.

"The fanciest." I smile back at her, although I'm sure mine feels more like a grimace than anything else. I'm still too rattled by Maddox's condescending words and derisive tone from earlier on the phone. My fingers are itching to grab my fountain pain, to let the ink stain my fingertips as I put all my darkest feelings onto paper.

If she notices anything amiss in my behavior, she doesn't mention it. Instead drops her eyes to the menu I'm clinging so tightly to, I fear my nails will cut through the hardened plastic. "Do you guys know what you want, or do you need a minute?"

"Oh, we're all ready," I tell her dryly. "My handsome companion will take a grape milkshake and the best mac'n'cheese dish this fine establishment cooks." I wink at her and lower my voice to ensure Ryker doesn't hear me—if by any chance sound travels at the bottom of the box he's currently rummaging through. "Maybe blend some broccoli, carrots, and peas in the sauce." Then say louder, "And for me, I'll take a small serving of fries and a small, pear and green banana milkshake."

She pats my hand and scurries off to place our dinner order. I sag back in my chair, my eyes unfocused, blinking rapidly in my stubborn attempt to keep my tears at bay. Regret tastes bitter on my tongue. The only reason I'm not running home right now to wash my poor decisions off my skin and hide under my covers is the little boy sitting in a corner with a picture-book on his knees, his curious eyes searching for me every two minutes as he reassures himself I'm still here.

Our food soon comes, and I coax him from his reading spot and into the booster chair at the table. If he can taste the veggies in the sauce, I can't tell, as he shovels a forkful of cheesy goodness in his tiny mouth, smearing it all over his T-shirt. I nibble at my fries, but they taste like ashes in my mouth.

I should've known better. It was arrogant of me to believe Maddox has even a smidge of human decency inside his body. There's a reason Tatum doesn't like him and, apart from Amanda, my older brother has never been wrong about anyone.

Fool me once...

Chapter Ten

Maddox

I grip the doorframe to my bedroom, hoping the room stops spinning with me in it, but no such luck. I woke up this morning feeling like five-days-old roadkill—my whole body aching and trembling, my throat sore and swollen, and a motherfucking death-metal-fest drumming in my head, on a hunt for my last two living neurons.

Ryker came bounding into my bedroom, dragging me out of bed to give him breakfast. It took forever to get him fed and ready for daycare, each movement a painful struggle. There was no way I could safely drive to drop him off. I had to ask Drake to come and help, since I knew my father was minding the store and my mom was busy with the vegetable gardens and spring crops. As soon as Drake picked Ryker up, I messaged my parents, asking them to take my son for a sleepover for tonight. Best to avoid the risk of passing whatever is actively trying to kill me on to Ryker.

And then it was me, the bed, feverish dreams of a silver-haired beauty, and the occasional puking in a trashcan I had the good sense of leaving next to the bed.

I woke up a sweaty, achy mess, just as the sun was about to set, to the grating vibrations of my phone against the black wood of my nightstand. My heart lurched in my chest when I saw Sawyer's name on the brightness of the screen, my stomach tightening painfully. It took every ounce of control in me not to answer the call. In my weakened state, I knew I'd be selfish enough to beg her to come here. My feverish mind had me nearly convinced that just the sight of her in my bedroom would be enough to cure any and all ails plaguing me.

I crawled out of bed and to my ensuite bathroom. By some divine intervention, I managed to stand up for long enough to take a hot shower and wash the sickness from my skin. While my body felt cleaner, and the almost scalding water provided some much needed relief to the bone-deep fatigue in my muscles, my head was left in a daze.

Hence why I'm now trying to milk dry the last ounce of energy in my body to walk myself back to bed. The sweaty sheets are completely unappealing, but I'm running on fumes as it is; I don't have it in me to change them with fresh ones. I barely reach the edge of the mattress and let myself sit when my phone flashes, reminding me of Sawyer calling me earlier. With a shaky hand, I pick it up and squint against the brightness of the screen. Twelve missed calls and one voicemail, and all from her.

Warmth surges in my chest as I stare at the voicemail. I might not be strong enough to talk to her directly without begging her to come here, but I, at least, get to hear her voice. I tap on the voicemail icon and put the phone on speaker, her beautiful voice filling the silence in my bedroom.

"Hey Maddox, this is Sawyer Carter. Please, call me as soon as you can. Hopefully, I'll hear from you soon. Take care."

Well... that's oddly formal for a booty call, but Sawyer is usually timid. It wouldn't be out of the realm of possibility for her to just reach out to... drop the ball in my court, so to say. Too bad this court is damaged beyond repair and nothing of substance can be found inside of me. I have nothing to offer her beyond the occasional fuck.

And, as spectacular as we are together between the sheets, Sawyer deserves better.

She deserves someone like Blake Hayes—soft, dependable, whole.

The memory of them strolling down Main Street—Sawyer's hand curled around his arm, the melodious happy laughter she rewarded him with, the bright smile that should've been mine but was aimed at him instead—rises at the forefront of my mind. My blood simmers in my veins, even though I have no right to feel the way I do. I have no claim on her.

I might have been her first, but I'll never be her only.

Downing the glass of stale water from last night, I pick up my phone and dial her number. I let the jealous rage bubble and boil inside of me. It's time to cut off any kind of obsessive fantasies right at the knee. That longing in my chest is just the fever talking. And it's high time she knows it.

"Hey, thank you for calling. Is everything okay?" Her sweet, cheerful voice hits me straight in my solar plexus. My whole body jolts as if pulled by invisible strings in her direction.

I bite my cheek, then sigh deeply, dispelling all the crazy thoughts in my head that push me to beg her to come see me. "Listen, Sawyer, I can see how my... actions from the courthouse might have been a little confusing, but we had a deal. You blew my phone up in the past half an hour. Sweetheart…" I stop when a bolt of agony, so searing I double over, hits my chest. I try to mask the gasp of pain with a derisive chuckle. "I don't do seconds."

I take her silence as acceptance, despite the irrational hope brewing inside of me that she'd fight me on this. I just about lower the phone from my ear when her voice—clear as day and ice-cold—sounds through the speakers. *"The daycare center's closing time was nearly one hour ago. I'm taking Ryker to Dine&Dash because he's hungry. You can pick him up from there."* Then she promptly hangs up.

Dumbfounded, I stare at the dark screen, her words making not one lick of sense. I vaguely remember messaging my parents this morning, asking them to pick my son up. With shaky fingers, I scroll to the group chat I have with them, only to see that while I typed a gibberish message, I never sent it. Which means… "FUCK!" I shout, my voice raspy and gravelly, my swollen throat throbbing painfully in protest.

God, I'm a fucking terrible father and an even more terrible man. I left my son all alone at the daycare center, and then I went ahead and fucking assumed the only reason Ryker's *teacher* would call me is for my cock. I'm a goddamn asshole.

Not only have I offended and hurt Sawyer for no good reason, I'm also not strong enough to stand, never mind drive to Dine&Dash. I call Sawyer back, my tail between my legs, ready to promise her half my liver and a kidney, if only she'd bring my son home. Unsurprisingly, she doesn't answer.

I try my father next, only to be told they're two hours away, having dinner with some old friends of Mom's from school. *Magnificent.* Aunt Ruth is next, but she doesn't pick up. She's either cooking up a storm at the diner, seeing as it's dinner time, or out with her church friends. Drake can't help either, since he's on shift at the fire station. Annalise is spending the night at Lalah's, helping her put everything together for the gender reveal party tomorrow.

Despite being sick as fuck, I still value my life. If I call Annalise and ask her to pick up Ryker for me, she'll find out why Sawyer can't drop him off. If she knows, Lalah will know. And then I'm as good as dead. She might have forgiven me for being a cunt to her, but she'll murder me in cold blood for hurting one of her friends. Which simply means…

I'm fucked.

Desperately, I try Sawyer again, and again, and again. To no avail. I wouldn't be surprised if she blocked my fucking number.

I start messaging her, hoping beyond hope that, while she's not willing to talk to me on the phone, she'll at least read my texts.

> *Please, answer your phone or call me back.*

> *Little fairy, I'm the lowest kind of asshole. I know. I'm so fucking sorry. Please, pick up.*

Me

Nothing.

The messages show as delivered but remain unread.

I scroll through my contact list, trying to figure out who I could ask for help, when I come across the diner's takeaway service number. Desperate times and all, I dial the number, hoping their services include delivering one three-year-old with a side of chicken noodle soup.

"Dine&Dash, Renee speaking. How may I help?"

I exhale a breath I didn't know I was holding and croak, "Renee, it's Maddox. Looks like I've caught that nasty virus making the rounds through the precinct. Sawyer is waiting for me to pick up Ryker from the diner, but I'm not well enough to drive there. Could you get her on the phone for me, please?"

"Sure thing, Maddox. Hope you feel better soon. I'll go ahead and put a 'care package' order in for you, too. Your auntie would have my hide if I let her favorite nephew suffer like that."

"Thanks, Ren. I owe you one." I listen as she places the phone down, my heart hammering in my chest. This is one sure way to get Sawyer to hate me. I'm pissing all over her boundaries right now by forcing her to take my call. She'd much rather gouge my eyes out with a rusty nail than do me a favor.

Relief rises in my chest, crashing inside my limbs like a tidal wave, when I hear her soft breaths on the other side of the phone. She remains silent, but I know she's there by how my stomach tightens and tingles just by hearing her breathe.

"Little fairy," I exhale, "I..."

"Don't. When are you getting here?" she cuts me off, her voice ice-cold and unforgiving. I deserve it, but that doesn't mean it's not cutting. And

cutting deep. She won't accept an apology now, and frankly, I'd be even more of an asshole pushing one on her just to make myself feel better.

"I'm not," I croak, my throat getting scratchier by the second. "I need you to bring Ryker home, please." Not giving her a second to refuse me, I launch into an explanation of how today went for me.

She remains silent for the longest time before whispering a quiet, *"Okay,"* and ending the call.

I sag against the headboard. The last of my energy flies out the window, but I need to find some spare strength to put on some clothes and unlock the door for them. My eyes scrunch shut as I push back to my feet. The towel secured around my hips drops in a heap on the floor. My feet drag to the walk-in closet, and after excruciating effort, I manage to get my weakened body into a pair of sweats and a sleeveless T-shirt.

My chest heaves with the shuddering breaths that escape my lungs. Every inch of my body shakes under the herculean effort of just... existing. Still, I push through. I take my puke-bucket, empty it, and rinse it in the shower. Because occasionally I'm a smart man, I move it back to the side of the bed. I have a feeling I might use it again before this nightmare is over.

I will my legs to move and carry me to the door. The hallway looks miles long. Daunting. But I steel my spine, vow to kick Carson's ass for getting me sick as soon as I return to full health, and start the long trek to the landing of the stairs. Another insurmountable obstacle on my journey to get the entrance unlocked.

Fuck me. Why did I ever think getting a two-story house was a good idea? I don't fucking need four bedrooms. Ryker and I would've been happy in a nice ranch-style house with no stairs to break my neck on if I tumble down.

I shuffle one step at a time with a death grip on the banister, although, with how weak I feel, if I do trip on my own two feet, it's not gonna do much to keep me upright. By some divine intervention, I find myself at the bottom of the stairs in one piece. I'll take the victory, even if it comes with a serious case of vertigo, black spots in my vision, and wheezing like I've never walked a day in my life.

A sharp knock on the door has me barreling through the fatigue and discomfort and rushing to open it. Except I overestimated myself. I pushed too much, too fast. By the time I fling the door open, my ears are ringing and my skin is on fire. The sweat peppering my hairline falls down my forehead in rivulets, stinging my eyes. My heart is about to jump out of my chest, the world around me blurring and fading, like the zoom of a camera gone haywire.

"Little fairy…" I whisper before my body tilts sideways, and my knees give up from under me. There's no time to catch myself on the door frame when the floor rushes up to meet my face.

"Umph." A breathy groan washes over the overheated skin of my neck. My hands grip onto silk and softness as a heavenly scent of pear and bergamot envelops me. "Good grief, Maddox. You're a mess."

I blink slowly, trying to dissipate the haze that settled over my eyes. My lips curl up in a blissed-out smile as I sway on my feet, my trembling hand cupping her soft cheek.

"You're here, little fairy."

And then it's lights out, with Sawyer's sweet voice screaming my name.

Chapter Eleven

Sawyer

I think I actually die here for a second as Maddox's face drains of all color, and he collapses in my arms. Only by sheer will and a stroke of luck, I manage to prop him against the doorframe to stop him from crushing me to the floor. My knees buckle under his weight, and my chest heaves as I strain to support him. The only thing that keeps me from freaking out is his even heartbeat under my palm.

"Is Daddy okay, Miss Sawy?" Ryker's scared voice comes from behind me. I gulp down the lump that settled in my throat.

Breathe, Sawyer. Don't panic, just… breathe.

"Sweetheart, why don't you go inside and wait for us in the living room? Daddy is okay. He's just very tired right now."

He blinks up at me, icy-blue eyes full of confusion and shiny with tears. If Ryker loses it now, I'll lose it, too. I force my lips up in a semblance of a smile and urge Ryker inside with a tilt of my chin.

"Please, buddy. Go inside. I promise Daddy and I will follow you, okay?"

His bottom lip trembles. With a last look full of worry over his shoulder, Ryker steps inside, his tiny feet slapping against the hardwood floor.

I scrunch my eyes shut and drag in a breath so deep, my lungs squeeze in discomfort. Now, to figure out a way to move Maddox's hulking form inside. I dare to move the hand planted firmly over the center of his chest to his cheeks, tapping the prickly scruff gently, trying to… wake him up, I guess.

He mumbles incoherently, his face ashen. An unhealthy flush blazes at his forehead and neck, his skin burning up under my fingertips.

"Come on, big guy. Wake up. Help me out here," I beg, trying my best to keep the fear crawling up my spine at bay.

Maddox stirs, and hope sprouts to life inside of me. "L-little f-fairy, am so tired," he murmurs.

My heart hammers in my chest. Every muscle in my body strains with the effort of keeping him upright. I quickly go over the mental list of who I could call for help, but I know everyone is either busy preparing for the wedding tomorrow or working, so I'm on my own. Worst-case scenario, I'll lay Maddox down and drag him by his arms. Let's hope his floors are slippery. Rolling my eyes at my stupid ideas, I slip his arm around my shoulders and bend my knees slightly as I take more of his weight.

"S-sorry, 'ucking sorry..." he whispers, his voice weak and raspy, as he sags against me.

I mentally curse all the meals I skipped lately. Not on purpose, of course, but being heartsick doesn't really lend the greatest appetite. I could've used a couple extra pounds of muscle. Alas, here we are.

Taking small, careful steps, we slowly make our way through the hallway. Maddox's dead-weight makes everything a thousand times more difficult. I wish he'd have just a pinch of awareness, just enough to at least shuffle his feet, but he's out for the count. I don't think of what it could mean. My body is about to crumble to the ground as it is. I can freak out once Maddox is safely tucked in, but not a second sooner.

The hallway leads into his open floor living room. His kitchen is on the far wall, separated from the main living space by a breakfast bar. Dirty porcelain bowls and a jug of milk lay forgotten on the gleaming black top.

I use the wall for support as I catch my breath and look around for a sofa, an armchair, or something similar. I nearly cry in relief when I see the massive L-shaped leather couch less than five feet away from us. The only problem? No wall to use as a crutch.

"This is it, Sawyer. Woman up. You can do this," I mumble under my breath, then louder to the room, "Ryker, baby, if you're on the couch, please move to the kitchen island." The last thing I need is for Maddox to squish the poor kid when I drop him down. Because it won't be a graceful dismount. A last deep breath, I ignore the shakiness of my limbs and take all his weight onto me.

My knees tremble and buckle even more. I bend them lower, shifting my position around so my center of gravity moves, and Maddox's weight is distributed evenly across my back. I don't want to think of his chest squishing all the food Renee packed for him and the state of my back-pack. There's no soup wetting my clothes or burning my skin, so I'll take that small win.

Good grief, ten days in a hot bath with all the miracle salts in the world won't be enough to heal all my stretched-out ligaments. If I don't end up with a hernia, I'll consider myself lucky.

When my shins touch the cold buttery leather, I take a deep breath. My face feels scorching-red. Sweat peppers my forehead, sliding down into my eyes. I ignore the burn. With a last effort, I tighten my stomach and spin us around, crouching as low as I can without falling face-first on the dark, fluffy carpet, then let go of Maddox. He falls back onto the cushions of the couch with a pained groan, his legs half on the floor.

"Can I come back now, Miss Sawy?" Ryker's small voice comes from somewhere behind me.

I inhale a shuddering breath as I straighten to my full height, my chest heaving. I prop my hands on my hips, trying to calm my racing heart. My head drops back, my eyes fixed on the ceiling, and I slowly count backward from ten. *Just a bit more, Sawyer. You can freak out soon.*

"Sure you can, buddy. Thank you for being a good boy for me," I tell him with a smile I don't feel.

With shaky fingers, I lower the straps of my backpack off my shoulders and let it drop to the floor. I move around the backrest and pull Maddox up until his head rests comfortably on one of the throw pillows. I then grip his heavy legs, one by one, and move them up on the couch. Even though his feet still dangle over the edge, he looks comfortable enough.

Ryker walks past me and crawls over the cushions, sitting near his father's head, laying his forehead over Maddox's. Tears spring in my eyes in earnest now. My heart squeezes painfully in my chest. There's so much love and worry on his sweet face, my insides turn to mush. I lower myself to my knees in front of him and affectionately brush his light brown hair with my fingers.

"Buddy, your daddy is not feeling too well. Remember a couple of months ago when your tummy was upset, and all you wanted was to stay in bed and sleep?" He nods gently, his bottom lip trembling, so I continue, "It's like that for your daddy right now. He needs to sleep so he can feel better. I'm going to give him some medicine, then I'll help you get ready for bed, okay?"

Ryker nods again, closing his eyes. He plants a sweet kiss over Maddox's sweaty forehead, his tiny hand patting gently his father's cheek. My whole body warms from the inside out. The passed-out man might be a first-class jerk, but he is the best father, and that's easy to see from how Ryker's adoration for him shines through.

Shaking my head to dispel all the warms and fuzzies for Maddox away, I march to the kitchen, rifling through his drawers and cabinets until I find the one that holds all kinds of over-the-counter medicines. One box of Tylenol secured, I snatch a bottle of water from the fridge before returning to the couch.

"Okay, sweetheart. I need you to hold this for me very carefully, so we don't spill it everywhere, yeah?" I figure giving him something to do will make Ryker feel helpful and less worried about his father. He nods eagerly and sits up, his hands at the ready. I loosen the lid on the bottle and pass it on to Ryker.

Sneaking one arm behind Maddox's neck, with gentle movements I lift his head, then pop two pills into his mouth. Maddox smacks his lips together and cringes. I don't blame him; those pills are disgustingly bitter.

I smile at Ryker, who's watching my every move. "You're doing such a great job, sweetheart. Now, hold on to the bottle. I'm taking the lid off, okay?" The lid slides across the coffee table as I angle the bottle at Maddox's chapped lips. The cool liquid trickles gently into his mouth, his throat bobbing as he swallows. When I'm satisfied he's had enough, I pass the bottle to Ryker and settle Maddox back on the pillow.

"Alright, buddy, let's get you ready for bed, okay? It's already quite late for you, isn't it?"

Ryker's eyebrows furrow and, with a concentration worthy of the bomb squad, he slides off the couch and places the bottle on the coffee table. He spins around, kissing Maddox's hand and nuzzling his cheek against the back of it. "Night, night Daddy. Love you," he chirps, then leads me up the stairs to his bedroom.

My eyes are begging me to look around, to get a glimpse of Maddox's home, of how he lives when in the sanctity of his house and doesn't have to play the serious Chief Deputy or the Cocky Playboy. But instead of snooping, I focus on Ryker. I might be curious, but they're entitled to their privacy. I also need to stop giving myself reasons to look at Maddox as more than he is. Just a man. A man who's not for me.

Ryker's bedroom is ridiculously big, bigger than my own bedroom at my small cottage. The walls are painted a soft blue, each wall adorned with a multitude of stickers—from cartoon characters, cars, and footballs, to princesses and butterflies. And this is one reason it's so hard to get over this unhealthy crush I harbor for his father. Maddox allows Ryker to be who he is, to enjoy what he enjoys without boxing him in with gender stereotypes.

A single bed, larger than the standard, is pushed against the far wall, one small nightstand next to it. To the right of the bed, the window looks into their backyard, a dark green desk just below it. Boxes, brimming full of toys, are littered around. Some Legos lay discarded onto the carpet depicting roads and rails, as if Ryker was interrupted mid-play and forgot all about them. A dresser with more stickers, in the same color as the bedframe and the desk, is pushed against the wall, with another door right next to it.

That's where Ryker leads me. His free hand slaps against the wall, and light floods the floor from inside the room. He pushes the door open to reveal a small bathroom, more toys peppered around. "Bath," he whispers, then starts stripping off his clothes, dumping them inside a car-shaped laundry basket behind the door.

I don't need more directions, and I step forward, plugging the drain of the bathtub and turning on the water. Ryker is fiercely independent for being so young and makes bath time an easy affair for me, although I'm not sure this is his normal behavior. At the daycare, he is always smiling and laughing. Tonight, he's subdued. Even if he gifts me tiny smiles as we play with some rubber animals, and I try to make all the correct noises, the light usually shining in his eyes is muted, dimmed.

Knowing I need to check on Maddox soon and not feeling comfortable enough to leave Ryker alone in the bathroom even for one minute, I take one fluffy bath towel and cut his bath short. Once I'm happy he is appropriately dry, I rummage around for a clean set of PJs and help him dress, then brush his teeth. Ryker runs to his bed, hiding under the colorful sheets, and I take a minute to drain the tub and tidy around his bathroom.

Once everything is put to rights, I make my way back to Ryker. He pats his hand on his nightstand where a children's book is waiting for me. "Night-night stowy, please?"

I take a seat on the edge of his bed, next to his pillow, and he shuffles closer, laying his head over my thigh. I turn on his nightlights, and hundreds of sparkly stars appear on the ceiling. Picking up his book, I start reading to him, silly voices, giggles, and gasps included, while I tenderly brush my fingers through his soft hair. Not even halfway through the book, his breathing evens out and his little body sags around me.

Slowly extricating myself from under his head, I tuck the blanket around him. With a kiss on his forehead, I tiptoe out of his bedroom, leaving the door cracked open a couple of inches.

I lock the child-gate atop the stairs, then rush to the living room. With the back of my hand, I feel Maddox's forehead is now clammy and slick with sweat, but not as hot to the touch as it was half an hour ago. Trying to make as little noise as possible, I pick up my backpack and take it to the kitchen. Much to my surprise, there's very little spill inside the paper bag. So, I take the containers Renee prepared for him, wipe the mess off, and shove them in the fridge. I'd have to wake him up later and try to get him to eat something. By the state of the kitchen, his last meal was this morning during breakfast.

I'm not sure what to do here. Leaving is not an option, since Maddox is not in any shape or form able to look after Ryker. What if his condition worsens during the night? I don't think this is a cold or the flu as I've not heard him coughing so far, and his breaths are not wheezy or labored.

I slide my phone out of my hidden pocket, then hit dial on Beth's number and explain the situation without telling her who my sick friend is. She's quick to reassure me that this is a virus doing the rounds around the county, but the antiviral vaccine we've had as part of a school program should have me well protected. I didn't even think of catching it myself. Tatum would kill me dead if I got Maevis sick as a wedding present.

Beth also tells me that while the virus makes you feel like you're knocking on death's door, *my friend* should feel better in twenty-four hours since the onset of the symptoms. Tylenol and proper hydration are all that's needed to get him over his hurdle. I hang up with her, sighing in relief. Maybe, because I spend so much time around kids who seem to attract germs like magnets attract metals, my immune system got used to the seasonal viruses and the likes, but I don't tend to get sick very often.

My parents and siblings also seem to be quite good in that department. I've never seen any of them so unwell. Not like Maddox is right now. So Beth's reassurance goes a long way to calm the fear storming inside of me. I feel my chin quivering, and I know I'm close to bursting into tears.

This is my bad habit. Every time I'm going through a stressful situation, as soon as it resolves and the adrenaline leaves my body, I start crying. It's my mind's way of washing away the heaviness of all those negative emotions warring inside me. So I steel my spine and start tidying up Maddox's kitchen. Best offense against my pesky tears is... to distract myself.

Once all the dishes are washed and put away and his countertops are sparkling, I check on him again. His skin is peppered in goosebumps and his T-shirt is soaked through, so I make my way up the stairs, looking for his bedroom. Every cell in me is screaming to abort the mission and run for my life, but I know I can't leave the two of them alone to fend for themselves. I keep my head down. I don't need to see where Maddox sleeps, probably naked. I, for sure, don't need those images in my head. Not when I know firsthand how his muscular, sculpted body looks and feels like when he moves above me as...

NO! Bad Sawyer. For goodness' sake, the man is passed out and ravaged with fever, and you're lusting over him.

Mentally admonishing myself, I find his walk-in closet and snag a T-shirt from the shelves, then run away from his bedroom like the hounds of hell are chasing after me. I close the door behind me with a resounding click and thump my head against it. That's it, upstairs is forbidden land. Well, apart from Ryker's bedroom, but not one step further.

I hurry to Maddox's side, huffing and puffing as I change him out of his soaked T-shirt and into a clean one. At least his fever seems to be going down by the minute. I help him drink more water, then bring a fresh bottle, just in case. With my trusty Kindle—always accompanying me wherever I go—I curl up in the armchair next to the couch and start reading, masking my yawns with the back of my hand.

I force my attention on the words flickering at me from the screen instead of the man sleeping so close, yet so far away from me. So what if butterflies are roaming free under every inch of my skin at his nearness? So what if my heart is playing tricks on me, trying to revive the feelings he's stomped all over earlier this evening?

Maddox is sick, and I'm reading in the armchair. Come morning, we'll part ways never to speak of tonight ever again.

Chapter Twelve

Sawyer

I don't know when I fell asleep, but I must have done so next to a heater. *Wait. Why's the heater turned on?* The hot wall behind me shifts and grunts. The steel band around my waist tightens around me, pulling me closer to the wall at my back. A large palm, firmly cupping my breast, squeezes me. Then a finger brushes over my pebbled nipple. I can't help but squirm as liquid ecstasy travels through my veins, pooling in my core.

Blinking my gritty eyes open, I find myself face to face with a leather cushion. My heart starts hammering in my chest in the ten seconds it takes my brain to come back online. I realize I'm on Maddox's couch, trapped between his hot—literally—body and the backrest of his couch.

What the holy ink...

I search my memory, trying to make sense of how I ended up in this situation, but the last thing I remember is sitting in the armchair with my Kindle. Slowly moving my arm under me, I push up on my elbow, trying to find a way of extricating myself from Maddox's death grip. He throws a meaty leg over mine, effectively trapping me in place. A breathy gasp spills past my lips when his erection pushes against my ass.

"Little fairy," he whispers, his hot breath washing over the back of my neck. His hand starts kneading at the soft flesh of my breast, and he grinds his hips against me. "Fuck, you feel so good. I missed you so much," he grunts.

"Maddox," I squeak, my fingers gripping his hand, trying to pry it away from my chest. He's sick, not himself. He doesn't know what he's doing.

"Don't push me away, fairy. *Please!*" His begging is my undoing. I know I shouldn't give into him. If I were a smarter woman, I would've jumped off his couch and run for my life. As it turns out, I'm not a smart woman. So I push my ass against his groin, rocking my hips onto his morning wood.

His primitive, guttural groan, ripped from the depths of his chest, vibrates against my back. Tingles spread through my body. Pure need coils inside of me. My clit throbs, wetness dripping between my legs.

One more time can't hurt, right? Just one more time, and then I'll put Maddox behind me.

He hugs me tighter to his chest, as if he can hear the thoughts floating around in my head. His mouth is relentless on the sensitive skin of my neck, kissing, nipping, biting, driving me absolutely crazy.

There's nothing tentative to his touch now. Every movement is intentional, precise, meant to make me lose myself in him and his skillful fingers. They tug and pinch my nipples, alternating between my breasts, until I'm a panting, writhing mess under his ministrations.

His mouth leaves my neck, peppering kisses across my shoulder, and my stomach flips and tumbles. The material of my dress bunches at my waist as I squirm. He grips onto one thin strap with his teeth and lowers it down my arm. The knuckles of his free hand brush over my belly, leaving goosebumps in their wake as they move lower and lower, past my navel and on to the lacy waistband of my panties.

"Maddox," I whine, anticipation building inside me as his fingers slip under my panties, feathering over my soaked pussy, but never touching me where I'm aching the worst.

"Tell me what you want, little fairy. You've been such a good girl, caring for me all night long. Tell me how to please you," he orders, his voice low, and growly, and oh so maddening.

"Touch me, please." I pant when his fingers brush again over my slit. The lightest of pressure against my clit makes me jolt in his arms. "More. I need more."

He chuckles darkly in my ear, his minty breath washing over me. A fleeting thought passes through my head that he must have woken up, brushed his teeth, then moved me to the couch with him, but as soon as his thumb circles my throbbing bundle of nerves, my mind blanches and empties. There is no other thought but Maddox, his tingle-inducing touch, his scent of cardamom and violet leaves, and the hard, thick cock rubbing between my ass cheeks.

My core clenches painfully over nothing. Lust and desperation burn a path of sin through my veins, and I rock my hips faster against him. I need him to fill me up and fuck me until my eyes roll to the back of my head.

"My, you're greedy this morning," he breathes in my ear, grunting when I push against his cock. "You're my slutty little nurse, aren't you?" My protest at his derogatory words dies on my lips when he plunges two thick fingers inside my pussy, and, without giving me a second to adjust to his intrusion, starts thrusting them in and out of me at a rapid pace.

My heart hammers, my chest heaves, my blood fizzes like champagne, and my brain short-circuits. I claw at the backrest of the couch, my hands unable to find purchase on the slippery leather. Pressure builds up inside my lower belly, burning hotter than the sun, threatening to incinerate me from the inside out.

"That's it, little slut, fuck my fingers. God, Sawyer. You're so tight, baby. Tell me you didn't let anyone touch this greedy pussy of yours. Tell me I'm the only one. Tell me, and I'll let you come," he orders, curling his fingers. His rough fingertips press against that special spot inside me that makes my limbs numb and my pussy flutter. I tremble in his arms, a helpless puppet at the hands of her master.

I'm tongue-tied, all my words trapped inside my chest as I grind against the heel of his palm, chasing the high that's just one breath away. His hand leaves my breast and grips my throat, squeezing enough that I struggle for air. My walls clench around him, a bolt of lust arching my back. My ass pushes into his groin, my hips thrashing and jerking. My eyes spring open when his grip tightens around me, his fingers a collar of punishment and desire around the base of my neck. His face, peppered with black spots, appears above me, his pupils blown, just a thin ring of icy-blue surrounding their black depths. His brow furrows. Agony and pleasure twist his handsome features as his eyes bore into mine, demanding submission and obedience.

Frustration rises inside me as he keeps me on that torturous edge, my orgasm just out of reach. My lips part on a silent beg, tears brimming on my lashes.

"Put me out of my fucking misery, little fairy. Tell me no one else has touched you but me," Maddox grits, his scruffed jaw tensed and clenched.

I swallow down the dryness in my mouth, and he hisses through his teeth when he feels my throat bobbing under his palm. "O-only you," I wheeze. A moaned scream rips from my constricted larynx when he bends his head and bites my pebbled nipple hard through the fabric of my dress.

The electric bolt of pain and pleasure travels from my nipple to the impossibly hot pressure swirling in my lower belly. And then I'm thrashing, clenching, crying, screaming, trembling, and soaring as my orgasm detonates through me with the speed of a bullet, ravaging everything in me.

"You're fucking mine," he growls, then roughly removes his glistening fingers from me, and shoves them inside of his mouth, licking them clean. "You taste sweeter than I remember." It's not a praise. His tone is sharp and bitter. Hateful, like he's displeased he's enjoying the taste of my desire for him.

He doesn't give my soul time to return to my body. Instead, hurriedly tugs his sweatpants down. His cock springs free from its cotton confines, slapping against his abdomen.

Maddox positions himself behind me. His fingers, sticky with my release and his spit, collar the back of my neck, pushing my face down into the cushion. His free hand hooks around my thigh and throws my leg over his hip. In one smooth thrust that makes me cry out his name, I'm filled with his angry, throbbing erection.

A litany of curses spills past his lips, his breathing rugged and harsh as he bottoms out inside of me. I'm stretched to the very limits. He's impossibly hard, monstrously big as he completes me. And all I want is more. More of his cock, more of his rage, more of Maddox, more, more, more, until he gives me everything and I dissolve into nothing.

"Godfuckingdammit. Why is it you of all women?" he hisses, disbelief and anger coating each of his words. And then he starts moving, his hips hammering into me like the end of the world as we know it is just about to knock on his door and I'm his lifeline, his saving grace. Fire licks at my insides, burning everything in its path. His hips pump relentlessly into me, his thrusts desperate and frenzied. My breath stalls in my chest, drool dripping out of my mouth where my lips rub against the leather cushion of the sofa. And Maddox drives himself into me, harder, faster, rougher. "Fuck, you're choking my cock, little fairy. You fit me like a glove, so wet, so tight, so perfect."

My core clenches around him, spasming and contracting; my oversensitive clit throbs in time with his jerks. His fingers fasten on my thigh, spreading me open to him. The couch squeaks under the strength of his thrusts. The living room fills with the sounds of his animalistic grunts, my blissed-out mewls, and skin slapping against skin. The inferno inside of me grows and spreads, consuming all my senses. All I know is Maddox is fucking me within an inch of my life, we're as close as two people can be, and it's not enough.

His hands grip my hips, flipping me around until my front is completely flat against the couch and my ass is up in the air. My weakened knees find purchase on the edge of the cushion, my face pressed down against the slippery leather. His fingers tangle in my hair, turning my head just enough so I can see him over my shoulder, dark and thunderous. The muscles in his neck are tense and corded, an angry vein pulsating on his forehead. A thrill runs through my spine at how easily he manhandles me, how easily he manipulates my body for his own wicked pleasure.

"Be a good little slut, Sawyer, and drown my cock in your cum. Show me what a good girl you are and fucking milk me dry," he grits, retreating until only the very head of his cock remains inside of me.

And then he unleashes. His thrusts are unforgiving, his thighs slap against the back of mine, a rhythmic soundtrack of the depraved power he has over me. My achy nipples rub against the slick fabric of the sofa, sparks of pain and pleasure traveling from the tight buds to my core. He bends his massive frame over me, his dark eyes boring into mine. I'm enthralled, hypnotized, lost in him. His arm sneaks around my waist, lifting my ass higher, his cock hitting all the magic spots inside of me.

Pure molten lava floods my veins, and all it takes is the softest brush of his knuckles against my clit to tip me over the edge and into the void. I'm floating with the stars, dancing with the unknown, all the mysteries of the universe revealing themselves to me. My eyes roll into my head, and my knees give out. I'm vaguely aware of Maddox shouting his own release in my ear as he slams into me over and over again. His cum, hot and sticky, drips between my thighs as he lazily moves in and out of me, pushing his pleasure back inside my quivering pussy.

I don't know how much time passes until reality hits me with the strength of a freight train, and I stiffen in his arms. He's holding me to his chest like I'm precious, but I know better. It's not sweet pillow talk and after-sex syrupy pancakes for us as we're waiting for the sun to rise. As soon as his own post-nut clarity strikes, he'll find a way to hurt me and get rid of me like the slut he keeps telling me I am.

Maddox nuzzles his face against my neck, pushing my sweaty hair away from the sensitive skin. "What's wrong?" he murmurs.

My stomach flips into itself. The jolts coiling inside my belly have no trace of pleasure or desire. They're coated in anxiety and dread instead. The smartest thing I can do is remove myself from the situation before Maddox does more damage to my already fragile emotional state.

Using the last of my strength, I plant my palms flat against the couch and push up against his weight. He sighs, a pitiful dejected sound, and shifts away from me, even as his fingers continue caressing my bare hip. I plaster a fake smile on my face, although I'm sure I look a sight—my hair a rat's nest, my face chaffed and red where my cheek rubbed against the leather. Can I get leather-burn like a carpet-burn?

I gulp down the lump of emotion clogging my throat, regret weighing heavily on my shoulders. *Time to face the music.* I lift my head, wane smile tipping my lips up. It takes everything in me not to let it twist into a grimace. My gaze scans over his face, stopping at dark circles under his eyes that I didn't see before because of the heady daze of lust he put me under. Worry swims in his cerulean eyes. I can practically see his walls building right in front of me. *Good.*

I push to my feet, smoothing the creased skirt of my dress with my palms, pulling the hem down over my hips and to my knees. My thighs rub together as I feel our combined arousal dripping out of me. Well, this is going to make for an interesting walk of shame home. At least, I don't need to concern myself with a surprise pregnancy, as I've religiously taken my contraceptive pills since I was sixteen.

"Nothing's wrong," I tell him in a small voice. "I need to get ready for the party. I'm happy you're feeling better." My eyes dart around until they land on my flats, discarded by the chaise, along with my backpack and blazer, and I slip them on quickly. "Thanks for the fuck," I throw over my shoulder.

The burn of his hurt chases me all the way home.

Chapter Thirteen

Maddox

What the fuck just happened?

I'm still sitting on the fucking couch like a confused duck, with my bare ass on the sticky, leather cushion. My eyes are fixating on the hallway she disappeared through, the resounding slam of the door as it closed echoing in my ears.

"Thanks for the fuck? THANKS FOR THE FUCK?!" I repeat to myself like a broken recorder, incredulity and disbelief venomous on my tongue. One minute she is in my arms, soft and pliable after the mind-blowing sex we've just had, me about to ask her to stay for breakfast, or just... stay. Next, she's rushing out the door like the house is on fire.

Pushing to my feet, I pull up my sweats, throwing my arms over my head and stretching my back. What feels like every bone in me cracks and pops, my muscles screaming in protest after the workout I just put them through. *The meaningless fuck.* She might not have said the word, but she thought it. Sawyer reeked of regret and bad choices as she ran away from me.

I start re-arranging the throw pillows when my eyes snag on a damp spot on the leather, a white, dried-out puddle of cum left behind on the dark material. Time stops. My blood freezes in my veins, and nausea pools in my mouth. "Fuck, fuck, fuck, godfuckingdammit stupid horny fucker!" My hand flies to my hair, gripping the messy strands in my fist. *What did I do? Shit.*

It's her. Sawyer Carter makes me lose my goddamn mind. I've *never* gone without a condom. Yeah, yeah, I have a kid. I have a kid because the universe aligned, and the condom I used was the failing two percent, and Katherine was just coming off a course of antibiotics that interfered with her pills. My son was meant to exist. But never in my life have I gone bare. The rule might as well have been tattooed on the head of my cock, *Wrap it up or tuck it back.*

And that's on me. I was the one rutting into her like an animal in heat. I was the one who didn't take a second to think. When I woke up just past midnight, and I saw her curled up in the armchair, I thought for a second the fever had incinerated my last remaining brain cell, and I was full on hallucinating. But my head felt clear for the first time the whole day, my body strong if a pinch sore, and my energy replenished. Then the events of the evening came back to me.

No one picking Ryker up from the daycare; begging Sawyer to drop him off; me using the last of my energy to unlock the door for them; snippets here and there of the disappearing fairy feeding me pills and helping me drink water; her changing my clothes and wiping my sweat off; her delicate fingers brushing through my hair.

I knew I had a choice then. The smarter decision would've been for me to march my ass upstairs into my bedroom and let her sleep. But the needier side of me won. The side that fantasized all day in my feverish dreams of having someone at my side, someone to care for me and make me feel better just by their smile alone. And if that someone had the sexiest dimple in their right cheek, hair so blonde it shined silver, and mesmerizing navy-blue eyes like the tumultuous depths of the ocean, who was I to fight against what my dreams dictated?

My longing made me weak, so I picked her up and moved her to the couch. I figured I'd get a redo. I'd find out what it feels like to wake up to Sawyer's smiling face, something she deprived me of after our night together.

Well... as it turns out, seeing her scramble to get away from me hurts just as badly as waking up to a cold bed.

If my desperation got her pregnant... I'm not going to miss the entire pregnancy like I missed all those milestones with Ryker. I'm a goddamn man, I'll face this head on.

All I need is a cloth to clean away any and all traces of my recklessness. Next up is a shower. The cold water does wonders for my abused muscles, the soreness in my body swirling down the drain along the bubbling foam. Once I feel more human, I go back downstairs and brew a full pot of coffee. With a steaming mug in my hand, I make my way to the back porch. The sun still isn't up yet.

Unease crawls up my spine. I didn't hear Sawyer's car start when she left. Which only means she walked here last night and walked back home. *Fuck me, in how many ways can I fail one woman?* With hurried fingers, I tap my phone, heaving a breath of relief when the call connects. My relief is short-lived when she doesn't answer and her voicemail kicks in.

She left about thirty minutes ago. She should be home by now. Maybe she's in the shower, scrubbing my touch off her skin like I washed hers away. Or maybe she's looking at the phone, seeing my name, and takes a hammer to the screen, wishing it was my face.

Please tell me you got home safe.

Me

Home safe.

Little Fairy

Then why aren't you answering your phone?

Me

What do you want from me, Maddox?

Little Fairy

...

Me

Everything.
Nope. Can't say that. Won't say that.

I didn't use a condom.

Me

Well aware. Now leave me alone.

Little Fairy

Sawyer, for fuck's sake. I didn't use a condom, you know, the little latex sheath called protection?

Me

> *What's your damage, Maddox?*
>
> *You know good and well I've only ever slept with you.*
>
> *Despite what you think of me, out of the two of us, you're the slut, not me.*

Little Fairy

My whole body recoils at her words. *What the fuck?* My stomach churns and my insides twist into painful knots. There's no denying that I've been around the block once or twice or a couple hundred times, but all the women I've been involved with knew what they were getting into.

Sawyer is the only woman I've shared a bed with more than once. Sawyer's the only woman I've allowed inside my house, apart from my mother and Annalise when she visits with Drake, which is *rare* because she's not particularly fond of me.

I'm not going to dignify her last sentence with a response.

"'*Despite what you think of me, out of the two of us, you're the slut, not me.*' What's that supposed to mean?" I mumble in my coffee, the bitter taste seeping into my taste buds, much like the bitterness in Sawyer's message burrows into my chest, leaving me hollow and cold.

> *I'm clean. And I was more worried about a potential pregnancy than an STD.*

Me

> *Rest well, Maddox. You're not going to be tied for the rest of your life to me.*
>
> *Feel free to sow your wild oats.*

Little Fairy

I see red. And black. And blue. And the whole fucking rainbow. My fingers, though, couldn't care less about the anger and unrest taking over me and seem to develop a mind of their own. Before I realize what's happening, my thumb presses send.

> *What the hell happened, Sawyer? I thought every-thing was well. Did I do something you didn't like? You were with me the entire time.*

Me

Message could not be delivered.

Tap the icon to retry.

She blocked me. She actually fucking blocked me.

The hollowness in my chest expands and throbs. My limbs grow numb, tingles spreading under my skin like a million fire-ants eating away at my flesh. I scrub my hands over my face, then press the heels of my palms against my eyes as the pressure behind them intensifies.

A moment of weakness. That's all this morning was. Yesterday scared me simply because I had no one to look after Ryker. I would've woken up this morning and felt fine with or without Sawyer. There's a reason I don't get involved with women. They always leave, and they always betray you one way or another. My life is my life, and I don't need a fucking wallflower to judge my choices and the way I elect to live.

I'll make sure I have a sitter on standby if anything of the sort happens again.

Ryker and I are a team. We don't need anyone to waltz in and disturb our routine, to make us fall in love with them, and then leave us bereft.

"WHAT CRAWLED UP YOUR ASS?" Lalah's voice chirps from somewhere behind me. I'm sitting in a chair, watching Ryker chase Clara around the extensive backyard. Balloons are littered everywhere you can see. The tables, heaving with what looked like everything edible in the county, are now empty.

I debated if I should show up for the gender reveal turned wedding for Maevis and Tatum, knowing she was going to be here. But my pride and the last of my common decency demanded I show up. After all, Maevis is the sister I never had. So, if I'm here and looking strictly at my son, that's because I'm a good father and I'm keeping an eye on my kid.

My eyes have never strayed to the vision in sky-blue silk. There was no eyefucking of any kind, nor any longing to be felt. My heart didn't stall painfully in my chest when she hugged her brother before the ceremony or when she shed happy tears as vows were exchanged, making her dark blue eyes lighten a shade or two. I absolutely did not want to rip Jackson's head off his shoulders, then Blake's, and the legs and hands of that Irish asshole, Rowan, when they each danced with her.

"Now you're ignoring me?" she scoffs and slaps my shoulder.

I tilt my head, enough to look at her towering over me in a hoodie and leggings, her beast of a dog sitting obediently at her feet. Of course, she ditched her dress as soon as the ceremony was over, while the rest of us were forced to wear monkey suits the entire day.

"Didn't realize you were talking to me," I mumble and gulp a mouthful of the warm, non-alcoholic beer I've been nursing all evening.

"Considering the *fuck off* vibes shooting out of you, are you really surprised there's no one else around I can actually talk to?

" She pops a perfectly arched dark eyebrow, pushing a strand of her long black hair behind her ear.

See, I'm not surprised I went for her that night at the club over a year ago. Lalah is a beautiful woman, in an understated, girl-next-door sort of way. But I look at her now and... nothing. Not even a twitch of my dick, or a single extra red cell in my blood rushing south, except for the ones required to keep the soldier behind my fly alive but dormant.

And I have a horrible feeling my lack of attraction to her is not because of the rock weighing her finger down.

"There are no vibes here, *fuck off* or any other kind. I'm still recuperating after the goddamn virus had its dirty way with me," I say. I would very much like to tell her to *fuck off*. But seeing as I am a guest in her house, and the entirety of Lost Hope would burn me at the stake in the middle of Main Street if I dared offend their favorite benefactor—or whatever would be left of me after Astrum and Cole had enough of killing me and bringing me back only to kill me again—I refrain.

"Ah. So we're blaming viruses now for you brooding at the grass in my backyard until it wilts. Gotcha'!" She winks and makes fucking pistol fingers at me.

I sigh and narrow my eyes at her. "What can I do for you?"

She smiles at me, and my balls shrivel and climb up into my stomach, hiding behind my kidneys. Lalah Hayes doesn't smile unless her husband and their adopted daughters are around. And if she does... run for your life.

"Here's what's going to happen, and keep in mind, you don't get to say *no*. First, you're going to go home and sleep off whatever virus crawled up your ass that has you throwing daggers with your eyes at any happy thing in a fifty-mile radius. Then, you're going to pack a bag big enough to keep you decent for a three-day trip. Last, you're going to drop Ryker off at your parents' and show your face at the airport at 3 p.m. sharp tomorrow."

I open my mouth to protest. Even if I wanted to get away, I can't just not show up at work, especially after I had to call in sick yesterday and took today off for the party. And most important of all, my son needs me. I failed him yesterday, so now I need to ensure he knows he is a priority for me, not an afterthought.

"Nah-ah. Zip it. This is not up for debate. I already cleared your leave with Sheriff Richards." Lalah crosses her arms over her chest and pops a hip. Oh shit, if that's not a fighting stance, I don't know what is.

"Ryker," I mumble weakly, but I know I don't have a leg to stand on. My son loves spending time with his grandparents and running around through their extensive gardens and orchards.

"While I commend you for being a doting father, we both know you're using him as an excuse. Come on, it'll do you good to get out of Lost Hope for a couple of days. I heard Castling Sands has some damn good beaches."

My eyebrows shoot to the middle of my forehead, and a sharp whistle that has Astrum growling at me slips past my lips. "Holy shit, you went all out."

"So don't waste my fucking efforts, then."

"Who's going?" I don't know what sort of drunk demon possesses me to ask that question, but the words are out of my mouth and into the world, and I can't shove them back in as much as I want. And believe me, I want. Especially as she gives me one of her smiles that promises I will absolutely regret both asking and going.

"Everyone, Maddox," she deadpans. "So pack up, buttercup, else I swear on the Kuiper belt and the whole Trans-Neptunian region, I'll wormhole your ass there."

I guess I'm going on the honeymoon organized for the brother of the woman I fucked less than twelve hours ago. And it's not just so I can make sure no man ogles said woman in a skimpy bikini at the beach.

She means nothing to me. Just another notch on my belt.

PART TWO

A season for hate.

"Adrift, my hollow soul cries for its half;
You're blind to my pain,
Enraged by my want.

A master puppeteer commanding the dark;
You pluck at my strings,
Then rip me apart."

SAWYER CARTER

Chapter Fourteen

Sawyer

"Are you sick?"

"What?" My head swivels in my sister's direction. Her corn-flower-blue eyes, much like my father's and brother's, scan me with the precision of a laser.

"Are. You. Sick?" she asks again, over-enunciating every word.

"No. What makes you think that?" Maybe the fact that I've avoided her like the plague until she plopped down next to me in the airplane and cornered me against the window seat so there was nowhere for me to run.

"You have dark circles so deep, they look tattooed under your eyes." She lifts one finger. "Your skin's ashen." A second finger follows the first. "A cloud of doom and gloom trails you around; I almost expect a lightning bolt to strike the plane down." A third finger goes up.

And that's the reason I've been avoiding her. Selena is my best friend, my confidant. We grew up together, we shared a bedroom for over fourteen years. She knows me better than I know myself. And I don't want her to know *me* right now. I want to wallow in my own stupidity and drink my body weight in mimosas on the beach till my liver screams *Uncle*.

"I'm going for the au naturel reverse-smokey eyes, thanks."

She blinks up at me, her beautiful long lashes brushing against her cheeks. Her lips, slicked in pink lipstick, purse as she tsks at me. "What are you not telling me?"

Okay, time to change tactics. I give her a small smile, widening my eyes. Innocence is my best defense.

"I'm just tired, Selae. We're rushing through the last mile to get Happy Bumblebees open. A lot of last-minute details are quite time consuming."

"We'll make sure you rest and enjoy this break, then. You need to take better care of yourself, sissy. I know HeeBee is your dream, but don't burn yourself out before opening day."

I rest my head on her shoulder, the lies leaving a bitter taste in my mouth. I've never lied to my sister before. My life used to be an open book, every page hers to read, every line hers to support. The steps I've taken as of late, the things I've done, I'm starting not to like myself anymore. It's not exactly shame that has me tongue-tied. I can't bring myself to regret the night I spent with Maddox. Either night.

What I regret is who I become around him—this desperate woman, craving every morsel of his attention. I thought my feelings to be an innocent crush. But what's crushing is my chest, caving into itself whenever he's near and not touching me. When we pass by one another, electricity crackles in the air, filling the empty space between our bodies, pushing us together and pulling us apart.

The violence of the feelings I have for him terrifies me to my very core. He both sees me and makes me feel invisible. Around him, I feel alive but also as if I'm screaming until my lungs are burning and no one hears but him. And he ignores me. I had barely a blip of his attention, and that blip grew into an addiction enslaving every single one of my decisions. Waking up, I have Maddox on the brain and longing in my heart. Going to sleep, impossible dreams plague the time I'm supposed to be resting.

Maybe Selae is right. I am sick.

My one and only boyfriend, Rob, has never made me feel this way, this... unhinged and out of control. I went days, weeks even, without seeing him when we were busy with exams, and I was just fine. Now, if a day goes by without a glimpse of Maddox, there's an itch deep in the marrow of my bones, urging me to just... casually walk around Main Street in the hopes I'll lay my eyes on him as he comes out of Suga'High or while he patrols the streets in his cruiser. Every morning for the past month, disappointment sat like a boulder in my stomach when Ryker was dropped off by everyone but Maddox. Hope danced in my chest every afternoon, only to be blown to smithereens, when everyone but Maddox would pick Ryker up.

I filled all the pages of a notebook in four short weeks with poems about him. Every word, every rhyme is an ode to the foreign feelings he evokes in me. The blue ink stains on my palms are permanently branded on each ridge and every crease making up my fingerprints.

It can't be love. I had love, and it was soft and nurturing, patient and kind. And when it stopped being the very comfort my days rested on, it stopped being love. When it scared me and made me cower, it was manipulation and gaslighting.

One thing I *know* I feel around Maddox is fear. He scares the very foundation on which I've built my life. What I never feel? The need to cower. His icy-blue eyes hold a feral urge, pushing me to rise to the challenge, to step away from the wall and shed those delicate petals, baring my sharp thorns instead.

Around Maddox I'm not a wallflower—delicate, timid, breakable. I'm a wildflower instead—strong, resilient, bulletproof.

Impossible dreams don't hurt me just because I know I don't get the man in the end. They hurt because, when his back is at me and his focus on someone else, I'm the same wilted wallflower with no thorns at all.

My father worships the ground my mom walks on. My brother is head-over-heels in love with his pregnant wife; he'd lay his life down at her feet if she'd only ask. I took the type of men in my family for granted. Until Rob proved me wrong. And then I went and took a nail gun to the coffin of my naïveté and got myself terminally ill with a chronic case of Maddox Lawson.

The rest of the flight passes in a blur, as does the drive to the resort. Do I admire the view even for a second? Nope. Why drool after the private island of one of the wealthiest men in the US when I can mope after the affections of the broodiest asshole? I don't even take a minute to admire the cabin Lalah rented for us, the one I'm sharing with Selae and Emma. As soon as the key is passed to one of us—not me—we walk to the cabin, and I march straight to the closest bedroom I can find and face-plant on the soft-as-a-cloud mattress. Eh, it's as good of a place as any to mope away my holiday.

The door bangs open against the wall, and in marches one Selena Carter, the sharp heels of her stilettos click-clacking against the hardwood floor. I groan and cover my head with a soft pillow. *What's a girl gotta do to get some peace and quiet around here?* I squeal and scramble to my knees when my dearest sister spanks me so hard, my cheek continues to jiggle one minute after impact.

"GOD, SELAE! What's wrong with you?"

"Oh, goodie, you're awake." She throws a garment-bag onto the bed at my knees. "Put this on, then come to the living room. Emma's doing hair and makeup." I sit on my calves, staring at her, my eyes blinking in slow motion. "What? Was I slurring? Chop chop, get dressed. Time's a-wasting."

My tongue finally unsticks from the roof of my mouth. "What are you talking about?"

"We're going clubbing." She spreads her arms wide, as if to present the club to me. Her foot is tapping impatiently against the floor. I almost expect her to break out a PowerPoint presentation and do a risk analysis for me on the advantages of staying in versus going out with them.

"I never agreed to come." My arms fold across my chest, chin tilting in a defiant pose.

"You want me to call Lalah and tell her that?" Selae smirks, wiping her nails on the shoulder of her dress before blowing on them.

My lips part on an outraged gasp, "You wouldn't!" I point my finger at her accusingly.

"Of course I wouldn't. As long as you're dressed and in the living room in the next ten minutes, my phone stays firmly inside my purse," the traitor says with a smug glint in her cornflower-blue eyes before turning around and marching out of the bedroom.

"Great. I guess I can mope just as well with a bottle of tequila in a club, instead of moping with a bucket of ice cream in bed," I mumble under my breath.

THE THUMPING BASS OF THE OVERLY LOUD MUSIC crashes through my body, my heart altering its pumps to match the beat of the song. My arms are up in the air and, with the three shots of whatever concoction Selae convinced me to down, my body is loose and limber. I don't care about the far-too-short silver sequined dress I'm wearing. I am absolutely not bothered by the brooding man flirting with every woman in this club just five feet away from me.

I am music. Music is me.

So I sway, and I shimmy, my hips undulating and gyrating, my knees bending and straightening. There's no heartache on the dance floor or pushover wallflowers. Only me, my friends, and the seductive beat of the song.

The club is mostly dark, strobing lights flashing here and there, but the atmosphere is obscure and sultry. The bar takes up the entire length of the far wall, although it's used more often than not as a dance floor too, with scantily clad women putting on a show and thirsty men hovering around for the flavor of the night.

I'm not one to judge, since I myself was just a few days ago one of those flavors.

Despite my lack of experience, I don't yuck in other people's yum. As long as *yum* is of legal age and consenting, how people spend their time in the bedroom—or other surfaces—is not my concern. There's too much bitterness in the world, too much malice and desire to inflict pain on others. What people do to release some negative energy and bring themselves joy it's their business and their business only, if everyone involved is in agreement and no one gets hurt.

Unlike me. I got hurt.

Well, I hurt myself, so I guess *that* doesn't count.

Annalise nudges me with her elbow. Her green sequined dress—identical to mine except for the color—sparkles when the strobing lights pass over her. The two-piece dresses were Emma's idea. She designed and made them herself, and I have to admit, even though I worried about the length, it fits me like a glove and wears like a cloud.

"Brought you some water," Annalise shouts over the loud music. "Figured we'd need all the help we can get to fight the monster hungover that awaits us tomorrow."

I laugh because I know she's right and unseal the lid of the glass bottle, gulping greedily at the cool liquid.

"Thanks," I shout back. "I needed it."

"Selae is ready to return to the cabins. She asked me to find you while she went to the bathroom."

I scrunch my eyebrows. This is so typical Selena. She'd bug me to go out, only to cut the night short for a business call or whatever strange email from a corporate ghost who doesn't sleep, eat, or have personal boundaries when it comes to time off demands her attention.

Grabbing Anna's elbow, I lead us to the booths in the VIP area Lalah reserved for our group. While technically on the same floor as the bar and the massive dance area, the VIP section is built like private rooms enclosed in glass. The music is still loud, but makes for easier conversation, and the seats are butter-soft, just perfect to rest your feet for a minute after dancing the hours away in four-inch heels.

Yes, yes, I too am rolling my eyes. But in my defense, I didn't go for the tall, strappy sandals. They've been chosen for me along with the dress.

I'm towering over all the women in our group, except for Emma. As the night started, I felt like a baby deer just learning to walk, all shaky knees and uncoordinated steps, but shots are fast-actioned that way. They steel your spine, increase your confidence, and lower your inhibitions. I don't let loose often, but when I do, that boost of liquid courage is the reason.

I hug my sister goodbye since I know once she gets in corporate-empowered-she-devil mode, there's no changing her mind. Drake and Annalise assure me they'll see her safely to the cabin and then come back here.

Taking advantage of the empty booth, I stretch my legs out on the leather seat, easing the pressure on my abused toes. My eyes scan the club, stopping briefly where Lalah and Cole are swaying gently at the edge of the dance floor. They're so enthralled with each other, they don't even notice the song has changed to something more upbeat.

Emma, Jackson, and Blake left about an hour ago, and I'm trying not to think about what I stumbled on in the women's bathroom. My heart lurches in my chest for my friend. Jackson and Blake have their own drama they're dealing with, and she ended up somewhere in the middle—literally. She's just been through her own ordeal—finding out her fiancé cheated on her with her supposed best friend, Maddison, almost the entirety of their relationship and then going as far as to put his filthy hands on her. But if a hot holiday thirst keeps her going... I just hope she's not like me, since apparently my heart lives right inside my vagina.

And that leaves... The Invisible Man.

So, basically, right now it's just me, Lalah, and Cole since I'm ignoring the broody, unwanted presence with all my might. And he's ignoring me right back.

No, it doesn't hurt. Why would it hurt that I'm wearing my sexiest dress to date, and I look at my most beautiful with the subtle makeup Emma has done for me—just enough to enhance my large eyes, high cheekbones, and the fullness of my lips. It doesn't bother me in the slightest that his eyes looked right through me, and then he disappeared out the door and into his rental car when we all met at the Main Lodge—Lalah, Cole, and Blake's cabin, which we all deemed to be our headquarters for this long weekend.

"Oh, hi," a feminine voice giggles. "We didn't see you there."

My body stiffens as I lift my eyes and scan over the generous body of the petite brunette attached to Maddox's hulking frame. Nausea pools in my mouth, the bile sour and bitter on my tongue. My stomach flips as if I'm free-falling, and the backs of my eyes burn.

"No, that's okay," I tell her, proud of myself when my voice doesn't betray the agonizing bolt of lightning hitting my insides. He owes me no loyalty, but I thought he'd at least consider not parading another woman in front of me just twenty-four hours after he fucked me into oblivion. "I was just leaving."

Somehow, I manage to stand, and my heroic legs don't buckle, but continue to support my weight. I plaster myself to the glass separating the booth from the dance floor, careful that no part of me touches any part of them. Of him.

"Sawyer…" Maddox sighs, but I pay him no attention.

I need to get out of here before I puke all over the beautiful white shirt he's wearing that's molding over all his delicious muscles.

He's not mine, and he'll never be. The sooner my heart accepts the reality, the better for everyone involved.

Chapter Fifteen

Maddox

All I've wanted for this shoved-down-my-throat holiday is to bury my feet in the sand and drink my liver to an early death, ideally, while avoiding Sawyer. Alas, here I am, music thumping in my eardrums, whatever-her-name-is grinding her ass against my crotch, and... I couldn't be less interested. Frustration mounts inside of me, my blood boiling with disappointment.

One month ago, she would've already been bent over the sink in the bathroom or the nearest cleaning closet. I'd be balls deep into her cunt, and we'd both leave a bit emptier inside, but fully sated. Now, there's not even a twitch behind my zipper. If my cock could yawn, I swear it would. How am I supposed to get over whatever this feeling is, twisting my insides into knots whenever Sawyer is nearby, or away from me, or just generally existing, if I cannot fuck another woman without feeling sick to my stomach?

I'd take the fucking nausea if it meant I'd be able to bury myself deep in a pussy, but I can't even get it up.

The dark-haired woman spins in my arms, her palms flat on my chest, slowly caressing me with her thumbs. "Buy me a drink, handsome?"

I hesitate for one split second, already well aware my cock is not ready to play. Or maybe he just has performance anxiety, and with everyone on the floor dancing and bumping into us, maybe just maybe, he'd be a more willing participant somewhere more secluded. My nostrils also flare because I'm convinced the stench of bullshit is heavy in the air. For some strange reason, I smell nothing but the usual tangy scent of sweat, a cacophony of perfumes, and the warm, spicy undertones of alcohol.

My fingers entwine with hers. The skin of my palm itches uncomfortably under the warmth radiating from her hand. Her fingers are too sharp between mine, too limp, too foreign. I pull her behind me as we make our way to the booth Lalah reserved in the VIP section, then open the glass door, and usher her in with my palm to the small of her back. I might be a horny cunt, but there's no reason not to have some semblance of manners.

"Oh, hi," she giggles, the childish sound of her laugh grating on my ears. "We didn't see you there," the faceless, nameless woman says in a high-pitched voice, her arm sneaking around my waist.

I freeze as I end up eye to eye with Sawyer's stony face. If it bothers her to see another woman plastered to me, I can't tell. She smiles pleasantly at my companion. "No, that's okay. I was just leaving," she responds, pushing to her feet. The silver strappy sandals with pencil-thin heels put her nearly at the same height as me. She's painfully beautiful, like a breath of fresh air and a punch to my solar plexus, all in one.

She shifts sideways, close to the glass window overlooking the dance floor, as she passes by. Ice travels down my spine and into my bloodstream as fear claws at my stomach. This is wrong, this is all wrong. *Don't let her leave, you supreme idiot.*

My arm stretches of its own accord, my fingers dying to grasp her forearm and stop her from running away from me. "Sawyer," I sigh, her name on my lips a blessing and a curse.

She ignores me, of course she does, the excruciatingly loud music drowning the expletives spilling out of my mouth as she opens the door and disappears out into the crowd.

"Finally alone." The woman next to me giggles again. Whatever feeling returned to my cock when I laid eyes on Sawyer crawls back into the depths of my stomach. My plan to get back on the saddle in a more private setting backfired *massively*. I plop into the first available chair and drag a generous gulp of air into my lungs. The scent of bergamot, freesia, and pear still lingers in the empty space Sawyer left behind.

I grunt when the pest of a woman I still don't know the name of drops in my lap. Only reflex has me gripping her hips with my hands, so that she doesn't topple over. My eyes are still fixating on the dance floor Sawyer disappeared into.

"How about that drink?" she asks again, her voice sultry, trying to be seductive, I think. All she manages is to annoy the fuck out of me. I'm ready to push her away and tell her kindly to fuck off. At this point, I'm sure my erection is on hiatus, without a return date in sight.

Just as I'm about to open my mouth and make her leave, the door to the VIP lounge opens again, Annalise, Drake, and Cole stumbling through it. Anna's eyes grow wide when she sees me and the... lady friend in my lap.

"Where have you been?" I demand of my best friend. What I truly want to ask is why the fuck is he letting me make mistake after bitter mistake. Isn't it in the best friend handbook or some shit that he's supposed to kick my ass when I'm being particularly stupid? Clearly, I have no self-control, so I need extra help.

Drake pops an eyebrow at me, dismissing the woman nuzzling her sweaty face against my shirt. Anna rolls her eyes at my sheer idiocy and slides on the leather bench of the booth, as far away from me as she can get. Not that I blame her.

"We took Selena home. She had a work thing. Cole was romancing his wife with his gyratory skills." Annalise snorts.

I grunt. I mean, what else is there to say? *Please, put me out of my misery and break a fucking bottle over my head—the heavier the better?*

Just then, the bane of my existence returns with a couple of fancy-looking glasses full with colorful liquids in her hands. She passes one on to Annalise, kissing her cheek and whispering something, and all the air rushes out of my body as if someone took a sledgehammer to the family jewels.

We've shared a bed twice, and not once have I felt her plump lips on me or the sweet caress of her tongue against mine. A hollowness sits empty in my mouth, the phantom touch of her lips feathering over me. I'm not drunk enough for this shit. Well, I'm not drunk, period. I figured with the sinful temptation that Sawyer Carter is in such close quarters, I'd better keep my wits about me. I don't need alcohol to destroy the last living neuron in my head and make a fool out of myself by kissing her—or worse—in front of all her friends.

This was a terrible fucking idea. Every time I'm with these people in a bar or a club, something terrible happens. That something right now is a five-eight out-of-limits woman, clad in the sexiest motherfucking dress I've seen in my life.

I shift in my seat, trying to discreetly adjust the hard-on raging beneath my fly. The faceless woman in my lap nuzzles my neck again and starts peppering kisses down my shoulder. Didn't I just say being with them in a bar is a bad idea? And an even worse one is rubbing her half naked ass on my aching cock.

The second I saw Sawyer in the main lodge, wearing that slip of a skirt made out of every man's wet dreams, I knew I was in trouble. Big fucking trouble. I figured the best way to remove her from under my skin was to get someone else under me.

Fucked, if it's working.

Because it's not.

My cock is an uninterested dick, unless Sawyer is around and then he's all party like it's '99.

She is poisoning me. She poisoned me when she gave herself to me a month ago, and then again, the other day, on my couch. She's poisoning me now with her chilly indifference. My eyes seek her out like they have a mind of their own. There isn't one single part of my body that listens to me where she's concerned.

"Sawyer!" Lalah shouts over the thumping music, "Come dance with us."

Oh, fuck me, don't go.

I'm about to push the brunette out of my way and stop this, but I'm too late when Annalise joins them. Whoever put Lalah and Anna together had no idea of the plague they'd be unleashing into the world. If these two get something into their heads, nothing changes their minds. And God deliver the fool who dares to stand in their way.

I watch helplessly as all three of them make their way to the bar, all dressed in the same combination of lace tops and sequined skirts hitting mid-tight, only in different colors. When Lalah stands on a stool, Cole flies out of his seat.

"Oh shit, what are these crazies thinking?" Drake curses and follows Cole to the bar, where all three women are now moving lasciviously to the beat, up on the bar top.

I swallow the current of unease lodged in my throat, but when BRKN Love's cover of "River" starts playing, I know I'm done for. My eyes remain glued to the fairy dressed in sparkling silver as she's sandwiched between Lalah and Annalise. Her hips are swiveling. Honey-sweet nipples, crowning teardrop breasts I have intimate knowledge of, push through the thin material of her top. Her dainty hands caress her collarbone.

I'm helpless to stop the groan ripping from my chest. My fingers bite into the wooden table in front of me in a futile attempt to keep me seated—my last line of defense.

And then it crumbles.

It rips to shreds as soon as those two evil motherfucking women rip Sawyer's skirt off, leaving her only in that godforsaken paper-thin top. The lace seam barely covers the top of her thighs, brushing over silver garter belts on each of her long creamy legs.

My heart pounds inside my ribcage, and all the air is vacuum-sucked from the club. My vision tunnels—all I see is her. Sawyer Fucking Carter, the bane of my goddamn existence, a vision in lace and silk, rubbing that ass-made-for-sin of hers against a jean-clad thigh.

Jealousy roars to life inside of me. Like a gunshot to the chest, my entire body jolts from the impact of seeing her lost in her movements, seducing a man who isn't me.

And I'm done.

I'm done fucking waiting. I'm done being over her. I'm done watching her forget all about me.

No one touches what's mine. No one gets to spoil what only I had.

I don't know the moment I leave the seat and get in front of the bar. All I know is that she is coming with me, and she's coming with me now.

My arms encircle the top of her thighs, and I throw her over my shoulder. With the last of my awareness, my palm covers her ass since, even with murder and hate-sex on my mind, I'm present enough not to want to give anyone a front view of what is only mine.

Her dainty, ineffective fists thump against my back. I feel nothing except for the need to have her under me and fuck out of her all thoughts of any other man.

I spin on my heel and briefly register the smug smirk on Lalah's lips and the middle finger she throws in my face, but I don't have the presence of mind to linger on the whys and the hows.

For the first time in weeks, my mind and my body are in agreement. My legs carry me out of the bar as fast as they can. Sawyer's knee hits me in the stomach, and I stumble but course-correct before we're both sprawled out on the floor.

She's angry.

Good.

I'll fuck the anger out of her, too.

I reward her with a smack at the back of her thighs. In a mirror image of our first night together, I push her soaked underwear aside and plunge my middle finger inside her tight heat, moving it mindlessly in and out—our sin covered by the lacy seam of her cami.

As soon as I push through the doors and into the darkness of the night, her moaned shouts reach me, "Put me down, you asshole! Who the fuck do you think you are? Put me the fuck down, you selfish prick." I nearly choke on my tongue at the filthy words coming out of her sweet mouth. Sawyer never curses. *Never.* I fucking love it.

"You're this wet for him, fairy, or for me?" I grit through clenched teeth as her tight pussy clamps hard around my finger, despite the contrary words coming out of her mouth.

"You're fucking insane, Lawson." My cock fights to break through my zipper when she moans my name, and I waste no time in sliding her off my shoulder and pinning her between me and my rental car.

My free hand goes to her throat, and I squeeze while I plunge another finger inside of her silky, wet channel and start finger-fucking her in earnest. I bury my face in her hair, letting her cries loose into the quiet of the night and the tremble of her body surrendering to me calm the caged beast inside me.

Her back arches, pushing those mouth-watering tits against my chest. I pay them no mind. I have an orgasm to chase and a woman to punish for driving me out of my fucking mind.

The fluttering of her pussy around my fingers and the mewling cries escaping her throat are my fucking undoing. I'll be damned if I let anyone else hear as she cries out her pleasure so prettily for me. Only for me.

I rip my hand from around her throat and plunge two fingers between her plump lips, sliding them against her velvety, slippery tongue. Just enough awareness is left alive in me so that I don't crush my lips to hers, my tongue conquering her mouth, desperate to swallow any and all sounds she rewards me with. Desperate to taste the obsession she flames inside my soul.

But that's the only thing I'll grant her tonight. Her last boundary.

"Come for me, little fairy. Be a good fucking girl for once, and come for me," I order with the last of my sanity, pressing my thumb to her needy clit at the same time I curl my knuckles inside her hot pussy.

"God, Madd, yes," she pants around my fingers, drool dripping down her chin. "Holy fuck, Maddox, yes, yes, yeeees."

Chapter Sixteen

Maddox

The drive from the club to the cabin is short. Sawyer is quiet in the passenger seat, her eyes staring unseeingly through the window. My body is tense, every muscle bunched, every breath labored. I'm white-knuckling the wheel, doing everything I can so that I don't stop on the side of the road and fuck her stupid in the backseat.

My cock might have been indifferent all night, but now he's threatening to burst through my zipper. I'm so hard it's painful. There's no damn cure to this hurt, except for her warm, silky pussy wrapped around me like a comfort blanket.

A savage war is waging inside of me. All my self-doubts, all the convictions I thought were cemented into the very depths of my being versus everything Sawyer represents, the possibility of love, of family, of devastation.

I'm losing my mind, and my heart, and the very foundation I've built my life on.

And all at the dainty hands of the woman sitting right next to me.

Throwing the rental into park, the tires squeal against gravel as I brake hard in front of my cabin. I jump out of the car and round the hood, opening the door for her. She doesn't look at me. Her contempt is palpable in the air. See if I give a fuck. I know she wants me. The wetness I'm sure is still dripping between her creamy thighs doesn't lie.

She can hate me all she wants, but she can't resist me.

And neither can I resist her.

"For fuck's sake," I bite when she just huffs and crosses her arms across her chest. "Get out of the car, little fairy. If you're not out in the next ten seconds, I'm gonna bend you over the hood and fuck you until the whole resort knows who's been inside of you. And then I'll fuck you some more, just to be sure no one missed your screams."

She tips her chin in the air, defiance and disdain bleeding out of her. Her pretty midnight-blue eyes roll, and I bite down a smirk since I know good and well, she'll roll them again soon enough as she takes me hard and fast.

Sawyer slips her long legs out, then stands to her full height, enhanced by the tall heels she's wearing. I can't wait to have her legs over my shoulders and those pointy, sharp needles digging into my back.

My skin is burning under my clothes. Anticipation runs free and wild through my blood. The last of my control hangs by a thin thread, and she's doing everything in her power to snap it off. I can't help the sigh of relief escaping my chest when my palm connects to the small of her back, the meaty flat of it curving perfectly around the slope of her spine as I lead her through the front door and to my bedroom.

I don't look around. I don't care what the one-bedroom wooden cabin looks like. There'll be plenty of time to explore when I have Sawyer on every available surface and free space of my holiday lodge.

The curtains are wide open, full moon shining through the floor-to-ceiling windows. The dark expanse of the ocean nearly reaches the deck just outside the French doors. She stops in the middle of the room, her hands fisted at her sides, zero emotion on her beautiful face.

She's disheveled. The white lace of her cami, streaked with silver threads, makes her look as if she's glowing. My own personal goddess of hate. And she was grinding against someone else in the club. As if they had any right to touch her. As if she has any right to give away what's *mine.*

The fire I kept contained in the pit of my stomach spreads through my chest and my extremities. I want her to hurt so prettily. I want her to cry, to choke on my cock until she's about to faint, and then to swear she'll only ever be mine.

The rational side of me is screaming in my head that I'm a dirty hypocrite. I was prowling for the same fucking thing in the club. But we've already established that in this twisted fairytale, I'm the asshole and she's the damsel in distress. Except I'm not here to save her.

I'm here to ruin her for any other man and have her crawl on her knees and beg for more.

"So you're just going to stare at me all night? Because I'm good," she hisses, her plush lips sneering in disdain.

I shake my head and chuckle, a dark, derisive sound bouncing off the four walls she's trapped in. Pointing at the floor, I bark, "Get on your knees. Earn my forgiveness."

Sawyer scoffs. She fucking scoffs in my face. "You're delusional, Maddox. Earn *your* forgiveness? I did *nothing* wrong. If there's anyone who needs to beg like a fucking dog, that's *you*." She steps closer, the thump of her heels against the floor muffled by the soft carpet at our feet. Her palm splays over my chest where my heart jackhammers so hard, it's about to break a rib or ten. "*You* get on your fucking knees. Down, boy. You want to be a big bad alpha cunt, then suck up like a big bad alpha cunt."

Her words hit me like a slap in the face. There's no trace of my delicate wallflower left in the woman standing tall and proud in front of me. She's all fire and brimstone, ready to rain hell down on me. Fucked, if my cock doesn't grow harder and the ache in my stomach rises higher, until I'm a mess of grueling desires and maddening lust.

I've never kneeled before for any other woman. But I drop to my knees for her.

If her forgiveness is earned by me surrendering myself to her, then sacrificing my ego for the ascending of my goddess is a small price to pay.

Her small fingers trace the lacy hem of her cami, hooking on a dainty loop of thread and pulling the material higher on her thigh, revealing more of her silky-soft skin to me. The damp material of her white thong appears before my eyes, so soaked with her need for me it's nearly see-through. I'm enthralled, hypnotized, completely taken with her bare sweet lips, as plump and delicate as the rest of her.

I startle when the heel of her sandal digs into the meaty part of my chest, the sharp pain sending a bolt of lust straight to my cock. She's splayed open in front of me, her enticing scent of sugared pears making my mouth drool. Her free hand claws at my hair, pushing my mouth flush against her pussy. I part my lips and suck at her sensitive flesh, welcoming the tangy honey of her desire on my taste buds.

"That's it," Sawyer moans. "Earn your forgiveness, fuck-boy. Show me what you're made of."

And so I do. I hook my fingers on either side of the useless fabric she calls panties and pull them down her long legs, shoving them in the back pocket of my trousers, then bury my face into her hot pussy, lapping at her clit, seeping her very essence inside my mouth. Her hips buck mercilessly, nearly smothering me in her warm, wet heaven. The desperate frenzy of her movements as she rides my face spurs me on. She'll come on my tongue, then she'll come on my cock as many times as I need to purge her out of my system once and for all.

"Fuck, Maddox, yes," she screams, when my hands dig into her plump ass cheeks, my thumb circling her dripping entrance, coating myself in her gushing arousal, then pressing against her puckered hole. She grinds harder against my mouth, and I spear my tongue inside her fluttering channel, teasing her throbbing clit with the tip of my nose, pumping my thumb gently in and out of her virgin ass.

Her hold on my hair tightens with every thrust of my tongue inside of her, and the sting on my scalp nearly has me coming in my pants. She's too sweet, too addictive, too much of everything. My free hand snakes over her waist, to the swell of her breast, and with expert fingers, I pinch her pebbled nipple through the thin material of her cami.

"God, Maddox, fuck, yes, yes, yes," she mewls, her voice raspy and scratchy, overcome with the waves of her desire. I grunt my approval as my lips suck hungrily at her needy pussy. After all, I've been taught not to speak with my mouth full, and Sawyer wants me to be her good boy tonight.

And then she floods my mouth with her delicious nectar, my tongue relentlessly lapping at her silky folds, as she jerks and convulses against my lips. Her orgasm is a thing of beauty, wild and unrestrained, and I don't hold back anymore. Hot ropes of cum stain the inside of my boxers as my cock twitches and spasms under my own release.

This goddamn witch of a woman has me under her spell and doesn't even know it.

When I finish licking her dry of everything she has to give, I press a sweet kiss to her oversensitive bundle of nerves, the hollowed-out softness of her quivering belly, and lastly to the center of her heaving chest.

Shakily, she lets her leg slide down my shoulder, and I seize her hips in a steel grip until I'm sure she's steady on her feet. Her eyes sparkle, and my skin peppers in goosebumps under her heady stare.

"Lose the clothes, fuck-boy. You're not done yet."

My mouth thins. Pain and lust swirl inside of me; both poison the blood flowing through my veins in equal measure. My hands, though, obey her as I rise to my feet. Button by button, I get rid of my shirt, drinking in the blatant admiration burning in her dark irises. When my fingers loop around my belt buckle, she stops me, her warm palm placed firmly over the back of my hand. I let my arms fall loose at my side, fisting my fingers until my nails dig into my palms to keep myself from touching her. This is Sawyer's show.

For now.

She unfastens the leather belt and sharply pulls it out of the belt loops. I don't miss the tremble of her fingers or the seductive way her gorgeous tits shimmy under the barely-there fabric of her cami. "Hands in front of you," the little bossy fairy snaps.

My lips twist into a crooked smirk, and I extend my arms in front of me as I pop an eyebrow. So... this is how she wants to play—the prey chaining the predator. She coils and loops the leather strap around my wrists, bounding them together. I test the restraint, the smirk on my face growing bigger.

"What do you plan to do to me now that you have me at your mercy, little fairy?" I tease, my voice gravelly and thick with need.

My dick doesn't care that we're nearing our mid-thirties, and I just came in my boxers less than five minutes ago. It throbs and hardens once more, until it strains against my hip, tenting my trousers. Her white teeth, the two front ones slightly overlapping, bite into the fleshy side of her bottom lip.

"Lie down on the bed," she orders, seemingly making up her mind.

I've been lucky so far, and despite everything I've done that had me convinced I'll end up dead, I survived through it all. But I'm not so sure I'll live through tonight. Death by orgasm, what a fucking way to go.

The mattress is soft under my back, with just enough firmness for it to be comfortable. My eyes track her every moment, the seductive sway of her hips as she stops at the edge of the bed, right by my feet. Her fingers hook into the bottom hem of her cami, and in one graceful arch, her gorgeous body is completely bared to me, leaving only her garter belts cradling her creamy thighs.

Gently, tentatively, Sawyer crawls on the bed, prowling over me. Her finger burns through my skin, branding me with her mark as she traces the edges of the anchor half-submerged in a stormy ocean just above my heart, Ryker's name and his date of birth permanently seared into my flesh.

Her palms slide forward until she reaches my shoulders, then trail down until they stop under my straining biceps. Her tongue darts out, licking at her lips, like she can't help herself but taste her want of me on her own skin first.

She pushes my arms back until my forearms dangle over the edge of the bed. The move makes her arch above me. Her hips grind against my groin, the decadent heat of her pussy seeping through the thick material of my trousers. Her gorgeous tits, heavy and perky, bounce right in my face. I don't resist the temptation but suck a pale-pink nipple into my mouth, grazing my teeth against the pebbled bud, soothing the sting with the tip of my tongue.

Her hips jerk against mine, my cock jolting up to reach the forbidden heat dripping just for me. A desperate mewl slips past her lips before she hisses, "No touching."

I suck harder, lap faster at her delicious flesh, until I feel her arousal soaking through my pants before releasing her with a wet pop, the cockiest of grins on my lips. She slides down my body, her fingers gripping my chin. "You're not being a very good boy. What am I going to do with you?" Her eyes roam over my face as if trying to find just the right punishment in the depths of mine.

I groan long and hard when fire shines through her dark irises, and she slides even farther down my body. Her velvet soft palms trail down my chest, over each ridge and valley of my abs, before sneaking underneath me, and finding what she's looking for in my back pocket.

If my grin was cocky, hers is absolutely wicked, a promise of euphoria and blissful torture. Her fingers fasten again around my jaw, thumb and middle finger pressing against the twin dimples in my cheeks. "Open up, pretty boy," Sawyer singsongs. And now I'm the one who can't control myself but buck up against the cradle of her thighs.

"My dirty, dirty fairy," I grunt through clenched teeth. Currents of desire bolt through my spine, tensing up my back. My wrist flexes against the rigid restraint of the leather. My patience is running thin. I need to be inside her. And I need it five minutes ago.

Her forefinger circles my bottom lip, and my tongue darts out to taste her exquisite sweetness. "Ntz, ntz." She wiggles it in front of my eyes, and I open my mouth to protest. In a lightning-fast move, slick lace presses against my tongue. The addictive taste of her arousal coats the inside of my mouth like the most potent aphrodisiac. "You push it out, I stop immediately. Understood? Blink once if you agree, pretty boy."

Fuck me. Sawyer really is determined to kill me tonight.

My body strains, my control stretched wafer-thin. I could have her on her back, jackhammering into her, in two seconds flat. I blink and mentally beg her to just put me out of my misery and fuck me already. Her plump lips smile, a thank you brighter than direct sunlight, and goddamned if it doesn't burn a path straight to my heart.

I swallow hard against the lacy panties stuffed in my mouth as she rips at my trousers, while I push my heels against the mattress to help her shove down the last of my clothing. My cock, straining and leaking, slaps back against my abdomen. All the blood in my body rushes south as Sawyer straddles the top of my thighs, the liquid heat of her pussy seeping against the oversensitive skin of my sack.

"Now, the internet is full of cocks," she murmurs, and I growl through my muzzle. I'll be fucking damned if she ever looks at another dick in her life. My trusted partner agrees as he tries to defy gravity and juts up, trying to reach her. My desperation is doubled. I don't just want to fuck her. I want to burrow so deep into her skin, she'll never know what it's like to live another day without feeling my brand in every molecule in her body. "Ah, you don't like that, do you? You don't like sharing what's yours with others. Then why force me through that misery?" she snaps. Her palm moves down between her legs, and she gathers the delicious moisture there, then cuffs my dick at the base, the hold borderline painful.

The little witch looks down at where her fingers can't quite meet around my length, fascination and awe dancing on her delicate features. She gives me a firm but tentative stroke, sweeping her thumb over the throbbing head of my cock. My back nearly shoots off the mattress, stars exploding behind my eyelids. My whole body feels electrified as pure animalistic need travels through my veins. I shout a muffled, "Fuuuuck," through the thong soaking inside my mouth.

She starts stroking me in earnest. Her hips rock in rhythm with the tugs of her hand around my cock, as if feeling each jerk of my body like a thrust up inside of her. If she ever wonders how much I hunger for her, the evidence is now coating her fingers. My desire lubricates her movements while she twists her wrist this way and that, driving me absolutely fucking crazy. The groan ripping out of my chest is pure, torturous agony. My mind goes through each line of the LHPD Code of Conduct. Like fuck am I going to come now. My next orgasm is going to coat her walls and drip down my balls from between her legs. All or nothing.

"Fuck me, please!" My beg spills past my lips, the words slurred and intelligible. Sawyer seems to understand me just fine because, in the next moment, my eyes roll to the back of my head as her ass cheeks slap against my balls when she impales herself onto my cock in one swift drop. Heavenly silky walls, molten lava heat, and my own fucking death wrap around my shaft as I roar my ecstasy.

"Maddox, god, you fill me so good, pretty boy," she cries out. "I feel you everywhere." Her words are a panting breath that has my hips bucking against her. Her palms plant on my abdomen, her eyes wide, glazed over with pleasure and a hint of panic. "Holy ink, you're big." A touch of hysteria darkens her voice, my stomach curling as I can't exactly ask what's wrong.

All my fear is forgotten as her walls clamp down around me, and for a second, I swear I've died and gone to heaven. On a reflex, my hips thrust up, and her blunt nails dig on the skin of my abdomen. Her wide eyes latch onto mine, and any trace of panic dissolves as she slowly lifts her hips until only the head of my cock is lost in the blissful snugness of her pussy. Saliva pools in my mouth as my gaze darts to where were joined, her tight pussy pink and puffy as it stretches to accommodate my girth. And then she drops down on my length, squeezing all the pleasure out of me.

Every inch of me feels every inch of her as she starts riding me in earnest, bouncing up and down on my dick. We're a maelstrom of mewled moans, muffled grunts, and wood thumping against wood. She takes me over and over and over, until I'm so out of my mind, I'm ready to rip through the restraints holding my wrists together.

She's so close, yet so far away. Not even the sight of the most beautiful tits I've ever seen in my life, bouncing against the corseted tattoo on her ribcage, is enough to dispel the longing raging inside of my chest. I jackknife up, taking her by surprise as I circle her waist with my still restrained hands, her arms coiling around my neck. A storm ravages through me as her soft skin touches me everywhere. We're chest to chest, nose to nose; I'm balls deep inside of her, and all I want is more. I angle my hips, my pelvic bone rubbing against her clit with every up and down swivel as she's incessantly using my body to chase her pleasure.

Tingles rush at the bottom of my spine. My heart thumps in my chest. I'm close to exploding, and all I need to take me over the edge and into the abyss is her permission. Because, willingly or not, I'll do anything for the woman fucking the very sanity out of me.

Her hips thrash erratically, losing all sense of composure and control; her walls flutter around me in a maddening rush of electricity and raging fire. Her head drops to my shoulder, her lips everything I've ever imagined against my slick skin. "Come for me, pretty boy!" She moans long and hard, each word a cry for release. I feel the sharp pain of her teeth against the top of my shoulder as she detonates around me, soaking my cock in silk and the molten lava of her release.

With a roar that rattles my ribcage, I dive head-first over the edge. Fireworks, stars, the whole fucking universe implodes inside of me, ripping me apart and gluing me together. Sawyer's very essence is the thread that fuses all my shattered fragments in place as I paint her quivering walls with my life force.

I fall to my back, taking her with me, our chests heaving as we return to a reality that will never look the same from this moment on. Minutes pass, or maybe hours, until Sawyer pushes weakly against me. My arms are still bound, but I drag my knuckles across every vertebra of her spine as she arches against me, pushing my straining muscles once more over my head, until my wrists dangle over the edge of the bed.

Her heart takes flight, beating so fast, I can feel it in my chest. Dainty fingers grip my jaw again, the hold much weaker than when we started. Sawyer stares into my eyes so intently, panic swirls inside my stomach. Her gaze is so earnest, so trustful, the cynical asshole in me doesn't know what to do with it. She seems to have reached a conclusion, the tips of her lips timidly tipping up before she lowers her mouth to mine.

I know what this means. If she kisses me, she wants more. Dread and shame wipe clean all traces of the desire I felt only seconds ago. Just before her lips touch against mine, I turn my head away, her kiss landing over the corner of my mouth and my scruffed cheek. Her smile grows larger against my prickly skin, cautionary alarms blaring in my head.

"Just like I thought," she whispers.

Sawyer stands up on her knees, severing our connection. There's no hint of what she's thinking on her face; her smile is the picture of serenity even as my seed leaks down her thighs. She gently pats my jaw, looking down at me.

"Stay away from me, Maddox," she throws over her shoulder as she climbs off the bed and pulls her cami over her head, hiding herself from me again.

A chasm opens up in my chest as I lie on my back, wrists bound, naked as the day I was born, a pair of lacy panties muffling my desperate pleas for Sawyer to come back.

Rock... meet really fucked-up bottom.

Chapter Seventeen

Sawyer

For the last two days at the resort, I hadn't gone out of my way to avoid Maddox. Sure, my chest felt like it was caving in when I saw him the morning after at the Main Lodge. I might have used Selae as an anti-Maddox shield since I could see it on his face, he wanted to talk. As far as I was concerned, actions spoke louder than words. I didn't need to hear pretty excuses or an easy let down.

I was... apprehensive Lalah and Annalise would jump on me, demanding explanations, or worse, look at me with pity for being the stupid girl falling for a sure heartbreak. Instead, all they did was provide assurance they'd have my back if I needed to talk and that my business was my business. Their lips were sealed, and their husbands were sworn to secrecy, too.

Foolishly, I went ahead and fell for the heartthrob. He doesn't—nor will he ever be able to—reciprocate my feelings.

Logically, I understand what the situation is. We part ways and move on with our lives. My heart, of course, firmly disagrees. It's absolutely possible for the wallflower to change the ways of the bad boy and make him fall in love with her irrevocably and irredeemably. The poor romantic pump, keeping me alive and sending distress pangs all over my body, still has rose-tinted glasses. A cliché is a cliché for a reason.

Pardon my French, but ink that.

So I gave myself a couple of days to mope around. Courtesy of Lalah, I could mend my bruised heart in style. Nothing heals wounds of the soul as well as golden sandy beaches, heady ocean salt in the air, and the gentle burn of the sun on a clear day.

When our holiday was over, I boarded that plane home, determined to leave my foolish hopes behind. And I almost succeeded, for the entire week we've been back.

I smile at my tanned image in the mirror. Well, tanned by my standards, and that's a faint golden shine to my usual milky-white complexion. Still, it masks the reverse-smokey eye situation I have going on, so I'm taking the win, no questions asked.

The witching hour spans the night. While I'm asleep, my determination wavers, and my dreams are conquered by dark promises and anchor tattoos. Every dream ends with that pesky feeling of free-falling, where, for a second, you gain an unwanted and up-close understanding of what it's like when your soul leaves your body. I wake up with a gasp, my heart pounding as if I've been chased by a feral wolf, my hand always pressed between my chest and my stomach where a chasm is wide open. There's five minutes every morning when hollowness threatens to consume me whole.

Then my eyes open, the sun is shining, and I'm one day closer to achieving my dream.

I'm twenty-six years old. My soulmate might be late, but he'll find his way to me eventually. Now that, I firmly believe.

The past week without Tatum and Maevis has been kind of lonely. All my friends have been busy. Emma is dividing her time between Mix'n'Match and Hope Haven, where she's started self-defense training. Violet is traveling more than usual to Billings to spend time with her new boyfriend. Lalah and Blake are more often than not locked inside her home office, with her tirelessly working on passing the assessor mantle for Lege et Lacrima to her brother-in-law. And Annalise works herself to the bone getting To Be Read Café marketed.

The distance has been beneficial to me. I usually wear my emotions on my forehead, the subtitles in multiple languages displayed on my skin. If I feel it, you'll know it just by looking at me. And the messy-Maddox-situation is something I need to process on my own.

Even so, my day is always happier when I get to see Maevis's bright smile as she greets me from behind the counter at Suga'High. My sense of security is always enhanced when my older brother gives me one of his signature bear hugs that leave me feeling as if nothing bad could ever happen to me. And even when it did, it was one of his hugs what helped me heal and stop looking over my shoulder every ten seconds.

Today, by all accounts, doesn't start great. I wake up half an hour late, only to notice my phone is dead on the nightstand since I forgot to charge it last night. To make matters worse, there's a bright red stain on my crisp, white sheets, and a dull pain in my lower belly. *Fantastic.* While my birth control pills help manage some of the pain, they don't erase it completely. All I want to do is curl back in my bed, hug a hot water bottle against my belly, and hide from the world. Alas, life doesn't have a pause button.

I quickly go through a shower, then change my sheets and soak them in cold water. Rummaging through my fridge, I fist-pump in victory when I find one open bottle of Chardonnay, then proceed to pour it over the stain on my sheets. I leave the soft cotton to marinate for five minutes before throwing a load of laundry in. Hopefully, I won't have to sacrifice them to the bloody gods who claim at least one pair of underwear a month and, yearly, my favorite pair of jeans.

Despite the gorgeous weather outside, I choose to drive myself to the daycare. Mid-seventies might be perfect walking conditions, but I don't know in what state I'll finish the day, and I'd rather have the option of a quick escape.

My day doesn't improve. I only have ten students attending today, and all ten of them seem to be in a grumpy mood. I've been running around, trying to console them and to stop them from throwing toys at each other's heads for the better part of the morning. When lunch time rolls around, I sag on a chair in the far corner of the room that serves as a cafeteria. This is the time when children of all ages who attend the daycare can mingle and socialize, while the teachers get an hour for adult conversations. I love children, I truly do. But there's only so much I can take on debates about who would win in a fight, Peppa Pig or Lightning McQueen?

The afternoon doesn't get any better. It takes longer than usual to settle the rambunctious kids for their nap. Once the little troublemakers are asleep, the spreadsheet with expenses keeps freezing on me.

I watch the clock, willing it with my eyes to move its tiny hands faster. Today I get to leave as soon as the last child in my care is picked up since it's Violet's turn to close. I vividly daydream with my eyes wide open about my comfortable sofa and the nap I'm going to take as soon as I get home.

Finally, 3 p.m. comes, and not a second too soon. Parents should start trickling about any minute now, so I make my way around to each of the blanket forts we've built for nap time and gently wake up my charges. I go through the normal routine of getting them ready for pick-up.

The dull pain in my belly spreads to my thighs and down to my knees. It takes everything in me to remain standing and smiling. I just have to make it through one more hour, hopefully. Usually, these sixty minutes pass fast. One by one, I say goodbye to my little troublemakers, until the only three remaining are Clara, Ryker, and Joel, a vivacious four-year-old absolutely fascinated with everything Lego.

"Well, you look like death," a feminine voice sounds behind me, startling the bejesus out of me.

My palm flies to the center of my chest as I squeak and spin on my heel to face her. "Wear a bell, would you?" I hiss, poking my tongue out at Lalah, who's doubled over, laughing at my expense.

"Sorry, doll," she chokes out once her laughter subsides. "You were... far away."

I roll my eyes but let go of my annoyance toward her when she pushes a takeaway coffee in my hands and a blueberry muffin. Well, I guess she can live to see another day. One sure way to tame the fire of a woman while her vagina is bleeding and her ovaries are trying to strangle themselves with the fallopian tubes is with baked goodies and coffee.

Lalah scoffs, crossing her arms over her chest as she leans against my desk. "Look at her, Miss Princess Pony Puff, so engrossed with that boy, she doesn't even see me. Cole's heart can't take it if she starts dating so young."

I rip a healthy chunk off my muffin top and shove it in my mouth to stop myself from laughing at her, chasing the delicious crumbs on my lips with a massive swig of dark, bitter roast. "Jealous much, Momma Bear?"

"You better believe it." Lalah winks. "That little girl has burrowed so deep into my heart, I couldn't love her more if I'd birthed her myself. Her sister, too." She lowers her eyes, scanning the top of her Converse. "Sometimes, embracing change brings the greatest happiness. I just had to be strong enough to accept I was deserving of it." She tilts her head, looking directly into the very depths of my soul. "I wouldn't change one second of the hell that was last year if, at the end, Cole and my girls are waiting for me. Cole's the only man in my life. He's my better half, the brightest part of my soul. Do you understand?"

My stomach flutters and flips. Ice and fire race through my veins, my cheeks flaming. "Lalah..." I breathe. "I know what you saw, but I promise you, there's nothing between us. Nothing more than..."

"You don't need to explain yourself, Sawy, but I'm also done with you tiptoeing around me and avoiding my eyes like you have a scarlet A painted on your forehead. Maybe it's presumptuous of me, but since provoking him to react in the club wasn't enough clue for you, then let me spell it out... I have absolutely zero issues here, okay?"

Luckily, I'm saved by a whirlwind of skirts and the trill of long beads chiming, as Avery Jennings pushes through the door. "Sorry, Sawyer, the traffic from Forrest Falls to home was something else. I swear, we were sitting in the lane more than we were moving."

I step out from behind my desk and give Avery a wide smile. "Don't worry, Joel is always such a sweetheart. If I put a Lego set in front of him, his engineering mind takes over, and nothing else exists for him."

"You're the greatest, thank you," she gushes, beelining to her son.

The commotion is enough to gain the attention of the three trouble-makers. Clara's face brightens up with the cutest smile as she sees Lalah. She drops the coloring book she was working on with Ryker and runs to us in a mess of giggles and squeals, launching herself in Lalah's open arms as soon as she's close enough.

"That's more like it, sweet girl." Lalah winks at me, and I shake my head at her playfulness, hooking Clara's backpack to her extended arm as she hoists her daughter on her hip.

I bend down and kiss Clara's chubby cheek. "See you tomorrow, sweet-heart."

And then it's just me and Ryker, sitting side to side, our backs against the wall, his head cuddled to my belly as I run my fingers through his hair. My stomach twists at the eerie feeling of déjà vu. I halve my muffin, sharing my treat with him, and we both munch in silence.

This is why Ryker is my favorite. Even at his very young age, he doesn't need to fill the silence with incessant chatter. Most kids would have abused their allotted limit of ten-thousand 'Why?'. Ryker is content to just sit and enjoy. Strangely, he reminds me so much of me in the way he holds back and observes the world around him, trying to make sense of every little detail, soaking in every morsel of information.

"I've gots somefing fo' you, Miss Sawy." He breaks the silence, once the muffin is all but devoured.

"What's that, buddy?" I ask, tilting my head to look at him, so he can see he has all my attention.

He smiles shily, his soft cheeks flushing, as he stands and wipes down the crumbs on his yellow T-shirt, before running to the fabric cube assigned to him. Not a second later, he returns, pushing a folded piece of construction paper in my direction.

"Thank you, Ryker," I tell him, affection dripping out of my tone, as I pluck the paper from his hand and unfold it with trembling hands. My eyes well as I look at a drawing of a stick figure with yellow hair, holding hands with a smaller stick figure with brown hair. Sure, their heads are bigger than their stick bodies, but to me this could've been drawn by DaVinci himself and I couldn't have loved it more. What looks like a five-tiered cake lies at their feet on a patch of green grass.

In shaky red letters, the color deeply affixed to the surface of the paper as if two hands put pressure on the crayon while it looped and twisted around each word, there's a sweet message, just for me.

Miss Sawy,

You are my favorite teacher.
Please come to my birthday party at my home.
I turn four on June First, and Daddy says I'm a big boy.

Love,
Ryker

I touch the letter to my chest and blink repeatedly, trying to keep the tears at bay. Butterflies explode in my stomach at the simple thought that Maddox took the time to hold Ryker's hand and guide the crayon over the paper, writing the invite for me.

It'll be awkward and painful to return to his home, but I'd do anything to see his boy happy on his special day. Who knows, maybe in two weeks' time Maddox will be nothing but a distant memory to me.

"Of course I'll be there, Ryker. I wouldn't miss your birthday for the world," I tell him earnestly. He cheers so loudly, I'm sure a couple of windows crack as the wave of sound slams against them, and throws his little, chubby arms around my neck.

"Fank you, fank you, fank you," he screams his excitement in my ear, making me wince.

By the time I retire from looking after children, I'm fairly certain my hearing will be gone from one ear, if not both. I'll never reprimand them for expressing their emotions. My ear can ring for a couple of minutes, then go back to normal. Reprimands, if not done right and with care, have long-lasting effects, turning happy, confident children into self-conscious shells of themselves.

I rub Ryker's back with my palm as he still squeezes my neck in a celebratory hug, and that's how Maddox finds us when he rushes through the door of the classroom. His light brown hair is a mess of tangled strands as he brushes his fingers through them, pushing them away from his forehead.

My palm tingles with the need to touch the silky softness myself. Instead, I grit my teeth and push to my feet. Ryker circles his legs around my waist, hanging onto me like a tiny spider-monkey.

"Daaaaddy," he squeals. *Again.* I wince. *Again.* The pair of lungs on this kid is something else. "Miss Sawy saided she comes to my bufday pawty."

Maddox prowls closer, like a panther trying to seduce its prey with the fluidity of its majestic body, until he crowds us against the wall while pretending to take Ryker from my arms.

"That so?" He purrs—*purrs*—and my body seizes. My belly clenches painfully. Heat travels through my veins and pools between my thighs, worsening the cramps wreaking havoc in my uterus. "Then it's going to be super special for you, huh, partner?"

Ryker jumps to his father's chest. Maddox has never looked bigger than right now as he's holding with one arm his nearly four-year-old son. But I'm made of sterner stuff, or at least that's the hope. I school my face into a neutral mask and paste on an indulgent smile.

"Thank you for the invite, Ryker. I love the drawing, and I'm going to put it on display right on my fridge for everyone in my family to see."

His chubby cheeks pink up, and he nuzzles his face in the crook of his father's neck. I avert my eyes and side-step them, walking to my desk and making a show out of locking up, hoping *he'*ll take a hint.

"Sawyer…" Maddox sighs. "Can we talk, please?"

I shuffle some papers on my desk, scrunching my eyebrows in concentration as if I'm defusing a bomb. And perhaps I *am* defusing one. I need to remain strong in my resolve. We agreed to one night; ended up with three. Three is a nice, strong number to put a stop to this train wreck. It'd be so easy to let myself be seduced by apologies and pretty words coming from a pretty boy. Even if I'm having a rare case of grandiosity, and he, in fact, just wants to… I don't know, check-in with me? Make sure our mutual friends don't blab after his idiotic display of possessiveness in that club? There's no need for a check-in, or an explanation, or whatever else he wants to say.

I'm cool as a cucumber. A cucumber with anxiety, but cool nonetheless.

"Ryker is doing great. I have no progress updates other than what was emailed to you at the beginning of the month," I say, my eyes roaming over the wall plastered in doodles, somewhere behind Maddox's wide shoulders. My response to 'can we talk' so he finally understands—the only things we have to talk about are pertinent to his son's education and nothing else. "You guys have a great rest of the day. See you tomorrow, Ryker." I wave like a moron, then promptly turn my back to them and pretend to rummage through my purse.

The second the door clicks shut behind them, a traitorous tear rolls down my cheek.

Chapter Eighteen

Maddox

My blood boils. Fucking boils. She's avoiding me at every step, looking at me as if our last night together never happened, as if I mean fucking nothing to her. It would hurt less if she took a knee to my balls.

It takes every ounce of control to keep walking to my truck and not turn right around to demand that she talk to me. I can't stand her indifference. I can't stand that wane smile on her beautiful face. And I can't fucking do anything about it.

I'm well aware nothing good would come out of getting my way and having a conversation. The best I can give her is a friends-with-benefits situation until I fuck her out of my system once and for all. Nothing about my wants is fair to her. But the simple thought of not being able to touch her freely, of Sawyer laughing and smiling with another man, of that man kissing her and caressing her sinful body like only I did, that fucking thought drives me crazy.

My skin is too tight for my body. Fire licks at my insides, and I'm overcome with the need to plummet something into the ground and stump on it until my feet grow numb. My blood *itches* and *aches* as it rushes through my veins.

White-knuckling the steering wheel, it's all I can do to keep myself focused on the road so I can get Ryker safely home. I go through the motions of parking, helping him out of his 'big boy' high-back booster seat, cooking dinner, and giving him a bath before bedtime story. I watch the rise and fall of his little chest. He's my only joy in this world, the only thing I've ever done right. Being Ryker's father is what fuels me and keeps me going every day, and now I'm failing him too.

I turn on the night lights and tuck the blanket around his body before silently slipping out of his bedroom and into my bathroom. My clothes fall in a heap to the floor, and I kick them toward the laundry basket as I walk inside my shower. A flick of my wrist has ice-cold water pouring down on me. It's the only way to slow down this maddening fever ravaging me from the inside out.

Sawyer Carter has shaken the foundation of every belief I've ever held true. As I shampoo my hair and scrub at my scalp with far more force than necessary, my mind is furiously working to find a solution or a way for this to end with a happily ever after, not with Sawyer broken-hearted. To no one's surprise, I'm coming up empty.

My twenty-year-old conviction that a woman brings absolutely nothing good to my life is not something I can just wipe clean as I do the water on my body with a soft cotton towel.

I felt my mother's betrayal like a thousand lashes over my back when Dad found out about her whoring ways. For a fourteen-year-old to bear witness to the destruction it caused my father, and the way his confidence was shaken, was devastating. I watched his worth as a man be put under a microscope and found lacking. The pain and misery of those six months when they constantly fought and shouted has shaped and molded me into the asshole I am today.

I'm too jagged, too cynical to believe in *forever*. It doesn't exist. The only real thing is 'for now'. The only convenient situation for me is 'for tonight'. So why can't I exorcize her out of my head? I'm not in the habit of lying to myself. It's not just a crush. It's not just physical attraction I feel for her.

Sure, it might have started that way back in November. One second, she was Sawyer Carter, my son's teacher and notorious wallflower. The next, pure fucking electricity crackled between us, some witchcraft-worthy chemical reaction that forever altered the cocktail of functionality in my brain. For the first time in my life... I wanted, not lusted.

And I spent the last six months feeding this irrational addiction.

I know I shouldn't, but I do it anyway as I lay naked in my bed, the ceiling fan working double time to finish cooling me off. My cock is painfully hard, bobbing over my abdomen. I'm tempted to take myself in my hand and give myself a bit of a reprieve as I replay in my head the moment those beautiful lips touched the corner of my mouth.

Before I realize what I'm doing, my phone is to my ear. Plans are made. Clothes clad my body once more. I'm on the move, desperation clawing at my heel. The beast inside of me has taken over, demanding more than I'm able to give. I'm having an out-of-body experience as I prowl the dark and quiet streets of Lost Hope until I find myself face to face with her living room window.

There's been many a night my feet have carried me here. I'm surprised she hasn't noticed yet the flowers wilting just below her windowsill. I stare at her through the glass separating us as she goes about her night without me.

It's so easy to imagine what it would be like to end a tiring day with Sawyer in my arms; my cock, snug and wet in her arousal, buried deep inside her tight pussy. I'd burrow my nose in the silk of her hair and inhale the maddening scent of pear, bergamot, hope, and filthy dreams.

It's fucking ironic that I'm the Chief Deputy in our county, when what I'm doing right now is not only illegal here, it's illegal in all fifty states. I grip my hard cock through my sweatpants, squeezing until the borderline current of pleasure and pain gets my spine stiffer than the steel pipe demanding to be let loose.

She moves out of view for a second, and my stomach falls to my feet. Her bedroom window is almost always covered by blackout curtains during the night. If she's going to sleep now, I won't have enough of her yet to sate me for today. And her absence would keep me up all fucking night long.

It's goddamn insane how I miss something I've never truly had.

My heart beats faster and faster as the lights in her living room turn off. Only the white, washed-out brightness of the TV allows me to still see what she's doing. The furious rush of my blood in my eardrums drowns out the annoying chirping of crickets outside and the muffled sounds of whatever she's watching. Her PJs are simple, no frills, no lace, just a pair of flowy black shorts and a spaghetti-strap black tank-top. This image of her, as she curls in a tight ball on the sofa in her simple, shapeless PJ, shouldn't be as sexy as it is.

But I still find myself palming my granite length and giving it two rough tugs to alleviate the pressure building at the bottom of my spine.

I stand rooted to the spot until I'm absolutely convinced she's asleep. Based on the bottle of painkillers next to the half-eaten box of chocolates on the coffee table, she'll sleep like the dead until morning. Painkillers knock her out, and I know she only takes them at night, and strictly when she absolutely cannot do without.

My eyes scan over her set up carefully. Understanding dawns on me. I ignore the disappointment coating my insides. There's absolutely no fucking way I'm upset I didn't get her pregnant, despite her reassurance that it wasn't going to happen. A dark and sick part of me wants her pregnant with my child, wants her permanently and irrevocably tied to me.

I release my cock and curse under my breath at the ache settling in my balls. The desperation of my want scares me, but I'm powerless to stop. Careful not to stomp on any more flowerbeds, I silently creep my way to her back door. I should probably tell her the lock is not working. Fat chance of that happening, though, until I've had enough.

My steps are quiet and precise, knowing exactly which slab of the floor creaks when I put weight on it and which is safe to walk over. I don't need lights to guide me to the living room, where she's sleeping peacefully, despite the hint of pain creasing the soft skin of her forehead. I bend down at the waist and coil my arms under her, scooping her up to my chest. Sparks prickle at my skin everywhere we touch. My body instantly relaxes as her warmth seeps into me.

She stirs slightly, but rests her head against my shoulder and doesn't wake. My breath is trapped inside my lungs, and even my heartbeats slow, in fear she'll open her eyes and bust me. I've never been this brazen before, satisfied with watching her from afar or lying in her bed when she wasn't at home. I'm excited and terrified in equal measure.

This is what she's reduced me to. A desperate, cowardly stalker.

With infinite care not to disturb her sleep, I take her to her bedroom, gently lowering her on the bed. I take a second—like I always do—to breathe in the scent of everything Sawyer is. Under my fingertips, I feel the softness of her sheets. For one forbidden moment, I allow the need to push the covers aside and curl up around her to inundate my bloodstream.

My chest rumbles, my dick hardening even more. A soft breeze would have me coming in my pants so fast my head would spin.

I pull the blanket up, her long legs disappearing from sight. The fluffy fabric settles over her hips like a mantle. My knuckles graze her nipple. I bite my lip until I taste blood on my tongue to stop the urge to cup her breast and suck the tight bud into my mouth until she screams my name into the silence of the night.

Straightening up to my full height, I tower over her sleeping form as she rests, blissfully unaware of the monster next to her bed she *should* fear. The moon shines behind me, casting my looming shadow over the pale bedding, and I make a mental note to close her blinds before I leave.

My eyes roam over her beautiful face and the slightly parted plump lips as she breathes softly. I want her with a desperation that leaves me weak in the knees. A dangerous thrill rises inside me. I could leave right now. I *should* leave. A touch was all I wanted, and I got it.

But my feet are rooted to the floor, shoulder-width apart, my cock tenting my sweatpants. Unease and blind desire war in my chest. After everything I've been through this past year, after all we've witnessed others survive... I'm still here right now, excited, wanton, and fucking sick to my stomach for what I'm about to do.

I shake my head to dispel the last shred of morality left in me. I'm going to hell anyway, I might as well lose myself to the inferno. A slight pull-down at the waistband of my sweats has my cock springing free from its confines. My hips jerk as the cool air of her bedroom hits my overheated skin. I palm my length, the proof of my insanity leaking from the angry tip. Swiping my hand over the head of my cock, I lubricate myself in my need for her, my grip hard and unforgiving. A slow stroke up, and then another, and another, has my knees buckle and hit against the wooden frame of her bed.

I'm so close to her, I can feel the warmth of her breath feathering over my cock. My grip tightens, and then I fuck my fist hard, fast, relentless. I force my eyes open when they threaten to close under the onslaught of emotion flooding my body. Desire, want, longing, possession, all battle inside of me, none winning, all losing.

My jaw clenches and my teeth grind as I suppress needy groans from spilling past my lips. My fist moves frantically against my cock, and I cuff myself just under the flare of my head. I tease the damp slit with the pad of my thumb, wishing it were her tongue lapping up everything I have to give her.

My hips buck against my fist, withdrawing as I swipe across the over-sensitive tip, thrusting forward when I squeeze the base. Tingles start in my toes, spreading up my calves with the speed of a supersonic fighter jet, shooting up my flexed thighs and into my balls. The pressure building in my lower spine makes me ache. My heart hammers in my chest in tandem with the wild drives of my hips. My fingers circle my cock, clenching and relaxing as I fuck myself in and out of my fist. All the while, I imagine the silk of her pussy swallowing me whole.

I chase, I hunt, I fucking hurt for her.

In a split second of absolute fucking insanity, I bend and touch the angry head of my cock against her pillowy lips, and I'm gone. I startle backward and cover myself with my hand as I unload in my palm, fire still licking at my skin. Rugged breaths push my chest up and down as I thrust shallowly into the sticky hot mess pooling in my fist. My cock is twitching with the last of my release spilling through my fingers.

I'm spent and empty. The absolute euphoria of my orgasm lasts but a minute. I drink in the sight of her sleeping. Soon, I'll have to turn my back on her and leave, when all I want to do is move her sleeping shorts aside and drive my softening cock into her bare pussy until we're breaking through the bed frame.

I tuck myself in with my free hand and clean the mess in my palm with some tissues from a box on her nightstand, shoving the used ones in the pocket of my sweats. There's just enough left on the pad of my thumb to fulfill the last of this depraved fantasy I made into reality.

My lips brush softly over her forehead as my thumb paints her bottom lip with my cum. I lean back and admire my best work, my arousal glistening in the silvery moonlight on her plump lips.

Closing the curtains, I shroud myself in darkness and slip out of her bedroom, unseen and unheard. Warmth radiates from my chest to my limbs. I'll sleep like a fucking king tonight, knowing she'll wake up and taste *me* on her lips.

Chapter Nineteen

Sawyer

"**Y**ou did what?" I hiss as I get in Emma's face.

She lifts her palms in front of me, a plethora of silver bracelets dangling on her right wrist. "It's just coffee, Sawyer, for crying out loud."

I lean against the sink in the Ladies' bathroom of a fancy coffee shop in downtown Billings, crossing my arms over my chest. "I don't appreciate being blind-sided. You told me we'd visit the Farmers' Market and the Yellowstone Art Museum. Nowhere in that conversation was I informed I'd be the third wheel to you and Blake making googly eyes at each other, or that I'd have to keep company to what's-his-name?" Emma rolls her large, coppery eyes at me as she dries her hands on a paper towel.

I was excited for the first Saturday off in forever. My plans were solid, too—lounge on a blanket in the tiny backyard of my cottage, scribbling poetry and reading a book or two. To say May was a busy month is the understatement of the century. I'm exhausted down to my marrow, both physically and emotionally. A day to decompress and build a fortress around my heart is essential, considering tomorrow is Ryker's birthday, and I'd have to be face to face with Maddox and interact with him.

The awkwardness in the air whenever we're sharing the same space is so thick, I can cut through it with a knife and get the knife blunt. Sure, the chemistry remains off the charts too. My skin tingles and the fine hairs on my arms stand to attention five seconds before he arrives anywhere in my vicinity.

I just about keeled over last weekend at JC's Pour, when we challenged the men to wear a period pain simulator while going head-to-head against the TBRC book club ladies, and he ended up on my "team". Not only that, but he also massaged my lower back in front of my brother, no less, when the pain got to me. As if these pesky, bothersome feelings I have for him need any more fuel to burn bright and strong.

My nerve endings have gone haywire as I constantly feel his eyes on me; even when I walk through Main Street and he's nowhere near, or when I'm at home at night, ready to sleep.

I woke up at least three times in the past two weeks, absolutely convinced he was in my bedroom with me. His alluring scent mantles my sheets. His imposing presence surrounds me. And then I open my eyes and find myself alone in bed.

"Liam. And when was the last time you've gone on a date, doll? Not that this is a date," she backtracks fast when I start throwing daggers at her with my eyes.

My friend has a point though. The answer would be... three, no wait, four years ago. Back when Rob still felt he had something to prove, when he still tried to reel in the poor unsuspecting wallflower. No wonder I fell prey so easily to the first pretty penis to give me attention.

"What's going on between you and Blake, anyway?" I change the subject. Right now, I'm still too annoyed with her to give her the satisfaction of being told she's right.

I watch in fascination as her cheeks rosy up, a delicate blush staining her face. Emma has elegance and grace embedded in her every cell. Low-key envy swirls in the pit of my stomach. My friend is drop-dead gorgeous, and she deserves the absolute best in life. I was shocked and enraged to find out everything her ex-fiancé had put her through. And now I fear she's only setting herself up for failure with Blake.

"We're... getting to know each other," she replies demurely.

"Emma..." I warn, but she cuts me off, a glint of malice flashing in her eyes.

"Don't, Sawyer. I know what I'm getting into. Despite what I allowed the demented trio to do to me, I'm not stupid."

"Never thought you were. I just don't want to see you hurt."

Her face softens, and she gently squeezes my shoulder. "Blake brings sunshine to my life. The kind of warmth I've lacked for a long, long time." Her bright-red lips tip in a self-deprecating smile. "He's in love with Jake, and I'm well aware of that. He's using me as a distraction. Blake knows Jackson can never return his love. I'm using him to break away from all the smoke and mirrors my past life drowned me in. We're both aware of what we're doing. We also are both deserving of a fucking break. I'm done making apologies for who I am and what I want."

I nod, letting her know I hear every word she's saying. Who am I to judge how they choose to live? I'm clearly not known for making the best decisions lately.

"You're both my friends, and I love you dearly. As long as you're happy... that's all I want for you."

She slips her arm around my waist and rests her head on my shoulder. "I'm just starting to learn what true friends are. I'll probably fuck up a time or two..."

"I'll be here to catch you when you do."

Emma gives me a soft squeeze, then straightens her dark-green silk top, smoothing the wide-leg pants over her hips. "Alright, love-fest is over. Let's go treat our taste buds with some coffee and our eyes with man candy."

I suck in a breath and slowly exhale the oily feeling in the pit of my stomach that feels very much like betrayal. Sharing a coffee with some friends, be they new or old, doesn't have to mean anything. Objectively, Blake's college friend is handsome, in a charming, surfer meets Wall Street kind of way. Nothing in my life stops me from enjoying his company. And who's to say I'll ever see him again after today?

We make our way to the outdoor terrace with a view of Billings' Downtown, the majestic Pryor Mountains as backdrop. Both men stand as we approach our table, identical charming smiles on their handsome faces.

I shake the unease itching underneath my skin as I accept the seat offered to me. Liam gently pushes the chair in for me, then takes the wicker chair next to mine. Emma and Blake cozy-up on the wooden bench on the other side of the table. A waitress in a flowery dress, matching the bohemian vibe of the coffee shop, comes to take our orders. I lean back in my chair, crossing my legs at the knee, and smooth the skirt of my pale-pink summer dress over my thighs.

We settle into easy conversation, Blake and Liam sharing stories of their shenanigans during their college years. Emma and I chime in with our own stories, although my college experience seems to have been extremely tame compared to the daredevils I'm sharing a coffee with. I slowly relax and actually make an active effort to participate. My first instinct still is to take a step back and let the people around me control what is being discussed, but I refuse to settle in my habit of being one with the wall.

Liam is charismatic and funny, making sure I'm included in whatever topic they jump into. He tells me he works for a PR company in Helena. The reason he's in Billings right now is because he's pitching their business to Lege et Lacrima. He doesn't share much about his work since, in his words, 'our outing is about friends catching up, and work can be tabled for a couple of hours'. I appreciate someone who is clearly passionate about their job and, at the same time, knows how to disconnect and just enjoy life.

I'm surprised to find out how much trouble Blake had gotten into since he seems like such a level-headed person, if a bit of a jokester. My worries about whatever is happening between him and Emma are also put temporarily to rest. There's a certain spark in Blake's gray eyes that wasn't there a month ago. Part of the dark cloud weighing down his shoulders lately also dissipates around her.

My palm is covering my mouth as I quickly chew through the strawberry-mousse cheesecake bite. I'm trying to suppress my laughter and not choke in the process, while the guys tell us how one of their Dungeons & Dragons sessions ended with Blake sneezing golden dust for a full week, after a girl from their dorm threw a glitter bomb at his face.

"God, the dumbfounded look in his eyes," Liam chortles, his palm pressed to his abdomen.

Blake snorts, and it only makes his friend laugh louder and point a finger at him. "Yeah, that was the white noise I went to sleep listening to that night as you tried to dislodge all the glitter."

Emma balls up a paper wipe and throws it at Liam. "You two were such nerds."

"Were?" Blake teases. "Still am, Dove."

A pang of envy hits my stomach at the bright smile Emma gives him. They may be just fooling around, but there's a comfortable ease to their teasing, a... partnership. Maybe Emma is right. It has been too long since I've been out on a date. Right now, it's not an ideal time for me to do so, not until Happy Bumblebees opens its doors. But, once I have the new daycare up and running and my professional life sorted, it's time to take care of my personal life.

The fine hairs at my nape stand at attention as a sudden chill washes over me. My breath hitches. My skin pebbles, and the sensation of being watched has me on alert. My eyes dart around the tables and, while the coffee shop is busy, none of the patrons are paying us—or me, specifi-cally—any attention. I turn slightly in my seat and scan the expanse of the street. My heart just about stops as my eyes land on a furious-looking

Maddox, holding hands with a distracted Ryker, on the sidewalk across the road.

Even with the distance between us, his displeasure is clearly written on his face. His jaw is tight with tension, eyes narrowed in my direction, and his lips pulled taut in a harsh line. My stomach flips, and I reflexively hug my arms around my torso, trying to shield myself from the onslaught of disdain radiating out of him. I pretend not to see him though, my gaze not lingering for more than a split second on him before returning to the table.

I busy my hands, playing with the cheesecake, smearing the strawberry mousse around more than eating it. There's a sick urge inside me, pushing me to turn around and drink in the sight of him, but I refuse to give in to my unhealthy obsession with the man. What is he even doing in Billings? Doesn't he have a county to patrol or something? If I'm being completely honest, the reaction I've just had seeing him scares the life out of me. I'm supposed to go to Ryker's birthday party tomorrow. How will I spend an entire afternoon around Maddox when he's rendering me speechless just by looking at me from fifty feet away?

The imprint of his stare on my skin remains with me throughout the entire time we sit at the coffee shop. I'm exhaling a breath of relief when, finally, Emma stands and declares we're ready to go. I say my goodbyes to Blake and Liam with a hug, then collect my shopping bags. We trek toward the parking lot Emma left her car in, while the guys head to their Saturday business meeting. Apparently, that's a thing.

The drive back to Lost Hope passes quickly, especially since Emma is heavy-footed on the acceleration. Normally, I'd grumble and tell her off, but I want to get home as soon as possible, shower the burn left on my skin by Maddox's hateful glare, and take a nap.

Her tires scream in protest as she takes a sharp turn into my modest driveway and brakes hard. "Jesus, good woman. What did my flowerbeds ever do to you?" I hiss, leaning as far as the seatbelt allows me to check through the windshield if they're still in one piece.

"Sorry, doll." She gives me a smile that shows me she's not sorry at all. "We lost track of time down in Billings, and I'm almost late to my self-defense class. Jackson does *not* tolerate tardiness."

A weird sensation crawls up my spine as I gape at her, pieces of the puzzle slowly slotting together as I start to make sense of her endgame. "You're playing Cupid," I gasp.

Emma grimaces, her eyes clouding over with a hint of... jealousy. Surely, I'm not reading that right. "I don't know what you're talking about. Had no choice in who the instructor was when I started," she chirps.

She can lie all she wants. Something smells fishy here, but I keep my mouth shut. She already tried to bite my head off when I warned her to be careful with Blake. Jackson doesn't need a warning, since he's a walking-talking red flag. I love the man dearly. I owe him my brother's life. But there's no denying the danger oozing out every pore of his skin. My friend is playing with fire and seems to miss that Jackson is a ticking-time bomb ready to incinerate us all if triggered.

I cross my toes and send a prayer up to whatever deity is willing to listen that Emma escapes unscathed out of this web of pain and misery she's weaving for herself. Giving her a side hug in goodbye, I collect my belongings and rush inside my little home. I don't stop until I reach my bedroom, where I drop the bags at the foot of my bed, then beeline to the bathroom.

I don't get the chance to turn the water on when sharp bangs come through the front door. My eyes roll of their own accord, and a dejected sigh slips past my lips as I exit the bathroom and pad to the entrance. Opening the door with a flourish, I ask, "What did you forget?"

It's not Emma's smiling face in front of me. No, no. That would be too easy. My eyes instead latch on a broad, heaving chest, corded neck muscles, and a jaw made of granite. Reflexively, I take a step back when he crowds against me, all righteous fury and raging betrayal. My back hits the wall as he steps inside my home for the very first time and closes the door with his foot.

Trapped.

"What are you doing here?" I squeak as he gets in my face, his icy-blue eyes cutting through me.

His arms are tight as his side, hands fisted so hard, his knuckles are white. "Who was he?"

I'm tongue-tied, speechless, as I cower away from his fury.

"The leech drooling all over you. Who was he?" Maddox insists.

I lean my head back against the unforgiving plaster, my voice small as I plead, "Please leave, Maddox."

His forehead touches mine as he plants his palms on either side of my head, his biceps straining the cotton of his T-shirt. The alluring, woodsy smell of his cologne seeps deep into my lungs. "I can't," he whispers, each word pained and distraught.

Tears burn the backs of my eyes while I struggle to find a semblance of a backbone. He can't do this to me. I can't continue to play this twisted game of his. He made his feelings toward me crystal clear when he refused to let me kiss him.

"Please," I sob. I don't know what I'm asking for right now. His presence overwhelms me. My heart is beating so fast I'm getting dizzy. He's too much to bear so close to me.

"Do you think I want to be like this?" Maddox hisses low in his throat, his voice pure gravel and grit. "I'm torn into fucking pieces over you. I live in debilitating agony. EVERY. SINGLE. DAY. Can't breathe, can't sleep, can't fucking function, obsessing over you every godforsaken minute of every godforsaken hour. You've *poisoned* me. I. DON'T. WANT. THIS!" he shouts, slapping his palm against the wall, punctuating each hateful word. The tip of his nose brushes over mine, the gesture so tender and caring, in such stark contrast with the menace emanating out of him.

I can't *not* touch him. Not when he's so close, not when he's hurting so much. I'll have time to regret this later when I'm all alone in my bed. So, I plaster my palms to his trembling chest, sliding them over his tensed shoulders, entwining my fingers at his nape.

My eyes remain glued to his, wide and unblinking, as he grips my thighs and circles his waist with my legs. The pleated material of my dress bunches around my hips. My breath hitches in anticipation as he unbuckles his belt, moves my underwear aside, and positions his hard, thick cock at my entrance. My fingers tighten in his soft hair, anchoring in the silky strands, as he reasserts his short-lived claim on me with long, powerful strokes. Our combined groans of pleasure and bliss fill the hallway.

My mind blanks while Maddox fucks any ability for logical thinking right out of me until I clamp down on him so hard I see stars, his name a gift and a curse on my lips. His hips jerk in frantic movements, my limp body thumping against the wall, as he drives himself into me over and over, spilling his agony and desperation inside me with a tortured roar. Breathing hard, Maddox squeezes his eyes shut, his lips feathering over the tip of my nose. He buries his head in the crook of my shoulder as he shudders in my embrace.

"Fuck," he murmurs, more to himself than to me before his hands untangle my legs from around his waist, and he lets me slide down his body.

A gasp of loss escapes my lips as he takes a step back and puts distance between the two of us once more. With more brutality than I expect, he tucks himself back into his jeans, then turns his back on me and strides right out the door.

He couldn't have said it any better.

Fuck, indeed.

Chapter Twenty

Maddox

I flip the burgers around on the grill, whistling softly under my breath. My backyard is full of children and adults alike, happy laughter, and cheerful music. Ryker is having the time of his life in the bouncing castle I hired for his birthday. I can hear his giggles and squeals of joy all the way from the back porch, where I'm keeping myself busy.

My son is four years old.

I shake my head in disbelief. Time simply... flies by.

One minute, I was called to rush to a hospital in Billings in the dead of the night as my son was getting ready to make his way into the world. Next, I'm blinking, and here we are four years later. If there's one thing I've done right in my life, that's choosing Ryker.

The night he was born, I stood frozen in front of the Maternity Ward, looking through the screen at the newborns sleeping in their tiny hospital bassinets. My whole body was overcome with dread. I was thirty and could barely take care of myself, never mind an actual baby. All I needed to do was sign my name on a piece of paper, and I could've been... Nah, that thought is not worth finishing.

My son is my most precious treasure, the light of my fucking life, and he'll continue to be until the day I take my last breath.

Look at me, the picture of normalcy, with a Lightning McQueen apron tied around my waist, and a cold beer in my free hand. Inside, I'm dying a slow, torturous death. As much as I want to be angry at Sawyer, I know I'm the only one at fault. This situation we're in... needs to come to a head. It's unsustainable to live like this, torn right down the middle between who I used to be and the lunatic I am right now.

I'm painfully aware of her presence. My body is attuned to hers on a fundamental level, even if she ignored the life out of me from the minute she graced my doorstep half an hour ago. My hold on the metal tongs tightens. It's all I can do not to throw them aside, run to where she is, and take her into my arms, never to let her go ever again.

"Dude, you look like shit," Drake greets me and slaps my back.

"Didn't sleep well last night," I mumble.

"The nerves to throw the perfect birthday party kept you up, Martha Stewart?"

I elbow his side and turn around, scanning the backyard. My face may crack with the smile tipping my lips up, but here we are. "It is a pretty perfect birthday party, isn't it?"

"You did good, Dad. Now, only if you'd hurry up with those burgers, so your guests won't perish away in hunger pains."

I snort and shake my head. Leave it to Drake to take me out of my funk. "I don't know how Annalise does it, man. I'm surprised you didn't eat her out of house and home."

He pats his abdomen, licking his lips. "I'm a growing boy. Don't you worry your pretty little head. I eat out my wife enough... in the house, at home, sometimes in the car."

I throw the cloth I use to wipe grease off my fingers at his face. "Shut up, asshole. If Annalise hears you, the next burgers I'm eating are at your funeral."

Drake gives me a cocky half-smirk and dismisses my words with a swipe of his hand. "Nah, dude. My wife loves me. And I love ea-"

"How did you know she was the one?" I blurt out. I don't mean to ask *that* question, just to say something to stop the next words from coming out of his mouth. Lifting the beer bottle to my lips, I take a healthy gulp. Maybe I need a plug to keep me from spewing shit that has no business being out in the open.

Drake, however, wipes the smirk off his face. His whiskey-colored eyes assess me from head to toe. He must have heard something in my voice to flip the switch from dirty-dog to dead-serious so fast.

"I don't know, man. At first, I wanted to be near her constantly. You know how angry I was those first few months after my father's stroke. Maevis was struggling with the divorce. All my loved ones were hurting left and right, and I was powerless to help them. Just seeing her, even from afar, healed something in me. She makes me stronger, kinder. I feel like I'm the best version of myself around Anna. The longing in me to have her near only grew as I got to know her."

I shake my head in disbelief. "Not to question what you have, but it can't be all that perfect."

"And it's not, Madd. Relationships are hard fucking work. We wake up every day choosing to love each other. I both love and like her. Some days I like her more, some days I like her less. Some days are pure fucking torture. I want to bang my head on a wall and give myself a concussion and permanent amnesia because she's pissing me off so much. And I'm sure she feels the same, too."

"I don't know how to trust someone so much with all the vulnerable parts of me," I tell him.

He leans against the wooden pillar of the porch, crossing his arms over his chest and his legs at the ankles, taking me in, dissecting my innermost fears.

"You trust me," he says, shocking the fuck out of me. I do trust him. Come to think of it, I also trust my father. Sawyer, too. She has my trust with the most important person in my life—Ryker. Even now, as I'm fucking with both of our heads, there's been not one single moment when I questioned her integrity, not one second I worried she might use her connection to Ryker to get to me. But...

"It's not the same."

Drake scoffs and rolls his eyes. "Isn't it, though? Just because you don't feel the urge to bend me over the grill and show me some love, doesn't make it any different. We've had our ups and downs; we've had our fights and our disagreements. We constantly work hard to forgive and understand."

"Not seeing you every day makes me wanna celebrate, not gouge my eyes out."

He flips me the bird, a hint of amusement twinkling in his eyes before he gets all serious again. "Sure, the degree of separation helps in our case, I'll give you that. My point is, you do know how to trust. You just choose not to. But... tell me this, do you love her?"

I suck in a breath. His words hit me with the force of a freight train. I lean against the wall to stop myself from doubling over. A fleeting moment of panic washes through me that everyone is aware of what Sawyer and I have been up to. Then I remember he saw my display of insanity last month, when I carted her out of the fucking club over my shoulder.

I've been so busy warring with myself over what to do with my feelings—whatever they are—for Sawyer, I haven't even stopped to assess the consequences of my actions and how I basically outed us in front of our friends. In fact, now that I'm thinking somewhat straight, I see more trust going around. Four people saw us that night, and none of those four are stupid. Yet Tatum hasn't set fire to my house while leaving me tied up in the living room to burn to death for touching his sister. And three of them are closer to him than me.

My knees weaken as a strange feeling warms up my chest and spreads to my limbs. My mind works at a furious pace, trying to understand the new reality taking shape in front of me. Each one of those four knows true and well the kind of bastard I am. And not a one protested when I left with Sawyer. They trusted me with her, even when I gave most of them absolutely zero reason to trust.

I'm startled out of my spiraling thoughts by Drake clasping my shoulder. "It seems like you have some shit to work through. You're my brother, Maddox. I've seen you struggle for twenty years. I've seen you acting rash and impulsive, self-sabotaging any chance at happiness you've been given. Take a good look at yourself and decide if you're willing to put in the work. But... if you're not, don't string her along. She's not your mom, so don't take Lucy's mistakes out on her."

With those parting words, he leaves me to my smoking burgers. My heart jolts painfully in my chest, each breath I force in, constricted and laborious. To pour gasoline on an already raging fire, I turn just in time to see my son running, as fast as his skinny legs can take him, straight into the waiting arms of the object of my obsession.

Sawyer Carter has both Lawson men well and true under her spell.

Chapter Twenty-One

Maddox

The sharp chime of my phone rouses me from my pitiful sleep. I yawn and stretch my sore muscles, sighing in satisfaction as my bones crack and settle. I drag my palm over my face and blink my eyes open, staring at the darkness of my ceiling. My phone chimes again, and I bite a curse, squinting as I unlock it and read through the messages blinking on my screen.

A call just came in, attempted break-in at Suga'High.

Disrupted by upstairs tenant.

Fight ensued.

Tenant has minor injuries; suspect fled scene.

4:07 a.m. Benson

Daniel attacked Blake. Kid has a fat lip, but he'll live.

4:10 a.m. Hayes

Drives an old Corolla. Blake couldn't make the license plate. Jake's looking into it.

4:11 a.m. Hayes

> *Wake the fuck up and look at the video. The motherfucker drives a '98 Corolla. Plates won't help as he keeps changing them.*

4:30 a.m. Camden

Shit!

I jump out of bed and run to my bathroom, showering as quickly as I can with ice-cold water to wake me the hell up.

The last few weeks—ever since Ryker's birthday—have been excruciating, to say the least. When Tatum brought me up to speed on the threatening messages Maevis was receiving, the broken windows at her apartment above the bakery, and the weird packages with dead animals and more threats, I dived deep into finding out who was after her. Sleep came in short supply. Hell, I can't even remember the last time I had a decent meal. The only thing that keeps me going is the half an hour I get each night as I watch Sawyer get ready for bed. My solace is the glimpse of her as she lowers the blinds on her bedroom window.

I increased the patrols around town, but none of my deputies have seen anything suspicious so far. The messages came from a restricted number, most likely a burner, so that was a dead end. The package with a dead rat was unusable since Rowan threw it away at Tatum's request. The culprit also knew how to avoid the cameras around the bakery. I was going in blind. That is until he got either too desperate or too brazen, two days ago, and attacked Maevis at Suga'High.

There aren't many things that scare me, but hearing their muffled argument through the phone and knowing I might not get to Maevis in time... It broke something in me. I don't see myself as invincible, but so far, I've walked with blinders on. Nasty shit happened to someone else, not to me. Not to my loved ones. The terror in Mae's voice transported me back in time, to another day Drake and I were almost too late. All I saw as I sped to the bakery was her face, bloodied and bruised, and the blank acceptance in her eyes, as if she'd made her peace knowing she was going to die.

I haven't slept since, pouring over every bit of information I had on Daniel Johnson, talking to his family, trying to uncover which hole the lowlife keeps crawling in and out of. I must have passed out on my bed out of sheer exhaustion just before the first message came through.

Drying off quickly, I slip into my work uniform of dark brown trousers and tan shirt, cursing under my breath as I redo the knot on the goddamn tie for the fourth time. I shove my work laptop into my backpack and hurry to the kitchen to make myself a coffee, hoping there's something edible left in the fridge.

At least, I don't have to worry about Ryker until Sunday. My parents and I agreed it would be best for him to spend this week with them, so I can focus on finding the son of a bitch harassing Maevis.

After quickly downing a cup of coffee—no luck in the food department—I make my way to my cruiser, throw my backpack onto the passenger seat, and drive with my eyes peeled open all the way to the precinct.

"Morning, Charlie," I greet our night dispatcher and office administrator.

"You're here early, Chief. Want me to get some coffee ready?"

I check my watch before answering and see it's only ten past five. My stomach grumbles, airing its displeasure for being fed shit-all for the past few days. "Nah. I'm clocking in, then going to the diner for a fresh cup and some breakfast. If anyone needs me, they can reach me on my cell phone."

"You got it, boss." He gives me a two-finger salute, brushing his long green hair out of his eyes. I prefer the purple from last week, but I'm the chief deputy, not fashion police.

I hurry to my office and scan my access card, then add the appropriate code that will show in the system I'm out patrolling, so they can track my cruiser if they really need to see me.

Less than five minutes later, I push through the doors of Dine&Dash and force a smile at Renee's tired face greeting me. "Do you ever go home?"

"Top of the morning to you too, brat," she scolds me. "You think it's wise to sass the hands who feed you?"

This time, the smile is genuine as I bend over the counter and kiss her cheek. "No, ma'am. I'm just looking after you."

"Better start with your own garden, because *you*, sir, look about as good as I feel."

I splay my palm over my chest, feigning hurt. "Ouch, Renee, that was brutal, even for you. My poor ego can't take it."

She swats at me with a cotton towel before pouring a cup of coffee for me, then leaves for the kitchen to place my order. I don't need to tell her what I want; she'll order whatever she wants anyway. We've been playing this game ever since Ryker was only a couple of months old. I came into the diner absolutely dead on my feet after being up with my son the whole night and took too long to decide what I wanted to eat. In all honesty, my eyes were so blurry, I could barely read the menu. So, she went ahead and made the decision for me. Now, our little game saves me a couple of minutes every time I come in here.

I bury my nose into the little paper cup and greedily inhale the rich, dark roast with a hint of caramel. My eyes close for just one second, but I can't trust this moment of serenity. If I let myself relax, I'll fall asleep here on the stool. So I slide my phone out of my pocket and go directly to the tracking app. It was not one of my finest moments when I broke into Sawyer's home one night in a fit of jealousy and installed a tracker on her phone. But, with everything going on with her sister-in-law, it soothes something in me if I know where she is. If something happens, I'll be able to find her.

At least, that's what I tell myself when the lunacy of my behavior keeps me up at night.

The red dot blinks at me as it moves slowly along Main Street. It must be one of the days she opens the daycare, since she's out and about so early. Maybe I can time it just right and exit the diner at the same moment she passes by.

Except, I can't do that. I promised myself I wouldn't be selfish anymore with Sawyer. Drake is right. I have a fuckton of issues I need to work through first before I approach her. Until then, I get to see her through a clear window, maintaining a safe distance and hoping like a simp no one else steals her from under me.

Despite my resolve, I swivel in my seat and wait with bated breath for her to pass. And she doesn't disappoint. Her platinum blonde hair shines in the barely there morning light. Her exquisite body is clad in one of her signature pastel dresses. This particular one is a soft pink, the color accentuating the slight flush in her cheeks. She's so goddamn beautiful, my chest hurts.

Adrenaline floods through my bloodstream as she disappears out of sight. Every cell in my body pulls taut, demanding I get up this fucking chair and go to her. Luckily, Renee chooses this moment to return and plops a plate of steaming, fluffy golden eggs and crispy strips of bacon on the counter behind me.

I barely get a sip of the hot-as-fuck coffee when Tatum's name flashes on my smartwatch. Slipping the phone out of my pocket, I connect the call and croak, "Morning, Carter."

"You better be fucking awake and ready. He tried to break into our god-damn house."

"Fucking hell. Tell me everything."

"About half an hour ago, Maevis and I were in the kitchen. He threw a rock through the window near the breakfast nook, then ran like the fucking coward he is when he saw me. I gave chase, but he jumped into a beat-up Corolla, parked just at the town's limits, and headed north."

My blood freezes in my veins. He's escalating quickly, if he tried to gain access to the bakery and broke their window in the span of less than an hour.

"Are you guys hurt?" I ask.

"No. I saw him a split second before he threw the rock and managed to push Maevis behind me just in time. Just your superficial scratches from glass flying about. Get your ass into gear, Lawson, and find this son of a bitch, or else I'm not responsible for my actions when I get my hands on him. He attacked my pregnant wife in our home," Tatum bellows. His rage is palpable even through the phone, and I can't blame him.

If anything like this happened to Sawyer... I'd burn the world to the ground and spit on the ashes as I break every bone in the body of whoever dared touch her. And if I feel this way about a woman I'm not even involved with, I can't imagine how Carter must be feeling.

"On it. I'll let you know as soon as I find anything," I promise, and this is one vow I intend to keep.

"See that you do," he hisses and ends the call.

I down what's left of my coffee in one gulp, taste buds be damned. They'll heal... eventually. My mind, however, needs to be sharp and alert. I shovel food in my mouth like demon-hounds are chasing me and throw a twenty on the counter to cover my breakfast. Like the good person she is, Renee refills my to-go cup. An idea forms at the back of my mind, and although it's far-fetched, stranger things have happened.

"Renee, darling," I say, throwing her my most lethal smile, dimples popping deep into my cheeks. She swats at me again with her towel, but I don't miss the pink gathering on her mocha-colored skin. I wink at her for good measure and thrum my fingers on the wooden top. "You know everything that moves in this town. So, tell me, has anyone new been sniffing around these parts?"

"Not in the past few weeks, no. We did get a new neighbor at the trailer park, though. But that must'a'been at least a month ago, if not more.

Doesn't interact, prefers to keep to himself. I haven't even seen his face properly, cause he's always wearin' one of those baseball hats with the brim drawn down to his nose. He ain't causin' problems, quiet sorta folk. I'll take him over the likes of Gertie, who's always up in everyone's business."

Gotcha' motherfucker.

"Thanks, Ren. I owe you one," I say as I lean over the counter and kiss her cheek. She pats my arm, and I throw her a goodbye wave over my shoulder, adrenaline mounting in my body as I hurry to my cruiser. My gut is telling me Daniel Johnson is hiding right under our noses, in the trailer park. He managed to fly under the radar for god knows how long, but it ends today. I have a pretty one-by-one cell just for him. My broom closet is bigger, but he's a slimy fucker, he'll make do.

I park my cruiser in the bushes, right at the bend before the entrance, and take off on foot. Normally, I'd call reinforcements, but I want to make sure my hunch is right and Daniel's here before we break through someone's door. Going in by myself might work to my advantage for a bit of sleuth recon. Huh, stalking Sawyer for the past seven months really comes in handy today. I've learned how to make myself invisible and avoid being detected in my... strolls.

Few people are up, so the whole area is eerily quiet. Seeing as it's just before six in the morning, it doesn't come as a surprise. The muffled thump of feet against metal makes me halt. I hide in the bushes behind one of the double-wides. It's not very well looked after, but it also doesn't stand out in this row of trailers. My eyes scan the area. Movement just above me gets my attention. A dark figure is crouched on the roof of the trailer. By the size and build, it must be a man, but I can't make out his face for the black hoodie covering his head. I suck in a breath and keep still and quiet, with only the hammering of my heart as background noise.

He looks around unhurriedly, then he must decide he's in the clear because, in a movement so smooth I could swear he's a stuntman, he jumps off the roof on silent feet. Not even a pebble of gravel is disturbed under the soles of his boots as he takes off running. I follow close behind, ensuring he doesn't see me or hear me. He crawls through a hole in the fence, then strolls casually through the woods nearby. I give him another minute or two, otherwise I risk him detecting my presence in the open clearing before the tree line.

The forest is darker, and it takes a second or ten for my eyes to adjust. *Who the fuck is this asshole?* It can't be Daniel. When I took Maevis to the hospital, she said he looked sickly. Tatum also mentioned earlier that he seemed out of shape, and the only reason he didn't catch up with the bastard was because Daniel had a head start while Tatum made sure Mae was okay.

I use the trees to hide as the stranger advances through the forest on sure feet. There's no rustling of leaves under his steps, no crackling of fallen branches. My blood turns to ice in my veins. I'm not a man to feel fear often, but the churning in my stomach can't be anything else but fear. The way he moves, the way he walks—if he finds me following, I'm not sure which one of us will emerge victorious in a confrontation.

The trees grow thinner and thinner, more light pouring through, and then I hear the traffic from one of the main roads. I walk faster now, curiosity driving me forward. Worse comes to worst, I have my work-issued gun on me. While I hope to not have reason to use it, if I must defend myself, I will. I just need to remember to turn on my bodycam. Not yet, though. Not until I have to.

He pushes up a slick-looking black motorcycle. I stop walking like I hit an invisible wall and take a step back as my body recoils. The hoodie goes down, confirming my suspicions, the black material replaced with a dark helmet. He mounts the bike before I unfreeze my feet. The rumble of the motorcycle vibrates through me, and then he's gone.

"Fuck," I hiss, pinching the bridge of my nose between my thumb and forefinger.

What the fuck did he do? And where do I go from here?

I walk back to my cruiser, debating on my next move. When a call comes through the radio, "*10-67. All available units. 11-71, fire reported at the trailer park. I repeat, 11-71,*" my stomach sinks to my feet.

With shaky hands I pick up the radio and respond, "10-97, Lawson. I'm already here, I'll check it out."

"*10-8, Benson. I'm on my way.*"

I make a show of turning on the siren and steering my cruiser into the trailer park. There's no surprise when I see thick, black smoke coming from the same trailer I was looking at earlier. I leave my car aside, so that LHFD has enough space to maneuver when they get here, and jump into action.

A frantic neighbor tells me he woke up earlier to walk his dog when he noticed the smoke. He'd been banging on the door for ten minutes without a response when he called 911. I don't believe in coincidences. And when LHFD gets here two minutes later, breaks through the door, and assesses the double-wide, I'm not surprised to have Emmett Benson, Theresa's husband, tell me the occupant was found dead.

What I'm surprised with... is myself. I knew since he put his helmet on that I'd get a call like this. But I thought I had more integrity, stronger morals. Turns out, when it comes to assholes harming my family—and make no mistake, Maevis *is* my family—all sense of right and wrong flies straight out the window.

For the sake of appearance and procedure, I start the investigation into the death of Daniel Johnson. Truth be told, I don't give a fuck why Daniel's dead, just that he is.

Chapter Twenty-Two

Sawyer

I regret not taking my car. My impulse control really needs a check-up because packing a bag at ten-thirty at night and hightailing it to my childhood home doesn't bode well for my mental health. But, in my defense, I couldn't take it anymore. I was having a good evening, a great one even, and then I felt it... the burn on my skin as if someone was watching me.

Out of nowhere, my heart started pounding and my palms went slick with sweat. I checked every window. Nothing was out there. I lowered every blind, turned on the volume on my TV. It helped not one bit. If anything, the sensation of being trapped under someone's stare only intensified. Goosebumps sprouted on my arms, the fine hairs at the back of my neck standing at attention. My little cottage suddenly turned from my safe place to suffocating and ominous, every creak and every rustle panic-inducing.

So I called my mom, like a child, and lied to her face about missing them and wanting to spend the night in my childhood bedroom. Of course, Sarah Carter—helicopter-parent extraordinaire—jumped at the idea of me having a sleepover there. With her, the hour of the night or day doesn't matter. One of her babies needs her, she's up and at them. My father may be a retired Marine, but my mom is the drill sergeant, hands down.

And so, I threw some pajamas into a bag, my *I hate Maddox* poetry notebook, and a change of clothes for tomorrow, locked my home, and took off at a run to their place.

Why? Why did I run instead of taking my car when I felt someone was watching me? Because *clearly* I'm the dumb blonde you see in every horror movie, who runs up the stairs and backs herself into a corner, making life oh-so-easy for the cold-blooded killer.

Do I think someone is actually watching me? That's a no. And I always walk everywhere if I can help it. The car is only used in bad weather or for longer drives, usually outside town. Familiarity overrode my common sense.

"Not that you have much common sense considering you've been sleeping with Maddox," I mumble to myself as I lengthen my strides, the thumping of my Converse against the sidewalk echoing in the silence of the night. That strange feeling still hasn't left me. It followed me from my little cottage all the way here, even though there's no one else around. I know, I looked.

Heaving a sigh of relief when my childhood home comes into sight, I hurry up the steps. The front door opens before I reach the porch, and my father's worried face is the first thing I see.

"Baby girl, what's wrong?"

I launch myself into the safety of his open arms, and he catches me with a surprised "Umph!", tightening his hold on me. Like when I was a child, I hide my face in the crook of his neck, breathing in his comforting scent of leather and home, with a faint hint of spice from his cologne. My adrenaline ebbs, relief washing through my tensed body. Once my breathing is back to normal, and my heart no longer threatens to pump through my ribcage, I release my hold around his neck and greet him with a kiss on his weathered cheek. "Hi Dad."

"For Christ's sake, Tatum, you're letting all the night bugs in," my mom chides from somewhere in the house.

My father looks down at me and rolls his eyes playfully before ushering me through the door. I snicker under my breath, allowing the feeling of home to settle inside me and calm the last of my anxiety. He hugs me to his chest one more time, kissing my forehead. "We're happy you're here, kid." Then passes me over to my mother, with a kiss atop her head. "I'll be in the bedroom if you girls need me."

My mom sneaks a hand around my waist and leads me to the kitchen, her chin-length curly bob bouncing around with every step. This routine is familiar. I drop my bag next to the island and take a seat on one of the rounded, tall stools. The light is dim, with only a crystal lamp in the corner of the counter turned on. She likes to read in the kitchen, away from 'Tatum's noisy baseball games'.

She flits about, picking up a teakettle and filling it with water, before placing it on the stove for the water to boil. Sarah Carter is old school like that. Claims nothing beats the shrill whistle of an old-fashioned kettle, even if an electric one works faster. Cabinet doors bang, drawers open and close, and I keep my mouth shut.

There's no talking until she's satisfied I have all I need, and she can focus one hundred percent on me. My eyes water as childhood memories inundate my mind. Me, snotty and cried out because I scraped my knee, sitting on one of these very stools as Mom would gently blow over my booboo. Her, intense and focused as she cleaned my wound with a paper towel and disinfectant, hissing at my brother to distract me from the sting. Tate, sour-faced as he sat cross-legged at the foot of the old leather couch in the family room, wearing a bedazzled crown and playing with my dolls with me and Selena. The 'Welcome home' parties my mother would throw every time Dad came home from a deployment.

I startle when a cup of steaming tea is placed in front of me. The soothing scent of chamomile with a touch of lemon envelops me as I breathe it in. A rounded plate with delicate golden flowers on the rim follows, perfect little squared brownies stacked up in the center. I snag one up and shove it in my mouth. *Uh oh, Sarah brought forth the big guns.* The scrape of metal on marble makes me wince as Mom pulls her own stool and sits next to me. She leans her head on my shoulder and takes dainty sips from her cup of tea, pinky finger in the air and all.

"Okay, Queen Sarah the ruler of the Carter household, that might be pushing it," I tease.

She snickers softly, plopping the teacup down on the matching saucer. "Thought so. I figured I'd give it a try. Thanks, daughter of mine, for calling me out. Have another brownie."

I narrow my eyes at the curls on her head, but do as I'm bid. Once I swallow the delicious square whole, I ask, suspicion lacing my tone, "What are you buttering me up for?"

She sits up straight, craning her neck to look at me. My mother is a tiny thing, her forehead barely reaching the top of my chest. My siblings and I have taken our height from our father—Tatum being just over six-foot tall, Selae and me five-eight. My mom always looks like a small, plumpy doll when she's around us. But as she says, strong essences come in small packages. And Sarah Carter is one of the strongest essences I've ever met. She could move the Earth out of orbit just with the power of her will if she so wishes.

Her navy-blue eyes, very much like mine, blink up at me, and her lips purse. My shoulders lift to my chin. *Not the mother-stare.* She always does this when she thinks we're hiding something from her, and we're in need of some good ole' coaxing to spill the beans. First the bribe, then the stare, after the stare...

I don't know what comes next because those laser-focused eyes dissecting me have always been enough to make me crack under pressure. But I can't crack right now. If the dam breaks, everything I've been up to will come out of my mouth, and there are just some things you don't tell your mother. Like... how a certain Chief Deputy sexed my brains out against the hallway wall of my cottage.

Her eyes narrow, and sweat peppers my hairline. *Oh, no. Stay strong, Sawyer.* I shove another brownie in my mouth, chewing slowly, methodically, but not daring to break eye contact. Her hand pats mine, and my heart pounds inside my chest. I sink my teeth into my bottom lip just to keep my mouth shut. *Oh god. How do Tatum and Selae keep it together?* I bring my teacup to my lips. Gently blowing the steam away, I take small sips, savoring the hint of honey and lemon and the dulcet tones of chamomile.

She huffs a breath and crosses her arms under her breasts, the pale-blue material of her nightgown stretching over her chest. "Fine, keep your secrets."

I almost smile. Almost. But if I do, she'll crack me right open. Instead, I bend my head and kiss her temple. "You're the best mom. I'm so lucky to have you."

Her eyes mist over and her cheeks pinken. She swats her hand through the air. "Flattery will get you anywhere, Missy."

"Right now, it needs to get me to bed."

"Go ahead then, I put fresh bedding on for you. Leave the cup, I'll tidy up in here."

"Yes, ma'am." I slide from the stool and envelop her in my arms. Maybe I can't talk to her about what's plaguing me, but just breathing in her sweet scent of apple pie with a hint of cinnamon makes me feel safe and loved. Feelings I've sorely lacked in the past few months of Maddox's twisted mind games. I press my lips to the top of her head. "I love you, Momma. Good night."

"Love you too, honey. Sweet dreams." I pick up my bag and turn to head to my bedroom when she clasps my arm. "Whenever you're ready to talk, I'm always here. This house, me, your father, your siblings, we're your safe spaces."

I nod, but don't dare speak. I couldn't if I wanted to. The lump of emotions in my throat makes speech impossible. So I run to my childhood bedroom. The one that still looks exactly as I left it eight years ago when I packed my bags and went a thousand miles away for college. The soft peach color of my walls, the posters of my favorite bands, pages and pages of handwritten poetry tapped around the mirror, the dozens of stuffed cuddlies, my favorite books on floating shelves Tatum took great care to mount—all is waiting for me as if I never left.

I told my parents to take my room and change it into something they could use, but both flat out refused. My siblings' rooms are unchanged too. My parents said, *"It doesn't matter where life takes you. How high it lifts you, how far it drops you. You'll never be left without a home. Whatever you do, do it with full confidence that you'll always have a place to come home to. A place to regroup and to heal if you need, a place to celebrate your success and share the joy. It was yours from the moment you were born, and it'll remain yours for as long as you live."*

The strange feeling of being watched hasn't lessened since I arrived here, but knowing my father is just at the end of the hallway settles the anxiety in me. Even though my skin pebbles under those invisible eyes as I go to the adjoining bathroom between Selae's room and mine. Even though the burning gives way to a strange caress as I crawl into my childhood bed and hide under the covers like I did when I was younger. I'm tempted to call my dad and have him check for monsters under my bed and in my empty dresser.

Except, same as when I was a kid, this monster lives in my imagination only—and sometimes in my dreams. I let my eyes fall closed and take comfort in my parents' nearness. Nothing can happen to me under their watchful gaze. I'm sure my body is just reacting to the second-hand stress of Maevis's nightmare with her ex-husband following her and threatening her.

But I have no excuses at the ready when I wake up in the morning, the chill June breeze threading softly through the lacy curtains in front of the window I know for a fact I closed last night. And maybe, just maybe, I could've played it off as being three fries short of a Happy Meal... if I didn't wake up the next day to the same window being cracked open again. And... as I look at the picture I took last night on my phone to convince myself that I indeed locked it, my blood freezes when I notice a figure shrouded in darkness just behind the trunk of the tree under my window.

Chapter Twenty-Three

Maddox

"And then Cla'a wan away with my gwapes, Daddy," Ryker tells me sullenly as he shovels more eggs into his mouth.

"We don't talk with our mouths full," I admonish, scratching my bare chest with my free hand as I fork a strip of bacon and bite into it. I swear, I *am* teaching this kid manners, but anything I say enters through one of his ears and exits through the other.

"Sowwy, Daddy," he mumbles, *still* munching on his eggs. "But my gwapes!" He throws his tiny arms in the air, egg yolk flying all over the kitchen island. I sigh and take a healthy mouthful of my piping-hot coffee, the rich aroma of the dark roast soothing my annoyance. I love my son, I truly truly do, but if I have to wash his hair for a second time this morning just to clean off his breakfast, I'm going to scream.

No, not at him. But like a proper adult, with my face in a pillow; the mature way of dealing with shit when the tension is mounting, and even the air around you seems to find your nuclear button and press it—repeatedly and forcefully.

It's not Ryker's fault that I'm in a piss-poor mood. It's also not his fault he has a cowardly bastard for a father, who prefers to burn to a crisp in a hell of his own making instead of dealing with his issues. No. Ryker is my only joy as of late, the only ray of sunshine in an otherwise dark sky.

I brought him back from my parents the day after Daniel's death. Sure, I had a fuckton of paperwork to fill in. The official investigation was *not* concluded by me, thank you very much. It stated Daniel had died of a myocardial infarction, as found by the coroner after his family agreed to an autopsy, and the fire started from a lit cigarette he dropped into a trash can filled with mottled papers.

I'm not upset he died, but I am torn up over how he died. The absolute truth of it is the investigation was thorough, yet no foul play was detected. I know better than that. Is there a possibility *he* just paid Daniel a visit to scare the fuck out of him and the visit is what possibly led to his heart attack? Sure. Except it's not what my gut tells me. Deep down, I know *he* had something to do with how Daniel died. But knowing, proving, and actually doing anything about it are three different things.

I've always considered myself a man of the law. The rules are written, and all we have to do is follow them. Simple as. Except, I broke my oath by keeping quiet and became jury, judge, and executioner. If I hadn't followed *him* and kept to my original plan of checking on Daniel, maybe he would've still been alive. And maybe he would've escaped unscathed just to harm Maevis later.

The truth is, while I'm mildly disgusted with myself for not being the man I thought I was, I'm not losing any sleep over Daniel's death. Oh, I'm losing sleep alright, just not over that scum of a man.

What keeps me awake at night is a pair of haunted navy-blue eyes and the cold indifference of the woman who owns my every thought. I can't lie to myself anymore. Unfortunately for me and the last shred of sanity I have left, I'm in love with Sawyer Carter. And I don't even choke on my coffee thinking those words. Love for a woman is not something I'd ever thought I'd feel. But here we are.

"Daddy, are you even lis'ning?" Ryker screeches from his booster chair.

"Sorry, buddy. I'm still sleeping in my coffee," I mumble as I take another sip. I really need to get it together and decide. Either grow a fucking pair and start working on my trust issues or let Sawyer go. None of the options presented are appealing to me in the slightest.

He scrunches his nose at me, his tiny forehead creasing in confusion. "Why are you sleeping in coffee, silly? You should sleep on the bed with the pillows and a stuffie to cuddle."

I'd cuddle a stuffie alright, after I stuff her full of me. *Christ!* I drag a palm over my face. These dirty thoughts really need to take a chill pill. I enjoy sex like any red-blooded male out there, but ever since I got my first taste of Sawyer, I'm like a horned-up-teenager with a porn addiction. If lust were the only thing I felt for her, I could live with that. There's therapy to cure a sex fixation, right? I don't think therapy would make me get over my feelings for her.

Obsession. Possessiveness. Being fucking sick to my stomach when a man gets too close to her. Protectiveness. Longing. Wishing for things my fucked-up mind has no business wishing, like finally kissing her, waking up next to her, holding her in my arms and just... sleeping.

Maybe I have a tumor. Maybe I ate raw meat and now a bunch of zombie-worms are wiggling their way through my brain, devouring all my gray-matter while dancing bachata with my pituitary gland. Or maybe I am in love and fucked to high heaven. Maybe that.

UGH.

"So, can I get more gwapes for lunch today?"

Maybe I need to get my will together, for Ryker's sake, because I'm definitely dying of an undiscovered illness. My stomach churns and flutters. Random boules of air form in my chest and make me feel hollow on the daily. I get pins and needles in my arms when she's near, and my blood feels carbonated. Clearly, sporting a boner twenty-four-seven has cut off the oxygen supply to other important body parts, and my cells are slowly decomposing and poisoning my heart. It sure hurts like that.

"Daaaadddyyyyy, can I? Please, please, pweeetty please?"

"Uh-ah. Sure you can, partner. Whatever you need," I mumble, distracted.

"Awe, thanks Daddy, you the best. Now let me down, I've gots to bwash my teef."

That gets my attention. *Shit. What did I just agree to?* I pull away from my chair and help him climb down, and he takes off at a run up the stairs. "Slow down, racer. Careful not to trip," I shout after him. Once I hear him thumping on the second-floor landing, I clear our plates, rinse them, and stack them up in the dishwasher. I wipe the top of the island, cleaning up all the eggs he spread about, including on the floor and the kitchen cabinet behind his chair, then follow him to ensure he doesn't paint his bathroom in toothpaste.

Ten minutes and half a temper tantrum later, after I *forgot* to pack the grapes I *promised,* we're on our way to the daycare center. My blood is fizzing in my veins, anticipation coursing through me, knowing that soon enough my eyes will feast on her.

It's been too long since I've seen her. Too long since I've touched her. The scratches on my legs and palms are a testament to the lengths I'm going to satisfy the complete madness she's reduced me to.

As soon as I park my truck, I help Ryker unbuckle and hoist him up on my hip. Sure, he could walk, but that would take ages, and I need to see her *now.* I throw a good morning over my shoulder to Brook at the reception desk and lengthen my strides so I can be close to Sawyer quicker. Ryker is giggling to himself as he bounces in my arms with every step I take.

My heart is hammering in my chest as I round the corner and stop dead in my tracks when confronted with the smiling face sitting behind the teacher's desk. *What the fuck?* My body cools off in an instant, as if doused with ice-cold water. She pushes her short, red hair behind her ear, waving at us with her free hand.

"Good morning, Ryker, Maddox!" She nods as she stands and walks to us. "You're just in time for our zoo lesson."

"Miss Lena," Ryker squeals and wiggles in my arms. I slowly unfreeze and let him down to run off to his teacher before I risk dropping him on his head.

"Where's Sawyer?" I bark, then feel my cheeks heating up. *Fuck. Way to be cool, asshole.*

If she's bothered by my frosty reception, Lena doesn't show. I know she's a teacher at the daycare center, but it's always been Sawyer looking after Ryker's class. Not finding her here when I need to see her so desperately unsettles me to my very marrow. A twinge of worry crawls up my spine, my mind rushing through the likely scenarios of what would keep her away from work.

"Sawyer is fine." Lena smiles wanly, waving my concerns off. "She had an appointment in Forrest Falls with the last of the permits for HeeBee. Her plan was to extend care for Forrest Falls residents too, since they're understaffed there as well. The legalities flew over my head, but she took today off." She bends at the waist, her palms slapping her knees as she looks at Ryker. "So you get me today, instead."

He smiles up at her, giggling when she ruffles his hair. "Fanks, Miss Lena. I always miss Miss Sawy, but I like you, too."

She laughs heartily and pats his shoulder. "You're good for my ego, kid. Now run along to your locker and leave your backpack there."

I drag a palm over my face and try to school my features into my normal mask of indifference. Truth is, I haven't visited Sheriff Richards in a good while. Maybe it's time I went and reported the closure of the Johnson's case in person. Forrest Falls' Town Hall being right across the street from the Sheriff's office has nothing to do with my decision. If I just so happen to run into Sawyer, then surely two neighbors can share a morning coffee, right?

While technically I'm responsible for the police department in Lost Hope, I report to Sheriff Richards. Our county is big enough to have separate police departments in neighboring small towns, yet all of them are connected through a central sheriff's office to coordinate us all.

My mind made up, I nod to myself. I stride to Ryker and crouch next to his chair. "Give Daddy a hug, partner." He launches his tiny body into my arms, and I kiss the top of his head, his scent of red grapes filling my lungs. Yes, my son's love for grapes extends to his body wash, too. "Be good for Miss Lena," I murmur in his hair as I squeeze him to my chest. "I love you, bud."

"I pwomise. Love you too, Daddy." Ryker smiles up at me, planting a kiss on my chin. I chuckle and wait for him to release me and go back to his desk. One thing I've learned is to never let go of a hug until my child is ready to let go first. I'll always be there for him to take from me what he needs. I might not be the cuddliest person, but if Ryker needs a twenty-hour-long hug, that's what he'll get. My son will never feel rejected by his own parent because I withdrew from a hug before he was ready for it to end.

I'm also well aware that these moments will be fewer and fewer as he grows up and becomes more independent. I had years during which I refused to let my parents touch me, denying them even a simple brush of a hand through my hair. While I'll never give Ryker the same reasons to refuse to be near me, as kids grow into teenagers and then adults, they become more and more independent. Those random acts of affection won't be sought from their parents anymore.

With a wave over my shoulder, I stride out of the classroom and jog to my truck. The drive to the police station takes but a minute. I'll quickly check in with Christina, who's in charge of dispatch, clock in, then take the cruiser to see Richards. She and Charlie alternate shifts, so that both day and night shifts are covered. Her husband, Christian—yes, we're always teasing them for their names—is one of my deputies, and currently eyefucking his wife over the reception desk.

I grip his shoulder, startling him, and bite back a laugh at his yelp. "Didn't know flirting with your wife was part of your duties, Deputy Holland." Christina laughs and rolls her eyes at me, while his widen, but then throws me a cheeky grin.

"You just signed a bonus for me last month, commending my performance for this exact duty, boss man," the bastard sasses me, leaning over to kiss his wife's cheek, before standing up to his full height.

He's nearly as tall as I am, but where I'm wide and muscular from hours on end punching a boxing bag and playing baseball in high school and college, he's lean, with a runner's build. He's also one of the fastest in my department. We walk together to my small office at the back of the station as he brings me up to speed with how the night shift went.

While I'm always on call if needed, unless Ryker's at my parents', I always come to work once I dropped him off at the daycare center. My workday starts anywhere between 7 a.m. and 9 a.m., depending on what time he wakes up. The shift changes at seven in the morning, so I rely on my deputies to give me the handover from the night before, if I miss them when I come in.

Just as he's wrapping up, Christina is knocking on the door. "Mrs. Ravencourt just called. Apparently, some kids have been messing about in her vegetable garden last night." She gives us a wry smile.

Mrs. Ravencourt calls at least three times a week to report one thing or another. Most of the time, her calls are just false alarms. She lives at the periphery of Lost Hope and has been alone for ten years, ever since she lost her husband. So she calls us, we go and check; she feeds us tea and finger sandwiches and chats our ears off for one hour straight. Everyone's happy.

"Anyone nearby?" I ask as I punch in the code in my computer to log the visit to Forrest Falls and send the case files I need to my tablet.

"Henderson and Landers are out on patrol. Paulski called and said he'd be late; Josie has a doctor's appointment, and he is minding the baby until she returns. He was supposed to do desk duty today," Christina tells me.

"Alright. I need to go see Richards. I'll drop by Mrs. Ravenscourt's on my way there."

And then *hopefully* I'll get to see Sawyer and calm the furious swirling in the pit of my stomach that demands her closeness with more insistence every passing day.

I huff a breath, blowing away from my eyes a tendril of blonde hair that escaped my neat little bun, as I scribble with my trusty fountain pen in my new poetry notebook. Dealing with administrators at the Town Hall is the devil's work. I was supposed to have Blake with me, but he and Lalah are on a super-secret-stealth mission, and he had to cancel on me.

Fair, before he canceled, he also gave me a folder with all the paperwork prepared and ready to save me the headache. But the lady with the pinched mouth and thorny stick up her bottom couldn't care less about how prepared I was. She huffed and puffed about how we're all trying to disrupt the good functioning of their town. Which makes no sense to me. Where Lost Hope is clustered in a valley between the mountains, Forrest Falls is spread out.

There are two mountain slopes flanking the town on each side, one bordering Lost Hope, the other Crestfall Peaks, another small town about an hour and a half away. The Main Street here runs along Forrest Falls River on each riverbank. Most businesses and government buildings in town are on—or close to—the river. Farms and households are scattered around on the two slopes. The majority of residents on the side of the mountain bordering Lost Hope would have a shorter drive dropping off their children to Happy Bumblebees. One glaring example is Lalah and Cole's situation. Their adopted daughters—and Cole's step-sisters—Clara and Eliza attend the school and daycare in our town, even though, technically, they live in Forrest Falls.

The gray-haired sour-faced demon of administration couldn't care less about my well-thought-out arguments. And now, here I am, sitting at a nice little outdoor café built on a wooden deck, watching the sun rays sparkle over the clear river waters as I wait for my appointment with the Mayor of Forrest Falls. Apparently, me trying to steal residents away from their wonder of a town must be approved by the top head.

I really wish Blake was here.

All he has to do is smile and flash those straight shiny teeth of his, and everyone trips over their feet to do his bidding. Being a pretty boy definitely has its perks.

My cheeks heat as an image of Maddox sprawled out underneath me, every chiseled muscle on his body straining and tense as I rode him and called him a pretty boy, flashes through my mind.

"Sawyer!"

My heart starts galloping as I hear my name in his low, gravelly voice, my core clenching. Holly inkwell, that memory is potent if it's actually causing me auditory hallucinations this strong. I startle when a large, warm palm settles on my back, tingles spreading through my skin at the contact. I bite back a yelp when my knee hits the table from underneath as I shift away from him and hurriedly close my notebook.

He's not here. I'm losing my mind.

"Are you okay, little fairy? You look like you've seen a ghost," he says, and I turn my head slowly, taking in the absolute glorious sight of one Maddox Lawson, decked in dark brown slacks and a tan-colored button down, his badge shining proudly on his belt. God, he's wearing the heck out of that boring uniform.

"Uhm... ah, y-you startled me." I clear my throat, squinting up at him, and try again, "What are you doing here?"

He smiles wide until his dimples pop, those full lips of his sinful and lush. My mouth dries out instantly. His icy-blue eyes sparkle in the sunlight as he takes me in. The air between us crackles as tension coils and ebbs. Good grief, he really is a pretty boy.

"Had a meeting with Richards and decided to grab a cup of coffee before returning to Lost Hope. Imagine my surprise when I saw you here." He bends down and kisses my cheek, the touch of his lips on my skin searing. "Is this seat taken?" He points at the lone chair in front of me, but I'm struck speechless, my words clogged in my throat. It's all I can do not to lift my hand and touch my cheek, the ghost of his minty breath still clinging to me.

Maddox doesn't wait for me to answer either, but grabs the chair and sets it as close to mine as possible before plopping down. He scoots down, man-spreading his strong thighs until the outside of his leg is firmly pressed to mine, his arm thrown over the back of my chair. *What is happening?*

"Did you order anything?" he asks as he reaches for the paper menu, still clipped to the pretty holder made of dark wood, butterflies carved on the base. I'm still staring at him like an idiot, my mind trying to comprehend and process what my eyes and ears are telling me. "Sawyer, baby, did you order anything?" He smirks now, a fully-satisfied, predatory smirk I want to wipe off his face with my mouth.

"I just got here," I manage to force out.

His warm, calloused palm squeezes my shoulder, and I swear lightning strikes through his hand straight into my chest. "Perfect, we can share something, then."

"W-what are you doing here, Maddox?" I demand, now that I've had a second to understand that he's not a hallucination plucked straight from my dirtiest memories.

He straightens in his seat. His fingers—still massaging my shoulder—tighten their hold on me. "Didn't we just go through this, little fairy?"

I shift away from him, so he's forced to drop his hold on me, and I cross my arms over my chest. "Last time I saw you, you hate-*effed* me against a wall, then ran away like the house was on fire. And now what, we're just having casual breakfast?"

His eyes glaze over, the hint of a smirk tugging at his lips. Pure fire rises inside my chest. I slap his rock-hard biceps and hiss through my teeth, "No. Don't do that. Don't go all... lusty on me as if that's a fond memory." I throw my hands up between us in frustration and yelp when he shackles my wrist in his large palm and pulls me to him, so close his plump lips feather over mine as they part.

"Oh, little fairy, but it's one of my *fondest* memories. I wouldn't mind a repeat," he rasps, his heart thrumming in his chest where he keeps my hand plastered over his crisply ironed shirt. I swallow down the lump of emotion lodged in my throat, my belly quivering. A different fire stokes to life inside me when his tongue darts out to sweep over his bottom lip. It takes all my willpower not to suck it inside my mouth and finally know what he tastes like.

A throat clears somewhere behind him, and I jump back as if burned. This is the power Maddox has over me. He makes me forget everything around me, where I am, who I am, my common sense. "Morning, folks. I'm Roxy, and I'll be your server today. What can I get you started on?"

She's a pretty woman, her dark hair pulled up in a slick ponytail, and her shirt unbuttoned close to indecency.

My cheeks flame as jealousy roars to life inside my every cell, and I surreptitiously peek at the paper menu Maddox dropped on his lap, trying to douse off my newly-found murderous tendencies. But I don't need to worry—queue the eye roll—since the overbearing man orders for both of us. And probably finds a way to flirt with the pretty waitress right in front of me. Because that's what he is, a manwhore, and I'd better remember it.

"Two dark roast coffees, please, with cream and sugar on the side for one of them. Two bacon, egg, and avocado bagels, and iced water. Thanks, darlin'!" He throws her his panty-melting smile that has me gritting my teeth, then turns to me, completely dismissing her. He bends his head, his nose nuzzling my hair. His lips brush against my ear as he whispers, "Jealousy looks so damn good on you, fairy. I love that you're possessive over me."

I huff and push him away from me. *The arrogant, conceited, big-headed... ugh.* "Not even in your dreams," I vehemently deny.

The smile he gives me is blinding, spellbinding. And I'm in *big* trouble. I just need to remain strong and remember nothing good can come out of this. Sure, my heart has currently relocated in my vagina, and right now, both are very fond of the man next to me. But that's because he's the only one my body has ever known.

Once I'm again in control of my feelings, I'll put him and my *temporary* lapse in sanity behind me and start dating someone more my speed. Someone who has the same goals and vision for the future as me. Someone I'll love and who'll love me right back.

"Oh, believe me, little fairy, it's definitely *not* your jealousy I dream about." He lifts both eyebrows at me as if to say *what are you going to do about it*, daring me to prod further, to demand he tells me what he dreams about. I'd rather poke my eyes out with a rusty butter knife.

He reaches his arm across my lap, his fingers curling over the spine of my pretty notebook, tracing the golden swirly patterns on the navy-blue background. My whole body stiffens. If he opens that notebook... "What's this?"

Act casual, Sawyer, don't give him a reason to get suspicious.

"My planner," I explain, happy when my voice comes out all confident and strong. Everything I'm not. "I was just going over the things I need to do today before you so rudely interrupted me." I huff and snatch it off the table, shoving it into my bag, all the while trying to school my face, so he doesn't see the relief I'm currently feeling.

"Busy day, then?" he muses, thrumming his fingers on the wooden tabletop.

My head is spinning with conflicting emotions. His magnetic pull hooked so deep inside of me, a faint sense of self-preservation demanding I put distance between us, relief he didn't read my poetry—everything battles inside my chest, making it hard to breathe.

There's only one thing to do. So I steel my spine and shift again so I can face him, my hands folded on my lap. "Now we're doing small talk?" I demand.

Maddox tilts his head and chews on his cheek as he regards me. His large palm envelops my much smaller ones as he covers them both, his thumb rubbing soothing circles over my wrist. He lifts a shoulder in a careless shrug. "Why not? The way I see it, we're both here, waiting to share a hopefully delicious breakfast. We can get to know each other."

"Get to know each other?" I shriek. "What's there to know, Maddox? I grew up in the same town you did. I know very well who you are. What's the purpose of this? We're not friends. We're nothing."

A shadow passes over his face, his eyes flashing with a hint of darkness. "You think I want to be your *friend*?" he bites out. "A friend doesn't spend every waking moment thinking of all the ways he could fuck you, Sawyer. A friend doesn't daydream about the taste of your lips, or the taste of your pussy, and how you feel like fucking heaven when I'm buried deep inside you."

I lunge at him, half out of my chair, slapping a palm over his mouth to stop him from talking, and nearly topple his chair to the ground. "Shh!" I hiss. "God, did you hit your head or something? What makes you think it's okay to say those things out loud?"

The insufferable man winks and licks my palm. The swipe of his tongue, wet and warm on my skin, sends an army of tingles between my thighs. It should gross me out, but all I want is to leap in his lap and kiss the arrogance straight off his lips. I snatch my palm away and make a show of wiping him off my skin on my pristine pale-pink skirt.

"You said we're not friends. I just confirmed how much exactly we aren't. People with an interest in each other can also get to know one another through small talk, Sawyer."

Gah. The audacity of this man.

He knows exactly which buttons to push to make me ignite, to make me explode, and to infuriate me to my very limits.

"Thank you, Maddox. If it weren't for your very thorough mansplanation, the meaning of dating would've flown straight over my head."

His clean-shaven jaw clenches. A faint vein pops on his forehead, pulsing under his skin. He's offended. *Good.* So am I.

"Don't do that, little fairy. I'm trying here. Please, I miss you so fucking much," he grits, his lips thinning.

My traitorous stomach flips. Butterflies explode to life inside of me. *Bad butterflies. Settle down. This is a no-fly zone.* This is what he does—swipes me off my feet with pretty words, and his pretty eyes, and his pretty boy moves. He takes what he needs when he needs it, then leaves me behind feeling used and foolish. And… falling a little bit more for him every time because, clearly, I have unresolved childhood issues I still haven't figured out yet.

"I don't understand what it is you're doing… or trying to do." I sigh, trying to choose my words carefully. "We had our fun, Maddox, and I'm grateful to you for making me feel safe and not being selfish… you know… in bed." My throat dries out and a blush blazes its way to my cheeks, but I power through. "But you don't want what I want. It's unfair to me and, ultimately, it's unfair to you to keep doing this. We agreed on one night. We repeatedly broke that agreement."

He flinches as if I slapped him. A sense of dread settles over my shoulders when his eyes, twinkling just minutes ago, turn ice-cold. "So that's it? We're what… just going to ignore what happened between us and move on with our lives as if it didn't matter?"

I force myself to keep my head high and look him straight in the eye. "It didn't matter, Maddox. We had sex, fantastic sex, even if I have nothing to compare against. But that's all it was. And now it's done."

He is not even blinking, his hands fisted in his lap, knuckles white. And so, I double-down to make sure he understands my stance. The mind-games are done. Being used and disrespected, that's done too. "I may be inexperienced, but I'm no one's toy. Just… leave me alone, please."

"Here you go, folks." Roxy's chirpy voice startles me as she plops two plates in front of us, the usually delicious smell of bacon and egg turning my stomach instead. "Can I bring you anything else?"

Maddox ignores her, pushing up from his chair and throwing a couple of crisp bills on the table. I shake my head at her, and she scurries away as he turns to me, his face holding no trace of the playfulness he had just moments before. Thunderstorm clouds gather all around us even though the skies remain clear, the sun still shining over us. The air turns to frostbite on my skin, goosebumps peppering me from head to toe.

His eyes bore into mine, searching and prodding. I hold my breath, trapped under his scrutiny. I should feel proud of myself for setting out clear boundaries, but as he tips his chin at me, then leaves without looking back, all I feel is hollow.

Chapter Twenty-Five

Sawyer

The air in TBRC is charged. I bet if I slashed my hand in front of me, I'd be able to cut the tension in half, it's so thick. Everyone is wearing grim expressions, and my stomach somersaults as my eyes dart over my friends before settling on my lap.

The only guidance I had for this meeting was to wear purple and teal, which meant I had to go shopping since most of my clothing is in calm, pastel colors. I smooth the pleated purple and teal skirt over my thighs, dread and anticipation building inside of me.

"Women of TBRC," Lalah calls out, leaning against the table brimming with snacks. "I have our next read. Before I give you your copies, I'd like you to know this is not an easy read. It's not enjoyable either. What it is… is necessary, imperative, and a goddamn fucking shame that we need to educate ourselves. Today, we're dressed to raise awareness for domestic violence and sexual assault."

Her hair is in a slick, high ponytail, the midnight-blue strands streaked with various shades of purple and teal. She really went all in for this session. I thought she'd cheat and wear her normal black leggings and sweatshirt, but no. I would've expected the touch of color to soften her up, but her lips are in a tight line, her hazel eyes hard and unforgiving. *What on earth is she making us read?*

"Every single one of us has experienced at one moment or another unwanted attention and unwanted touches from someone else. As women, we band together and support other women who have been sexually assaulted or survived through domestic violence. The overwhelming, cruel truth is survivors are everywhere, regardless of gender."

I draw in a sharp breath. This is about Tatum. My suspicion is confirmed when she helps Maevis stand from her chair. My sister-in-law is teary-eyed, her trembling hand cradling the curve of her belly. "We're all surrounded by strong men. Looking at them, it seems impossible that anyone could ever harm them. We've all also dealt with men who harmed *us*, or have been in situations where we've experienced on our own skin how futile fighting them was, and how easy for them to overpower us." Mae wipes furiously at her cheeks with the back of her hand and clears her throat.

Lalah squeezes her shoulder and takes over. "Which is why, rightfully so, there are a lot of resources available for women who go through the worst of life. Granted, not enough, and sometimes getting help is extremely difficult, but help is there. However, in our quest to protect women, we're turning a blind eye to the issues men are going through."

She looks at each of us, allowing her words to sink in. And she's not wrong. When we think of men, we think of protection and security for us. We don't consider they too need to be protected, they too need to feel safe and to have a sense of security.

My hands reflexively fly in front of my face as a booklet spirals through the air and lands in my lap. I glare at Lalah. A catcher, I am not. Put me any day in front of a notebook, and I'll write poetry endlessly. Give me a baseball and a glove, and I'm most likely to write rhymes on them.

"Hope Haven has been a shelter for survivors of domestic violence for decades. And while they did and continue to do a world of good, all their efforts are focused on women. In fact, to protect the women and children housed at the shelter, men are not allowed there, apart from a couple of volunteers. Even the volunteers are only allowed in the gym where the self-defense classes are taking place," Lalah tells us, her voice serious and somber.

Maevis points at herself, her eyes fixed somewhere over my shoulder. "It shames me profusely that it took seeing one of our own being hurt to recognize men can also be victims. It shames me that, after everything Daniel put me through before our divorce, in my head, an unjust divide was created. We're in a camp of women versus men when it comes to protection and support."

"And it starts from early childhood. Women are, in fact, more likely to report an abusive situation than a man is. It is more likely to believe a woman is being abused than believing a man. *We* are all people. *We* can all be hurt. And *we* all can hurt someone else," Lalah says, her cold eyes brimming with unshed tears. "In the booklet I gave you are testimonies from male survivors; the trials and tribulations they went through, not just during the abuse, but also as they tried to get out, to heal, to move on. The last part, well, that's the new direction I'm taking Lege et Lacrima. We leave no one behind."

My fingers are shaking as I skip to the end. I know what my brother went through in December; I've been at his side, supporting him, ever since he shared his pain with our parents, Selae, and me. My very soul mourned on his behalf.

A gasp spills past my lips as I read through Lalah's booklet. She bought Hope Haven. She also bought the building across the street from Hope Haven, a small ranch-style house that sat empty for the past five years.

"*Hope Equality* will be the sister shelter to Hope Haven, dedicated to supporting male survivors of abuse. Both shelters will be funded by Lege et Lacrima. Expansion plans are in place, but we're taking it one step at the time. Blake leaves next week for New York for two intensive courses in business management and psychological trauma response. My aim is to have the shelter up and running by January next year. Blake will lead Hope Equality." She moves aside, revealing the upright tablet behind her, my sister's serious face reflecting at me from the screen. "And Selena will lead Hope Haven."

Maevis places a palm over her chest as tears run unbidden down her cheeks. "For Tatum!"

"Everyone deserves a safe place, and all of us here have needed one at some point in our lives. Equality and Haven will be safe spaces. And I need your help. You each have businesses that can feed into the help, from employment to resources. I've outlined a plan at the end of the booklet, and what I think you could all bring to the table. Take it home, study it. Come find me when you're ready to talk."

My fingertips encased in velvet,
My feet secure on solid ground.
A second too late, a blink too slow,
I'm sinking, free-falling into chaos.
The velvet crumbles as darkness latches onto my skin,
The cage constricts. My body weighted,
I'm drowning.

I drop my fountain pen as goosebumps pepper my skin. Lalah's plans are weighing heavily on my mind. After a sorrowful TBRC book club meeting, her words have played on repeat in my mind for the rest of the weekend, guilt swimming in the pit of my stomach. Have I done enough for my brother? Have I shown him enough how much I love and respect him?

When Rob and I broke up, and I felt unsafe around him, my brother was my support. Tatum drove all the way to Chicago, helped me pack my stuff, and drove me home. He held me as I cried, slept on my sofa when I was afraid to be alone in my newly rented cottage, and repeatedly told me how brave and strong I was. And what did I do when he needed me the most? I sneaked around with Maddox, living my rebellious teenage phase at twenty-six.

I'm a living, breathing cliché—the spoiled, selfish younger child.

A soft tendril brushes against my collarbone as I shake my head to dispel those negative thoughts. Those were Rob's parting words. I allowed them to root deep inside my marrow and spring to life, making me second-guess my integrity.

I *have* supported my brother. I've also given him the space he needed to wrap his head around his feelings and what happened to him. While the trauma is still fresh and weighing heavily on him, he's also the happiest he's ever been—married to the love of his life, with a baby on the way. Tatum also prefers to make sense of things in his head first, valuing his alone time. We have different needs, and me showing up for him cannot be done in the same way he showed up for me.

What's concerning... my insecurities are rearing their ugly head again—insecurities I thought I worked through after Rob and I parted ways. Clearly, the stress of the past months has caught up with me. Opening the new daycare center, supporting my brother, dealing with my situationship with Maddox, the strange feelings of being watched, everything is coming to a head.

A thump at my back door has my heart racing. I swivel in my chair, standing on shaky legs. Yeah, I'm not the dumb blonde going to investigate. Instead, I tiptoe to the door and ensure it's locked, then make my way to the entrance, locking it too. With my breath trapped in my throat, I check that none of the windows are open and close all my blackout curtains. My house is now shining like a Christmas tree, with all the lights turned on, including the ones in the bathroom.

God, I hate this feeling. I'm like a goldfish swimming against glass walls, and a thousand and one pairs of eyes are watching me swish my tail back and forth. Every sound, every creak, makes me jump. This is not normal. I can't run to my parents every time I'm scared. Maybe everything my sister-in-law went through in the past couple of months has impacted me more than I realized, and now I'm internalizing her fear. Which makes me... well, a damsel in distress.

I'm not craving attention. I've never been one for the spotlight or to take center stage in anything. My place is next to the wall; being one with the furniture, that's my comfort zone. It also means I can't share my fears with anyone. The dust has barely settled for Maevis and Tatum. I can't make waves when all I need is to work through my stress. Sure, I have a picture of someone dressed in dark clothes hiding behind a tree, but that tree also borders a path between my parents' house and the neighbors. It could've easily been someone walking home, and creepy timing on my part.

With that resolve in mind, I tiptoe to my bedroom and go through my nightly routine, donning the hoodie I've taken to sleep in whenever I'm unsettled, before I slide inside cool bedsheets. With my blanket covering me from head to toe, I'm cocooned in safety. Nothing bad can happen to me under my plush and soft blanket. My fingers don't believe me, and tighten on my phone. At least, I have this small comfort. I can call for help if anything happens.

I let my eyes fall closed and try to even my breathing. My heart is still hammering in my chest, echoing in my eardrums, and doesn't make for the most comforting white noise to fall asleep to. But I'm safe. It's all in my head. I'm stressed. I'm overtired.

So I let my mind go to the one place I feel completely and utterly safe—Maddox's arms. While rationally I know the best thing is to forget about him because he'll never change his ways and settle with one woman,

I need the comfort of his closeness right now. My feelings for the cocky chief deputy are both unwarranted and unwanted but, at this moment, they're also what I need to calm down and fall asleep.

I burrow deeper into my pillow, my nose buried in the soft material of the light-blue hoodie. The scent of cardamom and violet leaves, with the faint spice of peppercorn, invades my lungs and allows my limbs to relax in slumber. I don't know how he found out last month what we were all supposed to wear for book club, but I woke up the morning before the meeting with his hoodie draped over the rocking chair on my porch. It wasn't just his masculine scent that told me who it belonged to, but also the huge stitching inside, declaring it his.

I walked on clouds all day that day, wearing it. Stupidly, it made *me* feel *his*, too. For a full day, I've forgotten about everything standing between us—his aversion for relationships, my dislike of overly dominant men, an extremely high chance my brother would murder him in cold blood if he ever found out—and just strutted about with a deep sense of belonging in my chest.

Yeah, I'm the dumb blonde who fell for the unattainable bad boy—a cliché as old as time.

With all the issues I have on my plate, getting over Maddox will just have to take a back seat. Especially with the comfort my feelings for him bring me in moments like these. Imagining his strong arms holding me, his wide chest at my back, the heat of his body enveloping me—it's all I need to fall asleep.

A screech at my window has me bolting upright in bed. I couldn't have been asleep for more than ten minutes, if that. My eyes feel gritty and full of sand as I blink them open. My hand is splayed over my chest, trying to contain my heart that's one pump away from jumping out, the other still clutching my phone. The screeching sound comes again, like nails scratching over a blackboard, and my stomach somersaults, bile pooling in my mouth. *Oh my god, someone's outside.*

Ice creeps through my veins at the thought of only a flimsy layer of glass separating me from whatever lurks in the dark beyond my blackout curtains.

I force my shaking body to move, slowly and silently crawling out of bed. With my feet planted on the cold hardwood floor, I lock my weakened knees in place. I'm trembling like a leaf, my legs threatening to give out at any moment, as I walk to the bathroom and block the door from the inside.

Luckily, there's only a small window mounted in the ceiling. It would make it very difficult for anyone to use it to break in.

I'm not even breathing as I hold my phone to my ear. One ring. Two rings. *Please...* Three rings.

"*Sawyer?*"

An overwhelming sense of relief has me sobbing. "Maddox, there's someone just outside my window," I whisper-cry.

A sharp intake of breath comes from the speaker, followed by his voice, hard and cutting. "*Where are you?*"

"Hiding in my bathroom. Please..."

"*Don't worry, little fairy. I'm on patrol; I'll be there in two minutes. Stay where you are. Don't hang up, but I'll have to mute the call. You won't be able to hear me, but I'll hear everything, okay?*"

I nod as if he can see me, then clear my throat and confirm verbally. "I can do that. Please, hurry."

Nothing but deafening silence comes from his end. I lower the lid to the toilet and take a seat on it, my knees high to my chest as I count the seconds in my head. That screech was definitely not in my head. Not a product of my imagination or of stress. It was right outside my bedroom window. I have no trees to brush against the glass. If someone's playing a prank on me, it's a cruel prank, considering everything my family's been through lately.

Tears are springing behind my eyelids, my stomach hollowed out. Relief that Maddox is coming and dreadful fear run rampant through my veins.

After what feels like forever, a rustling sound comes from the speakers, then Maddox's raspy, low voice replaces it. "*Little fairy, I'm at your front door.*" I'm up and out of the bathroom in an instant. "*I checked everywhere. Whoever it was, they're not here anymore.*" The slap of my bare feet against hardwood echoes through my empty house as I run to the entrance and swipe the door open as soon as I manage to get my fingers to cooperate enough to unlock it.

"I'll stay... Umph," Maddox grunts as I throw myself in his arms, my own coiling around his neck. I bury my face in his chest as sobs wrack my body. His large palm settles gently against my lower back, the other cradles my head. "Fuck, you're terrified," he breathes out, his hold on me tightening. "Come on, baby, let's get you inside." He gives my hip a squeeze, but I'm not letting go of him.

He's my safety net.

Maddox doesn't force me away but bends slightly at the knees and lifts me up, cradling me to his chest and walking inside. His heart drums away in his chest, the steady rhythm soothing my frazzled nerves. My eyes are scrunched shut, my face wet with tears. I'm sure I'm making a mess of his crisply ironed uniform shirt, but all I care about right now is that he's here.

We're swaying gently as he strides inside my home with sure steps. I gasp as I feel the softness of my sheets under me when he bends once again and carefully lowers me onto my bed. "Scoot," he grumbles, the vibrations of that one word passing through his ribcage inside of mine.

I untangle my arms from the chokehold I have on his neck and slowly shuffle to the middle of the bed, arranging the blanket over my legs with a shaky hand. His ice-blue eyes roam over my body, flaring when they take in my... *Oh! Well, that's embarrassing.* In my quest to run for the safety his presence promised, it completely escaped my mind that I am wearing *his* hoodie. Thankfully, he says nothing, just continues to watch me as he removes his gun from its holster and places it on my nightstand. The gun is quickly followed by his badge, phone, and the holster itself. And then he's lying in my bed, in all his uniformed glory, a wet patch on his shoulder.

"Come 'ere," he coaxes, his face unreadable apart from a slight crease between his eyebrows that I'm itching to smooth with the pad of my finger.

I listen. Of course I do, when I'm craving his strength with every cell in my body. My cheek rests comfortably in the crook of his neck, my leg thrown over his narrow hips. He coils an arm around my back, his palm splayed over my hip. I breathe in his comforting scent, my skin tingling everywhere we touch. My heart still races, but now because of his nearness, not because I'm scared out of my mind.

"Sleep, little fairy. I'll watch over you, I promise," he whispers in my hair, his lips brushing over the top of my head. I melt in his embrace and let my eyes fall closed once more. Nothing can touch me with Maddox here.

PART THREE

A season for growth.

"*Like the tide, you wash me ashore.*
I'll evolve and adapt
To illusions.

Like the moon, I'm tidal-locked to you.
I'll revolve and rotate
To your tune.

You're gravity in disguise;
pull me close, don't let me drift apart."

SAWYER CARTER

Chapter Twenty-Six

Maddox

I've been obsessing for a full week. Despite the numerous patrols I've done, both sanctioned and unsanctioned, at all hours of the day and night, in seven long fucking days I haven't come any closer to finding out who scared Sawyer out of her mind that night. And it's been eating at me ever since.

Sure, I've also contemplated she might have made it all up. Except, it doesn't make any sense. She made it crystal clear where she stood in terms of... me. I might not have a whole lot of trust in women, but Sawyer is not the kind to play stupid games. Plus, any doubt I might have had was completely decimated when she jumped into my arms, trembling and cried-out. She wasn't faking. She wasn't seducing me. She was genuinely terrified.

With all the shit happening around Lost Hope lately, I'm not even considering dismissing her concerns. If Sawyer gets hurt because of something I did or didn't do...

I push to my feet and start pacing the length of my living room. Frustration boils up inside my veins. This gets me nowhere—random stops at her house, the lack of communication, her stubborn attempts at ignoring me.

I know I've earned her indifference. It itches at my skin, eating away at my marrow and whatever is left of my sanity. We absolutely cannot continue on this path. I'm sick to my fucking stomach every time I stop at the daycare center, and she turns her back on me. My heart tumbles to my feet whenever I seek her eyes, and she looks right through me.

The conversation I had with Drake a month ago at Ryker's birthday keeps playing through my head. Sawyer is not my mother. I *am* capable of trust. And clearly, based on those rabid goddamn butterflies going crazy in my chest every time I think of her—which is all the damn time—I'm capable of feelings, too. It's high time to be a man and sort my head out, once and for all.

Before I have the chance to change my mind, I slide my phone from the pocket of my jeans and dial my best friend.

"*This better be good,*" Drake answers, his voice gruff. "*You really need to be bleeding to death to wake me up after a forty-eight-hour shift.*"

"Just about," I mumble. "I need... help."

Rustling sounds from the other side of the phone, and I walk to the kitchen window, keeping an eye on Ryker as he runs around in the backyard. Maybe I should buy him a puppy. It breaks my shriveled heart to think my son may be lonely.

"*Alright, I'm up,*" Drake sighs. "*What's up?*"

"Can you come over? It's about her..." I trail off. "I'll break out the grill and treat you to a steak."

"*Oh shit, that bad, huh?*" He laughs like the asshole he is. "*Yeah, man. Give me thirty to take a shower and bathe in coffee. Just a sec.*" More rustling sounds from my phone, followed by his voice, this time muffled. "*Going to Madd's. Not sure. Nah, love, I'm fine.*" I rub my chest when strange pangs of hurt probe at my ribs. This envy and sickening jealousy that hit me whenever I hear him talk to his wife are new.

The friendship, the companionship, the absolute confidence of knowing I have someone of my own to have my back, it's also something I pretty much want for myself.

"*Sorry, man. Anna was just telling me she's going to Lalah's. She asked if she could pick up Ryker and take him with her.*"

My eyes find my son again, and my lips tip up in a semblance of a smile at seeing him chase a butterfly around. "He'd just about marry Clara, if he could," I laugh.

"*Say no more. I'll be there soon.*"

Annalise's laugh replaces Drake's. "*I'm trading Drake for my best boy. Pack a bag.*"

I send off another message, inviting Joshua, too. If I'm making an ass of myself, might as well do it with witnesses. Besides, he's as closed off as I am. Doesn't hurt to have two different perspectives, eternally-in-love on one side, forever-alone on the other.

The sliding door opens with a screech, and I wince at the sound. I really need to get around greasing the rails and rollers. There are a couple of maintenance chores I could do around the house, but the past few months have been criminal—literally—and I've dropped the ball big time.

Ryker runs to me, pumping his arms with all his might as he reaches the bottom step. "DADDY, LOOK!"

"What's that, partner?"

He heaves a breath and promptly opens his fist, revealing a ladybug. "She's so pwetty, Daddy." His giggles fill the backyard when the little bug crawls over his palm. "Ticwish," he chokes out through giggles.

I ruffle his hair. "Set her free, buddy. We've got to wash all those grass stains from your knees. Anna's on her way to pick you up."

His icy-blue eyes sparkle in the early afternoon sunlight. "Whe' we going?" Ryker asks between gentle blows as he tries to get the little bug to fly. When her translucent wings slide out, he squeals, and she takes flight. "Buh bye, pwetty lady."

I guide him inside the house and to his bedroom as he tells me all about his treasure hunt in the backyard. A calming warmth envelops me. My son is not lonely. He's got good friends and many people in his life to love him. Still, a puppy might teach him early a sense of responsibility and give him a friendship that is his and his alone. *Something to consider.*

"Alright, bud. Clothes off and hop in the tub," I tell him as I turn the shower on and get the water to a lukewarm temperature. It's been unusually hot this past week. The tepid water will help him cool off before he starts running around in Lalah's backyard.

"Suwe, Daddy, but whe' we going?" he asks again, his voice muffled as he struggles to take his T-shirt off. My fingers twitch to help him, but he enjoys his independence. Basic tasks, such as getting dressed and undressed, those I let him do by himself unless he specifically asks for help.

"To see Clara with Aunty Anna. That is, if you want to go?" I smirk.

He scrambles to the tub, and I hold his arm to help him balance when he slips in his hurry. With quick moves, he picks up his bath sponge and dumps a healthy amount of liquid baby soap onto it before lathering it all over his tiny body. "Of couwse I want to go, Daddy. Clawa has gwape juice and you fo'geted to buy," he says in a serious tone, sputtering when water sprays into his mouth.

Sure. I forgot.

"Maybe play with her before you drink all her juice," I advise, because I'm the subject-matter expert when it comes to women and relationships and my son is not only four.

Once all the soapy bubbles are rinsed off, I turn the shower off and pick him up with a towel. His wet arms round my neck as I walk to the chest of drawers where most of his summer clothes are. "Daddy, you going to wok again?" he asks as he shuffles through the clothes, picking up a purple T-shirt and a pair of cotton shorts.

I lean against the wall as I watch him dress. "Not tonight, bud."

He stops abruptly and turns to me. "I don't want you to be home alone."

I nearly double over from the punch his words pack. Shit, I'm really doing a crappy job at showing my son I'm happy, if he's worried about me being alone. I drop to my knees in front of him, my hands clasping his shoulders.

"Uncle Drake is coming to visit me, bud. I'm not going to be alone. Even if I were, sometimes it's not a bad thing. I can do my chores, I can rest, and most important of all, I can miss you."

Ryker launches himself into my arms and squeezes my neck with all his might. "I miss you, too, when I'm alone, Daddy."

"Don't be a silly grape. You're never alone."

So, this is awkward. My eyes jump from Drake, sitting on a deck chair on my porch, to Joshua, leaning against the wooden porch rail. I mean, I invited them here so I can talk about all the shit swimming in my head. What I didn't figure when I made that *intelligent* plan was that I'd actually have to talk.

"As much as I'm enjoying a cold beer on a hot Saturday afternoon, I could've enjoyed it just the same at home," Joshua—the bastard—muses.

"I could've been asleep right now," Drake chimes in. I don't blame him; he looks like shit, and I told him as much.

"Fine!" I jump to my feet and pace the width of the porch, trying to expel all the nervous energy out of my limbs. "I think," I mumble, "*I think* I'm in love with Sawyer."

Drake whistles long and hard while Joshua spews a strain of expletives that would make a sailor blush.

"Jesus fucking Christ. You really *are* stupid, aren't you? At the very minimum, you have a death wish."

The glare I send the prosecutor's way does nothing to intimidate him. He pops an eyebrow up, daring me to deny my own stupidity. I can't.

"If Carter comes after you, I'll refuse to prosecute him, you know that. As far as I'm concerned, you went after his sister, you're fair-fucking-game, my friend."

I cross my arms and lean against the wall opposite Craig. What the hell was I thinking inviting him? I wasn't. That's the problem. Ever since the silver-haired fairy got under my skin, all my thinking capabilities vanished.

Drake drags a palm over his face, rubbing at his two-day-old scruff, but keeps silent otherwise.

"What do you want me to say?" I spit. "It's not like these feelings are *wanted*. I was just peachy before her."

Joshua shakes his head, his dark eyes narrowed in disappointment. "Keep saying shit like that. You're basically digging your own grave."

"That's why you two motherfuckers are here. To help me sort this out."

He opens his mouth to mock me, no doubt, when Drake cuts him off. "Fill us in, Madd."

Red-hot fury rushes through me. "If you think I'm going to tell you anything about her, you need to fuck off from my house."

He rolls his eyes at me and flips me off. "I'm not asking you to, you obnoxious cunt. For how long has this been going on? What's Sawyer's stance in all this? All I know is you were simpering after her like a damsel in distress a month ago."

Aw, fuck.

Joshua starts laughing. "If I knew you were going to be *this* stupid, I wouldn't have left you alone with her back in April."

"Longer than that," I mumble.

"How much longer?" Drake demands.

My eyes are pinned to the polished wooden floor of the porch. "Since Thanksgiving."

"You've been fucking her since November?" Joshua sputters in his beer.

I don't know when I'm moving. I have absolutely zero control over my body. But one minute I am leaning against the wall, the next my fingers wrap around his throat and squeeze. "Don't, motherfucker. Don't talk about her like that."

Drake's bear paws clasp my shoulders, pulling me back from a red-faced Joshua. "Christ, man," he coughs. "I mean no disrespect. I simply assumed it started in April, but now that I think about it, you were far too... crazed when you saw her at the club."

"I'm fine." I shrug Drake's hold off. He doesn't believe me—of course he doesn't—and positions himself between me and the foul-mouthed prosecutor. "Nothing happened until April, and that's all I'm going to say on this particular subject. My goddamn feelings started in November. And my feelings are what we're here to figure out, not anything sex-related between Sawyer and me. Got it?" I make a point of looking each of them in the eye. There will be no damn sex talk and no imagining the woman I love naked.

Ah, shit. I went and I said it now.

I walk to the cooler and grab three more beers, passing one to each of them. Flicking the cap off, I gulp a healthy mouthful of the icy-cold, bitter liquid as I gather my bearings. I don't do this shit. I don't talk about feelings, and I don't fucking have feelings. Not for a woman. Not the romantic kind.

My life used to be so simple. I saw. I lusted. I fucked. And then I moved on.

I drop back into my chair, resting my elbows on my knees, and then I open my mouth and spill all the fucked-up shit weighing on me for the past eight months. My best friends sip at their beers and listen to me waxing poetic about how I can't stop thinking about her, how sick to my stomach I get when she ignores me, how I show up at her house night after night and watch her sleep.

"Whoa," Joshua exhales. "That's why I was babysitting Ryker? God-dammit, Lawson. You made me an accessory to stalking, you damned idiot."

My eyes roll once again. "You didn't know what I was doing, Mr. Pros-ecutor. Who's gonna arrest you? Me?"

"I know NOW!"

I run my fingers through my hair as I lean back in my chair. "Can you take this seriously for a minute? If you're not going to help here, then just go and you won't be an accessory to shit."

All the outrage on his face slowly drains, leaving behind only pity and the kind of curiosity that makes my skin itch. "Not sure how much help I'll be, since I'm single in my late thirties, but I'm staying. Just... think of what you're doing, Madd. You're Chief Deputy, for fuck's sake. She has her claws so deep into you, you're willing to throw away your job for her?"

Drake's hollow chuckle echoes through the backyard. "He knows that. Why do you think we're here? You're new to Lost Hope, man. But I know Maddox like the back of my hand. He's never been in love. Hell, he's never been infatuated with anyone. All his feelings resided behind his fly and how fast it could lower."

"Thanks, Drake. Clearly, I can always count on you." I shake my head and chug another mouthful, willing the alcohol to wash away the oily feeling clogging my throat. Is this how everyone sees me? A manwhore? Good-for-nothing?

"I'm the last person to judge you. Come on, I've been right there with you before I met Annalise. I faced my truth, Maddox. Now, if you're really serious about Sawyer, it's time for you to face yours."

My eyes close, her pretty face and timid smile floating behind my lids. "For the first time, I want to try."

"Ntz," Drake clicks his tongue. "Not good enough. Not with Sawyer." The glare is automatic and aimed straight to my best friend's head. "Don't give me that bullshit," he chastises me. "You're like a teenager now, except not big feelings in a hormone-controlled body. All the feelings you suppressed during high school are coming back to bite you in the ass, and you have no idea what to do with yourself. But honestly, Maddox, before you try, before you break her heart and Carter breaks your neck, fix your issues."

"Relationships don't end only because of cheating," Joshua pipes in. "Trust is lost for many other reasons. Choosing work instead of your spouse." He lifts his right hand in the air and waves. "Guilty. Taking the person you're sharing your life with for granted." He waves again. "Guilty again."

"If you're serious about her, put in the work. Talk to your parents. Hell, write your issues on a goddamn whiteboard and sort through them. But don't fuck Sawyer or yourself over, if you're not willing to make the effort to fix yourself. It's been a long time coming, Madd." Drake stands, crossing his arms over his chest. "Do it for Ryker. No child should have to suffer because their father is a stubborn ass, holding on to a hurt that's not even his to hold on to."

Chapter Twenty-Seven

Sawyer

I take in my subtle makeup. A touch of nude lipstick, and I'm all done. "Today is going to be a good day," I tell myself for the thousandth time as I smack my lips together. It has been so far. HeeBee is nearly completed, and I just finished approving all the custom-made furniture. The warehouse was ridiculously big. For a second, I wondered where everything would fit, since all the bookshelves and desks and chairs seemed to take up what looked like a football field worth of space. Butterflies explode in my belly just thinking of how it will all look on opening day.

Next on my *tour* is an educational toys factory. I debated getting the books and stationery needed from a wholesaler, but Annalise made us a great deal, so we're sourcing everything through TBRC. It makes my heart happy to be able to support a local business.

I smooth my knee-length pastel-green summer dress over my thighs as I exit the car. The temperatures might be reaching low nineties, but I paired it with a light, half-sleeved cardigan. My blood hums as I hurry along the sidewalk to one of the coffee shops littering downtown Billings. Ever since that incident two weeks ago, when I called Maddox in a panic, convinced that someone was outside my window... everything startles me and puts me on edge.

Now, more than ever, I wish to be one with the walls. My skin prickles every time someone looks at me, even in passing. I'm hiding in my clothes, the plainer the better. As if a dress or a blouse would turn me invisible. If only.

I have nearly two hours to kill until my appointment at Teddy Knows It All factory. A nice chamomile tea and a quick lunch sandwich might do wonders to my frazzled nerves. I push the door to a cute little café open, my eyes scanning for an available seat. Disappointment sits heavily in my stomach when the only free table is in front of a large window, but beggars can't be choosers.

Pushing a strand of silvery hair behind my ear, I slide into one of the two chairs at the small, rounded table and study the menu. It's just my luck none of my friends were available to come with me. Emma is busy at Mix'n'Match, with a surprise order for a custom-made evening dress. Maevis is too pregnant to breathe at this point. Lalah is neck-deep into sorting out Hope Haven and Hope Equality. Poor Violet got roped into helping her family prepare for an event their church is organizing. And Annalise is glued to TBRC.

I could've asked Maddox.

No! Bad Sawyer.

I'm a wallflower, not a damsel in distress. Even if I were, Maddox is most definitely *not* my knight in shining armor. My head knows this. My heart... that's a completely different story. As if he's weaving black magic, he got under my skin and glued permanent rose-colored glasses over my eyes. He's the worst kind of news for my fragile heart, but feelings beat logic. I crave his brand of bad news with every fiber of my being. Based on the simmering heat in my lower belly, I'm not the only one with unhealthy cravings.

"What can I get ya', hun?" a bright-eyed teenager in a white button-down, with an apron tied around his waist, asks.

I give him a soft smile. "A chamomile tea with manuka honey and a ham and cheese tostati, please."

"You got it. Be right back." He winks as he spins around, hurrying behind the counter. I go back to inspecting the fine imperfections on the wooden table, tracing a hairline crack with the tip of my finger.

Despite knowing better, my silly heart makes me think back to a different coffee shop, in a different place, where the man who turns my knees weak awkwardly tried to share breakfast with me.

"I can't believe my eyes. Sawyer Carter, as I live and breathe."

I flinch. I'm not particularly proud of myself—like an idiot, I stopped paying attention to my surroundings. But I've never expected him, of all people, to be here. Plastering a smile on my face, I straighten in my chair and meet his gaze head-on.

"Rob, what a surprise." What an understatement, too.

The years I've not seen my ex-boyfriend have been kind to him. Of course, they have been. Life always seems to favor the assholes. His dark blue suit looks painted on him, tailored to his tall frame and gym-bred muscles. My stomach ties into knots as fear brews to life inside of me. His slanted eyes sparkle as he flashes me his million-dollar white smile.

Rob leans down, placing a kiss on my cheek, far too close to the corner of my mouth for my liking. "Darling, it's so good to see you," he says as he drags a free chair next to mine and sits.

There goes my lunch.

Instinctively, I scoot farther away from him, wishing the wall at my back would crack open and swallow me whole. My trembling fingers find purchase on the hem of my cardigan as I pull at invisible threads, trying to stop their shaking.

So, maybe I've kept a few secrets of my own. Maybe I haven't been entirely truthful about the reasons Rob and I have broken up. And maybe, just maybe, he terrifies every single cell in my body.

"Tell me everything. How have you been? How's Lost Hope treating you?" Despite his jovial tone, he can't quite mask the distaste in his voice as he practically spits out the name of my hometown.

I need to get out of here. All alone, more than an hour away from home, I can't cause any scene. I can't put it past him to follow me home. Or worse.

Sure, I'd like to give people the benefit of the doubt and admit that change is possible. To an extent, I believe it. Not Rob, though. In his eyes, he's perfect. There's no changing or improving on perfection, is it?

Clearing my throat to dislodge the fear clogging my vocal cords, I keep my voice even and small—just the way he likes it. "I've been doing well." A barely there, tight-lipped smile accompanies my words. "Helping at the local daycare center." This is not information he couldn't find out if he wanted to. Everything else, he doesn't need to know. "I'm surprised to see you in Billings. I thought Chicago was your home."

His fingers drum on the wooden table as he grins at me in response. A grin that never reaches his eyes.

"I'm happy for you. You always did want to be a teacher." My subtle nod encourages him to continue. Too bad he hasn't seen the *Go away already!* neon flashing in my eyes. "My law firm is opening an office in Billings, and I'm here to oversee it as they're relocating me. Isn't this amazing? Pure... serendipity."

As if all air has been vacuum-suctioned from the room, my throat goes dry and my limbs grow numb under the lack of oxygen. "Amazing indeed," I choke out. "Congratulations." I don't get to fumble through more lies when I'm saved by the waiter.

"Here's your tea and tostati, hun." He smiles congenially.

Rob scrunches up his nose, pushing the tostati away from me. "Double espresso, black. And a chicken and avocado salad," he barks, dismissing the kid before grinning indulgently at me. "Darling, I see nothing has changed with your eating habits. Those clothes of yours won't hide much if you keep building up those hips. But don't worry, I remember how much you love chicken salad."

I'm not one to curse. I'm really not. Spending as much time with children as I do, cursing is to be avoided unless I want to enrich the vocabulary of my bumblebees with fun words. But... what—and I can't stress this enough—the *fuck*?

God, how I wish I had Lalah's strength, or Emma's directness, or Violet's mean streak. Even my sweet sister-in-law knows when to straighten her spine and go for the jugular. All I do instead is duck my head and feel sick to my stomach. I sip from my honey-sweetened tea, tasting nothing but ash on my tongue.

"Actually, I don't have a lot of time," I lie through my teeth.

He pats my hand, and I swear my very bone marrow grinds to dust, trying to burrow deeper into my atoms just to get away from him. "Surely you can still have lunch with me." His eyebrows furrow, the falsest mask of sadness washing over his face. "I missed you, Sawyer. The way we parted ways... broke my heart. We were perfect together, darling. I... I can't apologize enough for my behavior back then."

My lips part, a vehement denial sitting just on the tip of my tongue, but my throat refuses to let any sounds escape.

"No, please. Don't try to excuse me," Rob says, interlacing my fingers with his. I'm frozen in my seat. I cannot move a muscle. The sheer audacity of this man is absolutely astounding.

Excuse him? As if I'd ever forgive or forget him.

"Believe me, Sawyer. I spent the longest time after you left, going over everything that happened during that cursed week. There's no excuse. I was fearful I'd lose you and the life we'd planned. My fear drove every one of my actions. I've grown since."

Suuuure, you have.

Maybe six months ago I would've believed his words. Six months ago, I would've looked at his dark blue eyes and the sorrow crinkling the slanted corners and given him the benefit of the doubt. But today's Sawyer knows better. My brother's ordeal brought up the rawest of emotions to the surface in a man with the greatest poker face. If I can read Tatum, I can read anyone. Today's Sawyer also knows the heartbreaker of Lost Hope—intimately, and more than once. If I can read Maddox, I can certainly read Rob.

He might be a lawyer, he might be successful—although I have my doubts he's earned all that success through his own hard work, since his one and only goal was to be a partner in the company his father has founded.

What he can't do is lie better than Maddox or hide better than Tatum.

I see his mask for what it is—conniving, full of deception, and with no empathy whatsoever.

I duck my head and peer at him through lowered lashes. Rob was always fond of my shyness. He liked me subservient and docile, the perfect trophy wife. *That* hasn't changed. And his predatory, victorious smirk confirms it for me.

"Let bygones be bygones," I find myself saying. Diffuse the situation, don't aggravate him, don't make it any worse. "We've both grown into completely different people than who we were when I graduated." To really drive the point home, I rub the back of his hand with my thumb—and fight nausea at the same time. My skin is crawling. "I'm happy for you and proud of everything you've achieved." My lips may be curved up in a smile, but my throat is burning with the bile flooding my esophagus.

With his free hand, he cups my cheek, caressing me. Dear God, this very well may be the moment I vomit into his lap. Would serve him well. He'd put distance between the two of us by himself, no need for me to be all sneaky and conniving.

"You're as gracious as always." His grin kicks up another notch. Of course it does. He thinks he has me line, hook, and sinker. "I can't help but think that life has thrown us back together for a reason. Perhaps, I'm asking for too much, but I'd love to get to know you again. I'd love to explore the possibility of us... again."

Fuck no!

There. I said it. Not out loud, because I'd need to be made of sterner stuff than the leaf shaking inside of me, but even thinking it is progress. My cheeks color, and the narcissistic douche nearly preens right in front of my eyes. He thinks he has me all flustered.

I smile through the anger simmering in my veins. "You've done all the maturing you needed to do, Rob. But I'm still growing. Far be it from me to tell you what you need." I lower my eyes, really stepping into my role. "What I *can* tell you is... at the place I'm in life right now, I'm not dateable."

My heart shrinks inside my chest at the flash of annoyance thundering in his eyes. He blinks it away and squeezes my hand. "I understand. Clearly, I still need to work on my impulse control. Coming on too strong is never a great move. At least, would you consider to still have me as a friend? I'm all alone here, after all."

I'd rather do a striptease on the counter at Dine&Dash in front of my father and brother, while Maddox sets me on fire.

"I'd love for us to be friends," I say instead.

Famous last words.

Chapter Twenty-Eight

Maddox

"**A**re you sure this is the costume you want?" I ask my son as I take in the green, sparkly dress he holds, together with the translucent, glittery wings.

"Yeeeees, Daaaaddy." Ryker stomps his foot to punctuate his words. "I want to be a fairy. Like Tinker Bell."

Now, see, he has no issues rolling perfect Rs when he's forming words that are forbidden to me. For everything else, he absolutely refuses, holding on to his baby-speech like I'd rob him of all his childhood if I dare insist on R-ing correctly. I've had a lot of nay-sayers, trying to convince me they could parent my son better than me and insisting I should take him to a speech therapist. If I hadn't heard Ryker before pronouncing all his letters fully, I truly would have considered. Despite my hard-headedness, I'd never do anything to put my son's health in jeopardy. But I'm not worried about his speaking abilities. He's four, for crying out loud. So, if he finds it funny to baby some words, I'm letting him be.

One day, soon enough, I'll wake up to correctly pronounced "grapes", and I'll know I won't ever hear "gwapes" from him. Sue me for not being ready for my son to grow up just yet.

Ryker twirls in front of me, and a scoff comes from somewhere behind us. I'm not blind. I saw the nosy woman at the end of the aisle, scrunching her nose at us. She can shove it up her ass as far as I'm concerned. If my son wants to dress like a fairy, or a mermaid, or a goddamn Disney princess, I'll be right there, holding his damn train.

"Come on, then. Let's go pay for it." I herd him back to the counter, keeping my stride slow, so he can skip next to me, the fairy wings bouncing around his skinny arms.

All rosy cheeks and ruffled hair, he halts in front of the cashier, the glass shelf hiding him almost entirely. That doesn't stop him. He pushes up on his tippy-toes, a smile wider than the Grand Canyon on his face, tiny teeth fully exposed.

"Hello," Ryker chirps at the girl who can't be older than eighteen. "I'm going to my best fwiend's buff'day. AS A FAIRY!" he squeals.

She nods enthusiastically, grinning at him. "Solid choice there. You'll look *just* like Tinker Bell."

His eyes sparkle with pride as he turns to smile at me, pushing the dress into my arms since he can't reach the counter. The girl leans over and whispers—loudly—to him. "You know, we have some fairy costumes for grownups, too. I bet your daddy would look good as Tinker Bell's sidekick."

I groan. I already know what's coming before the gasp has left his lips. Looks like Ryker isn't the only fairy at Clara's birthday. Just as well, Lost Hope could do with some education on how to nurture children's imagination. Even if it comes from a thirty-four-year-old man, dressed in a sparkly dress and wearing translucent wings.

It saves me the effort of fighting for Sawyer's attention, too.

One look at me in that glittery dream of a material, and she'll run for the hills, never to be seen again.

I FOLD MY ARMS ACROSS MY BLUE, sparkly chest, a scowl etched deep into my face. "Are you done yet?" I grumble.

She claps her thigh with one palm, holding an arm around her waist, laughing with all her might. Goddammit, I knew this was a bad idea. But I'm confident enough in my masculinity to pull off this fucking costume. So what if the frayed hem of the dress hits me mid-thigh? So what if the damn leggings end up somewhere below my knees and strangle the fuck out of my balls? Maybe it's just me and the Tooth Fairy—the only ones with minuscule wings, but that's because we're probably both packing somewhere *not* on our backs.

"Sorry." Lalah wheezes her poor-excuse of an apology as she tries without success to stifle her laughter. "I... just didn't expect *you* to be dressed as a fairy. Oh my god"—hysterical laughter—"Maddox! I can't breathe."

"Maybe I should get your husband to call 9-1-1, then," I hiss, rolling my eyes. "Seriously, do you need me to pour cold water on you or something? If I were a lesser man, I'd feel offended."

She slaps her cheeks as she draws in a deep breath. Then another. And then a fucking third, because clearly, I'm goddamn hilarious, and she needs all the slaps and the breaths in the world to calm herself down.

"I'm fine. I'm o-okay." Lalah stifles another bout of laughter. I bet she bit her tongue. Good, she deserves it.

"Besides, you're one to talk. What the hell are *you* wearing?"

Lalah hooks her arm around mine, leading me to the garden. "Duh, I'm Prince Charming. Clara decided pink wasn't my color, so I couldn't be a princess in her court. Guess whose color *is* pink?"

There's no guessing. Not when Lalah pushes through the sliding doors to her backyard, only to be met with the face of a smiling, tulle-layered pink pudding that looks very much like Cole, taking a curtsying lesson from a really bossy three-year-old.

"If *you* laugh, he'll shoot you," she warns me, dead serious.

I take the warning for what it is. "You do realize I am an officer of the law, and you've just threatened me." Besides, it's not amusement I feel right now but kinship. At least, I don't have to suffer alone, even if I'm showing considerably more leg than Cole does.

She looks up at me, her lips twitching from beneath the fake beard she's wearing. "Don't you mean a fairy of the law? Wha'cha gonna do? Cuff me with your magic dust?"

I grumble under my breath some very un-fairy words, but all curses and spells die on my lips as my eyes automatically find Sawyer. Her hair sparkles in the sunlight like liquid silver. The peach-colored cape around her shoulders flutters behind her as she chases around the pond an enchantment of fairytale creatures.

We may be all ripped straight out of the pages of one of Comtesse de Ségur's stories, but Sawyer is the queen of us all.

"Mhm, just as I thought. Drink in your fill, little butterfly, before the big bad brother gets here and huffs and puffs you to Neverland."

Sure, I hear her words, but they don't register. My ears are filled with the sounds of Sawyer's giggles, my whole body attuned to her. I'm rooted to the spot, smiling like a lunatic as she catches up to Ryker and lifts him in the air in one fell swoop, his wings sparkling as sunlight hits them.

As if she's just as aware of me as I'm aware of her, she turns around, seeking me out, Ryker settled on her hip. A chin nod, that's what I get. Not even a wave, or a twitching smile. I'd even take her folding in two, laughing her pretty ass off at my costume, but no. She lets my son run free, then gives me her back as she marches to the table where Annalise, Drake, Lalah, and Emma are sitting.

That cold shoulder is what I need to finally regain function of my legs. If she wants space, I'll give her space. For now. I still have shit I need to work through—an overdue conversation with my parents, looming over my head like a pending colonoscopy, and a greater understanding of where I stand and what I want.

I have no right hurting Sawyer if it turns out, eventually, I don't have what it takes to be the man she needs.

So, I grab a beer and make myself a plate with bite-sized sandwiches, then find a secluded spot where I can sit and watch over Ryker. I've been everything so far—an asshole, a manwhore, an arrogant bastard. What I haven't been is antisocial. Well, there's no place like the birthday party of a three-year-old to start.

I'm brushing crumbs away from the sparkly blue skirt of my dress when her perfume envelops me. Despite my resolve, I inhale greedily. She smells like late summer nights and pure sunshine, and who the heck knows when I'll get to be this close to her again? Even if I were to fix whatever is broken in my head, there's no guarantee she'll want me.

"You make glitter look grumpy." Sawyer laughs.

"I've been told it's a special talent of mine," I reply, giving her a lopsided smirk.

Her brow furrows as she looks at me, navy-blue eyes, like the darkest ink, searching mine. "If I'm bothering you, I can go." Her voice is small and uncertain, and I absolutely hate that she feels unsure of herself around me.

I lift my plate toward her, offering her the last of my sandwiches. "Have a snack, take a seat, welcome to my humble abode."

She rolls her pretty eyes, but lowers herself on the grass next to me, smoothing down the fabric of her skirt over her knees. Sawyer is nothing but prim and proper. And I want nothing more than to dirty her up—again.

Her dainty fingers prod at one of the sandwiches before she takes a small bite out of it. She nibbles around at the crust as we sit in silence. It should feel weird. Fire ants should be running around under my skin, my stomach knotting itself into painful twists, and the desire to flee should fire up under my ass. Instead, I'm content to just... exist next to her.

"I just... I wanted to thank you again." At my questioning eyebrow, she clarifies. "For the other night."

Now my stomach twists. "Have you had any more incidents?"

"No." Sawyer shrugs, and my eyes zero in on the soft-looking skin of her shoulder. I'd give just about anything to kiss the curve of her neck and freely nuzzle my face there. "I'm embarrassed, to be perfectly honest with you." And that embarrassment is obvious in the rosiness of her cheeks.

My hand twitches with the need to grab hers and give her a reassuring squeeze. "Why embarrassed?"

She picks at her sandwich, tiny crumbs fluttering down on top of her knees. "It feels like I freaked out over nothing," she mumbles as she stares at the children playing around with the one-thousand-and-one balloons in the backyard. "I've been under a lot of stress lately, and I can't help but think my imagination is playing tricks on me. Either way, I'm really thankful to you."

I nudge her shoulder with mine. It's the only touch I'm allowing myself. "It's my job, lit-Sawyer." I clear my throat, trying to mask the slip of her nickname. "I'd much rather you call me if you ever feel unsafe than dismiss something that frightens you as nothing, only for it to be a worst-case scenario."

Humming low in her throat—acceptance or dissent, I can't really tell—she nods absentmindedly, and I take a second to really look at her. There are dark circles under her eyes, barely covered by the thin layer of makeup she's wearing. She also looks thinner, more fragile. Maybe it's an effect of the stress she's under. Maybe she's not sleeping well.

I haven't... visited her in a while. Not since I'd promised Drake and Joshua I'd stop. Perhaps one more visit wouldn't kill either of us. Just to make sure she is sleeping. Just to check that she's not wasting her nights, alone and afraid, tossing and turning on her couch.

"Ryker is growing so fast," she muses. "I can't believe I'll only get to have him in my class for one more year."

I snort, I can't help it. "Tell me about it." Shaking my head, I let the normal disbelief I feel whenever I think back on the past four years run through me as I search for my little man. The smile rising on my face is undeniable as I watch him hold hands with Clara, sneaking away grapes from the fruit bar on the opposite side of the backyard, the birthday girl now wearing translucent green wings. "One minute, I was holding a newborn in my arms, terrified to the deepest pits of my soul. The next, I'm walking around with a sassy mini-me, with one set of persuasive puppy-eyes."

Goosebumps sprout on my skin when Sawyer does what I should've done minutes ago and clasps my hand in hers, feathering her thumb over my knuckles. "For what it's worth, I think you're a great father. I've never seen Ryker be anything other than happy. He knows he's loved and worships the ground you walk on."

The backs of my eyes burn. Her praise means the world to me. Parenting is the hardest thing I've ever had to do. I'm suffocating in worry every waking hour. Dad-guilt is my goddamn mistress, lying in bed with me every night. Am I giving him enough? Enough love, enough guidance, enough support, just... enough?

I lean back against the side of the house and fold my arms across my chest. "There are days when I look back, and I just don't get it. I don't get how she could look at him, all squishy cheeks and tightly-closed little fists, and decide she wanted nothing to do with our son." Bitterness coats each one of my words. I exhale all the pent-up resentment living in my chest whenever I think of Ryker's mother. "Other days, I'm grateful she's not in our lives. I'm goddamn selfish when it comes to my son. Ecstatic even that I don't have to share him or limit my days to a custody agreement."

Sawyer's fingers entwine with mine. She remains silent, but I know she's listening. Down to the last fiber of my being, I know I have her full attention. Apart from my parents and Drake, no one knows who Ryker's biological mother is. There has been speculation, gossip, but I remained a vault. I do not need to justify the existence of my son. Except, I want Sawyer to know. Regardless of what the future holds for us, I need her to know.

So here's the first step toward Maddox 2.0, building trust.

"Katherine is a trust-fund woman. But not the spoiled kind. The kind overly ambitious, with a chip on her shoulder the size of Texas. She was facilitating a merger in Billings, and I..." I'm cut off by the grimace on Sawyer's plump lips. I flip my hand, so we're palm to palm, and I can swipe my thumb across her silken skin in a silent apology. My voice drops to a near-whisper. "I told you before, and I'm telling you again. Never have I gone without protection. Not once until..."

She squeezes my hand. "I know. I believe you."

"I refuse to refer to Ryker as an oops-baby. Katherine was on birth control. I was all... suited up. My son is meant to be in my life. I may not believe in a lot of things, but this... this I believe down to my very marrow."

The tension lines around her kissable mouth soften, a dreamy smile gracing her lips. "And that's why you're a great father, Maddox."

I acknowledge her words with a feathering caress of my thumb over her knuckles. "Anyway, Katherine left, and I hadn't heard from her. Not until she gave birth, anyway. For whatever reason, she was back in Billings when her water broke. I think she tracked me down. The hospital had my contact details, and a nurse called me. As soon as I got to the hospital, her lawyer greeted me with a folder." I sigh as those frightful moments play on a loop in my head—the confusion, the anger, the anticipation. "She gave me two choices. Either I terminated my parental rights, or I'd have sole custody of the baby she was about to give birth to. I was told in no uncertain terms she wanted nothing to do with me or Ryker, if I chose door number two."

Sawyer shifts around on the grass, turning completely toward me. "You chose Ryker."

"Every day of my life," I declare with a smile. "Katherine allowed me to be in the room during the birth but made it clear, once the baby was... out, she never wanted to see or hear from us again." Sawyer's eyes hold a sadness that's not hers to feel. My arms are aching with the need to pull her into my lap and hold her. My stomach flips, weightless. But I stuff down all these foreign feelings. Right now, it's about building trust, not flirting. "I'm making her sound like a complete bitch. She's not. Once I signed the papers, declaring Ryker mine and only mine, we spoke. She sincerely felt she was not cut out to be a mother. Once she learned she was pregnant, she started looking for me, but also tried to get used to the idea of being a mom. Except motherhood was never a dream for her."

"And that's okay," Sawyer interrupts me. "A lot of people go into parenthood selfishly or to tick a box. When it turns out not to be like in all the fun internet videos, they lose interest in their children fast. The child ends up neglected and ignored. Doing what's best for a child doesn't always mean raising them yourself. Sometimes, it means ensuring the parents who get the honor of raising them are good people who want children and love them."

She sits up on her knees and coils her arms around my neck. My heart pounds in my chest at her nearness. Her sweet scent of pear, freesia, and bergamot envelops me completely. My whole body lights up as she hugs me gingerly, pressing her cheek against mine. "You're lucky to have Ryker." Her lips touch the corner of my mouth as she retreats, and my breath stalls in my lungs. "But Ryker is also lucky to have you."

"Sawyer!" Emma shouts from the other side of the backyard.

We both part as if electrocuted. Despite the smoldering heat of the late July afternoon, an icy chill washes over me as Sawyer stands, giving me a soft smile. I close my eyes, letting my head drop forward until my chin hits my chest. There's no way I can watch her leave my side, not after I cut myself open for her.

One thing is certain, though. I am in love with this woman. But do I have what it takes to be what she deserves?

Chapter Twenty-Nine

Sawyer

I huff away a tendril of silvery hair determined to stab my right eye out. My chest is heaving, sweat dripping down my spine. So, maybe I've gone a bit overboard with cleaning. Definitely, washing the walls with a damp cloth is not an activity suitable for the smoldering heat the end of July has brought.

But, if my sister-in-law and I have anything in common, that's stress-cleaning.

I fall back on my couch, stretching out my legs, then letting them fall limp on the floor. My muscles are strained and exhausted from my morning efforts. I should *really* take a shower, but I have zero energy left in my body.

To say I'm depleted is an understatement.

My blood is buzzing in my veins, my fingers itching for me to pick up my trusted fountain pen and just... rhyme.

Rob's move to Billings has rattled me up more than I care to admit. The responsibilities at the daycare center, the mental gymnastics of getting HeeBee up and running, the constant ache in the center of my chest whenever I think of Maddox—and that's all the freaking time—everything is weighing down on me. I feel like a bottle of champagne, shaken up and close to exploding.

I can't erase from my mind the image of him in that sparkly blue dress. When I saw him matching Ryker's costume, my knees went weak and my heart climbed into my throat, pulsing all the way down to my vagina. It's no wonder I can't shake my feelings for him. How can I, when he goes and does something like that for his son? That's the kind of devotion and love I want in my life. Then he tied whatever magic he sorcered over me by opening up about one of the most coveted secrets in Lost Hope. The man who trusts no one... trusted *me*.

My days are shrouded in confusion. Well, confusion, stress, and fear. Every day of every hour only seems to bring more questions and no answers.

I've lived my life plastered to the wall. My upsets, my concerns, all written down on paper, but never voiced. But I don't have to continue living this way.

My family will support me, no matter what. Sure, the dust has just settled over all the hurt and pain my brother has suffered. I'm not going to be the one to blow to smithereens the hard-earned happiness he's just starting to enjoy and give him my problems to worry about. But I'm not alone anymore.

The knock on the door proves just that.

In all fairness, they would've come even if I hadn't asked for help. I was careless yesterday at Clara's birthday. Too many people have seen Maddox and me talk, and some of those people weren't really in the know. They are now.

I groan as I push to my feet and drag myself to the door. Emma and Violet greet me from my small porch, both with arms crossed over their chests and eyebrows touching their hairline.

"I hope it's brewing because, doll, you have some tea to spill," Emma says, cocking a hip.

Violet nods in her direction, her wild curls bouncing around her head like a halo. "What she said. And we brought just the right thing to make your lips loose." She wiggles her eyebrows playfully, waving a heavy-looking canvas bag, full of what sounds like bottles clinking together.

I step away from the door and let them pass through. "Gotta shower first. I have dried sweat in places no sweat should ever be found."

"Yuck. Too much information." Violet scrunches her nose in distaste.

I slap her shoulder, then I point toward the couch. "Have a seat; make yourselves at home. And before you get any silly ideas, I was *cleaning*."

Locking myself in the bathroom, I hurriedly dump my clothes in the laundry basket and step under the cool stream of water, my hair bundled atop my head. It takes no time at all to lather myself up from neck to toe, then rinse up. My stomach ties itself into knots, knowing that once I get out of the shower, I'll have to open up to them. It's not such an easy thing to do when you've trained yourself your whole life to blend with your surroundings and make no waves.

I speed-dress in a loose T-shirt and jean-shorts and exit my bedroom, jogging to my living room where I can hear Emma and Violet laughing.

My once clutter-free coffee table now sports several bottles of tequila, a plate of freshly cut limes, and a saltshaker. Almost like an afterthought, a salted-pretzel bag is opened and dumped in the middle of the circle of bottles.

"Are those enough to soak up all that alcohol?" I question.

Emma waves my concerns off. "We'll order a pizza later. In the meantime, bottoms up." She points at the shot glass, full to the brim, waiting just for me. I plop down on my freshly-vacuumed fluffy carpet, folding my legs under me.

"Here's to friends and liquid courage," I say, lifting it in the air.

Violet's meets mine. "To stress-cleaning and dirty O's."

"To love triangles and closed doors," Emma finally toasts. Together, the three of us down the caramel-flavored tequila, chasing it with a bite of lime. In all truthfulness, there's no need for lime or salt. This is no cheap tequila. There's no bitterness on my tongue, no sharp aftertaste to mask the sweetness of my liquid courage.

It doesn't take it long to warm me up from the inside out, a pleasant buzz swirling right beneath my skin. My lips tingle with the lime's sour aftertaste, and I smack them together as I snatch a couple of pretzels from the bag.

Emma wastes no time filling our glasses again. "Courtesy of Jackson." She winks. "To broody bartenders and all their smoke and mirrors." She downs her second shot, and I follow suit. Yikes. At least, tomorrow's Sunday, and I can sleep off the wicked hangover that will for sure try its very best to kill me.

When she pours a third shot before my glass even hits the table, I'm starting to get just a tad concerned. Maybe I'm not the only one who needs to spill the tea. Does my concern stop me from lifting the third shot in the air? No, no, it absolutely does not.

"To spilled ink and gunpowder," I say, just briefly aware of my lips going numb and the slight slur to my words.

Violet giggles as she clicks her glass to mine. "Doll, what the hell toast is that?"

I sputter as the alcohol burns through me. My tongue is numb now. My lips just loose enough for me to blurt out, "I'm in love with Maddox Lawson."

Crickets.

A hiccup explodes out of me, and I slap my palm over my mouth. Both my girls jump out of their seats.

"Say what the fuck now?" Emma shrills so loudly, I bet Astrum heard her all that way from Lalah's soundproofed house.

"Jesus Christ on a pickled cracker, now you've gone and done it." Violet crosses herself. If she falls to her knees and starts praying for my soul, I'll cut this party short as soon as the room stops spinning.

As it is, I crawl backward until the wall comes to meet me and lean against it. My spine is made of jello, in dire need of extra support. Besides, a bit of distance between me and that cursed bottomless glass seems like a good idea.

"You heard me," I slur. "I sa'd what I sa'd."

"But what you said makes no sense." Emma stomps her foot, and I giggle. She really needs to stop waving with her whole body. My eyes cannot keep crossing and uncrossing just to get her into focus.

"Sure it does. When a girl meets a boy, she sees him naked and lets him do unspeakable things to her. Then her heart packs her bags and moves inside her vagina." I pause as my diaphragm starts doing the chicken dance in a series of hiccups, then point at Emma—one of the three Emmas, anyway. "If the unspeakable things are happening often and result in a lot of mind-blowing orgasms, her vagina grows three sizes and develops a serious case of the feelings."

Violet twirls around the table, and the table twirls with her. "Sounds to me like you got a sexually transmitted infection. Did you pee after the unspeakable things? You should alwaaaaays pee, Sawyer. Everyone knooooows that."

Have I peed after the unspeakable things? My mind is in a playback fury of sexy memories. I remember the exact shape, length, girth, taste, and feel of Maddox's penis, but I can't remember anything after.

"Oh, damn!" Emma squeals. "That's because you've been dickmatized. Dickmacharmed? Dicknotized? Dicka-"

I facepalm. Or try to, but the heel of my palm ends up bashing my nose. "Ouch, that hurt," I whine. Tears sting at my eyes as my nose pulses in time with my heartbeat. Three shots on an empty stomach are definitely *not* a good idea.

"Who knew you were such a cheap date? I brought *bottles*, and we're not even through the first one. And... five shots, doll, not three."

I'd roll my eyes, but that would only make the room spin faster. "Wait, five? When? How?"

Emma's pretty face blurs in front of my eyes. She must be a vampire to move so fast—one second, she was near the couch, now she's crouching down next to me. "Here, drink this." She pushes a glass of clear liquid into my hand, helping to guide it to my mouth.

"No more alcohol," I complain. My tongue is so thick in my mouth, it keeps boxing with my teeth.

"It's water, doll. Drink it," she insists, pushing the rim against my numb lips. I gulp greedily until I drain every last drop. "Atta girl."

Violet dances behind Emma. "I ordered pizza."

Pizza sounds like a great idea. My rolling stomach agrees, too. Pizza is like an anchor with magic powers. It gathers gravity, and soaks alcohol, and stops the Earth from spinning.

"Okay, boozy. Help me out here." My arms are pulled at, and I pretend they're made of Play-Doh. "Dammit, Sawyer. Stop playing dead and toughen up."

I like this pull-and-tug game we're playing. The rope swings and sways, and I'm rooting for Violet. Wait, I'm the rope? An outraged cry sounds from my left, and my knees find purchase on the carpet as I'm pushed to my feet. "Come on, pretty girl. Let's get you on the couch."

Clouds embrace me everywhere. So soft, so welcoming. Surely, a storm must be coming, otherwise why would they spin so fast? Look, rain is here.

"I'll get you an umbrella if you drink this, too," Emma promises.

I lift my hand and pat her soft cheek. "You're so pretty." I smile at her. She really is. Her coppery-brown eyes are big and round. Her lips, even without a stitch of lipstick, are a deep pink. Don't even get me started on her hair.

"Thanks, doll." She kisses my cheek, then forces another glass of water down my throat. That's okay. I was feeling a bit thirsty, anyway. A bag crinkles nearby before my hand magically fills with crispy pretzels. "Come on, eat something." Eating sounds like such a good idea. My stomach feels all sloshy, and I don't like it. I moan around the crunchy pretzel, and I shove another one in my mouth before I even finish chewing.

"I'll get some more water," Violet says from somewhere behind me. "We really miscalculated how much she could take."

A cascade of crumbled pretzels dusts out of my mouth as I scoff, indignant. "I can take a lot. I'm sick and tired of everyone around me thinking

I'm this fragile, breakable flower. You have no idea what you're talking about."

Anger rises in me, bright and hot, burning through the alcohol poisoning my blood. "I've been in love with Maddox for *months!* I didn't break, did I? Rob treated me like crap the whole time we've been together. I didn't break then, either. Someone is trying to scare me right now. I'M STILL NOT BREAKING!" I shout, throwing crushed pretzels in the air.

"Wow, we've got a bit of baggage to unpack." Violet nods sagely.

Emma tosses her red hair over her shoulder and plants her hands on her hips. "Oh boy, you'll be pissed tomorrow when you have to vacuum them crumbs with the mother of all hangovers for company." She then sits next to me, slipping her arm around my waist and squeezing my side. "Let's leave Maddox for when you're sober, doll. You've been holding out on us, but that's okay. Now spill. Who's trying to scare you?"

I sag against her, my head feeling as if it weighs a thousand pounds. "Don't know," I mumble. "There are always eyes on me. I'm just too stressed. But one night, I swear I heard something at my window. Madd said he didn't see anyone."

She lets us fall against the backrest, still half-hugging me. Hugs are nice. It would be even nicer if Maddox would hold me like this.

"Excuse me for not having the right equipment," Emma laughs.

"You're really good at reading my mind," I praise her. She really is. Best friends come in handy like that.

My head bounces against her shoulder as she laughs even harder. "It's not difficult, doll, especially when you're saying out loud every thought passing through that pretty head of yours."

Shock barrels through me hard and fast. "Oh, no! Maevis's pregnancy is contagious." I gasp as I jump to my feet. The floor immediately starts to jiggle under me, and I extend my arms to maintain balance.

"What are you talking about, Carter Airlines?" Violet is next to me in a flash—another vampire. "You're not pregnant, Sawyer. Just drunk as a skunk."

I wipe my forehead with the back of my hand. "Phew. But how come I'm thinking out loud? Only Mae does it when she's pregnant."

Emma pulls at my hand, and I plop down next to her with a huff. "Get her a coffee, Vi, would you?"

"Coffee is poisonous for dogs, and birds, and cats, and maybe hamsters, too. Is it poisonous to plants? Because I'm a wallflower."

"Dear Christ Almighty. Don't worry, Sawyer, I'll make a special coffee for you, babe, absolutely safe for sloshed wallflowers." Violet pats my head, and I preen under her attention. "Actually, I have an even better idea. How about we get you to bed?"

"Like a sleepover?" I beam. "I only ever had sleepovers with Selae."

"Sure, doll. Like a sleepover. Before we need to mop up your vomit, along with all the tea."

MY PILLOW IS ROCK HARD, cocooning me from head to toe. Hmm, when did I buy a full-body pillow? It's surprisingly comfortable, despite not having any give. I bury my nose in the pillowcase, inhaling the subtle trace of cardamom, my hand caressing the soft material. My fingers curl around an even harder lump. I smooth my palm over it, up and down, up and down, and the pillow moans under my cheek.

I freeze. A sharp inhale of air sends even sharper currents of pain through my head. *Holy ink, how much did I drink yesterday?*

"You're getting shy on me, little fairy?" Maddox's hushed voice, gravelly and sleepy, rumbles through me.

My heart gives a painful squeeze before galloping wildly in my chest. "Maddox, what are you doing here?" I croak. Oh god, my tongue sticks to the roof of my mouth, all the bitter tequila remnants gathering there.

He shuffles around, turning in the death-hold I have on him until we're face to face. His hips press deliciously against my belly, his morning erection nestled between the two of us. I might feel like seven-day-soaked roadkill, but even my alcohol-induced migraine likes his nearness. He nuzzles his face in the crook of my neck, chuckling softly when I bury my head in my pillow. We might not always be on the same page, even if we find ourselves far too often in the same bed, but he doesn't deserve to be punished with my morning breath.

His lips feather over a sensitive patch of skin just behind my ear, and I melt in his arms. It takes nothing for my body to ignite under his touch. The weight of him over me, the heat of his body, the coarseness of his legs rubbing against my smooth ones—Maddox is overwhelming me in all the best ways.

"This is the second time you've slept draped all over me," he whispers, his breath fanning across my collarbone. My thighs draw together on instinct, squeezing one of his legs between mine. "I have to say, it's a habit that doesn't upset me terribly."

Honestly, this is ridiculous. How am I supposed to speak with a dead rat in my mouth? I push at his chest, my fingers curling in the soft fabric of his T-shirt when the hard muscle underneath tenses and flexes. His teeth scrape down the column of my neck, and my hips rock in response as he sucks gently at the sensible spot where my neck meets my shoulder. His fingers tighten their hold on my hip, his thumb brushing just under the waistband of my panties. "Go on, then. Run away, little fairy," he says on a sigh, but the smile in his voice is undeniable.

I roll away from him and scramble to my feet. The whole floor tilts, my eyes pulsing painfully as I regain balance. Good grief, I'm still drunk. The bathroom beckons me, and I hurry through the cracked-open door. As soon as there's a safe slab of wood between us—as opposed to the unsafe one tempting me from my bed—I lean against the sink and draw a deep breath.

On shaky legs, I turn around, twisting the tap. The rush of cold water drowns out the gasp spilling past my lips. Oh my god, I don't just feel like roadkill. I look like it, too, with my hair taking front and center as the matted, tangled up fur. With the tips of my fingers, I gingerly remove a half-crushed pretzel from between the silvery strands.

Holy spilled ink, Maddox saw me like this. And he stayed and nuzzled against... all this? The sicko!

My face is the color of chalk, my eyes bloodshot and swollen. I shove my head right under the tap, letting the cool water pour over my skin. Blindly patting around for my face scrub, my fingers curl around the tube.

Carefully, I blank my mind. I refuse to think of the man casually laying in my bed, like waking up next to the ghost of agaves sacrificed to the tequila bottle is a normal occurrence. Ten minutes later, my teeth are no longer slimy, my skin is still milk-white, but all traces of my bender have been washed away. Most importantly, my breath can no longer kill any living creature in a ten-mile radius.

I smooth the bottom of my tank top, wishing I'd grabbed a pair of shorts in my haste to hide in the bathroom, and open the door, only to be stopped by a wall of crushing disappointment. The bed, empty and carefully made up, screams at me from the even emptier room.

Air stalls in my lungs, my stomach falling to my feet. My migraine returns with a vengeance, stabbing at my eyeballs until I'm forced to close my eyes. I lean against the door frame, trying to stuff down all the conflicting feelings warring inside of me.

What did I expect? Breakfast in bed and his penis as a painkiller, administered every thirty minutes until I felt better?

On wooden legs, I shuffle to my bed, falling face-first onto the *soft* pillow. Of course, it still carries his scent. Couldn't the hangover come with a stuffy nose?

My phone vibrates under my cheek, and I sniffle back my tears as I slide it from under the cover. I crack open one eyelid, just a smidge since my migraine doesn't like tears, and it *really* doesn't like light.

> *I unblocked myself. You called last night and invited me to a sleepover. Your words were more than slurred, but I did appreciate you saying my cock is pretty.*

Maddox

"Oh god, kill me now!" I moan, embarrassment flaming at my cheeks.

> *Couldn't resist seeing you three sheets to the wind.*
>
> *Of course, what I didn't expect was to find Emma and Violet in the same condition as you, passed out on your couch. I took them home, then returned to check on you.*

> *I did NOT appreciate the unlocked front door.*

> *I have to say, fairy, sultry becomes you. While you were far too drunk last night to get lucky—your words, not mine—I'm the lucky son of a bitch who finally got to sleep next to you.*

> *PS: Greasy breakfast is on the table. I also left a couple of Advils and a bottle of water for you. Go to town on them.*

Maddox

Those are not butterflies doing the bachata in my stomach. I'm also not squealing, holding the phone to my chest. I'm classier than that.
Scratch that. Nope, I'm not.

Chapter Thirty

Sawyer

Maddox likes to play games. He's on a constant loop of hot and cold that I simply cannot keep up with. It's impossible for me to reconcile the man who curled around me in my hungover and disheveled state, sucking on my neck like I was his favorite popsicle, with the man who has straight up avoided me for close to a month.

If we're walking on the same sidewalk, he'll find something demanding his attention all the way on the other side. I swear, the other weekend when we had the last pre-baby book club meeting, he jumped out of the bathroom window at JC's Pour, just so he wouldn't have to talk to me.

I might be inexperienced, but his attitude is telling. Gone is the man who cooked me breakfast. At least, this version of him is familiar. The version everyone has warned me about.

Of course, my friends didn't let a near-brush with an alcoholic coma stand between them and the details of our sordid affair. I was lucky to get two days for my brain to heal from the agave-based poison before they descended like a pack of hungry hyenas.

With the back of my paint-splattered hand, I wipe the itchy sweat gathered on my forehead. Anger makes me do crazy things. Such as... thinking I can sneak into HeeBee and paint my office, all by myself. It only makes me angrier, knowing I have no reasons to be angry.

Maddox made me no promises. If anything, he's finally keeping the promise he made the night he took my virginity. *"It can't be more."*

My agreement echoes, trapped inside my most cherished and hated memory. *"It ends with the sunrise."*

So it makes no sense why I'm feeling hollow inside, after months of back-and-forth, knowing exactly what the deal is.

I huff a breath, dunking the roller into the bright-yellow liquid paint. Pushing it against the ridges of the tray, I roll it until I'm happy it's coated evenly, then move to the last wall needing attention. Despite the hurt pulling at every muscle in my body—physical exertion and I are definitely not on friendly terms—there's something soothing about watching the paint cover bare walls, turning them from dull to magic.

Having something to do also keeps me from being sensationally stupid and seeking him out to ask a very pointed, but clear question. "What the ink?"

Oh, so maybe I'm not as angry as I was this morning, if my self-imposed censorship is firmly in place. If it rains in the next few days, it's because of me and the litany of profanities that spilled past my lips as I was waiting to be served at Suga'High. My black coffee was hot, my stomach eager for a cinnamon bun, fresh from the oven. Then the door opened, the chime trilled, and Maddox stepped inside the bakery. And step was all he did. As soon as those icy-blue eyes of his latched onto mine, he spun more gracefully than a prima ballerina, exiting through the same door not a second later.

Who needs a man, anyway? Certainly not me. Not when I'm just about to cut the ribbon on my dream and open my private daycare center. I blame all those romance books we've been reading lately at the book club meetings. They all wove stories of reformed bad boys who fall head over heels for their chosen. Like the naïve sucker I am, I... hoped. Yeah, go ahead and laugh. Go right ahead and say, "I told you so."

My arm is just about to fall off when my phone buzzes in the pocket of my summer dress. I press the roller harder against the wall, covering the last portion in need of my brand of TLC, then drop it next to the half empty bucket.

I spin in the center of the small room that will become my office in the upcoming weeks, taking in the absolutely awful job I did at painting. Ugh! Matt is going to have my hide tomorrow when he comes in and sees all the extra work needed to fix my anger tantrum.

Maybe I should take the leftover paint and dump it on Maddox's truck. I bet the yellow will really make it stick out.

"Holy ink, Sawyer. Get over yourself!" I huff as I drag the paint tray and roller to the bathroom across the hall. This too is a work in progress. At least, I have a functional sink, so I wash away the paint, soaking myself from head to toe in the watered-down mess.

Once I make sure all the tools I borrowed are in their proper place, I lock up HeeBee and take the short way home, crossing my arms over my chest. There's no need for a nip-slip. The dress is plastered to my chest—hopefully, it'll dry by the time I get home. My phone vibrates again in my pocket, but not for all the poetry in the world will I risk flashing my breasts to Lost Hope's Main Street.

Luckily for me, not many people are out and about. That's a Sunday afternoon for you. The weather has been blissfully kind to us lately, but August draws to an end. So everyone takes advantage of the sun, going to the Teardrop Waterfall, or hiking in the mountains. Even my friends are away, doing their own thing. Emma wandering god-knows-where with Blake or Jackson; Violet, all loved up with her boyfriend, is visiting him in Billings. Lalah had invited me for a get-together they're having with my brother and his wife. While I was tempted for exactly a nanosecond, I declined her invitation. Maevis is nearly two weeks overdue, and her attempts to start her labor became too pornographic for my sensible ears about two days past her due date.

I love that Tatum and Mae are so in love they don't see left from right, but there's no way I'm willingly subjecting myself to tales of my brother's bedroom prowess. Some things are better left to the unknown and the poor walls of their house. Even if I'm beyond excited for the first new Carter generation baby to be born.

The only one working today is Annalise. Maybe I'll pay her a visit at TBRC. I could use an iced coffee and a good book. Preferably horror, or crime, or something with absolutely zero romanticism.

Despite having more paint on my hair and clothes than on the walls, it takes me no time at all to wash the yellow streaks and grime off. I pair a silky, cream blouse with a knee-length, pleated skirt and brush my hair into submission, leaving it down over my shoulders. My phone once again vibrates, the sound muffled by my bed cover, where I dropped it before heading into the shower. I unlock my screen, only to see three messages from Rob.

My stomach flips and churns, the tips of my fingers turning strangely numb. I hoped our chance lunch in Billings would be a one-and-done occurrence. But I'm not that lucky. Where this past month Maddox has avoided me like Satan himself avoids frankincense, Rob has been trying to get me to meet him again tirelessly. Almost no day passes without a text from him, and when he's feeling extra brave, a call.

His messages are innocent enough—a simple "Hey, how are you?", or a picture of something he found interesting and wanted to share. My rare replies are mostly one-worded or a simple emoji, conveying my lack of interest. Not clearly enough, since he's able to carry on a one-sided conversation with no issues. The exchanges always end with an invite for coffee, or lunch, or dinner, or a walk through the park, and my refusal because I'm oh-so-busy.

The mascara brush in my hand shakes as I touch it to my eyelashes. Or maybe that's just my hand. Rob is definitely a complication I don't need in my life. He's poisonous to my self-esteem, worse than Maddox. I don't take Maddox's games as having anything to do with me. Sure, they hurt. But I don't think his behavior is because *I'm* not good enough.

With Rob... it's all about me lacking in every aspect that matters. Throughout our relationship, I was blind to his thinly-veiled barbs. I figured, a man as worldly as him, from a big city, knew what he was talking about. Of course, I had to watch the way I spoke. His friends were as worldly as him. I couldn't embarrass him with my small-town upbringing. Of course, I had to be careful how I dressed. The places he would take me out on dates weren't as keen on casual attire as Dine&Dash was.

But he was the man I was going to marry. I needed to work on myself, to grow and improve, so he'd be proud to have me on his arm. Too late I figured I was being played. I didn't even put the pieces together myself. Instead, I had to hear it from the man himself, as he was complaining to his friends about his redneck girlfriend. How he had to put up with me because, despite my lack of class and manners, I was dumb enough not to interfere with his life. Luckily for me—his words, not mine—I was pretty, so I could look stupid and beautiful, the perfect high-powered lawyer's wife.

The week following my eavesdropping was one of the worst weeks of my life. He was almost manic the entire time leading up to my graduation. I tried and tried and tried to no avail to talk to him. I needed him to clarify that whatever I'd heard was purely... out of context. When I brought it up the next day, he caught my arm, the grip of his fingers nearly bruising. He smiled down at me, pity and condescension in his dark-blue eyes, and told me in no uncertain terms my role was to obey my future husband, not to think.

I was too shocked to say anything else.

The next day, I brought up my job prospects and the interviews I had lined up post-graduation. His anger was quick and swift. *"You need a ring on your finger, not a job. We're as good as engaged, and you want to work?*

What time will you have for me and our children if you're out, working a minimum wage job so you can feel good about yourself?"

And maybe... his words I could've gotten over. But not the overturned furniture in his apartment, not the broken dishes, and definitely not the death-grip he'd had on my wrist as he forced me to my knees to tidy up the broken shards. Not the quiet whisper as he'd slammed the door, promising I'd get what's mine upon his return.

In the span of seven days, everything had changed. From a soon-to-graduate, happy woman, I turned into a shell of myself. Sure, I'd never been the most outgoing. I suffered through my fair share of bullying from Amanda and Maddison when Tatum's back was turned. Keeping to myself and hiding in a corner worked well enough for me. But to see all my dreams shatter in a matter of days... Yeah, I'm not excited to have Rob so close and persistent again.

While clearly, I'm slow on the uptake—and the recent experience with Maddox only proves that I need to repeat the same mistakes for half an infinity before I learn—I do eventually reach the point when I know better. As far as my ex-boyfriend is concerned, I *do* know better.

I take a seat at the foot of the bed, my legs folded under me, and swipe at the screen of my phone.

> *Hi, Sawyer. I hope you're having a great Sunday.*

> *I'd love to see you today and catch up, if you're free. As friends, of course. *winky face**

> *I'd be terribly disappointed to know you're avoiding me, pretty Sawyer.*

Rob Smith

Nausea flares in my stomach as my hand flies to my chest, trying to contain my galloping heart. This is what he does. It's not an overt threat. But it's a threat all the same. A vile attempt at manipulation. Yeah, he's a changed man. And I'm a Nobel winner in literature and poetry.

> *Hi, Rob. I'd be happy to see you. How about we meet at To Be Read Café in Lost Hope in one hour?*

Me

Two can play this game. He'll either refuse to come all the way to "Hopeless Bumfuck", as he used to call my hometown, or he'll be here with bells on. At least, at TBRC, he can't try anything. And, maybe, just maybe, if I'm really lucky, Tatum will see him and run him out of town.

Chapter Thirty-One

Maddox

I see red. And black. Goddamn nuclear explosions are happening in front of my eyes as I push through the doors of JC's Pour with the force of a battering ram. They slam closed behind me, the windows rattling in the nearly empty space.

Jackson glares at me from behind the bar. "If you break it, you buy it, motherfucker."

I wave him off. If I open my mouth, I'll end up arresting us both in the next twenty minutes, and that would help no one. Sitting in the lone cell of Lost Hope's precinct won't help me douse this fire incinerating me from the inside out. It won't erase the sickening image imprinted for eternity in my brain.

FUCK!

Fuck me! Fuck her!

Nope, fucking her is what has gotten me into this mess in the first place.

I plop my ass down on a chair in front of the bar and signal Jackson. "Whiskey. Neat. Bottle." I don't bother looking at him. There's a very fine thread keeping me sane right about now, and if he challenges me... I won't be able to control myself. Instead, I brood and glare at the sleek bar top, the distorted reflection of me glaring right back.

Fuck everything!

My hands fist at my sides as every muscle in my body is pulled taut. Running all the way here didn't help one bit to ease the rage burning deep in my gut. This is one of those moments asking—no, *demanding*—I either fight or fuck. Instead... I chose flight. If Jackson has any sense, he'll let me be, and we're not giving my demons what they want.

A glass hits the bar top, and the unmistakable sound of liquid being poured surrounds me. A bottle is magically pushed in front of me. "You can help yourself with the rest. I'm going to need your keys, though." His voice is low and even. He's a smarter bastard than I am.

"I don't have 'em," I mumble, snatching up the glass and downing it in one go. My throat bobs as I relish the burn of aged whiskey. I push the glass aside and go straight for the bottle. What's the point? It'll all end up poisoning me by the end of the night, anyway. By the time the bottle is dry, hopefully I'll forget about Sawyer being all lovey-dovey, holding hands with a sleek asshole at TBRC.

Fuck me!

That's why I don't trust women. One second, they booty call you in the middle of the night, sleeping their booze off in your arms, the next they're all loved up with suited assholes, prancing through Main Street.

If I'm really lucky, the whiskey won't just make me forget her moving on. It'll erase the whole fucking hard drive. Permanent whiskey amnesia. That's a thing, right?

"Grab your bottle and take your brooding ass to my booth. The night will pick up, I don't need you scaring away customers. Besides, you don't need the town talking." He's careful to keep his voice even. His words are harsh, but there's no malice or judgment in them. Maybe it's the alcohol talking, but I dare say I detect a hint of understanding.

I give him a two-finger salute and march to the booth usually reserved for him and his friends. *My* friends, too, if I'm being honest. Except, even with them, I'm a pariah. I made sure of it. At the end of the day, this is what I do. I push people away since I can't fully trust anyone. If my own family cannot be trusted, what can I expect from strangers?

Sawyer's shy smile flashes before my unfocused eyes. I wash it away with another healthy mouthful of whiskey. How the fuck can she just… smile like that at a random asshole? That's *my* smile.

I slide into the booth and slump against the leathery backrest, my fist clenched around the neck of the bottle. I'd clench it around that bastard's neck in a hot fucking second.

Four weeks—all it took for her to move on. I've been doing the work, trying to make myself worthy of her, and she went and made sweet eyes at someone else. What a goddamn travesty. Where did she meet him, anyway?

A glass of water is pushed in front of me. "Drink it."

"Fuck off, Camden," I huff.

His forefinger gets right in my face. "Drink it, asshole, otherwise, if you puke all over my goddamn bar, I'll make you get on your hands and knees and clean it all."

I roll my eyes—I'm not even tipsy—and grab the glass, downing it one go. "Happy, *Mother*?" I sneer.

"Fucking ecstatic," he replies evenly. "Tatum called me. Maevis is in labor. Just thought you'd want to know."

That gets my attention, a fleeting smile pushing at my lips, despite the rage still running rampant through me. "No shit." I lift my bottle in the air, toasting against nothing. "Congratulations to them," I say as I take another swig. At this point, the whiskey must have melted all my taste buds. I feel nothing as I swallow the hefty gulp. "How come you haven't rushed to the hospital?" Some friend he is. The leather seat is still glued to my ass, but Maevis is not my best friend. No one wants me there, anyway.

"I'm going as soon as an asshole cop is done feeling sorry for himself or finally drinks his liver away," Jackson replies tartly. "I've arranged for someone to pick you up, so if you could hurry on both those counts, I'd appreciate it." His middle finger taps on the table before he leaves me once again to my misery.

In a different universe, where I'm not a damaged bastard, I would've been right there at the hospital, celebrating with them. Sawyer's arm would've been wrapped around my waist, the ring on her finger gleaming in the fluorescent lights, as I shook my brother-in-law's hand. But in the universe I actually live in, I'm getting plastered at a bar while she fucks other men. Story of my life.

I can't really blame her, can I? She made no promises. And I haven't been the best man I could be for her. It didn't help that Drake caught me as I left her house the morning after Sawyer's tequila bender and delivered a sermon to rival all sermons. My good intentions didn't matter. He was crystal clear. *"Do the work, then woo the girl."*

Of course, the therapist he made me see twice a week sided with him. *"You can't get better until you recognize your triggers, Mr. Lawson. Keeping your distance for a short time, so you can focus on your own healing will serve both of you in the long term."*

And look where listening to them got me. Straight to the front row at the screening of a new small town romance, staring Sawyer as the female lead and the unknown cunt as goddamn Romeo.

The best of both worlds doesn't really work for me. I can't be around her and keep my distance. As soon as she's in my vicinity, all I want is to pull her into my arms and never let go. All I could do was keep an eye on her from afar and take care of her from the shadows. A loose word here and there about the old houses in her neighborhood having bad locks—the next day, Tatum sent Jackson to install all new locks on her entrance and backdoor.

Did it come back to bite me in the ass? Sure it did, since I lost my only means to get inside her house during the night. But I also promised Drake and Joshua I wouldn't visit her anymore, and I kept my word.

A few *Lessons Learned* meetings with the mayor; now we have a couple of cameras in strategic points around Lost Hope—all for the safety of our citizens. And to help me find out if anyone who's not me does nightly visits in her neighborhood. Of course, if all I get to see is the suited bastard she's fucking, going in and out of her house at all hours of the day and night, I might set fire to the camera, but that's a separate issue all together.

A huff of air escapes the leather bench when a heavy body plops down on the other side of the table. "I don't need any more water," I slur. Maybe I do, but isn't the whole point of this half-full bottle of whiskey to get me nice and plastered?

"Didn't bring any." The amusement in the voice has my head lifting, a full glare at the ready. It dies a quick death when my eyes make contact with Cole fucking Hayes.

"What are you doing here?" I bite out, taking another sip of my drink. Whiskey *is* liquid, after all. It counts to the recommended eight cups a day.

He shrugs all nonchalant, and I'd really like to punch him in his stoic, handsome face. "Being the designated driver, apparently."

"Don't need one," I huff.

A can of Coke slides over the table, stopped by Cole's huge paw. Maybe I need to reconsider that punch after all. If he doesn't pass out from it, I sure will when he retaliates.

"Like fuck you don't," Jackson hisses. "It's your prerogative to drown in alcohol whatever crawled up your ass. We've *all* been there. But you have a son waiting for you at home. Poison your damn liver, but get home safe, dickhead." Scowling, he turns his back to me.

As much as I hate to admit it, he has a point. Who would've thought our friendly, murderous bartender has a caring side? And most importantly, who would've thought it was extended to me?

"I'm closing down for the night," he carries on, ignoring me. "Xavier is still here, so don't worry about locking up when the party-boy here's done. I'll go check on Tate and Maevis."

Cole claps him on the shoulder and passes him a duffle bag. "Take this to them. I was on my way back to the hospital when you messaged me."

A paper bag with Dine&Dash's logo on it crinkles as he slides it over the table to Jackson, too. "For Lalah. She refuses to leave the hospital, and she hates their coffee. Tell her I took the girls to Matt's, and I'll be there in a couple of hours."

"Roger that. Don't let him puke on my goddamn floors," Jackson growls, throwing his thumb over his shoulder at me.

I don't look at Jackson's retreating back, nor do I look at Cole. My eyes focus on the shiny table surface, my vision blurring under the heaviness of alcohol. A hollowness in the center of the chest makes it hard to breathe. What is she doing now? Did she take him home with her? Are they lying in her bed together? My imagination takes me on dark paths, where the faceless asshole is hovering over her, ready to kiss her plump lips. Lips I never got the chance to know, to taste, to feel their softness for myself.

The smell of fried potatoes and garlic rips me from my sure-way-to-hell. "What's this?"

Cole, unconcerned with the contempt in my words, lifts his eyes from his phone and points at the unboxed fries. "Something to soak up the whiskey. Speaking of, you have exactly one hour to finish that bottle. Lalah's waiting for me."

"So what?" I slur as I wet my mouth with the rim of the bottle. "You're just going to sit here and watch me drink?"

He shrugs. "I'd say I got nowhere better to be, but I'd be lying. The faster you get shit-faced, the faster I drop you on your couch, and the faster I get to where I need to go."

I roll my eyes. He's whipped. I don't blame him. There was a time when I had the hots for his wife. Well, scratch that. I blame him for not punching me. I blame him for sitting here, watching over me. Who the fuck does that?

"Ah shit!" Cole mumbles, scratching his chin. "You're really going to town with that bottle. Jake might have joked, but if you puke in my truck, I'll kill you."

Just to piss him off, I take a chunky potato wedge, swirl it around in garlic sauce, and shove it in my mouth. I groan loudly. "Fuck, that's good." I take a fistful, making sure I coat them properly in sauce before inhaling them extra fast. There's nothing better than fried potatoes in a bath of garlic. I'm not kissing anyone anytime soon. Sawyer is busy kissing a suited dickhead, anyway.

You know what's *not* good? A swig of whiskey after a truckload of garlic. "Son of a bitch!" I shout. The combination is abhorrent. God, it would've been better if I licked a metallic dick straight from an unwashed asshole. I grab Cole's Coke, downing half of it in one gulp. Of course, all the carbonated drink does is fizzle on my tongue, melting every single one of my taste buds like acid. I sputter and drop the can as I frantically rub at my throat, trying my best not to gag.

"You're buying me another one!" Unfazed, Cole points at the rolling can spilling on the floor before he focuses back on his phone.

I shake my head. "You're buying me another whiskey bottle. Goddamn tricks-in-a-fry."

"How about a ride home, instead?" he asks, pushing to his feet.

I can't go home. I'm not drunk enough. If I can still walk, I'll end up on her doorstep, getting in a fight with the clown she's gracing with her presence. So, I grab Cole's arm and pull him back into the booth.

"How'd you know?" I snap, angry at myself for asking the stupid question. There's no more work to be done because there's no future for us. But I ask anyway.

Cole gives me a measured look, his eyebrows furrowing as he assesses me. "Know what?"

I drum my fingers on the table, forcing the words past my numb tongue. "That Lalah's the one."

He leans back, getting comfortable, a soft smile playing at his lips. "Everyone's story is different, Lawson. And it's always a work in progress. I wake up every day and choose to love her, even at her worst. While loving her is the easiest thing I've ever done, it's also the hardest." He exhales heavily, scrubbing at his face with his hands. "While Lalah and I just... fit, there were a lot of things about *me* I needed to evaluate and change. I know how to protect. I know how to fix a problem when I see it. What I don't know is how to take a step back. Lalah never needed me to fix her problems. She only ever needs me to have her back while she fights her own battles."

He rolls his eyes at my confused expression. "She's the only one to ever make me want to stay when all I ever wanted was to leave." His finger jabs my shoulder. "But I'm my own person. You have different needs and wants." Where he was jovial and friendly until now, the man who nearly crushed my hand in Suga'High when we first met makes an appearance right in front of my hazy eyes. "My loyalty is and always will be with Lalah. But make no mistake, just 'cause I'm keeping my mouth shut doesn't mean

I'm not going to bring a world of pain on you if you hurt Sawyer. And that's before I let Tatum loose on you."

I cross my arms over my chest and stare at him defiantly. "What if Sawyer hurts *me?*"

The motherfucker has the gall to laugh in my face before slapping my shoulder. "That's how you know, Lawson. When you're agonizing, on your knees, yet you still crawl to her, begging for her to hurt you more. When *her* hurt calls for more pain for you, and you crave her brand of destruction, you know she's the one."

I mull over his words the whole time we're cleaning the mess I've made with the Coke that tried to kill me, then for the entire drive home. He peels off my driveway before I even slam the door to his truck shut. I take one step toward my front door, and I freeze. With the heel of my palms pressed against my eyes, I turn my back to my home.

My steps quicken into a jog, then rapidly change to full on sprints. I run on three paths, searching for a fourth, but I still run. By the time I reach my destination, my lungs are close to exploding. With my palms firmly planted on top of my knees, I dry-heave a thousand times until my heart rate slows and the alcohol I've ingested decides it sits better in my stomach than on the pavement.

See? I told you... If I can still walk...

All worries leave me as my eyes latch onto Sawyer's sleeping form, curled up on the sofa, silvery hair fanned out around her like a halo.

Certainty settles inside my chest. I *still* have work to do. My reaction today proved I'm nowhere near done with her. Now only to hope we'll both still be standing when I'm done with us.

Chapter Thirty-Two

Sawyer

The bell chimes as I push through the doors at Lucy's Market. I wave to Pete as I hurry to the beautiful display of flowers.

"Please tell me the care package is ready," I call over my shoulder to him. "I'm so sorry for the last-minute request, but I've been running late since yesterday." The wince pulling at my lips is unstoppable. To say the coffee-met with Rob was a clusterfuck it's downplaying it.

"Got it right here for ya, girlie," Pete answers, his gruff voice drowned out by the crinkling of paper.

"Thank you," I yell as my eyes scan the rows and rows of flowers, finally settling on an enormous bouquet of multicolored zinnias. Grabbing it from the vase, I make my way to the counter.

Pete grins bashfully, and, for a second, an image of Maddox from the future flashes in front of me. "That for Maevis?"

"Sure is." I nod. "Heading to the hospital now to meet my brand-new niece." I beam.

Maevis, the incredible woman she is, gave birth this morning at a whopping 4 a.m. Seems like my niece likes to be up before sunrise. Like mother, like daughter. They'll be released from the hospital either later today or tomorrow. And I'm here to make sure their newly restored house is clean—to Maevis's standards—and their fridge and freezers are full. The first few weeks will be rough as they bond with their little bundle of joy. Sleepless nights are a parenting staple. So, if there's anything I can do to make their life easier, I'm on the case.

Pete's smile grows under his bushy beard. "Congratulations to them. Tatum must be out of his mind with pride."

I cup my mouth with my hand and lower my voice to a whisper. "And worry. I heard he fainted," I giggle. Uncool, I know, but what's the point of eternally being the baby-sister if I can't give my brother a hard time.

Pete's kind eyes take on a dreamy quality. "Good grief, I remember when Maddox was born. I nearly paced the floors down, waiting for the midwife to allow me to see my wife and baby. Back then, they wouldn't let anyone but the midwife and doctor in the birthing room." He shakes his head. "A different kind of pride I felt when Ryker was born. Everything was so... sudden. Finding out about him, scrambling to get everything ready for when he was released from the hospital."

I place my palm over his tanned forearm and give him a gentle squeeze. He throws me a knowing look—a look I don't want to read too much into. Sure, a lot more people have found out what me and Maddox got up to, but I'm fairly certain his parents are *not* part of that particular club. Involuntarily, I shudder. Dear god, imagine the horror.

Pete winks, his hands moving fast over the till as he rings me up. Once I pay for everything, he helps me take the flowers and two care packages to my car. "What's this?" I ask.

"A welcome to the baby, of course. We'll visit the new parents—Lucy is champing at the bit to get some baby snuggles—but we'd rather do it once they've had some time for themselves."

I give him a sideways hug before slipping inside my car. "Thank you, GrandPa. They'll appreciate it, I'm sure."

The drive to my brother's house—well, Maevis's family home—takes no time at all, like everything else in Lost Hope. I'm not surprised to find the door open, Clara and Eliza swaying about on the porch swing.

"Miss Sawy!" Clara squeals and nearly falls off the cushion. Luckily, Eliza catches her around the waist and keeps her little sister seated.

I pick Clara up and smother her chubby cheeks in kisses. Her blonde ringlets fly every which way as she giggles and laughs. "Hello, munchkins. Have you seen the baby already?"

My eyes go extra wide for Clara's benefit as she nods sagely in my arms. "She's so tiny."

Eliza gives me an unimpressed smile. "She's not allowed in the library until she's at least three years old. What if she drools all over my books?"

My shoulders shake as I force my laughter down. "You're quite right. There are special books for babies, and they can drool and play with those without damaging them."

Her round gray eyes sparkle. "That's right. I bet I can decorate a box for her in a corner of the library and add loads of soft pillows, because she's soft too, then get all the baby books for her there." She jumps to her feet, barreling into me as she hugs me tightly around my waist. "Thank you, Aunty Sawyer." She spins on her heel, startling the ink out of me when she screams at the top of her lungs. "Lalah! Moooommy!" Eliza disappears through the front door, her high-pitched voice still echoing through the walls. "We *have* to buy baby books."

Clara rests her head against my shoulder as I follow Eliza inside. As expected, Lalah and Cole are busy cleaning—well, Cole is cleaning while his wife is slumped on the couch with the biggest cup of coffee Dine&Dash sells, discussing books with Eliza.

Lalah's hazel eyes shine as she greets me with a wave. She gets teary every time the girls call her mommy. It never ceases to amaze me how she went from a woman who never wanted children, to love these two girls as if they were her own. Technically, in the eyes of the law and in her heart, they are.

"Hi guys. The cavalry has arrived," I say, dropping Clara in Lalah's waiting arms. My heart squeezes as she immediately snuggles up against her.

This is what I want, right here. I want lazy mornings, all cozied up on the couch, my children burrowing into me, and the man I love smiling sweetly from wherever he is as he hurries to give each of us forehead kisses. Maybe I'm still living my years of naivety, but I don't think I'm asking for too much.

"Want a coffee, Saw?" Cole asks from the kitchen.

I shake my head as if he could see me with the wall between us. "No, thank you. I'm jittery enough as it is. My newest niece doesn't need to be trembled to sleep when I finally get to hold her." I rub my hands together, eager to get going. "I wouldn't mind if you'd take the two care packages from my backseat, though."

"Put those hard muscles of yours at work, meus bellator." Lalah wiggles her eyebrows playfully.

Before he can respond with whatever dirty thing I'm sure is on his mind right now, I explode out of my seat and clap my hands. "Just a gentle reminder there are children here."

Lalah rolls her eyes. "And our daughters, too." I stick my tongue out at her in mock-outrage. "In all seriousness, what did you do to the man?"

I fold my arms across my chest. "Uhm, what man?"

Her eyebrows spring to her hairline. "You little minx, there's more than one involved? No wonder he was drinking like his liver was a nuclear plant."

"Lalah, honey, did someone make your coffee with almond milk, by any chance? 'Cause you're not making a lot of sense."

Seriously, if she rolls her eyes any harder, they'll get stuck to the back of her head. She untangles her hand from around the giant coffee cup. "Arm me, Eliza baby." Like the preteen she is, Eliza scoffs, but slaps Lalah's phone into her palm. A couple of taps on the screen, and then she grins like an evil emo princess before handing it over to me. Gingerly, I pick it up. I'm not crazy to have dread building up in my stomach, am I? As if the red device is about to bite me, I squint through my half-closed lids at the picture on the screen.

Even through the blurriness, I can make Maddox out. So I fully open my eyes, a giggle bubbling up my throat. His brown hair is deliciously messy, nearly falling over his eyes, as he slumps in a booth at JC's Pour. Long, thick fingers are wrapped around an almost empty bottle of whiskey, his plump mouth pursed around something that looks like fries. If I were to google the definition of dejection, this picture of Maddox would come up as the first result.

"So? What did you do to him?"

I pass the phone back to Eliza as I shake my head in denial. "Absolutely nothing. If a woman got him like that, the woman isn't me." And the bolt of jealousy striking me in the center of my chest is nothing but indigestion. "How did you get the picture, anyway? I thought you were at the hospital all night." Yeah, I'm not accusing or anything. Just casually... inquisitive.

"Cole was on pickup duty," she answers, giving me a defiant, challenging look. "Don't you think you've danced around each other enough?"

I let my head fall back, my eyes searching for answers—and patience—on the ceiling of my brother's living room. Once I find none of them, I look back at Lalah. "I might be dancing, but he's the one walking away." My smile wanes as I shrug. "Well, as fun as it was seeing you and Cole flirt through a wall, do you need any help before I leave?"

"Nah, doll. You go on and get some baby snuggles." Lalah waves me off, and I waste no time giving each of my girls a forehead kiss before I'm out the door and on my way to the hospital.

The entire drive to Forrest Falls, half my mind is dead set on the picture of a drunk Maddox. Maybe I should've sent it to my phone—*bad Sawyer, no pictures of Maddox, you obsessed, silly girl*. The other half is set on replaying every minute of my outing with Rob. It started innocent enough. A cup of coffee, surrounded by books, Annalise's watchful eyes bringing me a needed sense of comfort. He droned on and on about everything he's been up to in the past years. All the while, I daydreamed about a certain Chief Deputy riding on his gleaming cruiser to save me from being bored to death. Rob is narcissistic enough to not pay attention to me not paying attention to him. A well-timed giggle, a "No way!" or "Of course, you did it. You were always so determined."—that's all he needed as far as my participation was concerned.

It dawned on me yesterday, as the sun was setting behind the jagged mountains, how utterly and completely stupid he must think I am. Nothing but a pretty face with an empty head. It infuriated me as much as it scared me. I ate out of his hand for two years. If I couldn't see it then, what makes me believe I can now? And clearly, based on how I let Maddox treat me, over and over again, I don't.

The worst wasn't being bored to death for two hours over maddeningly good coffee, though. Rob grew bold, most likely thinking he once again had me wrapped around his pinky finger. It started with just a subtle brush with the back of his hand. Before I blinked, our fingers were entwined over the table. By the time I was saved by the bell—or Maevis's water breaking—he tried to kiss me. I averted my lips, sacrificing my cheek instead, at the last second.

His eyes turned cold and calculating when I jumped to my feet, pretending I had to get to the hospital. His "I'll be seeing you around" didn't sound like a promise, but a threat.

The soles of my flats slap against the cement as I jump out of my car, collecting the flowers and fluffy teddy bear I got for my niece, along with the boxed lamingtons Tessa, Maevis's pastry chef-in-training, baked for her.

The whole way to Mae's room, I'm convincing myself the best course of action is to ignore my ex from now on. He messages, I delete. He calls, I mute. He seeks me out, I turn invisible. And maybe, just maybe, I find enough strength somewhere deep down to do the same with Maddox. If he can jaywalk when he sees me, so can I.

I knock softly on the door, not wanting to wake the baby up. I know for a fact they've had people in and out since visitor's hours started at eight in the morning. Without a doubt, Maevis is exhausted. Slowly pushing the door open, all thoughts of deranged ex-boyfriends and cowardly ex-whatevers fly from my mind. My brother, exhaustion and exhilaration etched deep on his face, greets me from a chair pushed next to Mae's bed. I bite back a laugh at the sight of a huge black-and-blue goose egg on his forehead. My sister-in-law is curled up on her side, a fuzzy blanket drawn up to her neck, fast asleep.

But it's the squirmish bumblebee in Tatum's arms who gets all my attention. I swear, my ovaries start doing the tango with my fallopian tubes as I take in her rosy, plump cheeks, tiny mouth pursed, and the smallest fists known to humanity of my hours-old niece. My eyes well instantly, and I bite the inside of my cheek to stop myself from squealing.

Silently, I drop the gifts on a side table and throw my arms around Tate's neck. "Oh my god, big brother. You're a daddy!" I whisper-cry. "Congratulations!"

Tate gives me a drunk-in-love smile, his eyes lingering less than a second on me before he seeks out his daughter once more. "I thought I knew what love was," he murmurs. "But holy fuck. I'm... star-struck!" He kisses the side of my head. "Want to hold baby Lamington?"

Tears are pouring down my face as I choke back a laugh. "She didn't!"

"Oh, Maevis absolutely did. Apparently, pushing for hours on end and earning ten stitches for her effort gives me the right to keep my mouth shut and her the power to name our daughter." He nods sagely. Despite the trace of outrage in his words, he cannot pretend his happiness and pride away.

I cradle my niece to my chest as Tate stands, allowing me to switch places with him. Lowering my head, I bury my nose in her shock of blonde hair and inhale deeply. "She smells like a Lamington, too."

"It's 'cause she's over-baked." He chuckles as he stretches his back.

"Hi, Lami. I'm your Auntie Sawyer. I'm so so happy to meet you, baby girl," I coo at my niece, tears coating the back of my throat making it hard to speak. "You and I are going to have the best of time. I'll tell you all about Daddy's buttons and how to push each and every one of them."

She lets out the tiniest cry, like a little lamb calling for her momma, and my heart somersaults in my chest. Can you die of cuteness overload? Because I'm about to keel over just to hear her newborn cry again.

With a fingertip, I brush over each of her knuckles, her skin so soft it makes my teeth ache. I want to smother her in kisses and take a bite out of those chubby cheeks. How can you love someone so much just ten seconds after you met them? And if I'm feeling like I'm about to melt in a puddle on the cold hospital floor, I can't even imagine how Tatum and Maevis must feel right now.

Having my niece in my arms makes me yearn like nothing before. Will I be as blissfully happy when I get to hold my own baby? Will the father be so insanely in love with us, he can't bear to leave us out of his sight, not even for the time it takes him to blink?

Lami wraps her minuscule fingers around my thumb, and my heart just about disintegrates under the love flooding my chest. I lift my eyes to give Tatum a prideful smile, only for it to slide right off my face as icy-blue eyes connect with mine from across the room, and my heart disintegrates for a whole other reason.

Chapter Thirty-Three

Maddox

What is happening to me? I can't blink. I can't breathe. I cannot fucking move.

The hospital may have crumbled to dust around me. I don't care. All I see is her, the fairy of my fantasies and all my filthy dreams, cradling a tiny baby to her chest. I might be hallucinating too, since the baby looks like a bumblebee with chubby cheeks and a shock of blonde hair.

Drake bumping into me from behind finally breaks the trance I'm in, and I clear my throat awkwardly. Way to get Tatum to punch me in the dick, in front of his newborn daughter, no less. Luckily for me and my favorite appendage, he's too busy shitting love hearts at his sleeping wife to pay attention to me shitting love hearts at his sister. At least, I've got that going for me.

My best friend pushes me aside and in three large steps, he's in front of Sawyer. "Give me my niece," he demands.

Sawyer tilts her chin up, a stubborn line of determination bracketing her plump lips. "Nah-ah," she whispers. "I was here first. Wait for your turn."

Tatum clicks his tongue, glaring at us—me included, even if I'm silently minding my own business, lusting after his sister. "If you wake up my wife, there's a world of pain waiting for all of you."

Sawyer bats her unnaturally long lashes, her navy-blue eyes rounding. "Even me? I'm your baby sister, Tatum Carter. You're supposed to defend me."

No. I'm supposed to defend her.

As if pulled by invisible strings attached snugly around my dick and my heart—and not necessarily in this order—I walk closer to her, clasping Drake's shoulder. "Shouldn't your own sister be your concern?"

He waves a hand in the air, unbothered. "I shared a womb with the woman. She sleeps like the dead. I swear my first memory is of me kicking her in the back as we floated around in amniotic fluid. She wasn't disturbed."

"Really *not* helping your case," Tatum casually points out.

Sawyer snuggles the baby dressed in a black-and-yellow striped onesie closer to her chest, caressing her nose to Lami's forehead. My brain short-circuits. A thousand images flash through my mind. Sawyer in a white wedding dress, Sawyer smiling at me from the couch, her hand cradling her stomach swollen with my baby, Ryker proudly holding his baby sister in his skinny arms.

Fuck me sideways with a slab of white picket fence.

I shake my head to dispel the daydream of a fairytale playing behind my eyelids and turn to Tatum. His narrowed eyes do the job and calm the strange urge, simmering just below my sternum, to pick Sawyer over my shoulder and run, not stopping until we get in front of a judge, and she's declared mine for eternity.

"Congratulations, man!" I say to my frenemy, shaking his hand. "Welcome to the club!" I smile congenially.

In a move very unlike the Carter I know and occasionally hate, he pulls me closer and claps my back. "Thanks, Maddox. Any advice for a new and anxious father?" He gives me a sheepish grin that throws me off more than anything. The man in front of me is so different from the one I'm used to; I can't make heads or tails of the change.

"Stock up on grapes," Sawyer chimes, her eyes not moving away from Drake, defiance etched onto her pretty face despite the teasing note of her tone.

Call me crazy—I know I called myself crazy enough these past months—but a bolt of jealousy strikes me out of nowhere. Sawyer is usually mellow and pleasing with everyone, melting into the background. Up until now, I was the lucky bastard who got all her defiance and experienced that hidden backbone of hers. To see what's only been mine now directed at Drake makes me want to clock my best friend right in his handsome face.

I run a hand over my face and point at Tatum. "Ryker goes through grapes like a fiend. In all seriousness, you don't need any advice, man. It takes a village to raise a child, and lucky for all of us, Lost Hope is a tad bigger than a village. Every single person living there loves Maevis. All you have to do is walk out to your front porch and whisper for help for a line of at least a dozen people to form, ready to chip in."

The sound of rustling sheets diverts his attention. I swear I can see even his ears move in Mae's direction as she lets out a whimper while giving us her back.

"That's it. I love you all"—he points at me—"Not you, I tolerate you at best."

"Well aware," I mumble. All is right in the world, but I don't dare wipe my forehead in relief, because I know what's coming.

"Now get out. My wife needs her rest, and you're not helping with all your bickering." A blink later, he's in front of Sawyer, scooping his daughter up. "Come to Daddy, Mini-Muffin. The noisy people are leaving now, and you can sleep next to Momma." He doesn't even look at us as one-handed arranges the blankets around Maevis and points at the door. "Out!"

No one dares protest. I fully believe him capable of picking each of us up and shoving our asses out the door. We don't even say goodbye, since his complete attention is on his family, as we file out of the room. I don't blame him. I'd be the same if the situation were reversed.

That doesn't mean I don't fall back until Sawyer is walking in front of me. My hand finds the small of her back automatically, a silent sigh of relief leaving my chest at finally being able to touch her. I keep my palm fused to her back all the way to the parking lot and to where her car is parked. It doesn't escape my attention that, at no point, had she tried walking faster to get away from me. Hope blossoms in my gut and has me blurting, "Do you want to get a bite to eat?"

Sawyer stumbles as she turns to face me, and I hook my arm around her waist, pulling her closer to me. With a shaky breath, she pushes a strand of hair behind her ear as her eyes scan my face. "Uhm, I don't think that's such a good idea."

"Are you not hungry?" I play dumb on purpose. Of course she doesn't think it's a great idea. I haven't been boyfriend of the year so far. Not that I am her boyfriend. Manfriend? Lover? Whatever the fuck I am.

I can read the denial on her lips, but luckily for me, her stomach answers before she gets the chance to lie. A delicate blush spreads on her cheeks, her lips tilting up. "I'm not going to die of hunger if I wait until I get home."

I pull her closer to me, so close not even a sheet of paper could fit between us. It's a dangerous game I'm playing, but I'll be damned if I let her slip through my fingers before knowing we have a chance—a real chance. "Or you could come with me instead."

Her deep dark eyes turn glassy. There was no double-meaning to my words—not that I would mind one bit if she came with me, on me, for me; I'm not fussy. Taking advantage of her moment of hesitation, I wrap my hand around hers and pull her to my car. Despite her words, she follows willingly.

A throat clears behind me. "Excuse me, but aren't you forgetting something? *Someone?*"

Goddamn cockblocker.

"Where are your keys?" I ask Sawyer. She shows me her free hand, the keychain wrapped around her middle finger. We're still walking as I slide them off her finger and throw them over my shoulder. "Leave the car in her driveway," I say to Drake without looking back. I know if I falter for even one second, she'll find more excuses to leave alone. This way, she's stuck with me.

"Maddox," Sawyer whispers, a tinge of concern to her tone. "What are we doing?"

I stop by the passenger side of my truck and open the door for her. "Get in, little fairy," I murmur in her ear as I press a kiss to her cheek. She huffs in displeasure but does as I ask. No one can blame me for taking a second to admire her shapely ass while she climbs in. Sure, there's not much to see, since her dress does a good job of concealing her body. I can't even be upset about it. I've had her ass in my hands; I bit, and kissed, and spanked those perfect round globes; me and no one else.

Wasting no time, I shut the door once I'm sure her seatbelt is fastened around her, then round the hood of my truck and hop in myself. "That little café on the waterfront okay with you?" I ask as I place my hand behind her headrest, looking through the rear window as I back the truck out of the parking lot. It doesn't escape my notice how she draws near me, and I smirk in satisfaction to myself.

She might have gone on a date with a slick asshole, but she's still attracted to me. She still wants me. As long as indifference hasn't settled in, I still have a chance.

As soon as I merge onto the main road taking us to the café, I reach across and grab Sawyer's hand in mine once again, resting it on my thigh. Caressing the back of her hand with my thumb, I give her a little squeeze, willing her to relax. Of course, nothing is ever simple as she tries to escape my hold. All she manages instead is to make me entwine our fingers.

"Seriously, Maddox, what's gotten into you?" Her voice trembles slightly, her nervousness sucking all the air out of the cab.

I give her a quick look, just enough to see her chewing on her bottom lip. My jeans become unbearably tight at the simple sight of her white teeth pressing indents against the plump, deep-pink of her lip. "Answer me this," I say instead. My lust is inconsequential right now. The way things have been going for me for nearly a year now, I don't think there will ever be a moment when the sight of Sawyer or her vicinity won't get me hard. "Is that asshole getting another date?"

"What asshole?" To my complete and utter confusion, her shock is genuine.

"The one cozying up to you yesterday," I clarify. The words are grating on my throat like sharp razors. Just remembering his hands on her fills me with rage once again.

With the corner of my eye, I see her shaking her head. I keep my attention on the road, slowing as we approach the little parking area around Main Street. "We were *not* on a date."

"Just friends then?" I mock. I know I'm a rotten bastard right now, but jealousy is riding me and riding me hard.

Sawyer slaps my biceps with the back of her hand as she scoffs. I mean, I deserve it. I'm just glad her elbow didn't make friends with my dick. "Not friends either. Look..." She exhales but remains quiet as I park the car and kill the engine, then turn to face her. Her eyes are clear, even though there's still a faint blush caressing her cheeks. "The man you saw me with... he's my ex."

Fear, unlike anything else I've felt in my life, grips my insides. My stomach feels like a bolder as it careens down to my feet. I swallow around the lump in my throat as I ask, "Are you getting back together?"

"NO!" This time, when she pulls her hand from mine, I let her. "God, no." She folds her arms across her chest as she considers me cooly. "Rob and I haven't parted ways in the best manner. I'm not going to go into details." Her eyes narrow at me, issuing a challenge; I'm just happy she's opening up to me. The details? I'll find them out later. "Anyway, about a month ago, I ran into him in Billings. He used to live in Chicago, but the law firm he's working for is opening an office here. He doesn't make me feel... the safest."

My whole body freezes. Maybe I need those details right now. I don't realize how tightly I'm gripping the wheel until the leather screeches under my fingers. "What did he do to you?" I manage to growl out.

The warmth of her palm slowly seeps into my skin as she covers my hand with hers, untangling my fingers from the steering wheel, one at the time. "Nothing, Madd. And I mean it. Back then, his weapon of choice were carefully curated words posed as care but meant to break down."

It doesn't sound like nothing to me, but what do I know? Never mind, I know better than that. "And you went out with him again?"

She leans back in her seat, hands clasped in her lap as she stares through the windshield at the river trudging clear water in front of us. "I was afraid he'd follow me home or make a scene if I refused him outright. He insisted we'd reconnect... as friends. I ran out as fast as I could, but not before he insisted on getting his number on my phone and texting himself. Then he continued messaging me, and calling, and messaging some more." She trails off, and just in time, too. I'm about to snap like a thread wound too tightly. It takes absolutely every ounce of self-control I possess not to snatch up her phone and have a conversation myself with the bastard.

"So what was the outing at TBRC about, then?" I practically snarl the question. Honestly, I prefer the jealousy. I'd take being jealous every second of every day than enduring her fear and torment.

Sawyer sighs, and I can tell she doesn't want to explain herself to me. Too bad. I ain't moving an inch until I know. "I hoped Tatum would see us and run him out of town. Also, I felt more confident I could say no if I were somewhere I knew I was safe."

The horn of my truck blares as I hit the center of the wheel with the heel of my palm. "Motherfuc..."

"MADD! Stop! Stop, please, stop," she cries, pulling at my hands once again. Her dulcet perfume envelops me, calming the raging storm battering through me.

I shift in my seat, turning to face her, and cup her cheek. Our noses touch, and I see her eyelids fluttering close. I'm aching to kiss her, to feel the softness of her lips against my own, but I won't take anymore from her. Not until she's willing to offer. "Stop engaging with him," I whisper against her mouth. "If he contacts you again, let me know. If he pops in for a surprise visit, let me know. You're not alone, baby, you hear me? You're not alone."

Chapter Thirty-Four

Sawyer

I look in the rearview mirror and draw a deep breath. "You're not crazy, Sawyer," I whisper to myself.

Well, that's debatable, to be honest.

I must be a bit crazy to agree to have dinner with Maddox at his house after his mercurial behavior over the past months.

Despite all the warning alarms blaring in my head, being with him feels right. He is such an intimidating man, yet instead of shrinking into myself, when I'm around him I rise to the challenge. I give as good as I get, not just dreaming of retorts and having arguments in my head with people who cross me three months after the encounter.

Maddox Lawson makes me feel alive—mercurial behavior, hot-and-cold dishes, and all.

Of course, it helps that we've had a nice lunch for a change. He chose the same table we sat at months ago, pulling my chair out for me and caging my knees between his thighs. After the heavy conversation we've had in the car about Rob, the lunch was light-hearted. He joked, he flirted, he played with my hands and my hair, tugging teasingly at my misbehaving locks. On the ride home, he held my hand. Then he helped me climb out of his truck. I thought, for sure, he'd get back in the car and drive away, but no. With his palm firmly planted at the small of my back, he walked me to my front door, kissed my forehead, and *thanked* me for a great date. Yes, that was the word he actually used. Date. D-A-T-E. DATE!

Not even ten minutes later, my phone pinged with a text. Butterflies swarmed my belly, my skin overheating. I must have read it at least a million times since our D-A-T-E, four days ago.

> *Waiting whatever the recommended time is to contact you is an atrocity of a rule I refuse to follow. I want to see you again, little fairy, and I want to see you again soon. Have dinner with me, please. I'll cook for you. I even promise you'll like it.*

Maddox

That night, I fell asleep with his voice in my ear, on an hours-long call, like infatuated teenagers. We both wanted dinner to happen earlier than today, but between Lalah's birthday celebration, the "Welcome home" cookout for Lami, a late night at the precinct for Maddox, and me racing to the finish line for HeeBee's opening day, we had to be patient. Which is not a bad thing, despite the yearning bubbling under my skin.

The wait gave me time to come to terms with my decision to give Maddox a chance. A very much last chance. We both mutually agreed to keep our dates to ourselves for the time being. Not hiding, but not advertising either. The sneaking around, stolen glances, 'accidental' touches when around our families and friends were, in fact, a lot of fun.

I refuse to be a dirty little secret, though. If he's serious about us dating, then it can only happen out in the open. Most importantly, I'll take exclusivity or nothing. I'm not sitting around, sick to my stomach, while he's out sleeping with other women. So... light subjects to go with the salad at the dinner he's cooking.

With another deep breath, I gather my purse, the bottle of wine I picked up for Maddox, and the set of coloring books I got for Ryker, and step out into the balmy September evening. The weather is kind, still. But the nights are getting longer. Although the evergreens will keep their color, a lot of the trees around town have already started to change their leaves, just a subtle yellowing that makes everything brighter.

I lift my arm to knock on the door, when it opens abruptly. A blur of red and blue slams into my knees, forcing me to take a step back. "Miss Sawy, you're here!" Ryker squeals.

Heavy footsteps sound from inside the house. "Partner, what did I say about opening the door without an adult present?"

Still wrapped around my legs, the little rascal shouts right back, "But I have Miss Sawy here with me, Daddy, I sawed her from the window."

The shock of Ryker's welcome finally dispels, and I ruffle his soft, light-brown hair. "Your dad is right. You should never open the door by yourself, even if you know the person standing outside." I crouch down so we're at eye-level. "Promise me, next time you'll wait."

His icy-blue eyes, an exact replica of his father's, watch me with rapt attention as he nods solemnly. "I promise, Miss Sawy." I smile in response, kissing his chubby cheek.

I nearly trip over my feet when I move to stand. Maddox, looking all kinds of delicious, leans against the door frame. His jean-clad legs are crossed at the ankles, the dark-blue material sitting snugly over his well-defined thighs. A red T-shirt, similar to Ryker's, covers his hips and upper body. Not that the soft-looking fabric can hide the flexing muscles underneath. If anything, it clings to every ridge and valley of his abdomen, straining over his chest and wide shoulders. The cherry on top is the kitchen rag, hanging from his back pocket.

"Hi," I squeak, feeling all my blood rush into my cheeks. He gives me a wide-smile, well aware I was checking him out just a second ago. It's not like I've been obvious about it or anything.

Maddox pushes away from the wall and saunters to me. My whole body erupts in goosebumps, there's no two ways about it. Am I feeling ashamed of myself for lusting after him with a four-year-old still attached to my leg? You better believe it. Do I regret it? Not even a little bit.

He winds his arms around my waist, trapping Ryker between the two of us. "Hi, little fairy. You look beautiful tonight," he murmurs, bending down to kiss the corner of my mouth. A bolt of electricity travels from that point of contact straight between my legs. Discreetly, I rub my thighs together, trying to alleviate the ache blooming in my lower belly.

"Yeah, Miss Sawy, you're really pretty. Like a princess," Ryker echoes. His head tilts back so far, I worry for a second he'll end up getting dizzy. He beams at Maddox. "Did I do good, Daddy? I saided all my Rs."

Maddox barks a laugh, making my stomach flip, then touches his forehead to mine. My whole chest warms up. Why does this feel very much like coming home?

"You did very good, partner. Come on, let's show Sawyer inside. I bet she's hungry."

Ryker slips his small hand in mine and starts pulling me inside. "Come, Miss Sawy. We have salad, and steak, and daffodil-ease potatoes, and GRAPES!" He shouts his excitement on the last word.

I can't help my giggle, and neither can Maddox, as he chuckles behind me. "Dauphinoise potatoes."

"That's what *I* said, Daddy. Dolphin Noise Poh-tah-toes." Ryker continues to pull me through the hallway, past the living room, and to the artfully arranged round dining table between the kitchen and the living area. A large bouquet of multicolored freesias, wrapped in a delicate nude paper with glittery edges, sits in a glass vase in the center of the table. Plates and glasses are already set, cloth napkins included. Maddox really pulled out all the stops today.

He takes my purse from me, and I pass him the bottle of wine. His crooked grin has my knees buckling. The way it deepens tells me my reaction hasn't gone unnoticed. "Looks like you read my mind," he rasps. "This Cabernet Sauvignon will go like a dream with the steak."

My cheeks heat up as his eyes drink me in. "I figured we couldn't go wrong with it."

Maddox pulls out a chair for me, and with care not to flash anyone, I let him help me with my seat. His breath fans across my collarbone as he whispers in my ear, "I'm starting to think *we* can't go wrong, regardless."

And I'm starting to think I should've brought a change of panties just in case. *Breathe, Sawyer. Blink, for the love of all fountain pens.*

I'm left alone as he winks and saunters to the kitchen; I have to admit, he looks as good from the back as he looks from the front. Those jeans are tailor-made for his glutes, down to the smallest stitch.

"Miss Sawy." Ryker startles me as he climbs onto the chair next to mine, leaning over the table. "The pretty flowers are fo' you," he says as he gently pushes the vase closer to me. When it wobbles, he sucks in a breath, and I'm quick to help him stabilize it. "I wanted to get you grapes, but Daddy saided we give flowers to women. Do you love them?"

I ruffle his hair affectionately. "I love them very much. Thank you."

His eyes widen as his lips part. "More than grapes?"

My giggle echoes through the room, drowning out Maddox's snort. "Well, I love grapes, too. So if you want to share yours, I wouldn't say no."

Just then, Maddox returns to the table, carrying the bowl of salad and the steaming potatoes. A subtle scent of garlic reaches me, and my stomach growls in response. I can't find it in me to be embarrassed. It really smells *that* good.

"Sit back in your chair, Ry," Maddox advises. "The tray is hot." His mini-me nods sagely as he slithers his upper body off the table. "Just getting the steaks ready now. How do you like yours?" Two pairs of icy-blue eyes settle on me. The butterflies in my stomach take flight. This feels too right, too domestic, as if we just... fit. The three of us, together.

"Medium-rare, please," I croak, as emotion floods my throat. With trembling fingers, I reach for the glass of water and take a hearty gulp.

I could get used to this.

"Can Miss Sawy read me a good night story?" Ryker asks sleepily, half-splayed over his father's shoulder.

"Your old man ain't good enough anymore?" Maddox teases.

Ry lifts his head enough to look at him. "But you read every night. This is special. Like Christmas."

Maddox tightens his hold around my shoulder and kisses my forehead. Those butterflies in my stomach have not gotten one second of a break tonight. He touched me the whole evening. A forehead kiss, a shoulder squeeze, a graze of his fingers, a palm on my thigh—for the entire time I've been here, he was physically connected to me in one way or another. This is something new for me to experience with him. The other times we've been together, it was all about the physical. But, for some reason, I didn't expect him to be... touchy-feely when the clothes were still on and sex wasn't on the table.

After we ate the delicious dinner he had cooked, Maddox did the dishes—despite my insistence to do them myself—and me and Ry ended up drying them. We all cuddled up on the couch to watch videos of singing grapes, once the kitchen was put back to rights. When I sat on the other end of the couch, it was Ryker who insisted I move next to Maddox. If I didn't know any better, I'd think he was playing a little matchmaker.

"I'll be happy to do it, sweetheart" I say. Pushing to my feet, I extend an arm to Maddox, to help him to his feet. Ryker clings to his dad like a koala to a tree-trunk. Together, the three of us, we make our way to his bedroom.

Happiness and disappointment war inside me. I'm beyond honored Ry wants me to read to him, but I can't help the sadness of knowing the evening is coming to an end. Two hours, that's all it took for me to feel right at home with them. The thought of going back to my little cottage all alone brings me no joy.

I'm not sure how much Ryker understands what tonight means. But Madd seems very open in his interest in me. Maybe he's at ease because his son grew up knowing me. I would have been supportive of whichever way he decided to go with Ryker. If he wanted to keep us hidden from him, just easing Ryker in as we progressed, I would've been fine with that, too. What I get instead is Maddox full-steam-ahead. I can't say I'm too torn apart about it.

Even if whatever this strange spark between the two of us fizzles out, I'll always be in Ryker's life. So he won't be too impacted if the worst happens, and I stop coming over.

I pick up a book from the nightstand and flip through it as they finish getting Ry ready for bed. He's far more subdued than he was at the start of the evening as he crawls across the bed and wiggles inside the blanket. I lay on my side next to him, and he immediately cuddles against me. I have to clear my throat to start reading. My heart is too full, this little moment is too right. While my mouth spills all the sounds and voices and narration—a one person theater—my mind is running in circles, trying to pull the brakes on the hopes and dreams of my heart.

The simple truth is... regardless of where Maddox and I are heading, I'm heading straight for heartbreak. Despite all the caution I'm advising to myself, I know I'm already too late.

A large palm squeezes my shoulder as the book is removed from my grip. "He's asleep, little fairy. Come." I allow him to help me climb off Ryker's bed. Bending at the knees, I kiss the little sleeping boy on the forehead as I tuck the blanket around him.

The door closes with a soft click behind us. Maddox wastes no time gripping my hips from behind and spinning me around. My back hits the nearest wall as he looms over me in the darkness of the hallway. With a hand planted firmly above my head, he cups my cheek with the other one. My heart hammers in my chest, so loudly I'm sure he can hear it. My tongue darts out, sweeping at my bottom lip. Oh god, will he kiss me now?

I mournful whimper of disappointment escapes me when he buries his face in the crook of my neck. "Stay," he murmurs. "Sleep in my bed tonight and let me wake up with you in my arms."

As much as I want to, I also want the full dating experience. Every time we end up in a bed together, we sleep together, then he avoids me for weeks on end. As if he can read my mind, he sighs and whispers, "No sex. Sex is completely off the table. Couples share a bed, right? It's all I'm asking for, little fairy, please."

That plea is my undoing. I always know better when it comes to Maddox. It means absolutely nothing, since his intoxicating proximity overpowers any shred of sanity and logic I might possess.

"Okay."

His lips feather over the sensitive skin of my neck as he exhales his relief. "Thank fucking God!"

Chapter Thirty-Five

Maddox

I could walk on water just about now. The sight of Sawyer wearing one of my T-shirts, her silvery hair fanned out on my pillow as she waits for me to join her in my bed, leaves me breathless. She's exquisite, the most beautiful woman I've laid my eyes on. How I had ever thought of her as a wallflower is beyond me.

Her eyes widen as I approach my side of the bed and pull the covers away so I can slip under them. Every inch of my skin demands I pull her into my arms and never let go. But I made a promise, both to her and myself. Tonight is not about sex. We fit just right when our bodies are one, but I have to show her we fit just right in every other aspect of our lives, too.

She turns to her side, facing me, her palms resting under her cheek as she blinks at me through lowered lashes. "This is weird, right?"

I chuckle quietly as I tunnel my arm under the blanket covering us until my fingers grip her hip, and I pull her to me, tangling our legs together. "Not at all. Just... different."

With my fingertips, I trail a path over the dip of her waist, up her arm, and over her shoulder until her cheek is cradled in my palm. "Good different?"

I don't have to search for too long and too deep to find my answer. "The best different." Maybe it's the soft intimate darkness in my bedroom, or perhaps her sweet scent that speaks to something hidden inside me. Or maybe it's the anticipation of this new experience, where I get to really share myself with someone else. The fright of the unknown and the resolute decision to be brave and do it anyway.

Never have I imagined I'd get to share a bed with a woman and just enjoy her company. Yet here we are—Sawyer's body plastered to mine, me drunk on her scent and the silkiness of her skin, and my cock tucked snugly inside my boxers. Am I hard? Undeniably so. Will I do anything about it?

Absolutely not. Besides, I've had a lot of her firsts. It's only fair she has some of mine, too.

"I've never had anyone in my bed," I murmur. Strangely, I feel my cheeks heating up with my admission. "You're the first woman I've invited here. Little fairy, you're the first woman I *wanted* here."

She smiles shyly and kisses my shoulder. "Thank you."

I bury my nose in her hair as my hand tightens on the small of her back. My lips tingle with the need to kiss her, to give us that connection. But if I really want us to have a fair and real chance... I can't. Not until she's sure of me. Not until I'm sure of myself and her. Once I kiss her, all bets are off. Once I taste the sweetness of her lips, she's mine.

And I don't think either of us is ready for that kind of commitment right now.

Sawyer draws in a deep breath, her ample breasts pushing against my chest. My mind immediately flips to the precinct's Code of Conduct, otherwise all my good intentions go straight to hell to party naked. She tilts her head back until we're eye to eye and nose to nose.

"We need rules," she whispers, trepidation making her voice tremble.

I can't help but smile. "We're not good with rules," I counter.

She stiffens in my arms, and that simply won't do. "We're going to have to be good with these rules. I'm not playing hard and fast with my heart, Maddox." She pushes away from me and sits up, leaning against the headboard. I sigh but follow suit, mirroring her position so we can continue looking at each other in whatever scrap of light the moon casts through my windows. Sawyer grabs my hand, entwining our fingers. "I don't know who or what hurt you and made you blind to the goodness around you. But... you're easy to like, Maddox. And you're easy to love when the walls around you part and your marvelous heart is put on display."

The absolute sincerity in her words has my eyes stinging. Damn this woman and the black magic she was created from. The coiled tension in my chest pulls taut. My skin is too small for my body. She heals and punishes in the same breath, and I don't know if I'm strong enough to withstand her... or worse, survive her.

"What are your rules, little fairy?"

The dark depths of her irises bore into mine. "Exclusivity."

"That's a given," I say, mirroring her words from the night that propelled us onto this path.

As if I haven't said a word, she continues, "I know this is not how it's done, and the point of dating is to explore your options. But, if you have options to explore, I want no part of it."

I twirl a strand of soft, silvery hair around my finger and tug gently. "There's a reason I haven't dated anyone until now. The same reason I've never had a relationship." My words catch her attention, whatever protest she had at the ready vanishing on her pretty lips. "People can say whatever they want about me, but what they cannot say is I'm a cheater."

I shuffle around, making myself comfortable against the headboard. Sawyer crawls closer to me, leaning her head against my shoulder, the warmth of her skin against mine lending me the courage I need to bare the darkest corners of my soul to her.

"I've never led anyone on, Sawyer. If you believe anything, believe that." I run circles with my thumb on the back of her wrist, the feel of her anchoring me as I lay the poison in my heart at her feet. "It's not just an excuse to paint myself as less of an asshole. If I got involved with someone, the woman knew the score straight away. I knew what I was capable of offering, and trust wasn't on the list."

"Not commitment?" she asks in a barely there voice.

"Can you have commitment without trust?" I retort.

She shakes her head against my shoulder, and I take her silence as permission to continue. "Every year since I started playing in the Little League, my parents would send me to Florida during the summer holiday for a month. My mom's sister lives there, and she looked after me during baseball camp." My eyes lose focus as the painful memories of my past resurface with a vengeance. "During the holiday before seventh grade, something changed. I came home and noticed a subtle tension between my parents. My mother was standoffish, my father withdrawn, hitting the bottle more often than not."

Sawyer's sharp gasp echoes in the silent room. I don't hold her shock against her. No one, apart from Drake, knows the dirty past of my family.

"The tension persisted, although they tried their best to pretend all was well in front of me. The following year, I went for camp again. When I came back, shit hit the fan. There was no hiding the hell they were living in. Fight after fight started by my father in a drunken rage. No child should have to pick up their dad from the floor where he was lying in a puddle of his own vomit and waste." My throat is thick with emotion and restrained rage. Even now, twenty years later, it still hurts as badly as it did then. "My mother was not the woman everyone loves now. To this day, I still don't know the reason."

I chuckle ruefully as I pull Sawyer closer to me. Maybe I'm going crazy, but the feel of her in my arms somehow lessens the weight of my mother's betrayal. She nuzzles her face in the crook of my neck, her hair falling like a silk curtain over my shoulder. "Turns out, Lucy Lawson, the town's sweetheart, was also sweethearting with an out-of-towner on the sly. My father was... destroyed, to say the least. Did that stop her? Not one bit. Not until I've had enough of Dad's benders. Not until I saw her myself, sneaking around with that asshole, one night on my way home from Drake's."

"You lost your trust," Sawyer whispers against my skin.

I feel that loss all over again. "I don't know how my father ever forgave her. I never did. Sure, I tolerate her, but forgiveness? I simply don't have it in me. She didn't just betray my father for her selfish wants. She betrayed our family. So if I cannot trust my own mother, how can I trust a stranger? That's a blemish on my heart I'll always carry with me."

"So what's changed now?"

I thump my head against the headrest. "Drake says I'm like a teenager on steroids. All big feelings, and not a whole lot of logic. My therapist has me doing all these workbooks and exercises to help me recognize trust comes in many different ways. One speedbump on the road does not make for the end of journey."

Her fingers tighten in the fabric of my T-shirt as she looks right into the deepest trenches of my soul. "I can't be an experiment for you, Maddox."

I cup her cheek and bend my neck to kiss the top of her head. "You're not. I swear, baby, you're not. I'd never toy with anyone's heart like that. And most of all, with yours."

Her protest buzzes in the charged air between us, but I silence her with a finger across her plump lips. I only take a second—okay, five—to revel in the softness of her mouth and imagine the hungry noises she'd make when I finally get to taste her.

"I'm the first to admit I've been an asshole to you these past months. My issues are my own, and I've worked my ass off to reach a place where they won't stand between the two of us."

"But?"

"But it would be naïve of us to assume I'm all healed up. We don't know what life throws at us. My jealousy is far from healthy." I caress her jaw with my thumb as I try to make sense of all my messed-up thoughts. "Truth is, I don't know this side of me with feelings for someone else. We'll have disagreements. Would my innate selfishness and pride come before you in those moments?"

My heart sinks as Sawyer moves away from me. Before I can scramble after her, she throws a long, slender leg over my thighs, straddling me. Her soft hands cup my face, her dark eyes searching mine. My hands find purchase on her hips. *Fuck me.* The heat of her so close to my rapidly-hardening cock doesn't help me keep my resolve of not having sex tonight. Allowing myself to be vulnerable with her also makes me desire her with a ferocity that scares me.

"We're both new at relationships. We'll learn as we go," she murmurs. "You're trying to protect yourself from pain and heartbreak. So am I. So is everyone else. Overthinking helps nothing. Sure, we can play the what if game, but then we'll forget to live in the right here and right now. I can meet your issues with kindness, understanding, and respect if you do the same." She shifts in my lap, and I can't help the wanton grunt escaping my chest. Her plump lips stretch in a wicked mouth. "None of that." Sawyer wiggles a finger in my face as I bark out a laugh, dispelling the strange tension winding around us.

"So, exclusivity is your only rule? Because you've got it, little fairy. Hell, you've had it for close to a year."

Do you feel that second-hand embarrassment? Because it's burning with such force, I'm afraid I'll incinerate the sheets around us.

"What do you mean?" Sawyer whispers, a tinge of fear and incredulity in her voice.

I fight the urge to roll my eyes, since I'm pretty sure she'll take it the wrong way. Wishing I'd kept my mouth shut does me no good either. The words are out there, so I might as well own up to them.

Like the asshole I am, I smirk. "As it turns out, I've had big boy feelings for you for longer than I care to admit. We've never really been in the same circles," I confess, all traces of humor gone. If anything, all I feel right now is shame. "Sure, I've had brief crushes before, but they happened, then they evaporated." My fingers tighten on her slender hips as she bucks over my lap. "The night I drove you home from Lalah's Thanksgiving dinner, I think that was the first time we've ever been so close to one another. I was... shell-shocked. I thought it would go away, but then I'd see you again at the daycare center or in passing. Instead of diminishing, my feelings grew until I didn't know what to do with myself anymore."

"The night at the club?" she asks softly.

"Was the first time I went... out in months," I reply, unable to hide a wince.

Sawyer chuckles self-deprecatingly. "You wanted to get laid." Her tone might not be accusing, but I read well enough between the lines.

"I'm not going to sit here and lie to you, Saw. Maybe connecting with someone isn't my strong suit, but I love sex. I refuse to be ashamed of it. It was my way of having a temporary connection with no repercussions for the parties involved. Either way, in my head, to get over my irrational feelings, I needed to get under someone else."

"Except you got me instead. How did you figure sleeping with me would be a good idea? Everyone knows sex deepens feelings, not erases them." She tsks playfully as I pinch her ass cheek in retaliation.

"My jealousy got the best of me. Not that I have any fucking regrets. It got you here, didn't it?"

She slaps my shoulder as the sound of her laughter fills the darkened walls of my bedroom. Absolute pride unfurls in my chest. I made her laugh. She's with me here, in my arms. I'm the one who gets to hold her, and put her at ease, and wake up next to her smiling face in the morning.

"No more hot and cold?" Sawyer sobers up, the fear in her eyes diminishing the hope.

"I've fully accepted my feelings for you, little fairy. Maybe I don't always know what to do with them, but what I do know is... whenever I feel like running, it's to you."

Her arms wind around my neck as she rests her forehead against mine. Strange tingles run through my entire body. An unsettling warmth radiates in my chest. If this is happiness, I'll fight with my last breath to hold on to it.

"Who knew you had such a soft center under all that assholeishness?"

I kiss the tip of her nose as I scoot down until my head rests on my pillow and Sawyer is sprawled out on top of me. With my hand buried in her hair, I cradle the back of her head. "There's nothing soft about me where you're concerned, little fairy."

My eyes close as I breathe in the comforting sweet scent of everything Sawyer is. I might be falling asleep with my cock hard as a rock and my brain under-oxygenated, but I know I'll never have a more peaceful sleep than with her in my arms, right where she belongs.

Chapter Thirty-Six

Sawyer

I clap my hands to get the attention of the children running around in the outdoor area of the daycare center. "Alright, my little loves. You have five minutes to finish your games, then it's tidy up time." Just one step away from floating, I start collecting the discarded toys, so I can speed up the process.

Not long now until parents will start trickling in, and my day will finally end. I've been walking on clouds these past two weeks. My cheeks actually hurt from how much I've been smiling. I wake up with a smile on my face. I go to sleep with a smile on my face. Happiness practically shoots out of my eyes everywhere I look.

Although we're not going out of our way to keep our relationship hidden, for some reason Lost Hope has not exploded with the news of its Chief Deputy being off the market. We've settled instead into a routine—one that if anyone told me Maddox would participate in, I'd be laughing in their faces until my stomach cramped. Our days are spent either separately or sleeping over. Through a silent understanding, every second day, I'll show up for dinner and end the night in Maddox's bed and his strong arms.

When I'm not over at his house, it's like I'm living a forbidden romance. The stolen touches and glances full of longing when he's dropping Ryker off. The suggestive exchanges and naughty winks when he's picking his son up. Little stolen moments when we both find ourselves at Suga'High or at the diner.

Sure, it has helped that our friends and families have all been otherwise occupied. But it's working in our favor. We're getting to know each other without everyone else's preconceived notions about who I am and who Maddox is. While our friends would be supportive of us, my brother's reaction worries me the most. And if there's one person whose opinion I trust and respect, that's Tatum's. I'm afraid he won't be able to move past the vitriol they shared and the mistakes the man I'm in love with has made.

I'm loath to think I'd be forced to choose.

The happy bubble we've been living in will soon burst. There's no avoiding it. We might be acting like we're the only people on Earth, but real life spills your ink when you least expect it. Not much I can do—so I'm enjoying every minute I spend with Maddox and Ryker, reveling in my newfound happiness, while I hope we'll grow strong enough to withstand the storms about to hit us.

Of course, the question of us being certain of our relationship also looms over me. Two weeks of sleepovers, two weeks of dinners together, breakfast in the morning, plans and promises whispered in the dead of the night, and he hasn't kissed me yet. Of all the rules we made and broke, not kissing me is the one he holds true. It almost feels like a game at this point. How much teasing and taunting can we take before I get to feel his lips against mine, his tongue tasting me?

Sealing a promise with a kiss has taken on a whole new meaning between us. And so far, we're not promising.

I shake my head, forcing my mind to return to the here and now. With hurried steps, I head toward the side entrance of the building, pushing the door open, and clap my hands again. Little groans and protests rise from the playground. I bite into my cheek to keep from smiling. My bumblebees love the outdoor space with the colorful swings and sandbox. They'll be absolutely ecstatic when we move into the new building. Until then, I decided to take advantage of the few days we have left of sunshine and let them spend as much time outside as possible. During snowy days, we still come out and build snowmen, but the temperature doesn't always allow us to linger and play.

"Ready? Set! Go!" I holler. Despite their protests, a flurry of little arms and legs start pumping as, one by one, they run inside the classroom. I smile as my eyes scan over each rosy face before I quickly check no one is left outside. Pride blossoms in my chest as I see all the outdoor toys nicely tidied up in boxes lining the wall. I'll have to come out and lock them in the shed once all my kids have been picked up, but the effort is well worth it.

With a sigh, I close the door behind me, taking a second for my eyes to adjust to the darkness of the building. My flats slap against the carpeted floor as I follow my children to the classroom. I'm pleased to see each of them seated or laying on their assigned matts.

Our end-of-the-day routine starts. I help everyone who needs to use the bathroom, laughing and singing as we wash our hands and grass-stained knees. The classroom gets tidied up next, until every toy, book, chair, and piece of chalk rests in the designated place. One by one, parents trickle in. The afternoons are always happy-time, squeals and laughter echoing between the walls, hugs being passed around like candy.

I feel him before I see him. My skin flushes; the fine hairs at my nape stand on end. Butterflies explode in my stomach. Like incarnate electricity sauntering through the daycare halls, Maddox makes my heart pitter-patter a second before the scent of his cologne hits me—clean, masculine, intoxicating. With trembling hands, I busy myself, rearranging the papers on my desk.

The warmth of his hulking form radiates at my back, and I lock my knees to stop them from buckling. A whispered chuckle has lightning bolts coiling in my belly. "Good afternoon, Miss Sawyer. How are you on this fine day?" he rumbles in my ear. My skin sizzles where he brushes his knuckles against the back of my hand as he takes a step closer to me.

"Hi, Madd," I squeak. I can't help it. His larger-than-life presence is overwhelming in the best of ways. I shiver as a blush barrels over my neck and explodes in my cheeks. As if in slow motion, I tilt my head to take him in. Although we're standing side by side, it feels as if his entire body is curled up around mine.

Being the sole focus of those twinkly, icy-blue eyes leaves me breathless. A slight grin tugs at the corners of his lips, making the twin indents in his clean-shaven cheeks deepen. I realize with a startle I've never seen Maddox like this. His eyes always had a hint of coldness, a touch of distance in them. His smiles might have made his dimples pop, but they were holding only a crumb of happiness. Unwittingly, he'd built a wall around himself, forcing everyone out and at a safe distance.

I've always thought Maddox is a handsome man. There's no denying it. From his mesmerizing eyes, tall frame, and defined muscles, to the dimples in his cheeks and his gravelly voice, he's all grit and assholeness wrapped in a beautiful package. Now, he's absolutely exquisite as he slowly opens up, allowing me to see his huge heart and soft center. When he looks at me as if I'm the reason the sun rises and sets each day, I feel like I'm walking on clouds. Weightless. Untouchable. Loved.

"Ryker is spending the weekend with my parents," he tells me in a soft voice. "How do you feel about spending that time with me, just the two of us?"

Time alone with Maddox has been a precious commodity, not that I'd ever resent Ryker's presence. In fact, it was the first conversation we've had once we decided to give us a go. They're a package deal. Ryker will always come first for him. If I'm being honest, Ryker comes first for me, too. The little gentle soul has had too many people fail him. I will not be one of them. And most definitely Maddox will not be one of them. Not if I have anything to say about it.

Maddox is a father first, a boyfriend second. And I'm happy with that. I don't think I could fall in love with a man who would turn his back on his children as soon as a new woman comes into the picture. If things between us work out, and we end up a family, nothing will change. I love Ryker as if he were mine. Blood does not make a family.

"I'd love to," I whisper back, my giddiness not to be contained. He gives my fingers a brief squeeze, his thumb caressing my knuckles.

"I can't wait, little fairy. Friday cannot come soon enough." His smile turns wicked as he winks. "Neither can you."

My gasp is lost in the remnants of his chuckle as he strides to the back of the classroom where Ryker and Clara share a mini bag of grapes.

THE DAYS, OF COURSE, DRAG. As Monday turns into Tuesday, lingering glances and feathering touches are not enough anymore. As Tuesday turns into Wednesday, my skin itches, a constant throb between my legs makes me all squirmish and unsettled. My house feels too small, too cramped, too suffocating.

As much as I wish for the weekend to get here already, I cannot make time move any faster. I've cleaned the house from top to bottom, all my spreadsheets for HeeBee are up to date, the final touches are nearly completed—even my office was fixed after Matt grumbled at me for a full thirty minutes. I've even finalized the last interviews and hires for my new daycare center.

Emma took over planning for the opening day festivities in mid-October. The most sensible date was after the long weekend and Indigenous

People's Day. The week before, a series of activities and day trips are organized, supported by The Crow Reservation, to celebrate our Native communities. We'll use the weekend to move everything we bought from the Town Hall over to HeeBee's.

There will be no disruption to the children, nor will we cause any schedule issues for parents. I'd honestly dread the phone bill, considering how many calls I had to make to ensure parents and legal guardians were aware of the change, including the newest enrolled from Forrest Falls and nearby towns and communities. Luckily, Lege et Lacrima is footing the bills for the first year until donations and tuition fees come through.

I shrug my jacket on and slip into my flats. The door closes behind me with an audible click as I hurry down the wooden steps of my porch. A late evening tea would do me good to settle the anticipation and anxiety battling for first place in my chest.

My breath fogs in front of me as I fall into a brisk walk toward Dine&Dash. I know this weekend with Maddox will change everything between us. There's this unrest in the pit of my stomach. Hope and dread, love and despair. A lot of change is coming our way. HeeBee will take a lot of my time. Fall is always a busy season for Maddox, too. It seems like lower temperatures and increased darkness make people reckless, getting into all sorts of trouble. He's always constantly checking on the elderly residents who might need an extra hand.

We also need to come clean in front of our friends and face the firing squad, although I'm sure most of them will support us. Most, but not the most important. Am I being selfish if I'm planning to ambush Tatum when he's all loved up on Lami? Maybe I can buy my niece a matching bumblebee outfit to the one Lalah gave her and drop the news while he's too drunk on her cuteness. Surely, Daddy pride can soften him up? Maybe I need to wear a bumblebee onesie, just to be sure. Maddox, too.

The warmth of the diner makes my cheek flush. I shed my jacket as soon as I clear the door as I scan for an empty seat. The place is bustling, all the booths and tables occupied. I beeline to the counter, happy to see a couple of seats are still available.

A frazzled Renee scurries in front of me, wiping her forehead with a kitchen cloth. "Sawyer, doll, how are you?" She gives me a bright smile, although there's no denying the fatigue on her pretty face.

"Clearly, better than you," I tease. "What happened?"

She rounds the counter and plops with a huff on the last available chair. "Ruth went home. Poor thing, her hip is giving her trouble, what with the cold front that hit us today. The diner was quiet, so I didn't call anyone in. Can you spell bad idea, 'cause yikes?" She throws her hands in the air, gesturing at the crowded restaurant.

"Well, aren't you lucky?" I wink. "You've got the best waitress this side of Yellowstone at your disposal. I know my way to the employee room. You put your feet up for ten minutes while I get an apron."

Before she can protest, I'm out of my seat, sprinting to the back. I hang my jacket and tie a little black apron around my waist. The white shirt with pearly buttons screams regret, but I'm sure Emma will find a way to recycle it if I get it stained to death. At least, I had the good sense to leave home wearing a pair of black jeans. I hurry back to the counter and start preparing a tea for both Renee and me.

"You'll need to fill in a temporary work contract," Renee tells me with a tired sigh.

I wave her off. "It's fine. Just leave it out for me before we go home for the day. When's night shift taking over?"

She takes a sip of her chamomile tea, humming contently. "Marcia will be here just after ten, but you don't need to stay until then. Hopefully, things will start to slow down in an hour or two."

I gently pat her hand. "You're fine. I'll stay as long as you need me."

The hours fly by. Between taking orders, busing tables, serving food, and preparing drinks, I don't have a second to think or to breathe. It didn't take me long to slip right back into the role my teenage self held two summers in a row. All the businesses in Lost Hope are good to their youth. I flitted from babysitting jobs, to manning the reception at Tate's Shop, to waitressing for Ruth for the entirety of my high school years. It's like riding a bike, the first few feet wobbly and panic inducing, thinking you'll topple over, and before you realize, you're cruising down Main Street, all worries forgotten.

I'm wiping off the last table as Renee does the inventory at the back. It's been nice and quiet for the past ten minutes, giving me a chance to refill the sauces and condiments on each table. Once I make sure everything is ready for the night shift, I'll mop the floors, get a to-go portion of lasagna, and return home.

Water sloshes everywhere as I push the mop cart from the closet to the main floor. I hum softly as I sway with each swish of the mop against the checkered floors. A dejected sigh leaves my lips as the wind chime at the entrance trills sharply when the door opens. I plaster a smile on my face and shrug my aching shoulders.

"Hiya. Take a seat anywhere, I'll be right with you," I call over my shoulder as I display the 'Wet Floor' sign and push the cart away from view.

"Sawyer?"

I nearly trip over my feet as Rob's voice echoes through the empty diner. My entire body stiffens. I turn slowly and give him a wane smile, hoping my eyes don't betray my panic. "Rob, what are you doing here?" Unfortunately, I cannot mask the accusation in my question.

I've been dodging his messages and calls for the past weeks, hoping he'd get the hint and leave me alone. I can't believe he has the audacity to show his face in my town uninvited.

He rears back as if I slapped him, his skin turning red under the thin layer of dark scruff covering his cheeks. His slanted eyes narrow dangerously before he remembers himself and throws me a slimy smile.

"I was actually hoping to run into you," he coos as if I'm a baby. The urge to roll my eyes is nearly impossible to douse, but somehow I manage. Aggravating him will get me nowhere. "I figured I could grab some to-go dinner and hoped to persuade you to share it with me. What are *you* doing here?" His nose crinkles in disgust as he racks his eyes over my damp apron and stained button-up. "Didn't you say you were a teacher?"

I cross my arms over my chest. A wallflower I may be, but even wallflowers have their pride. "I *am* a teacher, Rob. In Lost Hope, if one of us needs help, we jump in and help." The disgust on his face only deepens with each word out of my mouth. With a shake of my head and a deep breath, I finally voice what I was too weak to say when he bumped into me down in Billings. "I don't think it's a good idea for us to keep in touch anymore. We outgrew each other."

He tsks, rolling his eyes, as he takes a step closer to me. I'm too slow to move when his hand wraps around my wrist. I flinch as his fingers curl around me, and he pulls me to him. "Sawyer, darling, you're confused. You've always been a bit... ditzy," Rob says with a condescending smile. "But that's okay. I didn't love you for your smarts, darling."

Although his insult *smarts* against my skin, I brush it off as I pull my arm from his grip and put some distance between us. "You don't need to stoop yourself so low and date someone like me. I'm happy in my hometown. But I mean it. I don't want us to keep in touch. I wish you all the best, but the past needs to stay where it belongs—in the past." I tilt my chin up. 'Yes, sir' Sawyer is nowhere to be seen.

His cruel smile twists around my spine with an icy grip. "We'll see about that, Sawyer darling!"

Chapter Thirty-Seven

Maddox

"Watch out, the po-po's on the prowl!" His arms go high in the air before placing his hands behind his grayed out hair. "Am I in trouble, boy?"

I shake my head, shoving my hands deep into the pockets of my jeans. "Cut the crap, old man. What the hell are you doing in the orchard at unholy o'clock?"

He rolls his eyes at me—ask me where I got that bad habit from. "Isn't the better question, what are *you* doing here at unholy o'clock? Where's my grandson, since we're interrogating?"

I clap my father on the back in greeting, not daring to meet his eyes. My words might be dripping with bravado, but my insides are quivering. "Daycare. You ain't gettin' him until Saturday morning."

His weathered fingers wrap around the closest apple, throwing one after another in a basket at his feet. "Your mother has a tinkering for apple pie. Can't say I mind too much. What I'll mind is her selling them instead of letting me eat 'em."

"So Maevis is out of commission for six weeks and Mom's monopolizing the baking market in Lost Hope?"

He rubs his chin, his hand nearly disappearing inside his bushy beard. "Nah. They're all for Maevis. She's selling them for free. My stomach kindly—and unkindly, if I'm honest—disagrees. What brings you here, son?"

I sigh, my breath fogging in front of me. What a difference a couple of days make. Just on Monday I was lazing around in my backyard in a pair of shorts and a T-shirt. This morning I had to dust out the Henleys and jeans. "We gotta talk," I mutter.

Not sure if my voice betrays the seriosity of what I'm about to bring up, or if Pete Lawson simply knows his son like the back of his hand, but his sun-leathered cheeks pale and his shoulders slump. "Ah shit. And you want to do this sober?"

I crouch to pick up the overflowing basket of apples, my knees popping in protest. Fuck me. Every twinge of my body is a sorry-ass reminder I'm not in my twenties anymore. It's also a reminder of the age difference between Sawyer and me. Eight years is... not scandalous. She's young enough that my fragile man-ego soars when I read the desire in her eyes. She could have anyone, yet, for some strange reason and fucked-up karma, she wants me. Sawyer's also old enough that I don't feel like I'm robbing the cradle.

Now only to hope her family will feel the same once we come clean to everyone.

With the basket secured around my forearm, I straighten to my full height and level my father with my best glare. "You haven't had a lick of alcohol in twenty years. Don't start on me now. Put a pot of coffee on and let's get this over with."

Together, we slalom along the numerous apple trees surrounding their home until we find ourselves on the back porch. I drop the basket on a wicker table and lean against the railing, my arms crossed over my chest, tapping my anxiety with the soles of my boots against the wooden deck.

"Aren't ya coming in?"

I give the back door a look, then a second. "Is Mom home?"

"Yeah," he sighs, the disappointment clear in that one word.

"Then no. It's you I need to talk to... for now. Go get that coffee, Dad."

His rubber boots shuffle along the floor, falling with a thump as he reaches the door. I close my eyes, trying to convince myself not to turn around and run home. Self-doubt and loathing are cramping my stomach. There's this hollowness in the pit of my stomach. I can't tell if my dread is caused by the answers I'm about to get or by revisiting those times I want to bury so deep, they'll find them on the Kerguelen Islands during the next excavation.

I know I'm being unfair toward both my parents right now, dredging up skeletons that are better off left buried. My father has forgiven and forgotten. I live in hell every day still. For my relationship with Sawyer to have even a modicum of a chance, I need to know. Burying my head in the sand doesn't work anymore. I'm scared shitless that one day I'll see something, I'll hear something, and jump to conclusions. My stubbornness is unparalleled. My impulsivity is insatiable. I'll do or say something to forever shatter us.

Even if we live blissfully our happily ever after, I deserve to heal. Sawyer deserves me whole. My son deserves a father who's not so irrevocably damaged, he'll end up damaged, too.

The door creaks on its hinges, making me wince. A waft of bitter coffee with a hint of cinnamon reaches me, and I inhale deeply, savoring the familiar smell.

My father clears his throat. "Go on then, sit!" he orders as he passes me a steaming mug of the bitter nectar of the gods.

Jesus fuck. Talk about a good time if he's ordering me around.

I stretch with a groan on the wooden chair opposite my father, the wicker table between us. He's not looking at me, his eyes fixed over the orchard across his backyard and the mountains looming in the distance. I slurp at my coffee, biting down a curse when it burns my tongue. My knee bounces incessantly, so much so, I worry I'm going to wear the scalding liquid instead of drinking it. My stomach flips and gurgles as the words practically rip from my lips.

"I met someone," I start. "She's... amazing. Everything I didn't dare hope for. Still, I'm scared shitless she'll pull the same crap on me as Mom did on you. How did you forgive her?"

My father's sharp intake of breath pieces through the early morning silence. "What are you talking about?"

"Mom. How did you forgive Mom?"

Coffee sloshes over the rim of his mug as he sets it down in front of him, stapling his hands together on the table as he leans closer to me. "I wasn't the one owed forgiveness, son. She was."

The fingers of my free hand drum over my bouncing knee. He must be getting senile at his age. Why would she forgive him for her cheating? "Explain."

"You're hurting your mother. Constantly dismissing her, ignoring her when she's right there," he snaps, pointing at the kitchen window. "We've let it pass. At the start, we figured you were a teenager. Then you were suffering because of your shoulder injury and couldn't continue to play baseball. But you went on to being an adult, and still being a shitty little prick to her."

His words are like a slap to my face. I explode to my feet, hot coffee spilling over my jeans. The burn hurts less than whatever poison he's spewing now.

"SIT!" he thunders before I even open my mouth to have my say. "You want to talk, after twenty years of being a constant goddamn terror and heartbreak to your mom. Sit and listen."

Fuck me, do I have to? I'm a thirty-four-year-old man. He single-handedly raised me while my mother was out, gallivanting with random men, living her best life. My father should know me better than this. It's a given—I *am* an asshole; but I'm never an asshole without a reason.

"So, you're telling me I should have what? Be grateful she turned you into an alcoholic while she tried on for size every man in a fifty-mile radius?"

My father's cheeks turn into an unnatural shade of red. If it were biologically possible, I bet steam would pour out of his ears any second now. "Fuck me, Maddox. I've never raised my hand at you, but so help me God, another unkind word out of your mouth about your mother, and you'll swallow your teeth."

Speechless—that's how I am. My throat is dry. My tongue is sluggish and stuck to the roof of my mouth. *What the fuck?*

"You might look just like Lucy, but unfortunately for you, you inherited every one of my shitty traits. I hoped... I prayed you'd outgrow my bad habits, but you've gone from bad to worse." He scrubs a weathered palm over his face as I sit back speechless.

Every part of my chest hurts with the insults my father is throwing at me. He's forgiven her, yet I'm paying for standing up for him. I'm the goddamn villain because I had more empathy for him, instead of my cheating whore of a mother. Dropping the mug on the table, I slap my palms against my knees and stand. "I came to you for help and advice. If you're just going to sit there and hurl knives at me, thanks, but no thanks. It makes me sick to my goddamn stomach to see you blaming *me* for her actions."

"SIT THE FUCK DOWN," he bellows.

"Nah." I shake my head, ready to hightail it out of here and into the next bar. "We're done here."

With surprising speed, he gets to his feet and in my face. "You're too stubborn for your own good, Maddox. And a damned hypocrite."

I scoff, my entire body jolting under the bolt of derision running freely through my veins. "I'm the hypocrite? You're holding me a sermon worthy of an exorcism about taking *your* side instead of a cheater's. Who's the hypocrite here?"

As if hitting the eye of a storm, all wind leaves his sails and he deflates before me. He grips my shoulders, his face a stone wall of seriousness and heartbreak. "Maddox, I'm the cheater, not your mother."

My heart stalls and sputters. I hear the words, but my mind is simply not able to comprehend them. As if shoved through a wormhole, I blink and I'm back in our living room. Like a black and white movie, I see my mom curled up on the sofa, her forehead resting on her knees as she hugs her legs to her chest. Her shoulders are shaking, heart-wrenching sobs echoing through the room. Dad is swaying on his feet, holding a bottle of rum he dangles precariously around. The rage on his face is palpable, thickening the air in the room. His pain brings tears to my eyes. I feel the betrayal in my own chest, curling around my spine and yanking.

"No," I croak. "I *saw* her." My breath is labored. As labored as it was when I pedaled like a mad teenager, eager to get home from my best friend's, taking advantage of the empty streets. The giggles gave me pause. The moans got me curious. Curious enough to stop, lay my bike in the grass at the edge of the road, then sneak around the fence of the old lodge. Only for bile to pool in my mouth when my eyes snagged onto the flannel-wearing asshole with his hand under my mom's skirt as he kissed her neck. The flowery red dress she wore is imprinted onto my very eyelids.

I ran like a bat out of hell, riding my bike faster and harder straight home. The disbelief was strong inside me, the disgust stronger. Yet I hoped. I hoped I'd get home and find her on the couch, watching one of her favorite soap operas. Or maybe in the garden, tending to her beloved vegetables. I really fucking hoped I'd get home and find my parents on the porch, having their evening glass of wine as they snuggled together in the swing Dad built just for her.

"Jesus Christ eating a rotten apple. All this time you thought it was her?" He squeezes my shoulders tighter, the pressure ripping me away from the memory of him passed out alone on that porch swing, and Mom breezing home not even half an hour later, her flowery red dress billowing around her knees.

My knees buckle and I let myself fall back into the chair. He crouches in front of me, his face a painting of misery and self-loathing. "This is *my* fault and my fault only. We... I-I n-never..." he stutters as he wipes a palm over his face. "Your mother is a goddamn saint. I'm thanking my lucky stars each day she didn't leave my sorry ass. I would've deserved it. And probably you'd be much happier for it, anyway."

Pinching the bridge of my nose doesn't help me keep together the reality fraying all around me. But I know what I saw. I'm not a complete idiot. "Did you hear what I said?" I grit through clenched teeth. Any second now, I'm expecting one to crack. "I. SAW. HER. WITH. HIM."

My eyes are scrunched shut, but even through the rush of blood mercilessly beating against my eardrums, I hear him shuffling and sighing. "Your mother and I married young. Too young, some would say. But we were madly in love, and at the time, it was almost expected. Soon after, responsibilities started piling up. Lucy did her best, she always did, but I grew restless and resentful."

A pained whimper claws at my throat, and I bite my cheek to keep it contained. You know that feeling when you just know the whole sky will rip apart above your head and there's nothing you can do but take it? Well, I have the feeling I'm about to be hit with the cosmic equivalent of a freight train.

"You came into the picture." His voice grows wistful for a brief moment before it cracks. His shame stinks the air between us, and I'm simply sitting here, holding my breath and bracing for impact. "We were happy for a time after. Lucy started working on the gardens, making millions of plans on how to grow them, sell the produce in our family's market. And I was drowning. My late nights at the bar became the norm. The alcohol on my breath replaced goddamn toothpaste. One afternoon, we had a fight. She begged me to stay home with her."

He scoffs, and I clench my fists so hard, I'm afraid I'll break the arms of the chair in two. Because I know what's coming and I don't know how to stop it.

"You know what I told her?" He doesn't wait for me to answer, too lost in his own misery. "That she's needy and controlling. That I wasted my life, a man in my prime tied up to a goddamn garden like a gnome. So off to the bar I went, drowning my sanity and liver in rum, then bedding the first willing skirt just so I could prove I was still a man."

I spring to my feet as if burned. "FUCK!" My throat is raw as I pace the length of the porch. "Where was I?" I ask with my back turned to the man I used to worship... up until five seconds ago.

"Baseball camp..." is his whispered answer.

"Fucking fuckitty fuck. What next, hmm?" I bellow, still staring at the mountains. If I look at him, I'll have to call one of my deputies to lock me up in jail overnight because I'm about to commit patricide and I can't find it in myself to care.

"I came home and told my wife she doesn't make me happy anymore. I told her I needed more. Freedom to... feel like a man." His voice is far away and choppy, as if I'm threading through water. "We separated but continued to live together. She refused to let you suffer and not have your father with you. When you were gone, so was I. It went on for two years." He clears his throat, and I barely suppress the urge to cry. My stomach gurgles and churns. We're a mockery of a family. And I'm a mockery of a man. A goddamn broken mirror-image of my father.

"Who was he then?" I manage to spit out. If he's poisoning me, he might as well finish the job.

"No one. Someone. A farm hand she'd hired to help her with all the jobs I was slacking off, too busy living my glory years." His regret is bitter in the air, sucking up all the oxygen, simmering, burning, consuming the both of us. "Until your mother called and demanded I return. She begged me for a divorce. And I lost my goddamn mind."

"That's when the drinking started?"

"Nah. Before. I like to think drinking myself to an early grave was my way of punishing myself. In all honesty, I was a selfish son of a bitch. Being three sheets to the wind every night felt like a good time."

"Why aren't you divorced then?" I snap.

"Because no judge in the county would've let me have custody of you. Lucy realized if she left with you, you'd blow up your future just to get back at her." He sighs. "The night you packed her bags was my lowest of lows. I got my shit together after that. I fought for my family. It's not an excuse, and it doesn't erase the hell I've put my wife through. It sure as fuck doesn't excuse the way you treated her."

Air leaves my lungs as if he kicked me in the solar plexus. I can't bear to listen to him anymore. I can't fucking bear to be in my own skin. Without acknowledging his words, I turn and run for the stairs. Betrayal wreaks havoc in my chest, incinerating me from the inside out.

"Maddox! Don't run away," he shouts at my back.

A bitter chuckle leaves my lips as I spin on the heel of my boots and spread my arms at my sides. "You already said I'm just like you. So why not? You've done it before."

Chapter Thirty-Eight

Sawyer

The UNLOCK button on my phone will probably self-detach and disappear into the ether, never to be seen again. I still press it. I still stare at the screen for the millionth time, only to find no missed texts or calls.

A whole day has passed, and I haven't heard from Maddox.

I don't want to be the obsessive girlfriend or the woman who can't let a day go by without hearing from her beau. But this... disappearance doesn't make any sense. Not for the Maddox I've spent all my time with this past month. My worry is eating me alive. Too many times in the last hour I've had to stop myself from putting my coat on and going to his house to check on him. That's the level of unhinged I reached.

The emptiness in the pit of my stomach leaves me breathless. I feel it deep down—something's wrong, something is very, very wrong.

It's not unusual for hours to go by without a peep from Maddox. Sometimes, things get busy at the police station. Other times, he'd go and help his parents with their gardens and orchards. Often enough, I'd be so busy with the kids constantly demanding my attention, I wouldn't even get thirty seconds to check my phone.

But to go the whole day with no signs of life... it just isn't something we do. All my messages have gone unanswered and unseen. All my calls have rung out, with only the voicemail to greet me eventually.

I didn't even realize I hadn't heard from him until Drake and Annalise came to pick up Ryker. All my kids have been restless today. Some, needier than normal, demanded extra attention, throwing tantrums when they didn't get their way. I've been running around like a headless chicken since 8 a.m.

As soon as my eyes connected to Drake's and I read the pity in his, it felt as if my blood had been replaced with iced water. I've been cold ever since. All I got as an explanation was, *"Maddox asked me to pick Ryker up and keep him with us for today."*

Since Drake is on Madd's approved list, I couldn't do anything but wave goodbye to Ryker and watch him skip out of my classroom, talking Drake's ear off.

"What if he needs space from me?" I mumble out loud as I change into a pair of warm PJs.

I can't really hold his need for space against him. We've gone from zero to one hundred in a very short time. Maddox values his independence; he's used to being alone and not having to inform anyone of his every move.

Not that he has to. But it wouldn't kill him to just send a message saying he's busy for the day, or the week, or the year.

Anything but this all-consuming worry, twisting my stomach around and giving me palpitations.

Once I make sure all my windows are properly secured and my doors are locked, I drag my socked feet to the bedroom and slip under the warm covers. Sleep is, of course, eluding me. I lay on my back in the middle of the mattress, eyes closed, as I try to slow my breathing and relax my body.

I'm sure there's a reasonable explanation for all of this. He got caught up at work and simply forgot to message me. I'll see him tomorrow morning, bright and early, when he drops Ryker off again. We have a weekend together, all to ourselves. Surely, I can bring up a small request for him to let me know in the future when things get too busy. Or even if he needs some distance from me. We're all adults here. I can handle it.

Right now, we're adjusting to each other, learning how to make space in our lives for a partner. Everyone has growing pains, right? Even the best couples I know have had their hiccups.

Once I manage to half-reassure myself and my body stops buzzing as if at any second I'd pop off like a bottle of champagne, I turn to my side, a restless slumber weighing me down. It feels like I've been asleep for only a second when loud bangs come from the front door.

With a shriek, I startle out of my blankets, my mind struggling to clear from an unfulfilling sleep haze. I untangle my limbs from the fabric holding me prisoner, my heart hammering in my chest with every pounding that echoes in my little cottage. Sure, the door will hold, but whoever's on the other side seems determined to break clean through the wood.

On silent feet, I tiptoe to the entrance. Hooking my index finger at the edge of the privacy curtain, I slide it over a fraction of an inch. Enough to give me a view of a slumped over form, light brown hair in disarray as he thumps his forehead against the door frame. Relief, unlike anything else

I've ever felt, washes over me. My clumsy fingers slip over the lock and drop the key at least three times before I manage a firm grip and open the door with a flourish.

"Maddox! You're here," I say and wince. In the dead-silence of the night, my voice seems to be amplified.

He lifts his head, taking me in. Icy-blue eyes bore into mine and a tired smile tugs at his lips. It doesn't escape my notice that his smile is not reflected in his dull irises. Maddox looks devoid of all light, pure resignation floating around him.

My self-preservation alarms are blaring at the back of my mind. Do I listen to them? No. Instead, I take a step closer to him, cupping his cheek. "Are you okay? Is Ryker okay?"

He winds his arms around my waist, plastering me to his chest. His lips press against my forehead. "I need you, little fairy, please," he murmurs, his voice scratchy and sad.

My fingers tangle in his soft hair as I pull his head down until we're nose to nose. "Tell me that everyone's okay," I order, fear clawing inside my belly.

"Everyone's okay," he retorts automatically, as if practiced.

He's lying to me and doing a poor job at it, too. I open my mouth to voice my protest. No sounds escape when his lips brush over mine, once, twice. A strangled noise vibrates in his chest. Electricity sparks through my skin, my entire body trembling in anticipation. My emotions are switching from one extreme to the other so fast, it makes my head spin. Or maybe my head is spinning because of the growl I feel at my fingertips, where my left hand is clutching at the soft material of his shirt.

He slants his mouth over mine at the same time my back hits the wall behind us. My whimper of need is muted by his hungry lips moving over mine, and my knees buckle. Maddox is kissing me. Maddox kissing me is everything I've been missing in life. He nips at my bottom lip, then soothes the sting with his tongue, and I melt into him.

His hands are everywhere; cradling my head, kneading at my ass through my fuzzy PJs. I rub against him, my belly exploding in a kaleidoscope of butterflies when his hips shift and all that hardness hiding behind his fly presses against me. My breath is labored and wanton as he consumes my mouth. The tip of his tongue traces my lips, tasting, licking, driving me absolutely insane.

"You're my punishment and my redemption," Maddox whispers. The pain in his words has my lips parting on a silent gasp. He takes advantage of my momentary stun and slips his tongue inside my mouth. I moan deep into my throat as he explores me with ravenous flicks of his tongue against mine. The taste of him invades me—mint and desperation and everything Maddox is—all coming to a head on my front porch as midnight strikes.

I daydreamed for months about his kisses. How soft his lips would feel as they tease mine. How firmly they'll coax me to open to him, all weak knees and wanton whimpers. My dreams don't do him justice. I'm spinning, I'm floating, I'm rubbing against him like a cat in heat.

Whatever alarm bells sound in my head that this kiss is not a sealed promise for a happy tomorrow are silenced by the masterful strokes of his tongue.

I'm kissmatized, and he's my kismet.

Vaguely, I hear the door close behind us. I don't feel us moving, yet I'm in constant motion. His arms surround me, his scent gets me drunk on him, the heat of his body plastered to mine makes my skin tingle. All my worries and fears from today vanish.

He's here. He's kissing me.

Maddox is here.

"I don't know what you're doing to me," he breathes, breaking our first kiss just enough to push the top of my pajamas over my head. Then his lips are on me again, tasting, nipping, biting, devouring me whole. And I'm here for it.

I'm ready to fall with him and raise alongside him.

His large hands palm my breasts, testing their weight, teasing my nipples with his thumbs. Burning need wraps around my chest, traveling directly to my core. My panties grow damp with every flick of his fingers over the hardened buds.

"You were made to drive me insane," he bites, his teeth scraping at my bottom lip. Goosebumps sprout to life on my skin as the rage in his words settles over me. My heart skips a beat and my stomach turns weightless. But I don't get to process his words as he picks me up and gently lays me in the center of my bed.

My hands fall at his waist, furiously pulling at his shirt, my frustration growing when I can't untuck it fast enough. He slows the kiss, the desperation in his need dissipating as quickly as mine is growing. "Maddox," I whine—a plea and a threat.

He pushes away from me, resting his weight on one arm. His eyes, tormented by too many emotions, resemble a storm brewing on the horizon. He feathers his fingertips over my chest, down to my navel, then finally hooks them around the waistband of my PJ pants. My throat dries under the intensity of his gaze. He bores into my very soul, as if he's welcoming me home and saying goodbye, all without a single word.

My breath is labored as he slowly peels the pants off me, leaving me completely naked under him. "You're so perfect and pristine. Little fairy, all I'll do is dirty you up. That desire brews just under my skin. I just want to soil you," Maddox murmurs as he settles between my legs.

He's still completely dressed, and my hands fumble anew, trying to get him rid of his clothing. I need his skin on mine. I need his harshness and his touch. After a day of stressing over his well-being, I just need.

"Do it, then," I challenge. "Soil me. Dirty me up." I push up on my elbows until our mouths are nearly touching again. "Do your worst, Maddox."

My words light a fire in his eyes. His plump lips twist in a crooked smirk. For a fleeting second, he's *my* Maddox, not the dejected carbon copy of the man I love I found on my front porch earlier. His hand collars my neck as he pushes me back down on the bed. His nose brushes against my hairline as he whispers, "I'm going straight to hell for this."

"I'll still call to see if you got there safely," I retort, as my patience wears thin. My nails find purchase on his shirt and my fingers grab at the soft material. As if my desire for him gives me an extra boost of strength, I pull with all my might, sending the pearly buttons flying. He growls deep into his chest as he sits back on his knees and gets rid of the offending garment, throwing it behind his shoulder. "There you are," I breathe.

Maddox Lawson is one handsome son of an ink. Framed by wide shoulders and well-defined pecs with just a smattering of hair covering them, the dark anchor inked in his skin draws me in. My fingertips itch to trace every swirl and loop, every interconnected letter making up Ryker's name and his date of birth. I lower my eyes to the valleys and ridges of his abdomen. I want to follow all those tensing muscles with my tongue, to feel for myself all that hardness encased in velvet staining the back of my throat.

I swallow over nothing as his deft fingers hook around his belt buckle and fist the sheets at my side. Anticipation is buzzing in my veins as I wait with bated breath for him to get rid of the last piece of clothing standing between us. With his eyes still latched onto mine, he crawls backward until he stands at the foot of the bed. Memories of the first night we shared batter my mind.

How he stood at the foot of a different bed, looking like an avenging archangel of darkness, ready to devour me whole. Not much is different now.

Maddox sheds his jeans, and I moan as his cock, heavy and thick, slaps against his abdomen. He cuffs himself at the root, moving his fist up torturously slow. "You want me, little fairy?" His voice is gravelly and low, but the hint of vulnerability in his words doesn't escape my notice.

My knees fall apart, showing him exactly how much I want him. I don't need a mirror to know I'm glistening and slick for him. He swallows thickly, his Adam's apple bobbing as if in slow motion. My nipples pucker in response, tight and achy for his touch. "Fill me up, pretty boy."

He gives himself another stroke, then climbs back into bed with me. He moves like a panther on the prowl, all grace and danger as he advances. Hovering over me like a sexed-up poltergeist of destruction and doom, Maddox plants his palms against the pillow and lowers his forehead to mine. "I'll break you, little fairy, and I'll never forgive myself."

I arch into him, my sensitive nipples feathering against his chest as my thighs cradle his trim hips. "Shatter me, Maddox. Do your worst and rip me apart," I challenge. My breath hitches as he drives his hips forward, coating himself in my arousal. "Once you're done dancing in the ruins of my destruction," I moan when he notches the head of his throbbing cock at my entrance, "love me enough to fuse me back together."

My high-pitched cry of ecstasy melts on his lips as his mouth descends over mine, and he enters me in one swift thrust. He weaves his fingers through my hair, holding me in place, kissing me breathless as I pulse and flutter around his intrusion. A raging fire explodes in my lower belly when he grunts his pleasure into my mouth and deep into my soul.

Tonight, I meet my end.

Tonight, we seal our beginning.

Chapter Thirty-Nine

Maddox

I'm the greatest asshole to walk the Earth, but my body still lights up. Sparks of pleasure and madness explode at the base of my spine as I slowly withdraw until only the tip of my cock remains sheathed in her majesty. I tighten my hold in her hair, my mouth ravenous and hungry as it moves over hers.

Sawyer Carter tastes like all my hopes and dreams wrapped in the most beautiful package I can never have.

I slip my tongue inside her sweet mouth as I once again drive myself into her, allowing her tight pussy to squeeze me like a vise. My lungs seize, restricting necessary air flow. I don't care. I'll die a happy man, right here, right now, buried so deep into her I don't know where I end and she begins. Then I'll never have to leave, I'll never have to break her.

Fury and maddening desire swirl in the pit of my stomach as I palm her generous breasts. My thumb flicks at one tightened bud, then the other, until she writhes and thrashes underneath me, seeking faster completion than I'm willing to give.

My whole body shudders as her pussy quivers, her wetness gushing around me. She's too much. She feels too good, too tight, too warm. Sawyer feels too mine, and I can't breathe.

"Please, Maddox," she urges me, her heels pressing against my ass, spurring me on. I keep my thrusts slow and controlled. I don't want this to end. I don't want us to end.

I nip at her chin instead, a warning and a praise, a demand for her to behave. "Patience, little fairy," I rumble against her fluttering pulse point. Her frenzied heartbeat swishes under my lips, soothing the pain rooted so deeply into my soul. My fingers grab onto the curve of her waist, pinning her to the mattress as I start loving her with deeper, faster thrusts. I love her with everything in me.

She fits me like a glove. She is made for me, and I am made to destroy her.

Her breathy moans drive me insane. Pleasure coils low in my groin as all the blood in my veins rushes south to where we're joined as one. The backs of my eyes sting, and I scrunch them shut. She undulates her hips around mine, and we move together in complete harmony. I'm making love to her with my whole body. And it's not enough.

All of Sawyer, all the time, it will never be enough.

I push up on my knees, my hands gripping her hips, and change the angle in which she's making me hers. Sawyer mewls a needy moan as I hit that magical spot inside of her that puts stars in her eyes and makes her pussy clamp down on me like a manacle.

She's near. And I'm obliterated.

Her arms coil around my neck as I bend my head down and take a pebbled nipple into my mouth. My teeth graze the hardened bud, and a new wave of desire floods around my cock. My restraint to love her slowly and tenderly crumbles to dust. The bed creaks as I fuck her in earnest, her tits bouncing against my mouth as I release her nipple with a swirl of my tongue and a pop. I kiss my way up her chest and suck up the graceful column of her neck.

In the morning, she'll wear my mark.

And she'll hate me for it.

"Maddox, yes. I'm so close. Please, don't stop, please, please, please," she cries out. My stomach flips as the nuclear bomb of pleasure reaches critical point in my groin.

I can't hold on.

I cant my hips, rutting into her like the mindless beast I am. Love, possessiveness, and world-ending agony unfurl in my chest as her back arches. A million flutters of insanity grip around my cock as she comes with my name on her lips. My mouth seeks hers once more as my control snaps. Painful throbs of desire shoot through me as I mark her quivering walls with all of me.

Her skin is slick and silky as I paw at her, obsessive desperation driving my hands to memorize each curve, every dip and valley. My hips are relentless as I push myself further into her in jerky, uncontrolled thrusts until I'm completely spent.

My heart is pounding in my chest as sweet exhaustion weighs me down. Sleepily, I blink at the ethereal image Sawyer poses. Her hair looks like molten silver in the moonlight, fanned in soft tangles across her pillows. Her bee-stung lips are swollen and red from my kisses. Dark spots I know for a fact would turn purple in the morning are peppered across the creamy skin of her neck and chest. Teardrop tits, crowned with puckered jewels, move up and down as she squirms underneath me.

Every one of my muscles is trembling as I plank over her and drop my head to kiss every inch of her skin. Her happy giggles are music to my ear and sharp knives in my back. I shake my head to dispel what I know is to come as I lick at her oversensitive nipples, her giggles soon turning into breathy moans. She gasps as I slip out of her and move further down the bed, tracing with my tongue the cursive writing corseting her waist.

With infinite tenderness, I kiss her belly, nuzzling my nose in her navel, and finally reach the sweet promise of her pussy. I inhale deeply, reveling in the scent of our lovemaking, and lick the length of her seam, tasting us on her. My spent cock twitches painfully against the rumpled sheets. He'll get his turn again soon.

I bury my face between her slick thighs, kissing, tasting, and loving on the sweetness of her pussy. Determination to make this the best night of her life courses through my veins. It's the least I can do. I know I'm a selfish motherfucker. I'll have my comeuppance; of that I have no doubt. My pain, I'll welcome. Hers, I'm causing.

She shakes in my arms, her knees locking around my head. Slender fingers tangle in my hair, pushing and pulling as her pussy flutters under my tongue. "Maddox, oh god. What are you doing to me?" Sawyer keens on a greedy cry, and I double my efforts. She seizes in my arms, going stiff as she explodes on my tongue.

Satisfaction and pride I have no right to feel flood my bloodstream as I sit back on my knees and take in the lovely painting Sawyer makes. I'll never see anything more beautiful. I'll never taste anything as decadent.

I flip her to her side and crawl behind her under the covers. Her ass fits perfectly against my groin, my cock nestled between her cheeks. I coil my arm around her waist as I pull her closer, my palm cradling her breast as I bury my nose in her hair. I hold her to me as if I'll never let her go, my throat thick with emotion. Boneless in my arms, sleepy and compliant, she's a fairy of the night put on this earth to show me that heaven is real.

Too bad bastards like me are not allowed past the golden doors.

Panic claws at my stomach. It's that panic what has me throwing her thigh over my hip and entering her tight heat once again. I groan my agony in her hair as I kiss the back of her neck.

"You're insatiable tonight," Sawyer moans, arching her back. She pushes against me until I'm completely sheathed in her warmth.

"I'm losing my mind tonight," I growl as I take her in slow, long thrusts. I'm losing my heart too, but she'll find that out soon enough.

My eyes roll to the back of my head as I move inside of her. Her pussy grips and releases me with every back-and-forth of my hips. Her tits bounce in my hand as I pinch her nipples every time I bottom out inside of her.

My despair threatens to overwhelm me, so I lift my head and slant my mouth over hers. She opens up to me so easily, like we didn't have our first kiss less than an hour ago. Like her lips were made to be savored, and bitten, and teased by me. She sighs dreamily into me when I grind my hips against her ass, circling them as my thrusts grow short and shallow. My cock jerks inside of her as pure electricity travels through my veins, ready to explode between the silken walls of her pussy.

"There's my good girl," I praise as she quivers around me. "Give it to me, little fairy. Let me have it. Break my goddamn mind and come on my cock." I withdraw slowly, letting her clench over nothing before I forcefully slam home. Sawyer detonates around me as I still inside of her. I drink from her lips her gasps of pleasure while her pussy milks me dry of everything I have.

There's nothing left of me to give.

My arms tighten around her as the clock strikes closer to the end. The scent of pear and freesia cocoons us under her blankets. I let my eyes fall closed for a second. Just enough for the *could have* future to flash behind my eyelids. A taunt of my subconscious, a cruel punishment born from my deepest desires, which just a day ago were a possibility.

Not anymore.

My dejection leaves my chest on a heavy sigh. "I never thought I could," I murmur, my lips feathering over hers, "but you showed me otherwise." Her lashes tickle my cheeks as she opens her eyes, reading into the very depths of my withered soul. "If you know one thing to be true, know that I love you, Sawyer." Her lips part, but I quiet her retort as I touch my mouth to hers. "Without a shadow of a doubt, you little fairy are the best thing to have ever happened to me." My arms release her and I shift away until I'm able to swing my legs off the bed and stand.

"What are you doing, Maddox?" she asks as she grips the sheet to her chest, hiding herself from me.

I'm thankful for the darkness in her bedroom as my eyes sting and tears fall unchecked down my cheeks. I run my fingers through my hair and pull, hoping the burn in my scalp overpowers the burn in my chest. "You're the best thing to have happened to me," I repeat. "But I'm the worst for you."

Sawyer scrambles out of the bed, the white sheet wrapped around her body like a toga. Her silky hair falls around her shoulders like a mantle as she advances on me. "Maddox, what happened?"

"I can't be who you need." I chuckle derisively as I tilt my head back, trying to find answers on the pitch-dark ceiling of her bedroom. "Sure, I'll try. I'll even get it right for a year, or five, or ten. You'll be happy and oblivious, thinking this is our happily ever after. Until I come home, a bottle of rum in one hand, reeking of another woman's perfume."

"Maddox," she gasps as she winds her hands around my neck, pulling my head down until our eyes are connected. "You're scaring me. What happened?"

"You deserve someone who'll respect you forever. Someone who appreciates the miracle you are in their life, who'll not search for happiness in seedy bars and between another woman's legs." My fingers wrap around her wrists as I gently push her hands away from me. I don't deserve the soothing powers of her touch. "I'm a cheater, Sawyer. This poison is embedded deep in my DNA."

I fist my hands at my side when her eyes well with tears. Every cell in my body is screaming at me to comfort her, to stop this madness. But I know... even if it hurts her right now, the blip of pain she's feeling is loose change compared to how I'll destroy her if I continue to leech off her love.

"Where were you today?" Sawyer asks as she takes a step away from me, her arms folded protectively around her waist.

I lift my shoulders in a careless shrug as I roam around her bedroom, looking for my clothes. Stabbing my feet through the legs of my jeans, I button them up, then start hunting for my destroyed shirt.

"Answer me!" She doesn't need to yell for me to hear the demand. There's nothing I can give her but space. I want what's best for her. And what's best is for Sawyer to be as far away from me as possible.

"To get clarity," I rasp once my shirt covers my shoulders and my boots are back on my feet.

"And what? You're all clear that the best course of action is to fuck and dump me?"

I'm the one fucked in the head as my cock twitches behind my fly because her pretty mouth spews curses at me. "I don't know what you want me to say, Sawyer."

She freezes in the middle of her bedroom, like a statue made of sin and gunpowder. I swear, I can smell ozone in the air. For a brief second, I'm suspended in time and space, expecting her to blow up at me. I flinch away when determination washes over her beautiful face and she steps toward me, resting her hands over my chest. My heart is pounding so hard, I'm sure she feels each beat and tremor in her veins.

"Don't do this, Maddox. Whatever happened, talk to me." She moves even closer, plastering her body to mine. Her head tilts back as her bottomless eyes bore into mine. "It is our rule. Whatever it is, we'll face it together. Please, don't do this."

My heart stalls painfully in my chest as I cup her soft cheek. Sawyer nuzzles the side of her face into my palm, and I nearly die on the spot. I lower my forehead to hers, breathing in for the last time her sweet scent of spring and hope. "Forget about me, little fairy. I'm no good for you—for anyone, for that matter. I love you too much to see you waste your life and time with me. Cheaters will always be cheaters. I don't deserve or want your forgiveness."

I once again wrap my fingers around her wrists and push her away from me for the last time. Not waiting to hear more of her arguments, I turn my back to her and rush out of the bedroom, nearly running away from her house.

I'm halfway down her driveway when she calls my name. My steps falter. The frigid air of the late September night finally registers as it bites at my skin. Slowly, I turn my head over my shoulder to see her still wrapped in that white sheet, leaning against the door frame. She looks like a goddess of the night, fallen on earth just to punish me.

Whatever sadness was on her face less than a minute ago has completely vanished now. Her eyes are colder than a snowstorm. Her beautiful face is marred by an icy smile. "Lawson," Sawyer calls, her voice clear and calm. "This isn't like all the other times in the past. When you wake up in the morning, continue to assume your decision. A month from now, when you pass me on the street, remain steady in your conviction. You're no longer welcome on my property or around me." She tilts her chin up, determination dripping out of each word. "I'm done fighting for you. I'm done loving you. I'm done."

My knees buckle as lightning strikes straight through my heart. I know I did the right thing. The very makeup of my DNA is rotten. The essence of two cowardly cheaters runs through my veins. My father said it right; I have inherited my mother's face and his twisted personality. At least, this way, she can move on and find her true happily ever after.

But even as I try to convince myself I did the right thing for once, I feel whatever ember of hope left in me crumble into dust at my feet.

Sawyer is really and truly done with me.

And I'm the only one to blame for the loss of what was never mine to begin with.

PART FOUR

A season for pain.

"Your eyes are frozen,
much like your cardboard smile,
Hair woven out of crepe paper,
colorless and dull,
You're just another lifeless doll,
Witness to an avalanche of rocks
Slamming against hopeful thoughts.
Icy knives stabbed into walls of dust,
Star dust or maybe of melted snow,
They guide you like the North Star
Rising only in the darkest of dreams.

When you loved me,
I was asleep."

SAWYER CARTER

Chapter Forty

Sawyer

My forty-eight hours of wallowing are soon coming to an end. That's all I'm allowing myself. After a pitiful night of crying and sobbing and regretting all my life choices, I woke up yesterday with a migraine determined to kill me and swollen eyes. For the first time in forever, I called in sick at work. The daycare will still run without me. I deserved to take a day to put myself back to rights.

The leftover tequila from our friendship-bender weeks ago winked at me from the door of my fridge, but I skipped right over it. As tempting as it was to drink myself stupid, I knew I'd cave and call him, begging him to reconsider. So I made the wise and mature choice to spend the day in bed, crying, sleeping, and eating my way to an ice cream induced diabetes.

My poetry mocked me from the shelves, all the rhymes, all the verses dedicated to him. So this morning, I wiped clean my off-white shelves of his mark, placed my notebooks in storage boxes, and heaved them all up in the attic. Let the dust settle on them as I hope it settles over the remains of my broken heart. If my heart doesn't kill me first with the way it's been aching beneath my ribs.

I should have known better.

This is what I get for setting my sights on the heartbreaker of Lost Hope.

There's nothing special about a wilted wallflower to make a man like him change his ways and settle down. Whatever magic karma is left in the world, twisting around bad boys' minds and making them fall for the washed-out, understated girl, it's all used up in romance books. Bitterness makes my eyes sting again, and tears leak unbidden. I've cried more in the past two days than I've cried my whole life. The bastard had the audacity to tell me he loves me. In one breath, he loves me. In the second, he rips my heart out of my chest. What an inking joke.

I haven't left the bed since I saw him walk away from me, except for the mandatory trips to the fridge for more ice cream and my shelving rampage. Even my anger was short-lived. As soon as the last box was stowed away between thick cobwebs and dust motes, I dived back between the sheets still smelling like him and—you guessed it—cried my eyes out.

I'm hollow—all wrapping paper and no substance.

For a short month, I've been happy. As happy as I've seen my friends and family be. Although timid in my hopes for our future, I could still see it as I laid my head down at night. I fell asleep on images of the three of us living together, loving together, growing stronger.

Now I don't even know how to pretend Ryker is just another one of my students.

How do I walk on the street and pass by Maddox and look the other way?

My only saving grace is HeeBee's opening day is closer than ever. I'll be too busy for the next year, ensuring it's up and running, dealing more with the administrative side than the classroom. The less I'm around him and Ryker, the faster I'll heal.

A tendril of resolve curls in the pit of my stomach. Yes, HeeBee will keep me so busy, I won't have time to think or remember my broken heart. So what if all my hopes and dreams are lying in a shattered pile at Maddox's feet?

It's this thought what gets me out of bed and through the fastest shower I've ever taken. My mind is blank as I rip the sheets off my bed and throw them in the laundry with bleach. No softener and no other frilly-scented liquids. I'll burn the smell of him from my bed if I must.

The air in my little cottage is stifling. Everywhere I look I see Maddox, his eyes drinking me in, his rumbly chuckle vibrating through the walls. I need to get out of here before my brain becomes oxygen-deprived. Searching frantically through my closet, I throw on a pair of warm leggings and a knee-length knitted sweater. Not concerned with my hair, I tie it up in a messy bun atop my head, then quickly shrug on a jacket and slip into a pair of flats. I barely remember to fish out my keys from the bowl at the entrance and my phone in my haste to leave the house.

The sun is close to setting, the air chilly and crisp. Most of the trees in town are painted in happy shades of yellow and orange, while the mountains keep their dark greens. Any other time, I would've taken a moment to welcome the fall. Now, all I want is rain and darkness to match the way I feel inside—barren, bereft, colorless.

With my head down and my hands shoved in the pockets of my jacket, I walk the distance to HeeBee's. The new daycare center used to be my happy place. Every tiny progress getting me closer to opening day brought me such joy. My soul needs some joy right now. I need a hug and for someone to promise me everything will be okay. Instead, I'm too ashamed to reach out to my family and friends. I'll have to settle with the half-hour walk and pray it numbs me enough not to cry anymore.

Logically, I know I'll get over him. I think. I hope. But my heart is screaming, *"Ink logic!"* No one has ever made me feel the way Maddox does. He owns my firsts, my highest highs and my lowest lows. He owns me. Like a fool with blinders on, I let myself fall. And now I don't see how I'm going to climb my way back up.

Sure, people go through breakups all the time. My misery is so common, I'm surprised there isn't an antiviral created for it yet. I'd be the first in line at my doctor's. "Jab me up, Doc! Make me immune to butterflies, wet panties, and dimpled cheeks," I mumble to myself.

Yes, I've reached that level of crazy.

I trip on a rogue pebble on the paved concrete and bite back a sob. Everything feels... unnecessarily unfair. I simply cannot wrap my head around his decision. Something must have happened for him to just... discard me like a used condom.

"Cheaters will always be cheaters. I don't want or deserve your forgiveness."

His words haunt my nightmares and my waking hours. Is that what he did? Did he sleep with someone else? Did he kiss someone else before he came and kissed me for the first time?

A gasp spills past my lips. Oh god, do I need to get myself tested? He didn't use a condom with me. Did he at least use one with her?

My stomach roils, turning and flipping. I stop dead in my tracks and bend over as dry heaves batter at my insides. My palms rest on my knees, supporting me upright, as I lean over a bush. Nothing but bitter bile burning my tongue comes out. I inhale deeply through my nose and exhale through my mouth as I give myself a second for my stomach to settle.

My skin itches under the knitted sweater. A rotten feeling of uncleanliness simmers inside my veins. Tears spring anew in my eyes as I straighten myself up. The world comes back into focus. Passersby give me a wide berth, their whispers and disapproval hurting like sharp stones. My head is swimming as I hurry my steps toward a side street at the edge of my neighborhood.

I don't need my reputation tarnished. People are quick to jump to conclusions. By morning, half of Lost Hope would hear I was drunk out of my mind and puking in my neighbors' gardens. Once I'm certain I'm out of direct view, I rest my back against a wall, drawing in deep, shuddered breaths.

It doesn't matter my heart is squeezed in a tight vise, sending sharp currents of pain through my chest with every second going by without Maddox coming back to me. I told him I was done. I meant it.

This back and forth between us is not healthy.

Maddox claims he loves me. You don't leave behind the people you love.

The desperate romantic in me keeps trying to understand what could've made him dump me so out of the blue. The reasons matter not one bit. Knowing won't keep me warm at night. Knowing won't bring love back to me. Sometimes, being on the outside of the truth is kinder. Either way I turn this puzzle, the missing pieces won't make the wilted wallflower bloom back to life.

"Did no one teach you dark alleyways are dangerous, darling?"

My heart just about jumps from my chest as my palm flattens over my jacket, trying to keep it contained. "Good grief," I exhale. "You scared the life out of me."

He chuckles hollowly as he steps out of the shadows. "Out for an evening stroll?"

His dark eyes assess me intently, and my throat dries out instantly. Something about the cruel smirk on his lips makes my skin pepper in goosebumps. Unease wraps around my spine as he walks closer. I inch my way against the wall, hoping to get out onto the street where at least someone might see us.

"Ntz. I wouldn't do that if I were you," he states, no inflexion in his voice. But I recognize a threat when I hear one. I also recognize the manic gleam in his dull irises, the same one he had just before Tatum got me out.

My shoulders rise around my ears as I flatten myself to the wall. I shove my hands inside my pockets, my fingers trembling against the screen of my phone. If there's one thing I learned from my sister-in-law, it's to always have a way to speed-dial in a pinch. I don't even know how many times I press against the up volume button and who'll be on the other side of the call. Worse, I don't even know if they'll pick up. But I have to try.

God, I was so stupid to think the interaction we had at the diner would be our last one.

"Do you want to go grab a cup of tea? It's a bit chilly today," I say, feigning nonchalance. I'm not fooling either of us. My voice is shaky and meek.

Before I blink once, he's in my face, his fingers digging into my shoulders. "You think I'm stupid, is that it? What's the matter, little mouse? You're afraid of the big bad sheep?"

"No, Rob. P-please... I-I..."

"I WHAT?" he shouts as he slams me against the wall. Sparks fly in front of my eyes as the back of my head connects with an uneven brick. My lungs deflate on a painful exhale as my body freezes, completely at his mercy. "Do you think I don't know about your lover?" He makes a show of looking around, laughing when he doesn't see anyone. "Where is he, anyway? Did you already bore him to death?"

"Why are you doing this?" I sob.

Rob shakes his head, his normally slicked-back hair in complete disarray as he releases one of my shoulders and stabs his fingers through the gelled tresses. "You thought you could just discard me? I move to this podunk state for you, and you repay me by fucking other men?" His fingers tighten their hold on me, digging so deep, currents of pain turn my arm numb. "I'm not going to lose my chance to join my uncle's ranks because of one unruly woman. Tell me, Sawyer, how is he going to trust me to control all the men under him, if I can't control a little sheep with no will of her own?"

My knees buckle as icy-cold fear replaces the blood in my veins. He's completely lost his mind. His ramblings make no sense. I need to do everything in my power to get out of here. There's no telling what he's capable of.

Why didn't I join Emma to her self-defense classes? I don't have false illusions I could ever overpower Rob, or anyone else for that matter, but I could've distracted him enough to run to safety.

"I'll help you," I hear myself saying. "Whatever you need to prove yourself to your uncle, I'll help you." Despite my voice cracking, I double down on my conviction. I just need him to believe me. Just for a second. "You're a smart man, Rob. I'm sure your uncle appreciates what an asset you are to him."

He pats my cheek roughly as if I were a toddler, a condescending move from a condescending asshole. But my anger is not enough to unfreeze me from the fear spreading through my limbs. He pinches my chin between his thumb and forefinger, tilting my head up so we're eye to eye. "Save your breath," he spits. "Your lies are as worthless as you are. Use your fucking head, you dumb whore. My uncle only respects powerful men. How strong do you think he'll see me, when I let you disrespect me the way you did?"

Blessed relief washes over me as he releases my shoulder, and my blood is once again free to flow through my numb arm. The pins and needles under my skin explode from my biceps through the heel of my palm. As if adrenaline is shot directly inside the chambers of my heart, as soon as I regain a modicum of feeling in my arm, I slam my hands on his chest. He's taken by surprise for a fraction of a second, forced to step back enough so I can dash away from where he's crowding me against the wall.

"HELP," I shout as I run toward the road, hope soaring under my ribs with each foot taking me closer to salvation.

The sting in my scalp stops me short, as he fists the bun atop my head and pulls me backward. "You fucking bitch" he roars. I lose my footing, and Rob takes advantage of my clumsiness, slamming me once again against the wall.

The first time, pain doesn't even register. Maybe it's the shock of seeing the gleaming silver blade in his hand. Maybe my mind is trying to spare me the hurt. My eyes follow as if in slow motion the arch of the knife as it disappears through my jacket. Time stops. My heart stalls. Oxygen is trapped inside my lungs. For one moment in time, the world doesn't spin. I'm suspended in disbelief and the complete, utter certainty I'm not leaving this alley alive.

An agonizing scream echoes between us. Belatedly, I realize I am the one screaming. When the blade leaves my body, crimson droplets stain the silver handle. Not even a blink later, it finds a new place to rip into me. My knees buckle as my lower belly catches on fire. Cried whimpers spill past my lips as I lay limp against the wall. My vision blurs, the world tilting sideways on its axis.

I force my arms to move, to fight, to stop him from plunging that knife into me over and over again. If I am to die, at least I want to die fighting for myself.

But I'm too cold. Exhaustion is paralyzing my limbs, keeping them limp at my side as I slide down the wall like the wilted wallflower I am. Icy tears pour down my cheeks while the fire in my belly grows. Blessed warm wetness spreads down my thighs, and I crumble to the dirty, dusty pavement.

The pressure around my body disappears as my lips part on a silent scream. Hindsight is twenty-twenty, especially when the Grim Reaper is storming into the alleyway for my soul. How fitting it is he looks exactly like my Maddox. At least, I'll have something pretty to look at as he carries me into the afterlife.

I should've stayed at home and drowned in a bucket of ice cream instead. It seems like a much gentler way to go.

Dirty alleyways are not poetic enough to be the place where wallflowers go to die. Silly me, why was I ever worried my broken heart would be the one to kill me?

Chapter Forty-One

Maddox

My phone vibrates in the pocket of my jeans. I throw a cautious look at my mom, knowing she'll rip me a new one if I answer it at the table, but being Chief Deputy and in charge of the Lost Hope Police Department doesn't leave me much choice. I might be doing shifts like all the deputies working under me, but some things require either my presence or the sheriff's. I don't see Richards coming all the way from Forrest Falls because answering the phone at the dinner table offends Lucy Lawson's sensibilities.

After all the shit they put me through, my parents should be goddamn grateful I'm still gracing their doorstep. Sure, I owe some damn belated apology to my mom. She's been the victim all along, instead of the villain I painted her to be. But it doesn't change the fact that their poor choices have led me to this moment. The moment I lost it all.

A peek at my screen has me biting my tongue. I hesitate to answer for a heartbeat or two. Nothing good can come out of this, I know that for a fact. But I also know I don't have it in me to just hit *ignore*. I push back from the table and hurry to the kitchen before connecting the call. My phone is plastered to my ear, my heart hammering in my chest in its desperate attempts to escape my ribcage and jump through the device straight into her soft palms.

"Hey…" I whisper, my voice soft and soothing, but the rest of my words die on my tongue.

A loud thump comes from the speaker, followed by a pained whimper. A rough voice grits from far away, *"You think I'm stupid, is that it? What's the matter, little mouse? You're afraid of the big bad sheep?"*

My blood turns to ice in my veins. A shiver runs up my spine and nausea churns in my stomach, the few bites of dinner I managed to choke down earlier sitting like lead in my gut. "Stay on the phone if you can," I bark, although I have no hope that she heard me.

A few taps of my finger against the screen bring up the map. The red dot blinks at me, mocking me with the distance between us. I have to get to her.

In three long strides, I'm back in the dining room. Three pairs of eyes fixate on me, my father lifting a questioning, bushy eyebrow. I shake my head, but I'm sure he can see in the pallor of my cheeks that something's not quite right.

Not quite right is a goddamn understatement. A fucking catastrophe is more accurate.

I kiss Ryker's forehead and bolt out the door as fast as my legs can take me. My limbs grow numb by the time I jump into my truck, turning the key so fast, for a second, I fear I broke it.

Fumbling with my phone, I somehow manage to keep my eyes on the road as I move the call on speaker and mute my microphone.

"You thought you could just discard me? I move to this podunk state for you, and you repay me by fucking other men?" His voice is muffled, sounding far away. As long as he's far from her, I still have time to reach Sawyer.

My teeth sink into my bottom lip to keep the curses at bay; to keep the rage contained. I grip the wheel so hard, my knuckles turn white. With a flick of my finger, I turn the warning lights on but keep the siren silent. My ears are attuned to the harsh exchange on the other side of the call.

"HELP!" Sawyer shouts, and I just about rip the wheel off the dashboard. Helplessness, guilt, and despair are clogging my throat.

This is all my fucking fault. What have I done?

Sawyer was supposed to be with me right now. We could've been cuddled up on my couch, watching a movie. Better yet, hiding between the sheets of my bed, naked and in love. She would've been safe.

Why is she with him now? I'll drive my fist through the windshield if he asked her out and she accepted. My jealousy is as unwelcome as it's unjust. Technically, she's a free woman. It's why I did what I did, so she'd be happy. Instead... all I've achieved is forcing us into a world of misery and putting Sawyer in danger.

The blood-curdling scream sounding from the speaker of my phone as my truck eats up the miles between us has my heart stop in my chest. Fear, unlike anything else I've ever felt, courses through my veins. My foot presses down the acceleration until the pedal is one with the floor. I'm flying through the streets, praying that the woman I love is safe, and no one gets in my goddamn way.

When I finally reach her neighborhood on the outskirts of Lost Hope, the blue dot showing my location nearly overlaps the red one, and I brake hard. My tires squeal on the gravel as I park my car on the side of the road and jump out, leaving the engine running.

Her whimpers reach my ears, and all I see is red. I'll fucking kill him. I'll rip him apart limb from limb. A high-pitched ringing sounds in my ears, drowning out any other noises as I tackle the motherfucker to the ground and start pummeling his fucking face. He tries to fight back, but I'm fueled by pure madness. His feeble attempts to shield his head are no match for the inferno raging up inside of me. When I'm done with him, there won't be a goddamned cell left for DNA match.

He shifts his arm, a silvery flash penetrating the veil of red settled over my eyes. I freeze. My heart stops. The ringing in my ears ceases abruptly. The world fucking stills with that one flash of the streetlight hitting the bloodied knife he's fisting.

No.

NO.

Fuck. *NO.*

He cries out when I twist his wrist until I hear a snap, and the knife drops to the ground. I kick it with my boot away from him in my haste to get to her. My hands shake, desperate to stop the relentless crimson river spilling out of her through my fingers and onto the dirty, dusty pavement.

I unzip her jacket, only to be filled with horror at the sight of her frayed knitted sweater and the blood soaking through the material. I shove it up to reveal the chopped-up mess her lower abdomen is. With one hand, I rip the Henley over my head and press it down against her wounds, trying to slow the bleeding down.

Numbness has me rooted to the spot as I quickly dial on my phone.

"9-1-1. What's your emergency?"

"Stab wound victim, female, twenty-six of age, actively bleeding and unconscious. Her name is Sawyer Carter." My tongue feels sluggish in my mouth, three times its normal size as I rattle off the street name and my badge ID. "Please, send help ASAP. She'll bleed out soon."

"Understood, Chief Deputy. EMTs are on the way. I've notified Forrest Falls General of your arrival. Please, remain on the line."

Remain on the line, my ass. I need all the help I can get. With my free hand, I dial up another number as my other keeps pressing against Sawyer's abdomen. Her eyes are closed, and her skin is turning sickly white.

"Lawson, to what do I owe the honor?" comes through the voice of the man who'll kill me dead as soon as he faces me. So he should.

"It's Sawyer," I croak. "She's been stabbed. EMTs are on their way. Meet us at Forrest Falls General."

"The fuck you've just said?"

"IT'S SAWYER!" I sob as the reality of her dying right in front of my eyes hits me with the power of a freight train. "I didn't get to her in time."

Her chest rises shakily on a deep inhale, and my own blood drains to the pavement as her head falls slack against her shoulder. "Fuuuuuuck! Gooooood, no! Get here, Carter!" I order through the phone. Turning toward where I left the asshole, it dawns on me that he ran like the coward he is. "I'm going to fucking murder him, rip him limb to limb, godfuck-ingdammit!"

My stomach turns as complete silence engulfs us in the alleyway. No more wheezed breaths, no more strained gurgles. My phone drops as I scramble with my fingers on her neck, trying to feel for a pulse, but nothing registers. Not a flutter, not a faint beat, nothing.

"Don't leave me, Fairy! Hold on just a little longer. Help's on the way. Please, baby, hold on. I'm here," I plead as I lean down and, tilting her head up to clear her airways, press my mouth to hers, breathing for her.

I'm torn with indecision. If I lift my hand from her abdomen, she might bleed out. If I don't start CPR, too much time is passing without her heart pumping oxygen through her body. Sirens sound in the distance, and I draw in a sharp breath as I press the heel of my palm over the center of her chest and interlock my fingers. It makes me absolutely sick to my stomach to sing in my head "Stayin' alive", but the beat helps me keep my rhythm as I press down hard and fast.

The sirens grow closer as the paramedics finally arrive. Sweat peppers on my forehead, my biceps burning through the motions, but I won't stop. I cannot stop until I feel her heart beating again. Pump her heart, breathe for her, repeat. Footsteps echo in the alleyway. I don't dare blink, but keep humming, keep pressing, keep willing her with all my might to gasp, cough, breathe, twitch. Anything.

"Maddox!" A hand clamps down on my shoulder, but I pay it no atten-tion. "Listen to me, I'll take over compressions. But you gotta let us work. We need to know everything, you hear me?"

I huff as my nose starts itching and my eyes sting with all the sweat pouring down my face. "Yeah," I bite back. Even though I'm not sure I can. Everything inside of me is screaming that as soon as I lift my hands off her, she'll be gone. And I don't know how to live in a world where she doesn't exist anymore.

Rowan must see the conflict playing out on my face; he bands his arms around me as soon as someone else kneels on the other side of Sawyer. He pulls me away from her, and I scramble back at her side, fighting his constraint. "Fuck, let me help her," I shout.

"You did, man. You did. Now let us help her." He turns me around, and I pull away, trying to reach Sawyer again.

There's no moving the Irish devil as he clamps down both hands on my shoulders and keeps me rooted on the spot. "Listen to me, I've been right where yer are. Yer dinnae need to look now. We'll get Miss Carter on a stretcher and into the ambulance. Behave, let us work, and come with us." I hear his words, but they don't register. All my senses are attuned to the bleeding woman lying lifeless on the ground. A sharp slap to my cheek gets some rationality back into me. "Lawson!" Rowan barks. "Pull yerself together, you bloody eejit. Freak out on yer own time."

I nod as if in slow motion. My body feels trapped under water. Regardless of how much I fight to pull myself to the surface, the chasm grows deeper and deeper. That rotten son of a bitch might have held the knife, but my choices got her here. My stomach churns, and before I realize what I'm doing, I run to the mouth of the alley and empty my stomach onto the pavement. The unease swirling in my chest doesn't end, but spreads to my limbs, threatening to consume me whole.

"There ya go! Drink now." Rowan passes me a bottle of water, and I want to shout at him for looking after me. I'm not the one dying right now, even though I'm pretty certain if Sawyer doesn't make it, I won't either. My body might be alive, but inside I'll die right there next to her. "Don't make me force it down yer throat," he barks, twisting the lid on the bottle and pushing it in my direction again.

I take it, swishing a mouthful to clean myself before spitting it on the ground. The next gulps I swallow, just to get him to let me be and look after Sawyer instead. My eyes narrow as I convey as much to him.

"Nah. She's well cared for. Now tell us what you know."

I notice one of my deputies behind Rowan, and I motion him here. I want an investigation started straight away. Regardless of the outcome, that sick son of a bitch is not getting away with this. I don't linger anymore as I see Sawyer being wheeled to the back of an ambulance and spit out everything I know as I follow the stretcher.

"Stop right there," Rowan snaps. I swear, if this motherfucker doesn't get out of my way, he'll need another ambulance to collect him.

"That's the love of my fucking life right there!" I shout, pointing to where the doors are about to close on a white-as-a-ghost Sawyer. "Get out of my goddamn face, Rowan, or else I'm not responsible for my actions."

The asshole does the complete opposite of everything I ask and gets in my face instead. "If anyone knows what you're going through, it's me. You're in no condition to drive. My colleagues have her. Her heart is weak but beating on its own again. Give me your keys and we'll get there as soon as they do. I promise!"

I push him away and rush to the ambulance before they shut the door in my face. One-handed, I pat around for my keys, throwing them behind my shoulder as I force my way into the cramped space.

"I'll be good," I say to Gregson, the paramedic in charge. "I won't get in the way. But she needs to know she's not alone. Sawyer needs me to be with her."

A heavy exhale fills the rig, immediately drowned out by the sound of a door slamming and the sirens crying into the silence of the evening. My bloody fingers tangle in her hair, my eyes focused only on the monitor counting her weak heartbeats. "We're getting you through this, little fairy. Just hold on a little while longer."

Chapter Forty-Two

Maddox

The thirty minutes it took us to get to Forrest Falls Hospital have been the longest of my life. My only saving grace has been that faint but steady line, moving up and down on the screen as it monitored Sawyer's heart.

The paramedics don't wait for me to exit the ambulance, immediately wheeling her out as soon as the rig stops in front of the Incoming ER entrance. I jump out, bursting through the sliding doors as they open, and follow the army of doctors and nurses surrounding the stretcher.

They shout orders at each other, most of the verbiage flying right over my head. I don't care what they say as long as they keep her alive. I feel like I'm having an out-of-body experience as I watch them working on her, while I'm rooted on the spot in the middle of the bustling ER. I'd give anything to be able to help her. I'd trade places with her in a heartbeat.

"Maddox!"

I sway on my feet as the noises of the emergency room rush through me and turn toward the person calling my name. Beth Anderson waves me to the reception desk, her curly hair in complete disarray atop her head. I give a numb shake of my head. I'm not leaving Sawyer out of my sight.

She sees my resolve and jogs to me, her stethoscope bouncing against the light blue of her scrubs. "I came as soon as I heard. Do you need anything?"

I shake my head again, my eyes hot and brimming with unshed tears. My teeth bite into the inside of my cheek. I can't lose it now. She needs me to stay strong for her. If Sawyer is strong and fighting for her life, then I need to be stronger. I can't fail her now.

Beth snakes her hand around my arm, squeezing gently. "They're taking her directly to an OR. You cannot go there." I grunt, dismissing her words.

Who's going to stop me?

"None of that. I know you're scared for her, but causing a commotion, all it'll do is delay her getting help." She pulls at my arm when the army of doctors working around the stretcher Sawyer lays in start wheeling her down the hall. My feet immediately walk me in her direction. "Maddox! We may be a small hospital, but we have excellent doctors here. You wanna help? She'll need blood. What's your type?"

"O neg," I mumble. They can take all my blood as far as I care. If I can do anything at all to help her, then let them dry me up.

"Perfect! Come with me."

This time, when she pulls at my arm, I let myself follow her. "I'm not taking you far. You want to be near Sawyer, and I understand that. I've already arranged for a private waiting room for her family."

My feet are wooden as she pulls me behind her until we're clearing some swinging doors. The noise of the ER fades in the ten-by-ten waiting room. I let myself collapse into a chair, my entire body sagging as the adrenaline drains from my veins.

I'm about to lose Sawyer, and it's all my fault.

Beth is fleeting around me as I stare numbly at the cream-colored wall opposite me. I don't flinch as a warm, damp cloth scrubs at my face, neck, and arms. There's no hitch in my breath when a tourniquet is fastened on my biceps, or when the needle prickles at my skin as it sinks into a vein.

"Once I'm done, I need you to stay seated," Beth instructs. "I'll bring you a cup of coffee and a chocolate bar."

"I'm not hungry."

Beth smacks her lips together as she fidgets with the bag rapidly filling with my blood. "And I don't care. You're donating blood. If you think I'm not going to force-feed you, you have another think coming." The deep crimson color reminds me of the puddle Sawyer was lying in. So much blood, everywhere. On the pavement, on her clothes, on my hands... She's so slight. How can she ever survive losing so much of it?

"How did you know?" I question. I need to call more people. My arm twitches as I make to search for my phone.

"Don't move your arm yet," Beth chastises me. "My boss called. I'm due to start at HeeBee in November. When she's heard Sawyer's name... Anyway, she told me."

I can't bear to think about how many lives Sawyer has touched. All the children in her classroom, their parents, her friends, her family. Ryker. Me.

An eerie chill spreads through my arms, expanding over my chest. Only my eyes burn as I finally let the tears fall. I'm not too proud to let *this* agony show. She's in the OR, alone and brave, as the doctors work to save her life.

I should be with her, holding her hand. Hell, I should've been with her today, and then none of this would have happened.

I hiss through my teeth when Beth removes the needle from my vein. "You're all done." She pushes the chocolate bar in front of me. "Eat this as I have the blood signed up into our blood bank. I'll be back soon."

She leaves me with a pat on my shoulder. I immediately shove the chocolate into my mouth, tasting nothing but ash and regret as I search for my phone.

"Fuck!" I choke when the stupid device is nowhere to be found. Through the haze numbing my mind, I remember it falling when I started doing CPR. I have no way of contacting anyone. "Stupid good-for-nothing asshole!"

I prop my elbows on my spread-out knees, letting my head hang down as despair and frustration bubble up inside of me. Here I am, a grown-ass man, crying my heart out in a deserted hospital waiting room.

I don't know how much time has passed, too lost to my self-loathing and bitter regrets, when the door opens and a middle-aged man in a pristine lab coat walks in.

"Family of Miss Sawyer Carter?"

I push to my feet, even though my knees are shaking so badly, I'm sure I'm one second away from collapsing. Like a dumb twat, I wave. "I... uhm... I'm her boyfriend," I croak.

His brow furrows as he regards me silently. "I'm Doctor Fieldson, head of the ER. Mr..." he trails off.

"Lawson. Tell me!" I demand, "Is Sawyer alive?"

"Mr. Lawson, since you are not an immediate family member, I'm afraid I cannot disclose any information to you about our patient's status. We'll have to get in touch with her emergency contact and have them come in."

I see red. He can't just leave and not tell me if she's at least still breathing. "I'm her fiancé."

He shakes his head. "Mr. Lawson, lying won't get you far. I'll come back once I get in touch with her family."

I don't know when I'm moving, but all the sudden, my bloody fingers are wrapped around his white coat. "Please!" I beg. "Just tell me she's still alive. Please. I don't need to know anything else, just that her heart's still beating."

Whatever he sees on my face—the absolute heartbreak I'm sure is tattooed on my forehead—has him softening. He gives me a barely-there nod.

"She's still in surgery." With that, he removes my hand from his lab coat and strolls out the door.

"What the fuck does that mean?" I mumble to myself as I pace the length of the waiting room. Agony bites at my heels. I don't dare feel any semblance of relief. Not until she's awake and smiling at me. For how long was I performing CPR? For how long has she been deprived of oxygen? Even if she survives the surgery, would she still be my Sawyer?

"It doesn't matter, you asshole!" I reply out loud to the questions tormenting me. She's my Sawyer, regardless. If I have to spend the rest of my days caring for her and tending to her every need, then that's what I'll do. Anything. Everything. If only she'd live.

The door opens once again, and I turn quickly. "Do you have any upda-" My question dies on my lips as instead of the doctor, my eyes find Tatum. I freeze on the spot. Every muscle in my body tenses and readies, bracing for the punch that surely is to come.

He takes a step closer, clear-blue eyes regarding me coolly, mouth downturned in a frown. I don't back down. Whatever punishment he has to dole out, I'll take it like a man. He can't hate me worse than I hate myself right now. My entire body seizes when he's on me a second later. Maevis's shocked gasp barely registers as the man who looked down on me with contempt and disgust my entire life gives me a brotherly hug I never deserved.

The pat of his palm on my back is what breaks me. My knees buckle, and I sag against him as completely unmanly sobs rattle my ribcage. "I'm s-sorry. I'm so so sorry. Wasn't fast enough. Didn't get there in time. I'm so sorry."

A second pair of arms wind around my waist, holding me upright. Not long after, two more come on each side of us. And I let myself fall apart. For a brief minute, in a sterile waiting room of a hospital, I let the horror and fear wash over me. The woman I am madly and desperately in love with is fighting for her life, on an operating table that seems too far out of my reach. I can't protect her. I cannot offer any words of encouragement. Within the circle of unlikely friends and family surrounding me, I let myself despair.

I have no pride.

Sawyer is special to each of us—a sister, a friend, an auntie, a teacher, the reason I breathe. And yet, everyone right now is rallied around me.

I thought seeing my mother with another man would be the darkest moment of my life. Picking up my drunk-ass father from the floor and cleaning up his vomit would be the lowest of lows I'd hit.

Amidst the devastation and pain bringing me to my knees, and the tears falling shamelessly, I also allow myself to draw strength from their support. When I have a modicum of control over myself, I open my eyes and take Tatum in.

"I love her," I state.

"I know," he replies, no trace of judgment or anger on his face.

"I'll never be good enough for her, but I'll never stop fighting to deserve her." If I'm trying to convince myself or him, I've no idea, but I have never been clearer about anything in my life.

"I know."

"She'll be the happiest woman to walk this Earth." Or I'll die trying.

This earns me a smirk. "Impossible. My wife is. But I'll take second place for my baby sister."

"You knew," I state the obvious.

Tatum's smirk deepens. "Everyone seems to forget I'm an observant motherfucker." He sobers up as he takes a step back and grips my shoulders. His blue eyes bore into mine, serious and deadly. "My sister always sees the best in everyone. I feared what would become of her because she chose to see the best in you." I tense under his hold, his words like acid against my skin, but he doesn't release me. "She's the peacemaker, so don't walk all over her. She might be soft on the outside, but I trust her judgement. Sawyer never takes a step without proper consideration. Being with you might very well be the only selfish and reckless decision my sister has made in her entire life." He closes his eyes and sighs deeply, his fingers digging into my shoulders. "I saw her coming out of her shell. I saw her happier than she's ever been. And if you were the one building up her confidence and happiness..."

"It was all her," I deny. All I got her was hurt and fighting for her life.

From the corner of my eye, I see Cole moving behind him—a silent wall of support. Tatum smirks. "Not even *you* are stupid enough to hurt my baby sister. But break her heart and..." He shrugs as he releases me. "I don't advise you to fuck around and find out, though."

Lalah pats Tate's back. "You were doing so well until the threats." She rolls her eyes. "That anger management therapy really paid off. Now, if you're done bromancing each other, I've got some clothes for you, Madd," she says, breaking our group hug.

I realize I'm still wearing the clothes caked in Sawyer's blood. I swallow thickly as I take a step away from Tatum. "Thanks," I reply, my voice cracking anew. Whatever lightness was in the room a second ago dissipates with the realization that this horror of a night is not over yet. Not by far.

He slaps my shoulder. "Go change. Our parents are on the way. My mom doesn't need to see..." He gestures toward the gruesome painting splattered over my chest and legs.

I take the bag from Lalah with a quiet thanks and slip out of the room, following the signs to the nearest bathroom. The fluorescent lights in the small space flicker, sending tendrils of pain through my head. I beeline to the sink, my eyes focused on the white porcelain. There's no need to look at myself in the mirror. I don't need any more memories of this nightmare.

Hot water spills in my palms as I gather as much soap as I can hold and scrub away all the congealed blood staining my hands. The water turns red, then pink, gradually lightening until it falls clear down the drain. I switch it to cold and splash it over my face, pressing the pad of my palms against my throbbing eyes.

Dark spots dance in my vision as I shed the stained clothes, the fabric rigid with dried blood and sticking to my skin. I wet some paper towels to clean up, although I could use a shower—or maybe a bleach bath. Once I'm somewhat decent, I quickly don the sweatpants and hoodie Lalah packed for me, then slip my feet into a pair of clean sneakers. I hesitate for just one second before folding up the horror clothes. These will have to go into evidence most likely, even though I'd happily set fire to them in the middle of the hospital. Preferably, using that sentient poison on humanity as fuel.

I tie the bag up, dropping it under a chair as I return to the waiting room. "Any news?" I ask. Maevis and Tatum sit together, little Lami strapped to Mae's chest, sleeping soundly.

"No," Lalah exhales from the other side of the room, burrowing closer to Cole.

Tatum clears his throat, a tendril of dread curling in the pit of my stomach as his eyes pin me to my seat. "I'm Sawy's emergency contact. When we got here, we were told she'd been stabbed four times in her lower abdomen." He fidgets around as Mae hugs Lami closer to her. "She's been given five units of blood, but she was losing more than they could replenish."

I'm on my feet in the next second as the room blurs out in front of me. "Don't say it!" I shout. "You came in here and looked me in the eye and let me believe she's still alive?"

"Lawson!" Cole snaps. My ears are ringing as I sway on my feet, the floor disappearing from under the soles of my sneakers. "Sawyer is still alive. They're still operating on her."

Through no will of my own, I'm walked backward until once again I'm seated. Cole forces my head between my knees as I drag in greedy gulps of air. Belatedly, I realize my outburst woke Lami up, her little cries echoing between the sterile walls despite Mae's attempts to soothe her.

"Goddammit. Do you think the hospital would still be standing if they'd lost my baby sister?" Tatum bites. Through the heavy pounding in my ears, I register footsteps moving away from me and the click of the door as it closes behind them.

"Are you ready to hear the rest?" Lalah asks softly, her warm hand moving up and down on my back.

I try to stand up straight, but I'm met with resistance. "Stay like this," Cole grumbles. "Trust me."

I nod against his hold. Lalah sucks in a sharp breath next to me. "I'm not really comfortable telling you this. Sawyer should know first. She should be given the time to come to terms with it once she's all better. It should be her choice to share."

Cole sighs. "Supernova, if you were the one in that operating room, I'd want to know. Sawyer needs support. How can he support her if he doesn't know?"

"Would someone just fucking tell me already? Tell me what I did to her," I snap, my fingers digging into the material of my sweatpants as I claw at them in preparation for the blow that is to come.

"They tried to save her uterus, but it wouldn't stop bleeding. The surgeon felt the best option would be to perform a partial hysterectomy."

For the second time tonight, I empty my stomach with no preamble.

If she lives through this, she'll never forgive me.

Sawyer loves children more than anything. I saw her with Lami; I saw her with her students. I know for a fact she wants to become a mother.

And my selfish actions took all that away from her.

Chapter Forty-Three

Sawyer

I'm encased in ice. Everything hurts. Whispers and distant beeping rouse me. I can't move. My eyelids refuse to respond to my commands. Where am I? My heart speeds up as one by one, memories of the confrontation with Rob surface from the haze keeping my mind captive.

Flashes of the argument return to me. The fear I felt when I realized he had stabbed me. Am I dead? Surely, the afterlife would not feel so cold. It shouldn't hold so much pain.

My throat constricts painfully, and I gag around whatever is lodged inside. My stomach roils as I cough and dry heave, currents of pain swirling in my lower belly.

"Relax, Miss Carter," a raspy voice orders me gently. "Easy now, breathe through your nose. This will feel uncomfortable, but we're removing your endotracheal tube now. You're doing so great."

The praise doesn't register as all my insides are suctioned out through my throat. *Please, please, stop.* The burn is too much. I'm too hollow. *Leave me alone.*

More coughs batter at my ribcage, my dried-out throat contracting painfully with every one of my forced inhales.

"Nurse Everton, please administer three milligrams of morphine."

Fingers probe around my neck as light shines in my unseeing eyes.

"Saturation?"

"Ninety-three and rising," a soft, feminine voice replies.

"Vitals?"

Quiet. Please, no more. Ice is climbing up my spine, and I want to disappear inside of it. *Leave me alone.*

More ice is pressing against my chest, in small pin pricks, a million at the time. "Lung function sounds good. No wheezing. You're doing so well, Miss Carter. Check her ABG. I want to see the results ASAP."

"Yes, Doctor," the same soft voice replies.

Blessed numbness weighs me down, and I let myself drift under the surface. "Miss Carter, do you want to say hello to us?"

No. I want quiet.

WARMTH ENGULFS MY PALM. It feels so good, so welcome amidst all the ice. *More, I need more.* I grab at it, trying to get a good hold. I'm sick of the cold.

"Oh god! Little fairy, are you awake?" The gravelly voice reaches me under the surface, drawing me out. "DOCTOR!" I wince as the gravel stabs at my eardrums and moan my displeasure.

"Baby," the voice says, a rough sniffle cracking those low, delicious sounds, "open those beautiful eyes for me, Sawyer. Please."

I want to. I know if I can open my eyes, I can break through the ice. My eyelids flutter but refuse to obey me.

"Baby, please. Are you awake? Can you squeeze my hand?"

More warmth coils around my wrist, my fingers brushing against crushed velvet as I fight to get a good grip. Anything else is just disconnected, out of my grasp.

"DOCTOR! BLAKELY!"

A whimper rips from my raw throat as my head throbs with each shout. I yank at my hand, the need to press it against my eyes uncontrollable, but it barely twitches, too heavy to move.

"Hush. I'm sorry, I won't shout anymore," he whispers now, and I let the low, melodic tones of his voice comfort me. So warm, so cozy, I want to nuzzle my cheek against it and have it soothe all my hurts.

"What happened?" a soft feminine voice asks, one that seems so familiar.

"She's awake. She squeezed my hand." The hope in his reply is unmistakable.

"Miss Carter, can you open your eyes for me?"

Despite my best efforts, my eyelids are still sewn shut. Exhaustion creeps on me, dragging me back under, even as I fight to stay close to his voice. He's my warmth; the dark depths hold only ice.

"I swear she squeezed my hand."

"Mr. Lawson, it might have been a muscle spasm. Sometimes these happen. She's lost a lot of blood. Her body needs time to regain strength.

I know the wait is frustrating, but she's healing now. Her vitals are strong, she's breathing on her own," the soft-spoken woman replies.

The warmth around my palm disappears, and I scream my protest. *Give it back.* All that comes out is a muffled moan.

"Blakely, there was no muscle spasm. Try it for yourself." A silken petal wraps around my palm, balmy and soothing. "Baby, if you're awake, can you move your fingers again? Please, for me?"

I try. Of course, I try. How can I ever refuse him anything when he's asking so nicely?

"That's great, Mr. Lawson. She's definitely responding to you. It looks like her sedation is slowly wearing off. I'll let Doctor Richards know of her progress. Continue to talk to her. Be patient. She's coming back to you."

I'm here. I'm right here.

Frustration mounts inside of me. Despite my best efforts to reach him, fatigue drags me back under the surface. In the dark depths, there's only one silver lining. Crushed velvet is once more wrapped around my palm, here to stay.

"Is Miss Sawy going to be okay, Daddy?" a sugary-sweet voice asks in a whisper-shout so familiar the backs of my eyes burn with longing.

"She will be. And she's going to love the stuffed quill you got for her," Maddox replies.

What is he doing here? My heart starts pounding in my chest as the memory of him turning his back on me and disappearing into the night plays behind my closed eyelids.

"She looks like the Sleeping Beauty." There's awe in Ryker's voice. My lips twitch up, a smile forcing its way through the exhaustion. We read *Sleeping Beauty* just a couple of days ago. The same day his father broke my heart.

What are they doing here?

"Did you gived her a kiss, Daddy? The pwincess always wakes up when the pwince kisses her."

My stomach flips as Ryker's Rs once again are lost to his childhood. Maddox's low chuckle hits me in the center of my chest, warming me up from the inside out. It's so cold in my bedroom. "You think it would work?"

"Yes, silly. You didn't readed in school?"

Soft, hot lips press against my forehead, and I sigh with pleasure.

"Did it wok?" A sharp clap echoes around me.

"Hmm, not yet. Maybe you should kiss her. I'm sure she'd like that very much."

"But I'm not s'pposed to mawy Miss Sawy. You are," Ryker accuses, his displeasure clear in the high pitch of his voice. "You kissed her all wong."

"Show me how it's done then, you little know-it-all." The bed dips around me. "Careful, champ. Her belly is hurt." My cheek tingles under the pressure of a short, wet kiss. The smack of his mouth against my skin makes the warmth in my chest spread further.

"Look, Daddy. She's smiling," Ryker squeals. "It's working, Daddy. Try again." I'm all pride and confusion as his Rs roll with no hesitation.

Maybe I had a nightmare. Maybe Maddox didn't really break up with me. His minty breath washes over my face. My heart slams against my ribcage as sparks burst to life across my skin. His plump lips feather over mine. He chastely touches his mouth to mine, and my lips part, welcoming his kiss. "I love you," he whispers. "Come back to me."

A shrill beeping startles me, and my eyelids finally spring open. Icy-blue eyes, tired and red-rimmed, find mine. "Maddox?" I croak. "What happened?"

"Sawyer, did you hear me?" Doctor Richards asks as she crosses her legs.

No, I didn't. My eyes are trained on the window behind her chair, staring unseeing at the dark, gray sky. I'm barren. Hollow. I feel the tears falling, burning a path of agony on my cheeks, but I do nothing to wipe them away. What's the point? It won't bring my uterus back. It won't rewind time and heal the stab wounds that left me bereft and wilted.

I'm exhausted. All I want is to curl up under the scratchy hospital blanket and sleep. They told me I slept a lot. Three days, to be exact. Two of which I spent with a tube shoved down my throat because I couldn't breathe on my own. They removed it when my lungs suddenly remembered how to perform their most basic function unventilated. Everyone was hopeful I'd wake up then. But I slept more.

I'm sure Doctor Richards is a very nice person. But she's blunt too. Too blunt for me to face her on my own. She still cleared the room, demanding Maddox and my family give us some privacy. At first, I craved it. The pity on my brother's face grated at my skin. The fright in my parents' eyes had guilt choking me up. But it was the hope and love practically pouring in waves out of Maddox what hurt the most.

My memories returned almost immediately after I woke up. Him dumping me; Rob stabbing me.

Even with all the pain I felt having him so near but knowing he was not mine—not anymore—I still wished he'd be here, holding my hand, when Dr. Richards told me my heart stopped twice and my uterus was gone. And then she went into details.

I'm not even sure if the blood flowing in my veins is mine anymore. I've lost a lot, she'd said. Whatever a lot I lost, new blood was transfused to me.

It's a weird feeling. My body feels foreign to me, while gratitude for all the people who donated and indirectly helped keep me alive washes over me. I have a hard time reconciling my emotions.

"When am I going to be released?" I ask instead.

"Sawyer, you've gone through a major ordeal. You just woke up this morning." She sighs, brushing invisible lint from her dark skirt with her fingers. "If your vitals remain strong, your oxygen saturation unchanged, and there are no signs of infection in the next four days, we'll determine a course of action then."

She pushes to her feet, her dark brown bob swishing around her face. "Try to get some rest. Tomorrow, we'll discuss more about how the supracervical hysterectomy affects your life. Our on-call psychologist will join us, too."

"What's there to talk about? I can't ever have children. But hey, at least I won't get any more periods. Yay me."

She pulls the blanket away, exposing my mid-section. After donning a pair of surgical gloves, she gently peels off the bandages covering my lower abdomen. "Your incisions are healing nicely. There's no excess swelling, no signs of infection, which is what we want to see. Our plastician did a great job closing the stab wounds, so scarring should be minimal."

"Excellent. I can wear a bikini when I go to the waterfall."

Without a word, she changes the bandages and tucks in the blanket around me. "We'll keep the course of antibiotics for the next four days as well, and we'll repeat your blood work in the morning, just to ensure we're staying on top of things." With a snap, she sheds the gloves, throwing them in a nearby bin. "The loss you've suffered is immense, and you'll have a lot of work ahead of you on your path to healing, physically and mentally. Don't hold back your grief, Sawyer. But through it, don't forget you're still alive."

I wish I could turn my back to her, but the pain in my lower belly keeps me rooted to the bed in the same position. I'll just have to settle on pulling the blanket over my eyes. Out of sight, out of mind.

Childish, I realize.

But right now, I'm childless. And will forever remain childless. This is my pain to live with, and if I want to hide away and lick my wounds, that's what I'll do.

I'm just about done with today. Why is it so hard for everyone to understand all I want is to be alone?

The first thing I did when I woke up this morning was to make it very clear to Doctor Richards that Maddox was not allowed to visit me. Petty, I know. But he broke up with me. I don't need his pity or whatever he thinks he owes me. All I want from him is space and distance.

I'm not going to lie and say my heart didn't hurt as he shouted his disagreement just outside my door when he was denied entry. But if I want to heal, if I want to move on, I need to do it far away from him.

My entire life is turned upside-down. All the dreams I held for myself are gone, just like that. I couldn't sleep last night, despite bone-deep exhaustion nipping at my skin. I've never not seen children in my future. Whenever I thought of what my life would be like, my arms were full of babies.

Grief has found a home in me now as I mourn the loss of all my future children, my actual future, and everything I held true for myself.

As the darkest hours dripped by, I played the blame game over and over. Would I still be in this hospital bed if I'd been upfront with my family about Rob's return? If I weren't such a coward when we first bumped into each other in Billings and told him I was not interested in reconnecting?

What will I do when I'm released from the hospital? As my body heals, and I learn to adjust to my new reality, how will I live knowing my own home isn't safe? The streets of my neighborhood, so familiar to me, now hold danger in their hidden corners and eerie shadows.

They haven't caught him yet.

His family is powerful. It'll be my word against his. They'll hide him and fabricate stories about me, to paint me in the most unfavorable light. I know this, just as I know I'll never be a mother. I hate him. Sure, Rob meant to kill me, that much I'm certain of. Instead, he killed my will to live.

His pettiness won't let him rest until he finishes the job.

And I'm afraid I'll welcome him.

"Sawyer, are you up for some visitors?" Blakely, my self-appointed nurse and bodyguard, asks from the entrance to my hospital room.

No. Fake smile at the ready, I arrange the scratchy blanket over my feet. My abdomen twinges and throbs as I push myself higher on the pillow. "Sure am."

Lalah barrels through the door, all dark clothes, dark hair, and purple highlights, arms full of bags, which she promptly drops on a round corner table.

"This room is fucking depressing. We'll change that, but first we gotta talk." She turns to me, hands propped on her waist, hip cocked, eyebrow arched high on her forehead—proper superheroine pose. "Drop the fake smile," Lalah orders me. An almost genuine smile tugs at my lips. At least she doesn't treat me like I'm breakable. Which, clearly, I am.

"What happened?"

She shuffles inside a tote bag, elbow-deep, until she finds what she's looking for. I barely have time to lift my hands to protect my face from the incoming missile as Blakely shouts, "Mrs. Hayes!" in outrage.

"What? She *can* catch." Lalah shrugs unconcerned. I'd laugh, but breathing and coughing have shown me my abdomen is bound to protest any kind of movement. "Your house is disgustingly barren of any notebooks. I got you some." She steps closer to me, her hazel eyes softening as she grabs my hand. "I cannot fathom what you're going through. I do know you are strong enough to get through this. Cole told me to keep my mouth shut right now, not to overwhelm you. But I need you to understand *you* have options. My heart breaks for you because I know how much you dreamed of being a mother. However, being a mother comes in many ways, Sawy."

"Lalah…" I try to stop her. My heart is pounding in my chest. This is not something I want to discuss. Not now when grief presses so heavily on my shoulders, making it hard to breathe.

"Sawyer." She gives me a wane smile. "You still have your ovaries. I have a perfectly good uterus and more money than I know what to do with. Say the word, and my legs will be in stirrups faster than you can blink. You want a child, I'll be your goddamn surrogate. Just don't make me give up coffee."

My breath hitches and tears spring in my eyes. I blink furiously as my mind scrambles to process her words. "You'd do that for me?"

She nods decisively. "You're my friend, Sawy. My best friend's sister. In our family, we help each other the best way we can. It just so happens I *can* do this for you." Her own eyes redden and shine. "So do me a favor, will you? Get stronger. Get better. Blakely here"—Lalah gestures toward the soft-spoken, dark-haired nurse—"doesn't work for the hospital. She's here to help *you*." Lalah smiles as Blakely gives me an awkward wave. "Officially, she's hired by Hope Haven. Once you're ready to kick ass and take names again, she'll look after Haven."

With the very belated introductions out of the way, she bends down and kisses my forehead. I'm still frozen to the spot, unable to breathe, unable to think past the bomb she dropped on my lap. "Now, she'll make this sterile hellhole look prettier for you," Lalah mumbles, heading to the door. "Which reminds me, put that sad-sack puppy out of his misery, his whining is grating on my nerves. As much as I enjoy him learning to be human, there's not enough coffee in the world to mend his heartbreak."

Chapter Forty-Four

Maddox

My breath fogs out in front of me as I run from my car to the entrance of the bar. A million bees buzz just underneath my skin—a barrel of gunpowder ready to explode and take down everything in my path.

Sawyer doesn't want to see me.

I can't blame her.

Everything in me strongly disagrees with the distance between us. It takes all my self-control not to turn on my heel and plaster myself to the door of her hospital room until she lets me in.

My mind is clear. My heart is set. I know what I need to do now, and there's nothing and no one in this world to stand in my way. I've had my head shoved so far up my ass, my nose was tickling my kidneys. Not anymore.

Sure, my head's still a fucking mess. But whatever mess my parents made with their lives, it doesn't mean I have to follow in their footsteps. What if Ryker follows in mine? I don't want my son to grow up a bitter, hateful man. Happiness and love were only mine for a month, but it's what I want for him every second of every day. I have to set a better example. He looks up to me. It's time I prove myself worthy.

I thought I was saving Sawyer from me.

But I was condemning us both to hell.

Those hours I thought she'd be forever lost to me also opened my goddamn eyes. I *can* take care of her. I know her. I love her. I'll make her so damn happy, she'll be randomly pulled for drug tests because all she'll do the rest of her life is smile constantly like a drunk-in-love lunatic.

But first... I'm a man on a mission.

I push through the doors, shivering when the warm air inside the bar replaces the frigid October air. My strides are determined and confident as I reach the sleek bar top separating us. "We gotta talk."

Jackson leans against the wall, folding his arms over his chest. His unholy silver eyes assess me nonchalantly. "Do we?"

I might be convinced he's a demon spawned straight from the darkest corners of hell, but for the woman I love, I'll take having my ass handed to me. Even though it makes me sick to my stomach, I maintain eye-contact. "Daniel Johnson."

He doesn't blink. There's no change in his breathing. He doesn't even so much as twitch. Yet the air between us carries an electric charge. My skin peppers and ice curls around my spine as he takes a step closer, shoving his hands inside the pockets of his black jeans. "My office," he murmurs, tilting his head in the direction I am to follow.

Follow I do, climbing the steps behind him. My heart leaps in my throat in the obscurity of the narrow staircase, with only the echoes of boots against wooden ledges for company. I gulp as I see him type a complicated-looking code on a panel affixed to the wall, before a metal door slides open.

"After you," he tells me with a flourish of his arm. If I weren't so angry, my blood would freeze in my veins at the half-feral smile he gives me.

Despite my very serious expectation of a dark dungeon, full of medieval torture devices and dangerous-looking guns displayed on every wall, only a dozen monitors, all turned off, dominate a large wooden desk in the middle of the room, an ergonomic chair facing them. That's it. Sparse. Empty. Not something you'd expect to find above a bar in the middle of nowhere, Montana.

"I'd tell you to sit, but as you can see... the floor is yours," he says, rounding the desk and sprawling in the sole chair. "What do you think you know, Lawson?"

Maybe blackmailing Jackson Camden isn't my brightest idea. I get the feeling I have sorely underestimated this man. My fingers twitch as I surreptitiously pat the butt of my service gun.

"Ntz. Ntz. I wouldn't do that if I were you. We're all friends here, aren't we?" Jackson smirks. "WHAT. DO. YOU. THINK. YOU. KNOW?" he thunders, all traces of amusement vanishing from his face.

Time to be a man, Lawson.

"I saw you," I say, swallowing down the fear crawling up my esophagus. "I know you killed Daniel."

"Do you now? 'S far as I know, the bastard died of a heart attack."

"The day Daniel died, you were at the trailer park. About twenty minutes before the fire was reported, you exited his doublewide through the roof. You wore black jeans and a black hoodie to cover your face." His eyes sparkle in the gray daylight streaming through the window. The goddamn psychopath is proud of himself, even if that small spark in his disturbing irises is his only tell. "You ran through the woods," I continue, "exiting northbound to where your motorcycle was hidden in the bushes. And I have it all on my bodycam."

Sure. The last part is a lie. But he doesn't need to know that.

Jackson spreads his legs and smiles mockingly. "Looks like you have everything you need, then. Are you here to arrest me, *Chief Deputy* Lawson?"

The psychopathic motherfucker may terrify the fuck out of me, but he's a psychopathic motherfucker I need right now.

"If I wanted you arrested, don't you think I would've done it back in June?" I throw at him. "My silence was free until now. Out of loyalty to Maevis, I didn't care how the bastard died, just that he did."

"And now you need something," he concludes, understanding dawning on him.

I lean back against the door, hands shoved inside my pockets—the picture of nonchalance. "Robert Smith."

That asshole's name is what gets Jackson. His face transforms into a horrifying mask. All the emptiness nesting inside of him out on the surface for me to see. It's at this moment I understand the danger living right on the outskirts of Lost Hope, and how fucking lucky we are he's seeing us as friends.

"I've lived my life on the right side of the law. Sure, I'm prancing around with a stick up my ass in a small town where nothing ever happens. Justice is easy to dole out when you're dealing with petty theft and neighborhood arguments at worst. The law won't touch him." My voice cracks, the horror of those minutes when I kept Sawyer's heart pumping and I breathed for her fills my veins with ice once more. "Sawyer needs to be safe. He needs to die. And you're the only one capable of finding him."

He regards me silently as he leans back in his chair, ankle crossed over his knee, fingers drumming against each other in his lap.

"You know what I find insulting?"

I lift my chin, staring at him defiantly. Of course, the bastard doesn't break. The silence is unnerving, making my teeth ache. "What?" I bark.

"That you thought I needed to be blackmailed into making sure my best friend's baby sister is safe." He points at the door as his screens flicker to life. The white light washing over his face makes his eyes look almost translucent. "Get out, Lawson. Next time you blackmail me, they'll find your DNA in the same hole Smith's rotting."

"How's Sawyer, son?" My father clasps my shoulder as I enter their kitchen. The smell of garlic and something delicious roasting in the oven greets me, and my stomach gurgles in appreciation.

"Haven't seen her today," I mumble, my head hanging low as I shrug off my coat and lay it over the back of a chair. "But I need you guys to keep Ryker for a little while longer. I have some shit to figure out."

Warm arms coil around my waist, the scent of apple pie and cinnamon overpowering whatever's cooking. A strange sensation floods my veins. How long has it been since I've had a hug from my mom? Awkwardly, I rest my arm around her shoulders, pulling her closer. My eyes sting as once more tears brim to the surface. I don't remember crying as a child as much as I've cried this past week.

Seeing the love of your life bleeding out in front of your very eyes would do that to the strongest man.

"Ryker can stay with us for as long as you want. Sawyer needs you right now."

I shake my head. Shame coats my skin as I bark a hollow laugh. "Sawyer wants nothing to do with me."

My mother breaks our hug as she takes a step back, and I feel the loss of her warmth in the very marrow of my bones. She cups my scruffed cheek as icy-blue eyes, identical to mine, bore into the depths of my soul. "We've failed you, Maddy, both your father and I. I can't begin to tell you how sorry I am for being so caught up in my own drama, I missed how much my child was suffering."

"Mom..." My voice cracks as I try to stop her. "If anyone should apologize, it's me. There's no excuse for all my lash-outs, taking my anger on you on matters I didn't understand."

She gives me a watery smile. "I should've done better. Your father should've done better, too. And that's on us. I know too much has happened in a short time, but I hope you'll give us a chance."

My father clasps my shoulder once more, squeezing me affectionately. "I was wrong when I said you inherited all the worst parts of me. I got complacent, and I gave up on my family. You never did, Madd. Not as a child, not as the man you've become."

The chain constricting my chest loosens. I hug both my parents close as I exhale a relieved sob. We're not miraculously healed. The trust lost between me and them will take time and patience to rebuild. But I know I can do it. There's no other choice. Not if I want to prove to Sawyer that I'm her only choice.

"Now, let's find that grandson of ours and get some dinner in our bellies. I believe you have a woman to win over."

I don't need to go far to stumble over Ryker. He's taken to playing on the back porch, where my mother has planted a couple of Frontenac vines along the rails. His impatience for them to yield grapes has him out here often, reading and singing to the vines. According to the little grape-monster, happy vines make for a happy Ryker's tummy. Hard to argue with his logic.

"Daddy!" he squeals as he sees me. I crouch as he jumps in my arms, and his tiny hands, full of dirt, coil around my neck. "Gammy saided Rosie, Tillie, and Nix will give me lotsa grapes next year. That's when I'm five and the leaves fall down."

"Who's Rosie, Tillie, and Nix?" I ask as I kiss the top of his head, tightening my hold around the squirming, wiggly eel in my arms.

He facepalms dramatically, leaning back over my forearm so I can get a full view of his 'Daddy's an idiot' frown. "The grape trees, silly. They still small until I'm five. I grow, the grape trees grow. That's what Gammy saided."

I roll my eyes playfully. "Silly ole' me. Well, if Grandma said so, then it must be true. How about we have some dinner, help you grow faster, hmm?"

"Yes, Daddy. The monster in my tummy is pretty mean," he whispers in my ear. "He growls a lot."

I rub his belly as I settle him down in his booster seat. "Oh no. He must be hungry. Let's feed him then. I heard he's particularly fond of carrots and broccoli."

"Oh boy. Not broccoli." Ryker crosses his arms over his chest, poking his tongue out to convey his disgust.

I ruffle his hair playfully as I dump a generous portion of broccoli into his plate. "Sorry, dude. The monster has spoken."

Dinner is a quiet affair apart from the appreciative noises coming from each of us and Ryker's sighs whenever his fork touches the florets on his plate. My phone pings from the pocket of my jeans. An eerie sense of déjà vu washes over me. Not even my mother grumbles as I take it out and check my messages.

We all know what happened last time it rang as we shared dinner.

I'll sneak you in tonight. Be here no earlier than 9 p.m. If she fires me, I'm coming after you, Chief. You better make it right with my best girl. Those blue puppies and dimples won't work on me a second time. It's up to you to deal with the Blakely hound. That girl might look small and innocent, but she bites.

Beth Anderson

A grateful smile graces my lips.

Thank you, Beth. I appreciate you. No worries for your job. I plan to grovel Sawyer right out of her hospital room and into my arms.

Me

Keep the pornography to a minimum, the hospital has THIN walls. You're lucky Annalise keeps me well stocked on romance.

Beth Anderson:

"Good news?" Mom asks with a hopeful twinkle in her eyes.
"We'll see. It's a start."

Since I still have some time to kill before I leave for the hospital, I take over doing the dishes. Mom dries them silently at my side as laughter comes from the living room. I'm grateful she's not pushing me to talk. My head is pulled in too many directions. I need to get myself on the right track. Get Sawyer to forgive me and give me another chance. Convince her to move in with me.

She'll need a lot of help in the upcoming months as she heals. I can be her support. I can look after her. Sure, Lalah hired Blakely specifically to help Sawyer, but from what I've been told, the dark-haired nurse has her own wounds to heal, even if they're not the physical kind. I'm sure she's tough. To hear Lalah say it, she's been in a plane crash just two months ago and lived to tell the tale. Blakely and four others were trapped in the woods for two weeks before they were rescued.

It made me see her in a whole different light after I grumbled for two days as I waited for her and Blake to make the drive all the way from New York.

But she's not me.

Blakely might be tough and a damn great nurse, but I love Sawyer. And if I have any say, she'll move into my house and make it our home. She'll be there long after her incisions have healed. She'll be with us forever.

The soles of my feet are itching for me to go to her, but I take my time giving Ryker a bath and getting him into his PJ and in bed. To my surprise, he doesn't protest at all when I tell him he'll spend the week with his grandparents rather than going to daycare. Instead, he gives me a tight hug.

"Tell Miss Sawy I love her," Ryker says as I tuck him in for the night.

"I promise. Love you, bud." I bend at the waist and kiss his forehead. "I'll see you tomorrow."

I close the door softly behind me and make my way downstairs. Once I shrug my jacket on, I crouch down to lace my boots.

"Going to the hospital?" my mom asks from the mouth of the hallway.

"Yeah," I mumble before standing upright again.

"I packed some stuff for Sawyer. She must be sick of all that hospital food. Nothing too heavy," she tells me with a shy smile. "I packed a blanket for you, too. Those chairs are the most uncomfortable things I've ever sat on."

"Thanks, Mom." Awkwardly, I give her a half-hug and kiss the top of her head as I take the tote bag from her.

"Give her our well wishes. We thought about visiting her, but figured she'd be overwhelmed."

The drive to the hospital passes in a blur. I'm half tempted to floor the accelerator, but with the temperatures dropping and the treacherous mountain roads, I'm not trying to gamble with my fate.

I burst through the hospital doors, beelining to the reception as per Beth's instructions.

"You're right on time," she says from behind me, startling the life out of me. "Come on, let's not waste any time. There are no more visits scheduled for tonight, and I made Blakely go home. Well, Sawyer's home."

"She's staying at the cottage?"

"Yeah. Sawyer's getting released in two days. She's to take it easy for the next month as her incisions heal. Lalah figured it's best they room together for the month. That dark cookie is cooking something, though."

That's an absolute surprise from the woman who has her fingers in every pot in Lost Hope.

Beth knocks gently as we reach Sawyer's door, signaling with her hand for me to wait outside. She pokes her head in as I hold my breath.

"You're all clear to go in. Do *not* wake her up. Chances are she'll kick you out herself if you do. Good luck, little grasshopper."

"I'll definitely need it," I mumble to myself as I tiptoe inside the darkened room.

I make quick work of replacing Sawyer's scratchy blanket with the one my mother packed for me. She deserves to be as comfortable as possible. Even though the lights are off, the monitor displaying her vitals is bright enough that I can notice all the little changes in the room. Baskets of gifts, multiple bouquets of flowers, even the drawings on the nightstand with hieroglyphic scribblings her students must have made.

Someone must have helped her braid her hair, as it sits like a crown around her head. Her plump lips are slightly parted as she breathes deeply and evenly. My stomach flips while I take in her ethereal beauty.

To think I was so close to losing her forever.

With her hand firmly enclosed in mine, I rest my head on her bed, next to her hip, and let myself fall asleep.

Chapter Forty-Five

Sawyer

I can't help myself. I know I should. His nearness should burn through my skin like the absolute sin he is. Instead... he soothes.

He's deliciously disheveled in his sleep. Light brown hair tousled, a deep sheet crease on his scruffed cheek, eyebrows slightly furrowed, as if even in his slumber he worries for me. I bury my fingers in his soft locks, and he groans low in his chest.

I woke up half an hour ago, only to almost startle myself out of bed when I saw him slumped in his chair, our hands entwined. It took some effort to extricate my fingers from between his, careful not to wake him up. The dark circles underneath his eyes tell me everything I need to know about all the sleep he's missed recently.

Try as much as I'd like, I can't find it in me to kick him out. I don't understand why he keeps coming back. If he's feeling guilty, he's a foolish man. The only thing he's guilty of is not wanting me. But then again, the heart wants what it wants, and his doesn't want me. The sooner I make my peace with it, the better for everyone.

My fingers tighten their grip in his hair as sudden rage courses through me.

I have to make my peace with too much. In two short days, I've lost everything I took for granted. I'm bound to lose even more. I can't even fathom returning to the daycare, looking at the smiling faces of my students, watching parents dropping off and picking up their children, seeing the love on their faces... all the while knowing I won't ever get to experience it for myself.

"Little fairy," Maddox whispers, his voice laden with sleep, unfairly low and gravelly. "I get the feeling you woke up and chose violence this morning. While I'm thoroughly deserving of everything you see fit to dish, I'm slightly concerned with the bald patch you're decorating my thick head with."

I exhale a watery laugh as I relax my hold on his hair. "Sorry," I croak. "Got carried away there for a moment."

He grunts in displeasure as he stands. His back pops painfully while he stretches, and I let my eyes roam freely over the expanse of his shoulders and the decadent way his Henley covers his chest, finally settling on the strip of skin visible just above his waistband.

"Do you need anything?" he asks.

I shake my head as I fidget with my hands in my lap.

"Okay. I'll go wash my face and get a cup of coffee." Maddox leans over me, cupping my cheek and tilting my head up. His icy-blue eyes bore into mine, full of concern and affection. "Please don't kick me out. I'm not leaving either way. If I have to camp out in the parking lot, I will, but I'd much rather be right here by your side where I belong." He touches his lips to mine, a feather of a kiss and nothing much, but my stomach still explodes in a swarm of butterflies. "We'll talk when I get back."

My throat is too dry to speak. I barely manage a weak nod as he straightens and shoots me a wink before disappearing out the door.

What the iambic meter just happened?

I shake my head to dispel the haze Maddox always seems to leave me in. With careful movements, I peel the soft, knitted blanket I'm covered in and drag my feet off the thin mattress. Each morning, I have a couple of minutes all too myself. No visitors, no Blakely barking orders in her annoyingly calm voice. I'm grateful for the outpour of love I received since I woke up, but I'm so so tired of it too.

Spoiled brat, that's what I sound like. But for someone used to living on the sidelines, being the center of attention doesn't come easy. Maddox is my only exception. I thrive being subjected to his whole focus.

My abdomen is tight and uncomfortable, the stitches pulling at my skin. Blakely helped me shower yesterday, even going as far as washing my hair. As humiliating as it was, being clean has made me feel so much better. I limp to the bathroom, my whole groin screaming in protest through each movement.

I've finally been cleared for solid foods. There's nothing like a doctor asking you if you've farted yet to put you off food forever. Nope, scratch that. It's your nurse confirming that yes, yes you did. Of course, flatulence shows your digestive system has resumed proper functioning and it works at optimal capacity. I just wish they gave me a form, and I ticked a box, and my optimal capacity farting wasn't announced to a room full of people.

Using the toilet is another monumental task. I cry out as I finally bend my knees enough to drop on the seat as my lower belly protests and the skin around my incisions tightens painfully. Once my bladder is once again the size of a peanut, and not a bowling ball bruising the rest of my internal organs, I flush the toilet. A lot of grunting later and more sweat down my back than if I'd run ten laps around the hospital, I manage to stand and make my way to the sink.

Tears shine in my eyes as I take my reflection in. A bit more pale than usual, cheeks sunken in, but otherwise no change. There's no red lettering on my forehead, screaming in capitals "BARREN". There's no "Here lie the embers of Sawyer's hopes and dreams."

I look the same, but wholly changed.

My hands shake as I splash cold water on my face, then gently pat myself dry. Washing my teeth is just another mindless chore, but I feel every muscle in my body trembling as my energy quickly depletes.

I limp faster back into the room. All I want is to lie down and hide under the blanket Maddox most likely brought with him last night. It smells like him—cardamom, pink peppercorn, violet leaves. And he smells like home.

"There you are." Doctor Richards claps her hands as I enter the room. "I'm happy to see you up and about."

"Can't say the same about you," I mumble under my breath. I know why she's here. This conversation I've avoided for the past four days. It's silly and stubborn of me, but if I don't understand my situation, I can still hope it's a bad dream. I'll soon wake up and be whole again. "Good morning," I say out loud instead. "No chance of postponing again?"

If she notes the hope in my voice, she doesn't let me know. Instead, she smiles indulgently, like a woman with her uterus still intact and inside her body, and helps me get settled in bed. Once she's happy that my pillows have been fluffed enough and I'm as comfortable as a pig in a mud bath, she sits in Maddox's chair, crossing her legs at the knee gracefully.

"I'm afraid not, Sawyer. I understand how daunting this is for you, I truly do. But I cannot sign those release papers until you've been informed of everything you need to know." Her warm brown eyes take me in, the dimple in her chin deepening as she purses her lips. "We have tried our absolute best to save your uterus. Unfortunately, the damage was too extensive, and the bleeding could not be controlled."

"We've been over this before," I reply petulantly, crossing my arms over my chest.

I'm honestly expecting her to roll her eyes, but all I get in return is a sympathetic smile. *UGH*.

"It takes a while to sink in. I was told you don't want to use our psychologist." That's a nice told-off if I ever heard one. "I cannot stress enough how important it is you get the proper support to help you navigate your new reality."

My cheeks pink up. I've always been the teacher's pet, goodie-two-shoes wallflower. So I'm eagerly interrupting. "My friend Lalah has arranged for a private therapist. Our sessions will start once I'm at home. Don't take this the wrong way, but the hospital doesn't help me relax. I need my safe space and to be surrounded by my own things. I believe the therapist specializes in grief management and depression, amongst a mile long list of acronyms I do not understand or care for."

She nods minutely. "That works. I'm glad to hear you are not dismissing the impact on your mental health. Your body will heal, but it makes all the difference in the world when your mental well-being aligns with your physical well-being." She taps her pen to the arm of the chair absentmindedly as her eyes return to me, silently asking for permission.

I steel my spine, despite the currents of pain rushing below my navel. "Okay. Lay it on me."

A knock on the door interrupts the speech she is about to give. I can't help but release a relieved breath as Maddox pops his head in. "Uhm... I'm sorry, I'll come back."

"No!" I shout.

At the same time, Doctor Richards tells him, "Shouldn't take more than an hour."

Maddox hesitates, his icy-blue eyes pinned on me. "No. You can stay." Maybe I'm weak because I need the comfort of his presence. I don't care. Somehow, sharing the burden of everything I'm not going to be and have in the future makes it easier to bear. And he's the unfortunate soul to hold my hand through it.

"Sawyer," Doctor Richards draws my attention as Maddox takes a hesitant step inside. "Do you give your consent for me to share sensitive information about your health with Maddox in the room?"

"Yes, you have my consent."

She nods, scribbling something on her clipboard. Maddox's comforting scent envelops me as he rounds the bed and takes a seat on the opposite side of her. I shift farther on the mattress and make room for him as I pat the empty space next to me. He raises a questioning eyebrow but doesn't hesitate to push his chair back and sit on the bed instead. His arm goes around my shoulders as I rest my back against his chest. Blessed warmth radiates through me. I didn't realize how cold I was until his body heat encircled me.

His large palm cradles my abdomen protectively, and I twin my fingers with his.

"Alright. If everyone's ready."

I feel him nod, his chin brushing the top of my head. "We're ready," I confirm verbally.

"As with most surgeries, taking into account the trauma which led to the supracervical hysterectomy, the expected healing time is between six to eight weeks. Because you have Miss Everton with you, I'll schedule an appointment in a month's time, and another check-up two months post-op. Of course, should anything happen—excessive pain, signs of infection, excessive vaginal bleeding, or blood clots—please call me immediately."

Maddox squeezes my fingers as I nod mutely.

"Now, during the healing period, you'll experience spotting or light bleeding. This can last a couple of days or as long as four weeks while your body recuperates and adjusts. You are to do nothing. Rest, rest, and more rest. All you're allowed is light walking around the house, no stairs. My recommendation is to try and walk about five minutes every hour. Depending on how the examination goes at our appointment, you might be cleared for light duties." She pauses as she waits for me to process, and I tip my chin to let her continue. "We're trying to avoid a reinjury or a hernia here."

"That's okay. I'm a couch potato, anyway." I laugh hollowly.

"Besides Blakely, do you have anyone living with you who can assist with meals, cleaning, and personal hygiene? Some activities we don't think about; we just do them. And they're definitely not light duty."

"Yes," Maddox answers confidently. My head whips around so fast, I'm surprised I don't give myself whiplash or whack him in the chin. He kisses my forehead as he lightly caresses my abdomen. "Yes, little fairy, you do."

Doctor Richards chuckles ruefully. "Alright. Sort that one out between yourselves." She looks at her clipboard, tapping her pen gently against the papers stacked there. "As we discussed before, with a partial hysterectomy, the cervix and ovaries remain intact while the top part of your uterus is removed. From what we've seen during surgery, they're healthy and in excellent shape. This brings good news on several fronts. With the ovaries functioning, they'll still produce eggs and hormones. You don't need to worry about bone density or cardiac issues—unless, of course, there are other causes. Early on-set menopause is also no cause for concern, as long as your ovaries do their job."

I swallow thickly as my cheeks pink up. Maddox is getting to know more about me than he'd bargained for. It's never a waste for a man to get properly educated on a woman's sexual health. Whoever he ends up with will thank me later. Jealousy rears her ugly head hard and fast inside me, my nails pressing down on the back of his hand. If he's hurting, he doesn't show it, instead just brushes his thumb against mine in silent support.

"Although it's mostly encountered with full hysterectomies, you may notice a shift in pelvic support. Should it happen, we'll recommend you to a pelvic floor specialist. Nurse Everton will also be able to assist you, once your incisions have healed up, with exercises beneficial for pelvic strength. All the information I'm relaying to you now, I'm also making available to your OB/GYN. They'll know what to look for to ensure you're on the right path to healing during your check-ups."

"Thank you," I croak. Looks like Kegel and I will become best friends.

She eyes Maddox pensively before clearing her throat. "As we've discussed, you'll experience no menstruation moving forward once your body is healed up. That being said, premenstrual syndrome is very much a possibility. Your ovaries still go through their cycles, your hormones still work as normal."

"So loads of ice cream runs in my future," Maddox quips like a know-it-all asshole. Why does he sound so proud and eager, like a way-too-happy golden retriever?

"And dark chocolate truffles," I sling back. He presses another kiss to the top of my head, causing my vision to swim. I'm almost convinced aliens descended over Lost Hope and replaced Maddox with... a super affectionate clone. Except, that's not true, is it? He's always been affectionate with me during our brief *let's give us a try* tryst.

"Looks like you've got that covered." Doctor Richards smiles kindly. "Lastly, partial hysterectomies rarely affect sex drive or sexual sensations." I freeze in Maddox's arms. Oh god, she had to go there. "However, hormonal changes may impact your libido. Any concerns, please feel free to address them with your OB/GYN. They'll be able to guide you through it.

But, no penetrative intercourse for the next eight weeks. Due to the nature of your injuries, my recommendation is ten weeks."

My cheeks flame. But sex is the last thing on my mind. Clearly, my one-night-stand history isn't exactly successful, and I have absolutely zero plans on dating anyone. We may have been together for only a short time, but my feelings were deeply rooted before then. As much as I hate to admit it—even to just myself—Maddox is not a man I'll easily get over. He burrowed so deeply under my skin, I feel him in every heartbeat and every flutter of my belly. Exorcizing him from my soul will take longer than my body needs to heal.

"You okay with that, Sawyer? Non-penetrative sexual activities are allowed after the six-week mark. We'll re-evaluate during your first check-up. Okay?" the good doctor asks, and I squeak in embarrassment and surprise. I nod like a bobblehead, drained of all words and bleeding mortification. "Alright. I have some pre-release tests for you scheduled in an hour, and Nurse Everton will draw some blood. If the results come back with no anomalies, you're free to leave in the morning." She removes a stack of papers from her clipboard. "There's more information about everything we've discussed in here. I also added a list of books and medical journals you can read, if you're interested in more literature."

She pats the papers, drawing my attention to them. "The most important thing to remember, Sawyer, is to take care of your mental health. Let yourself grieve and let yourself heal."

Maddox strokes my arm gently, barely saying goodbye to Doctor Richards. I clear my throat as I try to put some distance between the two of us. A light headache is pressing down on me as I process the slew of information dumped on my lap. My eyes well once again as a hollow feeling throbs and grows inside me, where my uterus used to be. He pulls me to his chest, running his fingers over my spine, as I hide my face in the crook of his neck and let myself cry.

"You're going to be just fine, little fairy," he murmurs, his voice low and soothing. "I've got you." My hair shifts as his breath fans through the rogue strands escaping my braid. "Tomorrow morning, we'll get you home. I moved all the furniture from my bedroom into the spare room on the first floor, so you don't have to go up and down the stairs until you're all healed up."

I swear, my brain short-circuits for a moment as his words soak through my ears but don't compute. If my mind was Windows-operated, I'd get the blue screen of death and the infinite *404 Error* message.

"I'm sorry, what?" I croak through my tears as I lift my head so I can look him in the eyes.

His face is set in granite, determination resolute. "You're moving in with me."

I slap his shoulder, then wince in pain when my abdomen protests the vigorous movement. "Oh, hell no!"

Chapter Forty-Six

Maddox

Should've figured she'd kick me out.

It's fine. A lot of information was dumped on her today, and I just went and stuck the cherry on top with her impending move. What Sawyer doesn't know yet is that our friends—her brother included—have descended onto her little cottage to pack her up and unpack her into my house. Our home.

Lalah worked her scheming magic and has the paperwork ready for Sawyer to sublet to Blakely. I figured it would be a bigger battle to get the nurse on my side, but she's been eager to help and keep quiet about our sneaking around. Of course, someone got to her before I called her earlier this morning and did half the job for me. Can't complain, since my sole purpose right now is to get Sawyer into my house.

With the basket of fruits, vegetables, wine, and flowers that Mom prepared for me anchored around my elbow, I climb out of my truck and make my way up the three steps to the porch. I should be nervous. But after all the ways I've been threatened by Emma, Violet, Annalise, and—surprisingly—Drake, I don't think there are any new threats Tatum Sr. can come up with.

However, I've been surprised before.

It doesn't matter. I'm not here to ask for permission. Sawyer is capable of making her own decisions. But I want to do this right. No more hiding. No more sneaking around. My intentions are clear, and I plan to broadcast them loud and wide.

My knock is strong and precise. I rock back on my heel as I wait for someone to answer the door. Luckily, I'm not kept waiting for too long.

"Afternoon, Maddox," Mrs. Carter greets me. "What brings you by?" she asks, her navy-blue eyes, so similar to Sawyer's, twinkling.

"Good afternoon, Mrs. Carter. If I'm not intruding on your plans, I'd like to talk to you and Mr. Carter."

She steps back, opening the door wider. "Of course you're not intrud-ing. Come on in. You're just in time, too. I have a blueberry pie just about done."

"If that boy thinks he's taking my daughter and *my* pie, he'd better turn around and leave the way he came," Sawyer's dad barks from somewhere inside.

His wife smiles widely at me, although the dark circles around her eyes and the red veins webbing around her irises betray the worry and stress she must be feeling for her daughter. "Don't listen to that old fool. If he knows what's good for him, he'll keep his trap stuffed with pie and his ears wide open."

I let her usher me in, following her like a puppy until we reach a large kitchen, with a huge island towering in the center of the room. Tatum Sr. straightens from his bent position, quickly closing the oven door.

"If *my* pie collapsed in the middle because you couldn't help yourself, you better run, Mister. And you better run fast," Mrs. Carter threatens, her hands firmly propped on her hips.

So maybe it's not Tatum Sr. I need to fear. Maybe it's the curly-haired pixie with the attitude of a bloodhound and the smile of a saint who has my balls shriveling and hiding behind my stomach.

Something must really be messed up in my head as my heart starts pounding in excitement while I imagine Sawyer having a go at me in *our* kitchen.

I place the basket on the gleaming surface of the island. "My mom sends her best wishes," I say. "If you need anything, just reach out. She's been keeping her distance, thinking the attention might be overwhelming."

Tatum Sr. clears his throat as he grabs Sarah's hand and pulls her to his side, his arm resting around her shoulders. Even though one is still smiling and the other is trying to glare me out of his house, they're presenting a united front. I want what they have. I want it with every cell in me. But right now isn't the time for me to mentally berate myself for being so incredibly stupid and blind, I haven't allowed myself to be happy sooner.

"Thank you, Maddox. That's very considerate of her." She smiles sadly as she sniffles. "This past week has been... excruciating. But my daughter is a fighter. If Sawyer can be strong and brave after everything she's been through... then so can we," Sarah tells me. "Have a seat. Would you like some tea?"

I already know Sawyer's mother thinks a cup of tea cures everything. On all the late nights we've spent just... talking and getting to know one another beyond the crazy chemistry we have and the surface image everyone else has seen, my little fairy has told me all about their spilling-secrets-over-tea ritual.

"I'd love some, thank you."

"Kiss-ass," Tatum Sr. coughs, immediately grunting when his wife jams her elbow into his side.

"Behave!" she snaps, then turns to me and winks. "Why don't you tell us why you're here while I make our tea?"

She flits about the kitchen, picking up a kettle and filling it with water. I don't flinch when her husband takes a seat directly across from me. The island might be between us, but I have no doubt he'll leap over it and strangle me if I so much as breathe in the wrong way.

So maybe I need to fear them both.

Tatum Sr. is an imposing man, as quiet and as threatening as his son. There's no doubt Tate has learned everything he knows from his father. They're spitting images of each other, just thirty-years apart.

"I'm sure you already know, Sawyer will be released tomorrow. Doctor Richards ordered a new set of tests earlier this morning, and everything came back as expected. However, she mentioned Sawyer needs to rest for the next four weeks. Based on her progress, only then she'll be cleared for light activities."

The frown on Tatum Sr.'s face deepens. "Looks like we're getting our girl back for the foreseeable future."

I drum my fingers on the island top, nodding gratefully to Sarah as she drops a steaming cup of tea in front of me. The calming scent of chamomile envelops me as I inhale deeply. "Sawyer will stay with me as she recuperates. She'll stay forever if she wants to," I declare, like an overly confident asshole. At least, I'm self-aware, even if it's after the fact.

His fingers curl into fists that look big enough to pummel me into the ground. "Is that so?"

I ignore the threat in his voice. If I cower, I'll never win his respect. He needs to trust me to take care of his daughter. And I need to earn it.

"Yes, Sir. Nurse Blakely will be on hand to look after Sawyer and ensure she's on the right path to healing. But it's my duty and honor to be the one at her side." I square my shoulders as I straighten up.

Sarah places a gentle hand on my biceps, giving me an encouraging squeeze. She assesses me from head to toe, like only a mother can—mouth downturned in sympathy and eyes crinkled at the corners. "Are you doing this out of guilt? I got the whole story out of Tate when I found you sleeping outside her hospital room and wondered why... I knew you found her... and saved our baby girl, but it still didn't explain you camping out there."

I choke on pure air, a cough hissing through my teeth. "No, Ma'am!" I deny vehemently. "Sure, I'm guilty of being a coward and not fighting for her." My cheeks heat up as I speak, but I'll own up to my actions, and I'll redeem myself eventually. If Sawyer finds it in herself to forgive me. "I love your daughter. There isn't anything in this world I wouldn't do for her."

"What makes you think you know how to care for her better than us?" Tatum Sr. snaps.

I face him, looking directly into his eyes. "With all due respect, Sir, I know you love Sawyer. You're her parents. But ask yourself this... what if—God forbid—something happened to your wife? Would you let her out of your sight? Would you not move heaven and earth to know she's safe and cared for?"

He folds his arms across his chest and shoots me a defiant look. I can see how he commanded his Marines into submission. One glare from those sky-blue eyes and my soul froze inside my chest. But I'm not backing down. "She's not your wife."

"Not yet, Sir. She will be as soon as she decides she'll have me."

It is possible that I'm driving ten miles under the speed limit. There's just no fucking way I'm speeding up when Sawyer's white as a sheet, sweat peppering her forehead.

"Are you doing okay over there, little fairy?"

She huffs and rolls her pretty eyes. "Shouldn't you be looking at the road?"

"I'm looking," I murmur. Well, one eye on the road, the other on her. I might get a serious case of vertigo by the time we get home, but I'll gladly suffer through it.

"Seriously, how did you convince everyone to get busy right as I needed a ride?"

I shrug, all nonchalance and innocent-like. "No convincing involved, pinkie promise."

"And no cabs and absolutely no ride-shares were available in the entire county?"

My shoulders come down from around my ears as we're finally entering Lost Hope. She needs a bed, right fucking now. I can't have her pass out on me thirty minutes into my care.

"What can I say? It's the middle of the week. Probably all are booked out with school letting up just about now."

"You're taking me home," she demands. If she weren't in so much pain, I bet she'd stomp her foot, too.

I bite back a smile and answer in my most serious voice, "Yes, ma'am!"

Silence reigns supreme for a couple of minutes as we cruise down Main Street, heading in the complete opposite direction of her cottage. "Lawson!" Sawyer shrieks. "This is not taking me home."

"Yes, it is," I declare as I ease my foot off the accelerator and steer the truck into my driveway. Before she depletes her last ounce of strength, I jump out and round the hood to pop open the passenger door.

"You obstinate, pig-headed man. You should be nominated for gold in audacity. Take me home, Maddox!" She bats my hands away as I grip her hips and slide her out of the truck and into my arms.

"Careful now, little fairy. Remember, you're not supposed to strain yourself."

I mean, in all fairness, I should get gold for being an asshole, too. She can't fight me. She barely has enough energy to walk five feet from her bed to the bathroom. Getting free of me is out of the question. Especially when I have all our friends, my parents and hers—well, hers reluctantly—supporting this harebrained plan of mine. But I'm nothing if not determined.

There's rarely anyone to outstubborn me.

Much to her chagrin, this is not a battle she'll win. So, like the good girl she is, she winds her arms around my neck while Blakely opens the entrance door.

"Traitor," Sawyer calls after the nurse.

Blakely rolls her eyes and gives her a wide smile. "I've been called worse. I'll let you guys settle in and will be back tonight to check on you. Try not to pull your stitches when you're killing him. And remember, I'm not cleaning any blood off the floor."

"Thank you," I tell her. "We'll see you tonight. Dinner's at seven."

Sawyer groans as she slumps in my arms, a yawn overtaking her. "Why are you doing this, Maddox?"

I drop my chin so I can watch her eyelids flutter closed, her cheeks still much too white for my linking. "Because I love you."

Careful not to jostle her around too much, I lay Sawyer down in bed. It'll take me a minute or two to get used to sleeping in this bedroom, but with her cuddled next to me, I'd stay under a bridge if I have to. My stomach flips with disappointment that she's fallen asleep before she gets a chance to see how... right our things look blended together. But that's just me being selfish.

She'll get another one when she wakes up.

We'll get another chance with every breath she takes and every pump of her heart.

"Maddox?" she whispers sleepily.

"I'm here, little fairy," I reply, gently caressing her silky hair.

"Where's Ryker?"

I chuckle as warmth fills my chest. *This fucking woman.* "With my parents. He'll stay there another week or so. Give you time to adjust."

"Maddox?" she asks more forcefully, her eyelids fluttering.

"Yes, little fairy?"

"Bring him home."

We've gotten into some sort of routine over the past week. Every morning, I wake up before her and spend half an hour staring at her like a simp. I'm sure she's awake during that time, but pretending to be asleep and allowing me to satisfy my obsessive needs via staring. I have to. It's the only way my freaked-out mind understands she's right here, in one piece, still alive, still breathing. I've had to stop myself one too many times from splaying my palm over her heart to reassure myself it's still beating. I felt it stop. I saw her chest still and her breaths vanish.

Once whatever panic attack waging war inside of me lays down its weapons, I get up, take a shower, and cook breakfast for us. The first meal of the day is always a quiet affair. For all the sunshine Sawyer brings into my life, she's morose and withdrawn. Not that I blame her. If she's thunder instead of pure sun rays, I'll buy a goddamn raincoat and put an umbrella over our bed. I'll take her in whichever manner she comes.

The main bedroom has become my office. My deputies have been more than understanding of my need to work from home. Sure, police work is not done from the confines of a bedroom, so I make sure I'm at the station for at least a couple of hours every day while Blakely keeps Sawyer company.

She's lost to her grief. More than once I've found her crying with her face buried in a pillow or a blanket. I'd give anything to take the agony away from her and feel it myself instead. It's beyond excruciating to witness it; I can't even imagine what *she* must be feeling. I'm helpless to make it better for her. So I show up every day, instead. I'm there, just in case she needs me. Just in case my presence might ease the grip her grief has on her.

I wish she'd see how loved she is. Not just by me, but everyone around her. Her family, my family, our friends, her students, the residents of Lost Hope as a whole. The news of her attack spread like wildfire. My deputies have been on high alert while we were waiting for her to wake up at the hospital, considering the backlash we'd face as people would start to feel unsafe in their homes. For a small town where nothing ever happens, we've had to deal with more crime in the past year than ever before.

Instead, the townsfolk banded together. Neighborhood watches increased. As did the random acts of kindness. One negative side effect seems to be an increased mistrust for out-of-towners. A few complaints from people visiting from nearby towns have reached my desk. While no one has been outright hostile, the stares got to be too much.

Mayor Brown works incessantly to convince the fine people of Lost Hope that while the vigilance is appreciated, we don't really want to live our lives in distrust and suspicion of any newcomer. So far, it's going as well as expected. A pure and complete shitshow.

I don't care. If Sawyer is safe, people can glare out of town whoever they want. And if it escalates, well, they can cool off in the precinct's jail overnight.

Payroll's a bitch, and I scrub my face with my palm as I let my eyes travel from the screen of my laptop to where Sawyer is perched on the sofa. She's surrounded by pillows, bundled up in a fluffy blanket I took from her cottage. The sight of her shy smile hits me right in the chest. They're so rare these days. I'm more likely to share coffee with Bigfoot than see her plump lips tip up.

The only one who brings her happiness to the surface is Ryker.

He cuddles closer to her, and I bite my tongue, shoving down the impulse to warn him to be careful. Last time I did, I could swear the ground under my feet shook and electricity crackled in the air. I'm certain she wanted me struck by lightning, and she almost got her way by sheer willpower.

My son doesn't understand exactly how fragile Sawyer is and the extent of her injuries. He knows she has a pretty big booboo he's taken on himself to kiss better. Instead, he walks on cloud nine to have her live with us and fights me each morning as I get him ready for daycare. In his mind, Miss Sawy is in our living room, so class can be held right there between my couch and the coffee table.

Of course I'm the asshole jealous of his four-year-old child. They're bonding and I'm simpering. But I'm fast in my resolve not to push her any more than I have to.

That doesn't mean I'm not... loophole hunting. Like right now.

I push to my feet, stretching and groaning as my shoulder blades relax and pop back into place. "What are we watching?" I ask as I pad toward where they're cuddling on the couch.

"*Lilo and Stitch*, Daddy!" Ryker whisper-shouts. "Miss Sawy says you're as grumpy as Stitch is."

The troublesome fairy coughs in her palm, hiding her eyes behind her slender fingers. Despite her best efforts, her cheeks blaze red. She's learning the hard way a preschooler is the worst secret keeper in existence—unless questioned about the number of grapes he's eating on any given day.

"Does that mean I'm your *ohana*, little fairy?"

"What's ohana, Daddy?" Ryker pops to his feet like a Jack-in-a-box at her side. She's trying her best to suppress a wince but doesn't quite manage it. I pick up the little troublemaker, propping him on my hip as I settle next to her myself. Our fingers entwine under the blanket, and I give her palm a gentle squeeze.

"Ohana means family," I say, quoting Lilo.

"And family means no one gets left behind," Sawyer completes the quote for me. Much as she completes me and our little family.

Chapter Forty-Seven

Sawyer

I swear everyone around me is high on ink. There's no other explanation for their behavior. Sure, some of our closest friends knew of the little dalliance between Maddox and me. But to have absolutely every person in my life working against me and pushing me into his arms is beyond ridiculous. I expected at least my hot-headed big brother to protest or, you know, be vehemently against us, considering the lifelong contempt he's held Maddox, but no. He's all for our forced cohabitation.

My mother gushed—*GUSHED*—for an entire day when she came to visit me.

"Oh Sawyer, look at his garden, isn't it so well kept?"

"Oh Sawyer, look at Ryker's bedroom, isn't it so precious?"

Thankfully, Blakely noticed I was right at my wit's end and put a stop to her visit before I blew up.

"Oh Sawyer," I mumble to myself, "isn't he so handsome with his stupid badge and his stupid khaki uniform and his stupid dimples?" as I hobble to the kitchen, in search of a bottle of water.

I've had just about enough of being cooped up inside. As comfortable as Maddox's couch is, I daydream of dumping it in the middle of his 'well kept garden' and setting it on fire.

My head's a mess. My body is slowly but surely healing. Strength returns to me, a little more, every day. I'm finally able to do small things—things I used to take for granted—for myself, like... using the toilet without some-one guarding the bathroom door or brushing my teeth without feeling dizzy and faint after standing for five minutes.

But my heart... my heart still aches painfully every morning as I remem-ber I'm as hollow as an orange peel. There are five minutes when I wake up, and Maddox curls up around me like a cocoon of warmth and safety.

For those five minutes I forget.

I forget he broke up with me.

I forget I won't ever be pregnant and able to carry my own children.

For five minutes every morning, I nuzzle my cheek against his chest and I'm happy.

And then I blink open my eyes and grief hits me with the power of a freight train, robbing me of breath and any semblance of joy.

I don't know what Maddox's game is this time. Guilt, most likely. Pity, probably.

Every night, as we settle beneath his warm sheets, he tucks me in, kisses my nose and my forehead, tells me he loves me, and wishes me goodnight. A month ago, I'd have given anything to hear those three little words from him. In fact, I did. Just before he disappeared into the night. So, if love wasn't enough just five measly weeks ago, why would it be enough now?

His feelings for me weren't strong enough when I was whole. It's impossible to believe now that I'm hollow, I'm worth staying for.

I'm selfish, too. My family might be fooled by whatever lies he's telling himself and everyone else, but I'm sure if I said I didn't want to be here, they'd pack me up and have me in my childhood bedroom faster than Maddox could blink. But his house has something mine doesn't.

Someone.

The one person who brings me such unexpected joy. The one person I thought would bring me the most pain is, in fact, helping me heal faster.

Ryker.

His happiness is contagious. It's impossible to feel sorry for myself when I see the love in his icy-blue eyes, the smile on his lips every morning he wakes up and finds me still here. Sticky hugs and sweet kisses on my cheeks, tales of daycare adventures—these are all unexpected bonuses. Ryker acts like I'm his favorite person every time he lays eyes on me. He lights up from the inside-out, chasing my darkness away with his bright little personality.

He gives me hope.

In that hospital bed, I worried I wouldn't bear to be around my students. I feared that seeing them with their parents would bring too much pain as the future I planned for myself has been literally stabbed out of me. Being around Ryker has shown me my fears are unfounded. If anything, my pupils are exactly what my soul needs to thrive.

Which, of course, makes me sad all over again. My recovery has pushed HeeBee's opening day back by a month.

"What?" I snap at Blakely as she crosses her legs, obstinately propping her chin in her palm.

"You're thinking awfully hard over there," she quips, a devilish smile on her lips.

She's unfairly pretty. Round hips I envy, small waist, boobs for days, curves I'd drive my BMW on if I played for the right team, sleek black hair—she's the plus-sized, bombshell version of Wednesday Adams. If she wouldn't treat Maddox like the obstinate pest he is, I'd be jealous. But she has no interest in him. And truth be told, he's looking at her like he looks at Maevis. With respect, gratitude, and the occasional roll of eyes when she puts him in his place.

He hasn't checked her out, not even once. If anything, whenever she's near, he'll always find a reason to sit closer to me, touching me in one way or another.

"I'm sick of being cooped up inside." I pout like the spoiled brat I am.

"So what's stopping you from going outside?"

"Usually, you."

She downs her peppermint tea and pushes away from the table. "Doctor Richards cleared you for light activities. You're the one who's stalling," Blakely accuses. I poke my tongue at her in response. Nobody likes to be called out on their Ballad Stanzas.

Here's my conundrum. My teeth are aching, that's how badly I need to get out of the house. But every time I take a step toward the door separating me from the outside world, my blood fizzles in my veins and my heart starts pounding. Cold sweat drips down my spine and my breath grows labored and choppy. I'm afraid.

What if he's somewhere out there, lurking and waiting for me to feel safe? What will he take from me next? It took every ounce of self-control in me to not show how utterly terrified I was when we went for my check-up. And I had a whole protective convoy. Between Maddox, Tatum, Blake, and Drake, I felt like the wild daughter of a president. Not even Liam Neeson could've touched me.

I startle as my coat is dropped in my arms out of nowhere. "What the... What are you doing?" I cry.

"Put it on. I feel like blueberry waffles for lunch." Blakely doesn't wait for my protest, but disappears down the hall, only to return with my sneakers dangling from her fingers.

"Sit!" she barks. I'd make a comment about how I'm not a dog, but she'll find a way to point out how much of a sandy beach I'm being. So I plop down in a chair, only to squeak as she starts putting my shoes on.

"Please don't," I croak, mortification staining my cheeks red. Blakely waves me off as she busies herself with my other shoe. "I'm fairly certain this is not in your job description."

"Would you stop complaining already?" she huffs. I honestly have a hard time understanding how someone can bark orders while soft-spoken. She doesn't need to raise her voice for me to feel properly chastised.

Once I'm bundled up, she hooks her arm around my elbow and leads me to her car. She doesn't give me time to overthink or stress, even though my eyes are frantically scanning the street for any lurkers.

The air is crisp, tiny frozen crystals sparkling on the wilted grass in Maddox's driveway. Blakely opens the passenger door and helps me get situated inside. While my incisions are healed on the outside, there's still a lot of tenderness below my navel. The weeks I've been confined to a bed or the couch have taken their toll on me. My muscles are soft and weak.

I keep my eyes glued to the window as she drives us to the town center. She's humming under her breath to whatever song comes on the radio, and I relax, lulled into a false sense of safety.

"You're feeling up for a walk, or should I drop you off first?"

My stomach falls to my feet. Panic rises in my veins swiftly and without mercy. "I-I-I d-don't know."

I'll be alone in the diner if she drops me off. But walking next to me, when I have the speed of a snail after snorting chili powder, might put her in danger if Rob's lurking nearby.

"Illegal parking it is. I really hope having the Chief Deputy wrapped around your little finger comes in handy when someone sticks a fine on my windshield."

My shoulders drop from around my ears as I exhale in relief. "I'll pay for it."

"All I need is for you to talk to your therapist about this anxiety. If kept unchecked, it might evolve into agoraphobia." Blakely turns in her seat to face me once she parks alongside the curb in front of Dine&Dash. "At first, you don't even notice. Home is safe, like when you get scared at night and hide entirely under the blanket. Nothing can touch you there, but peek a toe out—you're monster food." She gives me a soft smile. "Same as my fear of flying."

I open my mouth to deny her very astute observation, but she deserves more respect than a blatant lie. "I'll bring it up."

She gives me a brisk nod, then exits the car, wasting no time to round the hood and help me out. Together, we walk inside the diner. Much to my surprise, it's nearly empty. Mrs. Jennings from the Post Office waves at me from a booth, and I wave back. I say hello in passing to a couple of people as Blakely leads me to a window booth.

"We're not hiding," she tells me as I take off my coat and slide onto the vinyl bench.

"Dollie!" a hoarse voice greets me before I can address Blakely's comment. "You finally came to see me."

The scent of glazed apples and maple syrup envelops me as Ruth throws her hands around my neck. She cups my cheeks as she tsks, pursing her lips. "What's that good-for-nothing nephew of mine been feeding you? We gotta put some meat on those sharp bones of yours."

At least she's blaming Maddox now. She thinks my bones are sharp every time I step foot into her diner.

"Been missing your pancakes, that's all," I reply, smiling as I half-stand from my seat, the table digging into my thighs. I press a kiss to her ruddy cheek and give her shoulder a squeeze. "He's been taking good care of me."

"He'd better, else he'd be banned for life." She takes a step back as I make myself comfortable once again and props her hands onto her generous hips. Her black apron pulls taut over her belly as she taps her foot impatiently against the checkered floor. "Well, let's get you those pancakes," she muses, her brown eyes shifting to Blakely. "What about you, sweetheart?"

"I'll have a blueberry waffle, please," Blakely replies, rubbing her stomach. "And a peppermint tea with lemon."

Ruth winks as she spins on her heel and disappears behind the counter.

"She's Maddox's aunt?"

"She is," I confirm. "His father's older sister, and doesn't let anyone forget it."

Blakely laughs, but her laugh immediately turns into a cough. "Incoming!"

"What?" I shift my knees just in time as a frantic-looking Maddox pulls me out of the booth, one arm banded around my waist, the other cradling the back of my head as he forces me onto my tiptoes.

"Fucking hell, Sawyer. Are you okay? Ten years out of my goddamn life went right out the window." His pupils are blown, eyebrows pulled tight on his forehead, as his arms coil around me.

I slap at his shoulders. "Put me down, you brute. You're making a scene."

"Fuck the scene. I came home, you're nowhere to be found. I call, your phone rings on the fucking coffee table. Are you trying to kill me?" he grits, his neck corded and tense. "Is that it?"

Shame rises in the pit of my stomach. I didn't think he'd come home so early. He was supposed to be at the station all day, then pick up Ryker in the afternoon. Instead of pushing him away, my fingers curl into the cold fabric of his uniform.

"I'm sorry," I whisper. "I didn't mean to worry you. It was an impromptu trip."

He rests his forehead against mine. His heart is pounding in his chest so wildly, I can feel each pulse against my ribcage. "I know I have no right to ask anything of you. You owe me no explanation of where you're going and why. But please... keep me in the loop next time. Just so I know you're safe. Just so I know you haven't left me."

My eyes flutter closed as I wind my arms around his neck, burying my fingers in his hair. "Maddox, you left me first."

He exhales heavily as he playfully rubs his nose to mine. "I couldn't leave you if I wanted to. I'm yours for the taking, little fairy. Unfortunately for both our hearts, I'm a slow learner and an asshole to a fault. Not a second has gone by since that blasted night that I haven't regretted leaving you. Not as I broke our hearts, not as you closed the door in my face, not as I dragged my feet home cursing myself for single-handedly destroying my happiness." He touches his lips to mine in a chaste kiss.

"Maddox..." I whine when he doesn't fully kiss me. Butterflies swarm my stomach as warmth floods my core.

"I've never been in love, Sawyer. Not a day in my life. Not until you blew your magic fairy dust on me. Ever since then, I can't sleep, I can't eat, I can't fucking breathe when you're not around."

He grips my chin, tilting my head back. Icy-blue eyes with blown-out pupils bore into mine.

"I. Love. You." He stresses every word as it rolls out of his mouth. "And if I have to crawl on my knees for all eternity to regain your love and your trust, I'll do it. No hesitation, no second thoughts."

My eyes well with tears, their burn deep and heavy. "You loving me wasn't enough for you before."

"*You* are always enough, little fairy. I was a coward, assuming someone else's demons for my own and bowing down instead of fighting them. I'm ashamed that it took seeing *you* come back to me, fighting for every heartbeat and breath, to finally understand *I* am also enough."

Chapter Forty-Eight

Sawyer

"They're being ridiculous!" Maevis huffs as she bites into a slice of banana bread. I eye her stealthily. Banana bread and lamingtons dominated her craving palate the whole time she was baking Lami in her oven. Clearly, I'm not stealthy enough as she glares at me. "You're being ridiculous, too. For the last time, I'm *not* pregnant."

I shrug nonchalantly while narrowing my eyes at her. Everyone's coddling me, thinking I'm going to break if they so much as mention pregnancy and babies. I don't deny that I'm still mourning my loss but, despite the extreme jealousy I will certainly feel if she's indeed pregnant, I'll also be extremely happy for them.

"Eighteen months!" Mae stomps her foot as she flips her braid behind her shoulder. "That's how long we're going to wait until we try again. I'm allowed to like banana bread, for fuck's sake."

I quickly cover the ears of the little bumblebee cooing to herself on my knees. "Your momma has a potty mouth," I whisper to her as I trace her little nose with my fingertip. Lami squeals and kicks her chubby legs, her cornflower-blue eyes round and wide as she gives me a toothless smile.

"They're still being ridiculous, with or without a bun in your oven," Emma quips from where she's lying on the floor on her belly, her heels touching the back of her thighs as she swings her legs back and forth.

"Pretty, but ridiculous," Violet sighs. "Pretty ridiculous."

Lalah plops down at my side, making grabby hands at me. "Gimme that baby!"

I give her my back, trying to protect the little treasure blowing drool balloons on my knees. "Get your own." My cheeks heat up instantly as I realize what I just said, so I turn back to her. "I'm sorry. You'd think *I'd* be more sensible about what comes out of my mouth."

She waves me off as Emma and Violet continue to bicker somewhere in the background about the pretty and ridiculous sentries outside. "Nah, doll. Don't sweat it." She shrugs, the black hoodie with *Smut makes my kitty purr* written in neon-pink stretching across her chest. "Truthfully, babies are cute and all. But as soon as diaper duty is calling, I'm out the door."

"I'm pretty sure Cole would help, unless he's just rubbing around the mint."

Her hazel eyes bore into mine, the green more prevalent as her face smooths into a somber mask. "Apart from freezing his nadas off currently"—she throws her thumb behind her shoulder, pointing at the *yes, pretty* but ridiculous men lined up in front of TBRC—"I've never really wanted kids. Not in a biological sense. Then Lady Luck decided to actually bless me, for a change, and brought Eliza and Clara into my life. Those girls are my daughters in every sense that matters. And I think someone chose *you* as well."

I couldn't stop my smile from spreading wide on my face if I tried. And I don't want to try. Ryker has woven his way into my soul way before I even looked in his father's direction. My favorite student, even when I wasn't supposed to have a favorite.

Lalah nudges my shoulder. "I'm not trying to downplay your feelings. Losing the ability to carry a child is devastating. But it doesn't make you any less of a mother, Sawyer."

My eyes well, and I suck in a watery breath. "I can be a mother in every way that matters, be it biological or not."

"You *can* still be a biological mother if it's what you want. My offer still stands. It will remain standing for as long as my health allows. When you're ready for a biological child, I'll be your surrogate."

"Me, too!" Emma shouts as she flips to her back and thrusts a hand in the air.

"Hey, I'm her older sister. I take priority!" Selae yells through the tablet propped on a coffee table in front of me.

"You gotta move home first," I hiccup-sob as the love of all these amazing women warms me from the inside-out.

My sister winks at me from the screen and blows me a kiss. "January cannot come soon enough, doll. But I'll see you at HeeBee's opening day first."

"If you don't mind your baby with a side of crazy, add my womb to the list." Violet twirls a wild curl around her finger. "Apparently someone told

Father Dearest I have ideal birthing hips." She smacks her palms over the curve of her hip to point out their roundness. "Give 'em a try, baby girl."

Tears are pouring unbidden on my face. My insecurities and grief are still strong, but seeing all the support I have from my loved ones heals some of the cracks in my heart.

"Well, now I'm just feeling left out." Maevis pouts.

"Weren't you waiting eighteen months?" I throw back, trying to keep the levity going.

She brushes my question off. "I am, but in eighteen months you get a prime baking oven. You should know, you're swinging on your knees my first masterpiece."

"There you have it," Lalah declares, sweeping her arm out to point at all of us. "A choice of wombs. A sanctuary of wombs? A cradle of wombs?"

The laugh that spills out of me startles Lami in my arms, and I shoosh her gently, swaying my knees back and forth so she settles. "Don't give yourself a concussion," I tease.

Lalah jumps to her feet and throws her arms in the air. "A genesis of uteri."

"What did I miss?" Annalise asks, her cheeks red as she carries a heavy-looking box. The storage door closes softly behind her as she drops the box on the bar top, next to a spaceship-like coffee maker. "Isn't the plural of uterus actually uteruses?"

"I like the Latin version better." Lalah shrugs. "Speaking of formal and dead languages, where's Blakely?"

"How did you make that connection?" I question, but she just rolls her eyes in response. "And Blakely messaged me this morning, excusing herself. Apparently, some mystery visitor from New York turned up on her doorstep, and she's dealing with that situation."

"Great. Now I need to find another nurse for Hope Haven." Lalah pouts, but by the wicked gleam in her eyes, she knows more than what she's letting on.

Violet taps a deep-purple fingernail against her chin. "Maybe she has a secret lover who's every bit of a caveman like the display Annalise put in front of her shop. Do you pay them by the hour? How much if we ask them to whip off their shirts?"

"Can we not ogle the merchandise, please?" Anna laughs. "In all seriousness, should we put them out of their misery?"

Lalah slaps her knees as she stands. With decisive steps, she strides to the entrance. "Yeah, this book club session is a bust, anyway. Plus, we need to discuss HeeBee's opening day. Emma and I just so happen to have a mile-long list for the idiots watching us through the window," she says as she opens the door with a flourish. "Fucking cavemen," she bites while one by one, Cole, Tatum, Maddox, Drake, and Blake *stalk* in.

MY KNEES ARE TREMBLING. All eyes are on me. *All the inking eyes.* I gulp and grip Maddox's arm tighter. Why did I think it was a great idea to let Lalah make such a circus out of Happy Bumblebee's opening day?

A normal day with me locked up in the office, pouring over spreadsheets as children just... changed buildings would've been best. But, no. There's a huge red ribbon blocking the entrance doors instead, and what looks like the entirety of Lost Hope and half our county crowding the grounds of our new daycare.

"I can't do this," I mumble, hiding my mouth in the collar of my winter coat.

Maddox turns to me, his dazzling smile making my stomach flip. The sight of his dimples and pearly white teeth, with the two front ones slightly overlapping, almost makes me forget about my nerves. *Almost.*

He grips my shoulders, rubbing his thumbs over my collarbone. "Yes, you can." He kisses my forehead, my eyes fluttering closed as I soak in his presence. "Every single person here wants to support and celebrate you. Just think how happy your students will be when they see their new classrooms. Think of why you are doing everything you're doing. HeeBee will be a safe space for children to play and learn. It's an ease for parents as they go about their day, knowing their kids are cared for and looked after so they can continue to provide for them." He steps into me, burying his nose in my hair. I nuzzle my cold face in the crook of his neck as white flurries fall all around us.

I draw a deep breath as I steel my spine and square my shoulders. "Thank you," I murmur. "Having you here for support..."

Maddox cuts me off as he cups my cheek, stroking my jawline lovingly. "You never have to thank me for supporting you, little fairy. I know your focus right now needs to be on healing and HeeBee. I know you still need time to forgive me and trust in me again. But I'm here. I'll always have your back. And when you're ready, I'm yours if you'll still have me."

He touches his cold lips to mine, our breaths clouding out between us. "Now go show them what a wallflower is made of." Maddox doesn't give me time to process his words or for the butterflies inside my stomach to overwhelm me. Instead, he pushes me gently in front of the entrance, where Mayor Brown stands with a pair of oversized scissors in hand.

"Without further ado, our own Sawyer Carter. Give it up for the woman behind Happy Bumblebees. She has fought tirelessly to ensure our children have a safe space with modern amenities where they can play and learn."

My cheeks flame up as applause and sharp whistles thunder all around me. My feet trip over themselves, and it's only by a stroke of luck I don't faceplant right in front of the massive red ribbon. I give the crowd a shy smile as I build up the courage to open my mouth. My smile grows as my students clap and cheer from the first row, all holding banners with their own interpretation of a bumblebee.

"Thank you all for being here," I say, raising my voice so it projects over the noise of the crowd. I clear my throat when my voice shakes. "Happy Bumblebees has been a lifelong dream of mine. I grew up watching my amazing and loving parents torn between their jobs and their children. While they did the best job at raising two rambunctious kids," I laugh as I point at Tate and Selena, "and one extremely well-behaved daughter," I point to myself, "I also wished I could make their lives easier."

My confidence grows as understanding chuckles sound from the crowd, and I see my mother blowing me a kiss.

"As parents, you want what's best for your little bumblebees, while also sometimes craving a bit of time for yourselves. I've seen my mother battle parent guilt every day as she hid with a cup of tea to take ten minutes for herself. I've seen the same guilt in my father's eyes as he left for each deployment and had to kiss his family goodbye once more."

My fingers tremble as I wrap them around the handles of the oversized scissors and poise the blunt blades on the mark drawn across the red ribbon. "Happy Bumblebees represents the assurance I want my parents to have that they did their absolute best for us and—I think I can speak for both myself and my siblings—we love them. It's my wish that every child passing through these doors feels the same about their parents." The ensuing cheers drown out my voice, so I pause for a second. I allow the joy of accomplishing my lifelong dream to wash through me.

"This would have not been possible without the financial backing we received from Lege et Lacrima; Anderson's Constructions for the wonderful job they did at remodeling the building into the beautiful daycare it is today; Lalah Hayes for being the unstoppable force she is, taking over for me as I recuperated; and last but not least, Blake Hayes for navigating with me the absolute jungle of administrative tasks, permits, and impossible spreadsheets."

I cut through the ribbon and, as the red fabric flutters before falling at my feet, I spread my arms wide. "Welcome to Happy Bumblebees."

PART FIVE

A season for hope.

"I'll take my leave, singing in muted notes to the cloudy skies.
I'm going to hope, and I'm never coming back.
I'm falling asleep muttering words...
Whispers of yearning and punishment.

Punish me with tears forged in your obsession;
Punish me with agony encased in strength;
Punish me with perilous dreams of oblivion.
But mostly...
Punish me with fiery vows of love undue.

Punish me today and tomorrow,
because tomorrow we're starting our forever
And we lose hope.

All we've hoped becomes our forever;
Tomorrow."

SAWYER CARTER

Chapter Forty-Nine

Maddox

I'm living in hell. A hell of my own making, and many would go as far as saying it's a well-deserved hell, but... still hell.

"Get back out there, Lawson!" I pat my cheeks roughly as I pep-talk myself in the mirror. "Be a man."

I'm hiding like a coward in the downstairs bathroom of my own home. It says a lot about my character that all I want to do is burst through the door, pick Sawyer up, and beg her to put me out of my misery and take me back. She pleaded with me not to leave her two months ago. I still left. And now I'm hanging on by a thread, making more demands.

She's been living with me for eight weeks. Fifty-six times in a row, I woke up with her in my arms. Fifty-six times in a row, I went to sleep curled up around her, my entire chest caving in with the fear that come morning she'd be gone.

Yeah. I did this to myself. I did this to her. Ultimately, I did this to us.

Sure, she's slowly opening up to me. She's not shying away as I pull her to my chest and hold her tight. She's not putting distance between the two of us, and she certainly hasn't packed her bags and moved back into her cottage, now that she's able to fend for herself. But she's also not... initiating.

Before I almost lost her for good, she didn't hesitate to seek me out. Her palm on my thigh, threading her fingers through my hair, kissing my cheek in passing as if kissing was as ingrained of a reflex as breathing. None of that exists anymore, and it's killing me inside.

It's physically painful for me to hold back. By some divine intervention and a sense of self-control I didn't know I possessed, I do. All day, every day.

How do we move on from this? How do I prove to her I have staying power?

I splash some cold water onto my cheeks and pat myself dry with a towel. I'm certainly not going to find those answers hiding in the bathroom.

As soon as I open the door, sounds of laughter greet me from the living room. The sight is nothing short of a miracle. Who would've thought Tatum Carter would one day be sprawled on the loveseat in my home, his wife perched on his knees, making casual conversation as if we're family? Certainly not me.

"Daddy, baby Lami smiled at me!" Ryker shouts as he barrels into my knees. A sharp shot of pain travels through my shins, and I bite back a curse.

I ruffle his hair before he twirls around like the mini-tornado he is and runs back to the couch where Sawyer is blowing raspberries onto Lami's naked belly. "She must've liked the book you read to her, buddy!"

"Yes, she did! But, Daddy, she then farted so long, it soundeded like a truck." He fans his fingers in front of his nose before quickly pinching his nostrils together. "Nappy changing is stinky business."

I bark out a laugh as I make my way to them, dropping down on the couch next to Sawyer. With a finger, I tickle Lami's belly. She rewards me with another long fart for my efforts.

"Ewwww!" Ryker squeals, jumping on the cushions that somehow ended up on the floor.

Lami smiles once again as Sawyer holds her at arm's length. "Mommy, you're up again." She scrunches her nose adorably as she waves the baby around.

"Sorry guys," Maevis says, smirking sheepishly. "I shouldn't have eaten broccoli last night."

"She's also conveniently leaving out she stir-fried them with onions and garlic," Tatum quips.

"HEY!" Mae protests as she jumps to her feet. "Garlic helps with the milk supply." She shoves a finger in the center of her husband's chest. "Go change your daughter, sir. Clearly, she inherited your poor digestive system."

I hide my face between Sawyer's shoulder blades as I bite down a laugh. The last thing I need is a Mae-lecture on nutrition and breastfeeding mothers.

"I can feel you shaking," Sawyer whispers as they disappear into the bathroom. "You're not as sneaky as you think you are." She turns to face me, and I drink in the sight of her eyes, sparkling with amusement and happiness. I miss seeing her smiling freely. The ever-present hollowness in her dark irises calls to the deepest parts of me to chase away, to fill it in with love until there's nothing left of it but a bad memory.

Ryker plops down on my lap, stretching around until his head lands over Sawyer's thighs. He grins up at us, all his baby teeth on full display. "Wha'cha whisperin' about? Is it Santa?"

I roll my eyes as I catch a squirmy leg in my palm and pretend to take a bite out of his calf. "There's gonna be no Santa if I'm eating you whole like a jellybean," I growl. The sole of his foot shoves at my shoulder just as Sawyer's palm pushes against my forehead, and I cry out in fake defeat as I slump against the cushions.

"No, Daddy, no!" he squeals, scrambling off my lap, his knee pressing down on my groin until I cry out for real as he hides behind Sawyer.

The wicked fairy flicks my nose as she giggles. "That's what you get for being a hungry knucklehead." Her arm goes around Ryker as she shields him with her body. "I've got you, sweetheart. Next time his teeth are itching for a yummy bite, we'll tickle him into submission."

Ryker winds his arms around her neck, his eyes narrowing in my direction from behind a curtain of silky hair. "You're a meanie," he tells me. "You give me five grapes right now." He stomps his foot ineffectively as the leathery cushion just bends around him. "And no goodnight story for you, Mister."

I clutch at my chest as he savagely wounds me. My mouth betrays me, though. For a dude with shattered pride, I'm grinning so widely, my cheeks. But I'll take second place in my son's eyes when he's clearly chosen his favorite. Having Sawyer live with us has brought out a different side to him, a lightness that was missing in his cheeky smiles.

There's much to be said about parental guilt. Seeing them bond so completely has made it rear its ugly head from time to time. I've questioned myself, trying to understand where I was lacking, where I have failed my son by not giving him everything he needed. But as the days progressed and their bond flourished, I slowly understood how Sawyer and I bring different things to the table—both sides equally important.

I'm always affectionate with my son, mindful of his needs and thoughts. But the magical fairy cuddling with him in front of me gives him the kind of nurture I'm not able to give. I support his passions and hobbies as he slowly grows into his personality—the goddamn fairy costume in my walk-in closet is proof enough. But she takes the time to understand his thought process, where I take him at face value.

She makes even story time a learning experience for him. One he looks forward to every night. She's been his choice ever since she moved here. Every night without fail, he'll take me by the hand and lead me into his bathroom. He'll take a shower, dry off, and get dressed in his PJs without complaint, choose a book, and dash down the stairs to Sawyer. I've been reduced to a ferry service. As soon as he falls asleep, I pick him up and carry him back, tucking him in for the night.

And then I get to pick Sawyer up and tuck her in.

I *got* to pick her up and tuck her in.

I'm not allowed to anymore now that she's stronger.

"Does anyone else think this is weird as fuck, or is it just me?" Tatum asks as he returns to the living room, Lami strapped to his chest.

"Would you stop with the swearing, for ink's sake!" Sawyer snaps.

I shake my head as I chuckle ruefully. "Nah, man. I'm with you. It's going to take me a while to get used to you not wanting to kill me."

He smirks in response as he cradles the back of his daughter's head. "Who says I don't?"

"No killing in the house." Ryker crosses his arms across his chest as he frowns at Tate. "Gampy saided blood is a bleach to get out of the carpet."

I choke on my tongue as Sawyer turns fifty shades of red trying not to laugh. Maevis grins ear-to-ear as she passes by her husband, and leans down to give Sawyer and Ryker a hug. "Thank you for dinner *and* entertainment. We're gonna get going, guys. I'm trying to get some semblance of a sleep routine for my little farting-machine. I swear the kid keeps baker's hours."

I push to my feet and help Sawyer up too, letting Ryker hang by my neck instead. As strong as she is, I'm still careful she doesn't strain herself and sets back her recovery. Tatum slings an arm around her shoulders as he kisses the side of her head.

I help Maevis shrug into her coat as the siblings whisper to each other in the background. Ryker tightens his feet around my waist, holding onto me like a wiggly spider-monkey. I'm dying to know what Sawyer and Tatum are talking about. I swear, I can feel my ears burning. But they deserve their privacy. She's not had much time to herself in the past two months. Between me hogging her during the night, Ryker, Blakely, and the stream of constant visitors during the day, I'm surprised she hasn't run for the hills yet.

"Thanks for having us over, Madd." Maevis beams at me. "Tate has been worried sick about her. It does him a world of good to see his sister almost back to her former self." She gently squeezes my forearm. "Hang in there. We're all rooting for you. My husband included, believe it or not."

I PACE THE LENGTH OF THE LIVING ROOM LIKE A CAGED LION. I know I'm an idiot. No one needs to tell me. I'm a self-aware idiot, thanks. That knowledge doesn't stop me as I find one of those twelve-hour-long videos of a fireplace on my smart TV. Yeah, laugh away. This is my pathetic attempt at romance.

But even in my supreme idiocy, the living room looks cozy. The crackling of fire is a soothing background in the stillness of the night, as yellow and orange flames dance on the screen. Snow is falling unbidden outside, in big icy flakes. I've left the curtains open, just enough so that we can see outside without fear of anyone looking in.

I'm just... at a loss for what to do.

I don't want us to just wordlessly go to sleep, each on our side of the bed, until I finally cave and pull her against my chest. Tonight has been great on so many levels. Seeing Sawyer interact with her brother and her sister-in-law, her eyes sparkling as she cooed with Lami, her blinding smiles directed at my son... I want that magic to continue.

Our interactions used to be so effortless.

Now we're chained to a self-imposed awkwardness I don't know how to fight.

Her soft footsteps sound on the stairs, and I turn just as she reaches the landing. She pushes her hair behind her ear as she smiles uncertainly at me. "What's this?"

The black magic of her proximity has me tongue-tied. A strange sort of timidness has me rooted to the spot. I grip my nape as my stomach flips. "I thought we could spend some time together." Her eyes widen and her lips part.

My stomach bottoms out. Ah shit, she's going to reject me.

"It's okay," I rush out. Dammit, I'm not trying to make things more awkward. "We can go to sleep if you're tired."

She watches me quietly for the longest thirty seconds of my life. "I'm actually in the mood for some hot cocoa. Do you want some?"

My heart is hammering so hard in my ears, for a second her words don't compute. My knees sag as relief barrels through me when I finally understand she's not running away to sleep. "Yeah. Yes, please."

She passes by me, her scent of sweet pear and bergamot coiling like a leash around my neck. I follow after her like a lost puppy, shadowing her every move. "Fireplace, huh?" Sawyer says as she picks up a pot and fills it with milk. Off to the stove she goes, moving about my kitchen as if she owns the place.

"Figured it was relaxing," I grit as embarrassment stains my cheeks. "I'll turn it off if you don't like it."

She rolls her eyes at me over her shoulder as she picks up two mugs. "Ink around and see what happens," she threatens as she dumps a generous portion of cocoa powder and mixes it with maple syrup.

Her playful side emboldens me. My cock thickens behind the fly of my jeans, and I take a step closer to her. My hands find purchase on her hips, her back nearly touching my front. Pure fire licks at my skin, tingles sizzling through my veins at her nearness. "You can say 'fuck', you know?"

Sawyer leans against me as she watches the milk simmering. "Just because I can, doesn't mean I have to."

I lower my head, tracing the curve of her cheek with my nose as I whisper in her ear, "I know you want to, little fairy."

She leans her head on my shoulder, her ass rubbing against my crotch. That's all the incentive my cock needs to go from half-mast to proudly calling the troops to battle. All the feral butterflies zombying inside my stomach dissipate into thin air when she stiffens against me. I give her hips a gentle squeeze and take a step back.

I pushed too far, too fast.

With jerky movements, she pours steaming milk in the mugs and sprinkles a dusting of cinnamon. I turn the stove off and rinse the pot in the sink before sticking it into the dishwasher. With my fingers hooked around the porcelain handles of each mug, I let her lead the way to the couch.

I have half a mind to melt my tongue off and chug the hot cocoa in one go, then go hide in the bedroom.

I mentally berate myself as we take a seat, each on opposite sides of the couch. *Goddamn insensitive asshole.* For sure, she now thinks I have sex on the brain. Well, I always have sex on the brain where Sawyer's concerned.

I yearn for her every hour of every day. But right now, I simply got caught up in the moment, in her responding to me like she used to.

Blowing gently over the top of the mug—I'm not stupid enough to punish myself by burning off my tastebuds—I slurp quietly at the sweet, warm concoction. A happy noise crawls out of my throat. I don't even like hot cocoa, but of course, she made it, so I love it. Everything she touches, she somehow makes it better.

I chance a peek at her out of the corner of my eye. She's barely perched on the edge of the couch, holding her own mug with both hands over her knees. Her thumbs drum silently against the rim as she stares at the steam rising from her hot cocoa.

"I'm sorry I'm making things more... difficult for you," Sawyer murmurs. I shift in my seat, the leather crinkling under me as I face her. Panic grabs around my throat. She refuses to look at me, keeping her eyes downcast.

"I don't understand," I finally manage to grit out. The slight clang of my mug as I settle it on the coffee table echoes through the room.

She takes a dainty sip, licking at her bottom lip as she leans over, resting her mug on the corner closest to her. Her fingers entwine in her lap as she squares her shoulders and finally looks at me. "You have needs, Maddox. Needs I'm not able to fulfill anymore."

I sputter as I jump to my feet. "What's that supposed to mean?" She visibly flinches away from me, and I immediately drop back down. I need her to feel safe to speak her mind, not intimidate her with my height. I shake my head, trying to keep my mind clear, but it's close to impossible when my very soul feels heavy with lead.

She closes her eyes. The pain etched into her delicate features robs me of my breath. "I see them, you know? Every time I shower, every time I get dressed. Those red jagged lines pull at my skin every time I stretch, constantly reminding me how hollow I am."

I fall on my knees on the soft carpet and crawl to her. Cupping her beautiful face between my palms, I kiss her forehead and the tip of her nose. "You're too full of life to be hollow, little fairy. Too full of love." An anguished sob escapes her lips, and I chase it down, touching my mouth to hers. "Those scars are a reminder of how strong you are. They're part of you. You look at them and see emptiness. I look at them and see the reason I'm still whole." I splay my hand in the center of her chest, feeling against my palm the strong, rapid beats of her heart. "I felt you dying, Sawyer. I felt your heart stop and your breath vanish. Those scars are the hope that brought you back to me."

"I can't give you any more children," she cries, the words hoarse and whispered as tears track down her cheeks. I press another chaste kiss to her mouth.

"You're more than enough for me, little fairy. If children are your hold-up, I'll book a vasectomy first thing in the morning. Then I won't be able to give you any either."

Her arms come around my neck, her fingers tunneling through my hair as she pulls gently at the strands. "You have Ryker."

I chuckle darkly. "Have you seen the kid lately? If he could tie himself to you, he'd do it. As soon as he learns to work a knot. You might not have given birth to him, but you're the only mother he has."

"You'll never get to experience me pregnant," she counters. "Or hear the baby's heartbeat for the first time. You didn't get the chance with Ryker either."

"But I'll get to experience life with you. Same as I get to experience life with Ryker." My head replaces my hand, the drumming of her heart a nightmare-chaser soundtrack in my ear. "All I need to do is walk upstairs and listen to his little heart beating." I sigh against her chest as her fingers tighten in my hair. "I choose to experience you in any way I can get you. And if you want more kids, we can always adopt."

Her fingers feather along my jawline, settling under my chin as she tilts my head back. Red-rimmed dark eyes stare at me incredulously. Her lips part, her final argument settling like a nuclear bomb between the two of us. "You broke my heart."

My throat constricts as I suck in a wheezed-out breath. "I'll fuse it back together if you let me," I vow. "I lived my life thinking my choices were limited because of the poor choices others made for themselves. *You*, little fairy, taught me the only choice that matters in how I live my life is mine. And I choose you. My heart, battered and shriveled and bruised as it is, chooses you."

I close my eyes as I whisper, "Please, choose me back."

Chapter Fifty

Sawyer

My heart stalls painfully in my chest. I smooth my fingers over his cheekbones, savoring the roughness of his scruff against my skin. I'm on the precipice of a cliff. Should I take a step back to safety or should I jump?

There's no net to catch me if I fall.

Maddox blinks his eyes open; icy-blue irises shine at me as the flickering orange glow of the TV fireplace dances with the shadows in the living room. He's completely splayed open for me. Mine to take. Mine to walk away from. He's a sorcerer, of that I am sure. There's no other explanation for the spell woven beneath my ribs and coiled around my heart—*his* heart—tugging me in his direction.

I lower my head until we're nose to nose and our breaths intermingle. "I choose you back," I whisper. He sucks in a watery breath, his relief palpable between the two of us. "I might be the most foolish woman alive to risk my heart twice. You put a spell on me. When you're around, I feel invincible and strong. My need to hide away vanishes into thin air. You drive me absolutely insane. And I love you for it."

Maddox cups the back of my head, pulling me down to him. I slide over the buttery leather, right into his lap as I straddle his thighs. The skirt of my pastel-green dress fans around us. His mouth slants over mine, his lips firm and tender as he coaxes mine open. For a breath, time stays still. Fireworks explode somewhere around us. The world could go up in flames, for all I care.

"I'm sorry," he whispers against my mouth. "I love you," he murmurs. "I. LOVE. YOU." Maddox insists between gentle pecks. His tongue traces my bottom lip, and I nip playfully at him before sucking it inside my mouth. He tastes like hot cocoa and winter wonderland dreams and everything Maddox. He tastes like mine.

I whimper in his mouth as his tongue explores mine, grunting his pleasure when my hips buck against the hardness straining to reach me from behind his fly. His large hands are everywhere. Feathering against my neck, holding my hips as I rock against him, cupping my breasts, and playfully tugging at my taut nipples. My core hits up as electricity travels through my veins.

My fingers find purchase on the hem of his Henley, and he growls in displeasure when I pull back from our kiss just enough to push the soft fabric over his head. His skin is feverish, sizzling hot as my palms roam all over the expanse of his wide chest. His mouth chases mine once more, relentless in its pursuit, and I let myself be caught.

Rough, callused fingers trail over my thighs, tunneling under the pleated skirt. His thumbs toy with the hem of my panties as my breaths grow labored, my whimpers needy. "You're so goddamn beautiful, it's physically painful for me to look at you," he grunts as he gently sucks at my tongue. "I hurt for you, and I'll gladly hurt the rest of my life if you let me."

I gasp as my dress is ripped over my head, my hair fanning out over my shoulders. His hand cups one of my breasts as he thrusts up against me, the stiff material of his jeans chafing between my legs. He lowers his head and sucks a pointy nipple into his mouth through the lace of my bra, biting gently at the hardened bud. I swear there's a ley line between my nipples and my core as my walls clamp painfully over nothing.

He lavishes my breast with his undeterred attention, licking, sucking, biting, loving until I'm squirming on his lap, a boneless mess of need and desire. Only once he's good and ready, he trails open-mouthed kisses across my chest, then doubles his efforts on the breast he's been neglecting so far.

"Hmm," he hums, his lips fused to my throbbing nipple. "You're so responsive to me. I wonder if you can come just from me loving on these beautiful tits of yours." He flicks his tongue rapidly against my bud until my eyes roll and my back arches. "I'll never get enough of these tits. God, you fill my palms so well. Look at you, a handful and then some." I tighten my hold in his hair, to pull him closer or push him away, I don't know.

A seed of doubt swirls in my stomach. "What if... what if I can't?" I whisper.

He releases the clasp of my bra, my breasts spilling in his awaiting palms. He growls his pleasure as he buries his face between them, licking a path of love to the center of my chest. My heart hammers beneath my ribs, anxiety and anticipation warring in my mind.

"What if we find out?" he asks, his gravelly voice muffled by my breasts. He tilts his head back, his pupils so dilated, the fathomless darkness almost overtaking the icy blue of his irises. My breasts, heavy and aching, are trapped by his chest as he tilts my chin with two fingers. "I know we cannot have sex. Even if my balls turn purple and fall off, I'll never risk you, you hear me? But if you want, there are other ways for me to pleasure you."

I tremble in his arms as desire starts to give way to panic. "But what if I can't, Maddox? What if I never can?"

He stands up on his knees as he lays me back on the couch, my ass half-hanging over the edge. He looms over me, and my thighs find purchase around his hips. "Do you trust me, little fairy?"

I swallow the lump in my throat as his eyes bore into mine. "I do." I nod jerkily.

He rewards me with a crooked grin that has a dimple popping in his right cheek. "Then let me take care of you, baby."

"But what if I..."

"Then I'll pick you up, tuck you into our bed, and we'll go to sleep. And tomorrow, we'll try again. And again, and again, and again for as long as you're willing. Your orgasms are a thing of beauty. While I'd miss them like I'd miss a limb, sex is not a make or break for me. I want *you*, little fairy. My entire life I've chased after a connection in all the wrong places. You give me *everything* I need. Your trust, your backbone, your love, you—all that matters to me." He runs his thumb over my bottom lip as I squirm underneath him. "Will you let me take care of you?"

I suck his thumb into my mouth, swirling my tongue around it. His hips buck into mine, the length of his hard cock rubbing against my center. Maddox lowers his head, giving me a rough kiss as he moans into my mouth. He trails his lips down the column of my neck, across my collarbone, nipping at my breasts in his path. He takes his time nuzzling his nose around my belly button. And then, his eyes latch onto mine as he gently, reverently, kisses all four of my incisions. There's only love and adoration in his gaze, not a shadow of doubt or confusion.

His mouth settles between my legs, just a breath away from where I'm aching for him, a thin layer of lace separating us. As if in slow motion, he brushes my underwear away, revealing me to him. "Fuck me, you're so pretty, so pink, so mine," he breathes over the center of me as I squirm in his grasp. Leisurely, he licks the length of my seam with the flat of his tongue, groaning as if he's never tasted anything better.

My clit throbs in response, and I fight his grip on my hips as I chase his mouth for more. A fire kindles in my lower belly, roaring to life with each flick of his tongue, every caress of his lips lifting me higher and higher and higher. My fingers claw at the leather cushion under me, finding no purchase.

"Maddox!" I cry out as he starts feasting in earnest, giving me no reprieve as he sucks my clit into his mouth, his tongue circling it with unrepentant flicks. My hips buck against his mouth, my thighs holding him in place as I rub against his face, chasing my pleasure, letting that slow kindling fire spread through my limbs and consume me whole. Pain and pleasure seize my body as I explode against his mouth. "God, yes, please, please, please," I beg as his mouth keeps making love to my pussy through all the tremors and aftershocks of my orgasm.

I slump against the cushion, boneless and exhausted, as Maddox places a chaste kiss to my throbbing clit. "That's my good little fairy. You taste better than I remember." He pushes to his feet as my soul returns to my languid body. A different kind of fire rises in my chest as I bask in the afterglow of my orgasm.

I didn't really consider my sexual desires, overwhelmed by the grief of not being able to bear children. I didn't realize that one reason I couldn't look at my body in the mirror is because I see myself as faulty and unattractive, now that a fundamental piece of my identity is missing.

Maddox crouches at my side, wrapping his arms around my waist. "Let's get you into bed, baby."

"No!" I protest. Empowerment runs rampant through my veins. "Get rid of your jeans."

He looks at me incredulously. "You don't have to..."

"I want to. Jeans. Off. Now!"

He steps away, his hands settling over his belt buckle. "Little fairy," he murmurs, but does as I ask, his fingers looping around his belt and unfastening it in slow movements, as if giving me time to change my mind. Maddox never treated me like a porcelain doll in bed. It'll break my heart if he starts now. His need for my body was always all-consuming. I want... *No!* I *need* him unhinged for me.

I shift on the couch, swinging my legs up on the cushion as I stretch my whole body over the buttery leather. "Straddle my chest," I order him.

His lips part as he gapes at me, but hurries shedding his jeans. A brisk shove of his underwear has his cock springing up like an erotic

Jack-in-the-box with a pink and angry head and dark veins throbbing on the surface. *I do this to him!*

He steps closer, trailing his thumb on my jawline. "Are you sure?"

I grip his hard cock in response, moaning as I feel all that hardness encased in velvet jerking in my palm. I stroke him tenderly from root to tip, circling the damp head with my thumb. My tongue darts out, licking at my bottom lip; my mouth drools as I imagine the weight of him slide across my tongue and hit the back of my throat. My fingers tighten around his shaft as I literally lead him by his cock to straddle me.

His strong thighs settle on each side of my chest as I continue to jerk him off in slow, tender strokes. Maddox looms over me, all mighty and powerful, his hips chasing my fist as he thrusts shallowly into my grip. "Sit, pretty boy," I tell him, my voice all raspy and seductive. I brace my elbows around my breasts, the creamy soft mounds pushing together as I guide his cock between them. His leaking tip disappears in the valley between my breasts, and he throws his head back and moans as I stroke him with my tits.

"Goddamn, you're set on killing me, aren't you? You're a wicked, wicked little fairy. Fuck, fuck, fuck," he grunts as he fucks himself between my tits in slow, shallow thrusts. A veiny forearm braces on the backrest of the couch as his free hand cups my nape, tilting my chin. I have a first-row view of his cock tunneling between my breasts, sliding in and out, as he holds himself above me.

Maddox slowly retreats, driving himself up harshly until the angry red head of his cock nearly touches my lips. My stomach flips as my core once more throbs with desire. On a whim, I part my lips and fasten them around the very tip of him, swirling my tongue around the sensitive flare of his head.

He throbs in my mouth as he retreats, and I lick my lips, savoring the salty, masculine taste of him. "Fuck, who taught you that?" he bits, but doesn't hesitate to thrust back into my mouth. I hollow my cheeks as I suck him to the back of my throat, gagging around his length. He trembles above me, moving in long, controlled thrusts.

"That's it, you wicked woman. Suck me, baby. Choke on my cock and show me how much you want me." I trail my fingers over the backs of his thighs and splay my palms over the round globes of his ass. Goosebumps rise on my skin as I feel all those taut muscles tensing and relaxing with every thrust, every drive of his cock inside my mouth. My breasts bounce and jiggle, the couch squeaking rhythmically beneath us as he chases his pleasure wildly, relentlessly, and with abandon.

"Fucking hell, little fairy, your mouth is made of dirty fantasies and all my best goddamn dreams." I relax my throat when he slides against my tongue once more, my breath trapped in my chest as he stuffs me full of him. "You're so damn beautiful with your lips stretched out around me. Look how well you take me." His fingers tighten at my nape as my mouth rings the very root of him when he bottoms out between my lips. He is so impossibly hard, but somehow grows thicker as I caress the underside of his length with my tongue.

"God, you're going to make me come." His words are rough and gravelly. His entire body strains over me as he holds himself back. I sputter a breath, tears falling down my cheeks as he retreats, his cock once again disappearing in the valley between my breasts.

"Do it," I rasp, a challenge to him as I voice out my desire. "You had your taste. Now give me mine, pretty boy. Fuck my mouth and flood my throat with your cum."

He roars as he parts my lips again, the head of him sliding down my throat in rapid, shallow thrusts. The entire couch is shaking under the strength of his lust. "You're the absolute death of me. Fuck, my little slut, take it," he grits, "fucking take all of me."

His cock jerks across my tongue. I hollow my cheeks again and suck hard. My jaw aches, the corners of my lips stretched painfully around his throbbing length. My palms press down on his ass, pushing him further down my throat until my face is flush with his groin. My mouth floods with the taste of him as he paints my throat with his hot, salty cum. I swallow roughly around him, milking him dry of all he has to give.

Gently sliding out of my aching mouth, he collapses at my side, breathing hard as he nuzzles his face in the crook of my neck. "I think my soul left my body for a second there," Maddox murmurs, his hot breath fanning across my collarbone. I turn in his arms as he hooks his arm around my waist, pulling me to his chest. His eyes flutter open, and he gives me a blissed-out, sleepy smile. "I'm never letting you go, little fairy."

"No little slut?" I ask, my voice scratchy and rough. For everything we do to each other in bed, that moniker is what gives me pause.

His smile widens as he winds a tendril of my hair around his finger and tugs playfully. "You're my prim and proper wallflower everywhere you go, in everything you do," he murmurs. "But when it's just the two of us, you're wild and free. You trust *me* enough to be wild and free."

I giggle against his chest as understanding washes over me, and I playfully pinch his side, making him yelp. "Oh god. You're *proud* of yourself. Calling me your *little slut* is..."

"Reassuring myself you're comfortable to be wild and free with me and only me, little wildflower." Maddox kisses me hard, his tongue forcibly swiping inside my mouth. "You taste like us," he rasps, pecking at my lips. "You taste like forever, and I've never experienced anything better."

Chapter Fifty-One

Sawyer

A delicious throb between my legs wakes me up. I blink my eyes open, only to be greeted with Maddox's wide shoulders propping up my thighs, blowing gently across my aching center.

"Has no one taught you not to play with your food?" I tease, my voice laden with sleep. "What time is it, anyway?"

"Just after six," he murmurs. "I... we never discussed... uhm... initiating anything while one of us is asleep." Maddox grins bashfully, like a devious cat caught pawing at the pot of cream.

"But... staring at my pussy while heavy-breathing it to death is acceptable?"

He nips at my thigh in warning. "I love it when those pretty lips of yours spill filthy words. Even if they are at my expense." He soothes the sting of my smarting skin with a chaste kiss. "I want you to always feel safe with me."

I stretch my arm until my fingers reach his hair as I scoot down the bed. "I told you before, I'm willing to try everything once. If I don't like it, I'll tell you as it happens. Besides, how fun would it be for me to have a one-on-one with your favorite appendage as you snore away?"

"You're talking too much, and I'm hungry." His words are muffled by my moans as he buries his face between my legs, licking, sucking, and slurping. His large hands grip my thighs, spreading me further. I open up to him as he feasts, his growls of pleasure sending bolts of electricity through my navel. The sun doesn't even breach the horizon as Maddox eats me to an early orgasm.

"Good morning to me," I sigh as he kisses my lower belly gently before crawling up over me.

The dopamine rush in my bloodstream dries out instantly at the serious look on his face. His eyebrows are drawn together. His lips, swollen and slick with my lust, are pulled taut. I caress his scruffed cheek. "What's wrong?"

"I have a confession to make."

My stomach churns, ice flooding my veins. "If it is about you sleeping with that other woman two months ago, I don't want to know," I snap. "Infidelity is something I'll never accept between the two of us. You're all mine or not at all."

His eyes round comically as his lips part. "What other woman? I've already told you, there's been no one else but you for a year, little fairy."

"You said"—I lower my voice, in a cheap imitation of his—"*Cheaters will always be cheaters. I don't deserve or want your forgiveness.*"

He drops his head to my shoulder as he groans. I squeal as he coils an arm around my waist and rolls to his back, taking me with him. Maddox settles against the headboard as I straddle his thighs. His cock, perfectly cradled between my legs, throbs against my slick core, hard and thick. "Goddammit, I *didn't* cheat on you. Not before, not now, not ever."

The oily feeling crawling up my spine deserts me as I suck in a breath of relief. I grip his shoulders as I rock against the hard length trapped between my thighs. He stills my hips with his hands and a hissed, "Behave."

"I went to visit my father that day. I promised you I'd work on my trust issues, so I wanted to know how he forgave my mother for cheating on him." His eyes flutter closed, shame practically pouring out of his skin in waves. "Turns out, they were separated. *He* cheated on her first." I lean down and kiss him in encouragement, coaxing him to continue. "After I got the full story, my mind was a mess. I'm the product of two cheaters. Two people concerned only with *their* wants and needs made me. I felt dirty down to the last strand of my DNA. I just... I *knew* deep in my bones, I wouldn't be any better. I could love you desperately and still ruin you."

"Maddox," I breathe, rubbing his chest tenderly, "you're not your parents. You choose how to live each day."

This time, he kisses me. Hard. Fast. Unapologetic. "I know that now. You show me how, every day." His fingers tighten on my hips. "But that's not my confession. I haven't cheated, but you might hate me for it, anyway."

I freeze in his arms. What's worse than cheating? "Say it," I beg. Better to rip the band-aid off. A spark of anger kindles to life in my chest. I was happy for exactly six hours, and now he's trying to take it away.

"Ever since I drove you home from Lalah's Thanksgiving dinner... I became restless. Unsettled. I considered I might have a brain tumor. Poison was also on the list of possibilities." He gives me a wry grin, but I don't feel like smiling. Not until I hear the full story. "It just didn't make any sense. The sparks in my stomach every time I'd see you. The way my knees went weak and my palms sweat."

I swat at his shoulder. "Don't try to get cute with me right now."

He sobers up as his icy-blue eyes, barely visible in the darkness of our bedroom, bore into mine. "I'd go to sleep, only to toss and turn for hours. So... during the nights when Ryker was with my parents—or when I'd get desperate enough and call Joshua to stay with him—I'd go for a run. And always, *always* end up at your house."

I suck in a breath as my heart starts racing so wildly, I'm certain he is able to hear it. "What are you saying?"

"It started innocently enough. Just a run up and down your street. Soon, it wasn't enough. I needed more. So I'd watch you through your living room window." He swallows harshly, his cheeks blazing so fiercely, not even the lack of light can hide his blush. "Sometimes I'd..."

My gasp echoes through the room as I slap a palm over my mouth. "Dear god!" I mumble. "YOU WERE JERKING OFF AT MY WINDOW?"

The absurdity of his confession rocks me to my core. His eyes scrunch shut, as if the shame of his actions is too much for him to bear. My body shakes on top of him. My lungs constrict. My throat closes off as I wheeze in a breath. And then I explode. Laughter spills past my lips. My ribcage feels too constricting. My mind blanks as I struggle to process the ludicrousness of his words.

"You?" I laugh. "You stalked me?" I can't breathe through the throaty laughter still torturing me. "Oh my god. That's what you meant when you said you had big boy feelings and no idea what to do with them."

I collapse against his chest, my abdomen cramping as I try to stifle the bouts of giggles still threatening to escape. "No wonder those flowers kept dying down."

Maddox grips my nape, his fingers splayed through my hair. "God, you're such a fucking weirdo, and I love you for it." He kisses the top of my head. "Better hope Blakely won't ask about them come spring."

I rest my chin on top of my hands as I give him a lazy smile. "Technically, you're the weirdo. Luckily for you, it just so happens that I love you, too."

I touch my lips to the column of his neck. "Don't worry about Blakely. I have a feeling her New York story might not be over yet."

"I broke in too, but only once when you were at home," Maddox blurts out of nowhere. "You fell asleep on your sofa, so I carried you to bed. Uhm... I also might have spent a couple of nights up in a tree and opened your childhood bedroom window when you stayed for a weekend with your parents."

"Don't tell me..." I groan. Not because he might have... pleasured himself as I was sleeping—I'm dismissing completely his climbing adventures; Dad with a shotgun, yeah, he'd be a goner. But because I missed the show. He nods against my head, his heart pumping wildly under my palm. "Holy kinky ink, Maddox. You owe me an encore." A memory hits me hard and fast as I jolt on top of him. "Wait... the night I thought someone was at my window..."

"Wasn't me," he cuts me off. "I swear to you, it wasn't me."

"A few times," I confess, my voice low and timid, "I felt like someone was watching me. Sure, on occasion I thought I smelled you in my house or felt your eyes on me. I simply thought I was too... infatuated with you, so I was seeing you everywhere. This, though, was different. Frightening. Do you think it was him?"

His fingers dig into my hips, almost to the point of pain. "I do." He sighs. "I looked into it, you know, after you called me. Drove around your house—my deputies were worried about all the night patrols I volunteered for. The bastard was careful. But," Maddox says, relaxing his grip on me, his thumbs brushing gently against my skin, "he's gone now, little fairy. You never have to fear him again."

"The police haven't found him."

"No, the *police* never did."

Suspicion blossoms in my gut. Call it feminine intuition, call it whatever you want. "What did you do?"

He drags his fingers over the curve of my spine and over my shoulder, then tilts my chin until we're eye to eye. "I did nothing. *Lady* Luck works in mysterious ways. Some assholes get the girl." He winks at me. "Others get what they deserve."

"He's gone forever?" I murmur. Truthfully, I don't care what happened to Rob. He could rot in hell as far as I'm concerned, as long as there's at least one level of distance between the two of us.

"You never have to worry about him again."

THANK THE HOLY FOUNTAIN PEN, Maddox has this parenting gig down pat.

After his morning confessions, he redeemed his stalking tendencies with another orgasm as we showered together, then dressed me up in a pair of sleeping shorts and one of his T-shirts. Just in time too, as I barely finished brushing my teeth when Ryker came barreling through the bedroom door.

The last thing we need is to have him walk in on us buck-naked and traumatize the child.

Of course, the shock of the little good morning alarm wore off, only to be immediately replaced with a freak-out of massive proportions. Ryker came down the stairs all by himself. What if he tripped? What if he fell? We'd be none the wiser if he hurt himself, as we were lazing it up in bed.

So, after I had to reassure Maddox a thousand-and-one ways that I was strong enough to use the stairs—and a phone call to Doctor Richards so she could confirm those stairs wouldn't kill me, plus a second one to Blakely who laughed in his face and ended the call—I got to spend the morning watching him and Drake move all the furniture back into the master bedroom.

I'll have clothes to refold until the New Year, but at least Ryker can barrel into our room to his heart's content safely.

I guess this is what being a parent means. Having your child's well-being at the forefront of your every decision. Worrying about their safety until your stomach churns and you develop an ulcer. And hiding grapes from the four-year-old hound with more cravings than sense. I'll take it. I'll take the tantrums, the sticky fingers, the scrambled eggs plastered all over the kitchen floor and sometimes the ceiling, and whatever else he's throwing our way.

I'd never imagined how much I'd get to love someone who, by the traditional definition, isn't mine.

Because that's so *fucking* wrong.

There. I cussed it.

How can Ryker not be mine when he owns my whole heart? His toothy smiles fill me with pride. His eyes shining with tears bring me to my knees.

His every accomplishment has me beaming like the North Star. He might not have my DNA, but yes, he's mine in every other way that counts.

"You're missing out on all the fun, little fairy," Maddox taunts me. I pull my coat tighter around me as I watch on from the edge of the porch.

Father and son, side by side in a thick layer of fluffy snow, are sprawled on their backs. Their arms sweep in a wide arch, Ryker's just a smidge slower than Maddox's, while their legs fork apart, then back together. Big, white flurries continue to fall from the sky, settling over them. Cheeks rosy from the biting cold, labored breaths clouding above them, and matching wide smiles—what a sight they make.

My heart is so full of love for both of them, I feel as if I'm bursting at the seams.

"I'm fine right here," I laugh. "It's a big no thanks to snow down the collar of my coat. There's hot chocolate waiting for you when you're done trying to become the next *Jack Frost*."

"Oh little fairy, I'll grow a big carrot just for you."

Looking at the man sprawled out in the snow at my feet as he drinks me in like I'm god's gift on earth, handpicked just for him, I know I'm staring at forever right in his icy-blue eyes. Gone is the heartbreaker of Lost Hope. In his place is now the man who owns my heart, treasuring it like a dragon treasures its hoard.

We've stopped hoping. In the land of certainty, there's no space for hope. I choose to leave the anonymity of being a wallflower behind me and blossom as I take Maddox's hand. He chooses to be my wall instead—hiding me when I need to, supporting me upright when I can't stand on my own. Every single day.

My happily ever after might not look like in the faded scribblings wished upon paper by a shy teenager. I wished for wallflowers and a mellow partner to hide with in dark corners to avoid attention. What I got is the asshole, dragging me into the darkest corner. Not to hide, but to prove to me eternally how much of a wildflower I really am.

Epilogue

NEW YEAR'S EVE

My palms are sweaty. My knee is bouncing in place. The anxiety is overwhelming. I gulp and fidget with my bow tie as Sawyer sashays her way through the crowd. She's a vision in silver. Light catches onto whatever magic is sewn into her gown, making the fabric glimmer. One blink, it sparkles silver. Next, it matches the exact color of my eyes. A strange sort of calm descends over me, the kind only her presence brings. I'm so fucking gone for her, I don't even recognize myself.

And I wouldn't change it for the world.

I don't care much for who I used to be—a coward hiding behind his own ignorance and flippancy. Everything Sawyer touches, she makes better. And I'm the son of a bitch who lucked out in life. She makes me better every day.

She steps between my parted thighs, gripping the lapels of my midnight-blue tuxedo. I'm even wearing a vest for the occasion, for fuck's sake.

"Whatcha doin' brooding in dark corners?" she teases, her plump red lips spreading into a blinding smile.

I can't help it. I chase her mouth and nibble at her bottom lip. She's sugary sweet with a hint of ripe pear, and I want more. So much more. My hands find purchase on her hips as I pull her closer to me.

"I'm not brooding. I'm nervous," I confess.

Her fathomless dark blue eyes lose their sparkle, worry clouding them over instead. "Why are you nervous? Did something happen to Ryker? Is he missing us? Cause we can go if he is. We'll ring the New Year with him."

I chuckle against her mouth. "He's probably fast asleep by now, little fairy."

"What's the problem, then?" she asks, smoothing her hands over my chest.

Rising to my feet, I still hold on to her hips. My eyes close as I draw in a deep sigh. My mind blanks.

I debated having Ryker here with us, but I wanted to be selfish for a change. He had his turn at Christmas, asking her to be his mommy. For a man with deep trust issues, I've proven my trust in her as she ripped through the ink-colored wrapping hiding the adoption papers. Sawyer has my trust with my son. She has it with my heart, too.

I had a plan. A well-thought-out plan, with a grand gesture and over the top romance, like in those books she likes to read. The New Year's Eve party at JC's Pour felt like the best occasion. We'd be surrounded by friends and family, and I'd show my cards in front of everyone. No more hiding of any kind.

But now that she's standing in front of me, looking so beautiful it makes my chest ache, and smiling up at me like I'm her favorite person, I don't want an audience. Our moment feels too intimate, too precious to share.

So hiding in a dark corner, knowing she'll find me anywhere, is a sound compromise.

I take a step away from her and sway on my feet as black spots fill my vision. Eagles swarm in my stomach as my hands cover hers entirely. I lift them to my mouth and kiss each knuckle in turn. Sawyer tilts her head and regards me quietly, a befuddled expression on her face.

She gave me her forgiveness five blissful weeks ago, but I'll never stop groveling. It's why, instead of lowering to one knee as is customary, both of mine touch the floor as I kneel in front of her.

"Holy ink, what are you doing?" she gasps. "Get up, you silly man."

She pulls at my hand, but I hold steadily. It's make or break time. "Little fairy, you've changed my whole life. I don't know what I did to ever deserve you, but somewhere out there, the stars aligned and pushed you right into my arms. I was a man without a reason until you unwittingly cast your spell on me and had this fool fall head over heels for you. I made mistakes." My throat grows dry as my eyes well. "In all truthfulness, I'll probably continue to make mistakes."

Sawyer gives me a watery laugh that eases some of the tension swirling in my stomach. "I plan to train you." I smile like the infatuated loon I am in response.

"I took from you more than I ever gave. And now, I'm asking you to do me the honor of taking once more, forever." My eyes seek hers as I'm drawing in the calm she always brings me. "Sawyer, you're the love of my life. I beg of you, please let me wake up next to you for the rest of our lives. Please, let me fall asleep wrapped up in you for as long as we shall both live.

Please, let me be your rock as you are my tranquillity in a storm." I slick my tongue over my bottom lip as I draw in a deep breath. "Sawyer, will you marry me?"

She's as still as a statue for what feels like eternity. The noises of the party quieten. My vision tunnels, the ethereal woman in front of me my sole focus. Everyone and everything else disappears from view as I wait with bated breath for her to put me out of my misery.

"I love you, you silly obstinate man. YES! Yes, I'll marry you," she shouts as her eyes well. Pretty sure tears are pouring down my cheeks as relief barrels through me with the force of a tsunami. She launches herself into my arms, peppering my face with kisses, whispering a disbelieving yes between each of them. I chase her lips and slant my mouth over hers, kissing her hard and fast. My tongue laps at her bottom lip, begging for permission. Permission to taste my fiancée for the first time.

I moan wantonly as her lips part, granting me access. She meets me half-way as I slowly slip my tongue into her mouth, savoring her sweetness, knowing she's mine forever. A needy whimper reaches my ears as I cup her soft cheek and deepen our kiss. There are no more barriers between the two of us, no more secrets. "Maddox, I need you," she cries out as I stroke a taut nipple through the silky fabric of her dress.

Slowing our kiss, I nip at her bottom lip when she mewls in protest. I push to my feet and help her up, swaying when our bubble bursts and the noises of the party explode all around out. "I'll take you home," I rasp hoarsely.

Sawyer blinks up at me with wide eyes, pupils blown-out with lust. "I need you now."

I thrust my hips against her lower belly. She moans softly through her swollen pretty lips when she feels just what she does to me exactly. "We're not making love for the first time in months in Jackson's bar."

Her fingers claw at the lapels of my jacket as a wicked glint flashes in her eyes. "How about the parking lot?"

I chuckle ruefully as I shake my head. "It's freezing outside, little fairy. I'm not going to risk you getting frostbite."

"I guess it's a good thing you got heated seats, Mr. Lawson. Now stop protesting and fuck your fiancée in that monster truck of yours."

If she continues talking like this, our friends and family might get a bit more from the New Year than they bargained for. As it is, I bend my knees and attack, carrying her over my shoulders. My steps are hurried as I exit through a side door and beeline to my car, her giggles echoing behind us in the darkness of the night.

I throw the door to my truck open and slowly slide Sawyer down my body. Our labored breaths condense in front of us, but I don't feel the cold. My body is a furnace, ready to burn through the clothes separating me from her. I climb in the passenger seat, pushing it as far back as it goes as I lower the backrest, then grab Sawyer around her waist and settle her on my lap. The door slams shut, sealing us in the close confines, away from the rest of the world.

"Do your worst, little fairy," I rasp as she straddles my thighs, her silky dress bunching up around her waist. My eyes snag on the flimsiest triangle of white lace, barely covering her pussy. I groan low in my throat. "That's what you've been wearing all night?"

"Will you cry if I tell you my dress has a built-in bra?" she taunts as she slowly rocks her hips.

The friction caused by her movements and the image of her tits bouncing freely has me so hard, I'm in actual pain. "Put me out of my misery, baby," I beg.

For all the urgency in her eyes when she had me race to the car, she takes her sweet time now, the little vixen. Her fingers wrap around the buttons of my vest, undoing them one by one as she swivels her hips seductively over my lap. The need I have for her overpasses the remaining shred of common sense I possess. My hands find her thighs, pushing up her dress until I see exactly how small and sheer her underwear is.

I press my thumb against the little bundle of nerves, hidden by white lace, and she moans low in her throat. I circle the hardened bud, and her hips speed up in return. "Fuck, I love how responsive you are to me. Be a good girl, little fairy, and take what you want. Let me fill you up, baby, until you're so full of me, you'll walk around that goddamn party leaking my cum down your thighs."

Her fingers attack my buckle, ripping the belt out of the lops and tossing it on the backseat. The button of my trousers is shown no mercy as Sawyer tears into it. I thank my lucky stars when she shows infinite gentleness to the zipper as she lowers it slowly over my straining cock.

My thumb rubs faster circles over her clit, her breathy moans and timid flutters against my skin letting me know she's close. Wetness gushes over my fingers as she palms my length through the fabric of my boxers, giving it a rough stroke. She shoves the waistband down only enough for my cock to spring free. Her enthusiasm falters as her fingers feather over the underside, making me groan in response.

"What if it'll hurt?" she whispers, her voice full of uncertainty.

I cup her nape and pull her down to me, meeting her lips with my hungry ones, kissing the doubt out of her. Brushing her underwear aside, I moan as my fingers make direct contact with her silken flesh. She's so wet for me, so swollen and warm. "I've got you," I promise. "You'll take me nice and slow, one inch at the time, until you're so full of me you struggle for breath." I lick at her lips, swallowing down her whimpers as I slide my middle finger inside of her tight little pussy. She clamps down on me, her quivering walls pulsing around my finger as I pump it slowly in and out of her. "That's it, baby. Relax for me. It's just you and me. Always. Forever." I flick her clit with my thumb as I slide in a second finger, scissoring them, stretching her out.

"I'm so close," Sawyer moans, and I thrust my tongue between her plump lips as I finger-fuck her to completion.

The heat inside of her grows, threatening to incinerate me. She bounces on my lap, my eyes glued to the magical place between her legs where my fingers are disappearing to. "Come for me, little fairy. Come for your fiancé for the first time," I grit as my cock throbs in time with the flutters of her pussy.

Sawyer throws her head back as wetness floods my palm. Her whole body seizes as she comes with my name on her lips. I stroke her gently as her orgasm tears through her, prolonging her pleasure. As much as I'm dying to feel her wrapped around my cock, I need her relaxed and ready. I'd rather take my own life than hurt this woman ever again.

She'll only know love and safety with me. Complete adoration and absolute devotion, that's what she deserves and that's what she gets.

Her eyes flutter open as she gives me a blissed-out smile. "You look mighty neglected over there."

"Then you better do something about it, little fairy." I pat her still quivering pussy as I gently remove my fingers. They're glistening in the dim lights of the parking lot, and my mouth waters. I make a show of licking them clean, watching as Sawyer's eyes cloud over with desire.

I push up on my forearms, cursing the tight space in the cab as I hit the door with my elbow. Blindly, I pat around until I find the central armrest and flip the cover open. My fingers wrap around the little bottle of water-based lube, and I pass it over to Sawyer.

"Drown my cock in this," I order.

She gives me a timid smile, but does as I ask, unscrewing the lid and pouring a generous amount into her palm. The thin, silky gel feels icy against my feverish cock as she spreads it in slow strokes up and down my shaft.

"We can try different ones," I whisper roughly as sparks of pleasure explode at the base of my spine. "We'll try them all until we find the perfect one for us."

Sawyer splays her free hand over my chest, pushing me down against the backrest. "Thank you," she murmurs against my lips as she twists her hand around the head of my cock, making me see stars.

"You never have to thank me for taking care of you." I grunt as she notches my cock at her tight entrance, rolling her hips seductively until only the very tip of me slips in. "You're *my fiancée*. It's my privilege and my right."

I grip her hips, helping her balance in the tight space. Gently, she works herself up and down my cock, taking me in another inch. She mewls as I stroke her clit with tender caresses.

"Your privilege and your right is to fuck me now," Sawyer declares, easing down on my shaft, taking more of me with each swivel of her hips until she's fully seated. We still for a breath as she adjusts to having me once again inside of her. *Finally complete.* I grit my teeth so I don't come in the next second as her tight heat envelops me whole, making me lose my goddamn mind.

She's too tight. Too warm. Too silken. Too fucking perfect for an asshole like me.

"That's it, my little slutty fairy. Take your fiancé's cock for the very first time. Weave your goddamn spell on me."

I tilt my head as I kiss her lips, coaxing her to relax with each stroke of my tongue. She softens in my arms, her hips rocking slowly. I thrust up on instinct, slowly, gently, shallowly, the desire too fervent to be contained.

Sawyer grips my jaw, her eyes, as dark as midnight, boring into mine. All her dreams, hopes, and fears let loose between the two of us. I show her all my love, my incurable obsession with her. She owns me. Heart, mind, body, and soul.

Her tight walls ripple around me, and I just about come. "I'm the luckiest son of a bitch. Getting all your firsts. *I'm* your one and only." She nips playfully at my bottom lip, her breathing choppy and wanton.

My hands shift to her plump ass, my fingers tightening on the round, soft globes. Up and down, up and down, I help her move on my cock. My stomach tenses under the fire chasing at my veins, begging for relief. My balls draw up, aching for a release they've been long denied.

"You fuck me so good, baby," I murmur against her lips. "Look how well you take me. Fuck, I missed your pussy strangling my cock. You bring me the best kind of pain."

Sawyer braces her arm beside my head, fucking me in earnest. There's no more hesitancy to her movements as she bounces on my cock with dizzying speed. She's hungry. She's relentless. She's my goddamn wet dream made into reality. The car shakes. The dark-tinted windows are all fogged up. Anyone coming outside would know exactly what we're up to.

I don't care.

All I know is the woman above me is fucking the life out of me, all while conquering another one of her demons. And I'm here for it.

"God, Maddox. I feel you everywhere. I'm so close, I need more." She arches her back, pushing her tits right in my face. I nuzzle them, biting and sucking at her tight nipples through the soft material of her dress. "Yes!" she screams as she tightens around me. "Make me come, fiancé. Fuck me, pretty boy!"

I grip her ass, spreading her cheeks as I thrust up into her. She meets me halfway, raising on her knees and dropping down on my cock. There's no semblance of control left between us. We're fucking like rabid animals as the truck groans in harmony with my grunts and her mewled cries. I circle my hips and ground against her fluttering pussy, rubbing my pelvic bone against her clit. She explodes around me with the rawest of screams as her quivering walls clamp down on me so hard, she's choking my cock and cutting off blood supply.

I've reached the end of me inside of her as she moans our beginning at the cusp between the old and the new year.

My back arches as I rut into her, my release barreling over me as I spill into her months of pain and pent-up frustration, all my fears and worries, and most of all, all my love.

She slumps against my chest, breath heaving as my cock still twitches with the aftershocks of my orgasm and the frenzied flutters of her walls. I stroke the small of her back as I whisper incoherent nonsense in her ear.

"You're wrong, you know?" she murmurs, tracing indecipherable patterns with her fingertips across my chest. I hum in response, waiting for her to continue. "You give me more than you realize. Courage, confidence, a pep in my step, a steadfast belief that I am worthy to be seen. With you, I never feel the need to hide away." She tilts her head back, pressing a kiss to the underside of my chin. "You make me feel like I matter. Even when you were running away from me, I was never overlooked."

I shove my hand into the pocket of my jacket, thumbing open the velvet box hidden in there. I poise the ring above her finger, sliding it down over her knuckles, until it settles in place where it belongs. Gripping her hand, I kiss the princess cut diamond, tracing the delicate engraving of a feather quill in the golden band with my lips.

"I have another confession to make," I say as I unbutton my shirt, just enough so she can see the still angry skin and fresh ink resting over my heart.

All we've hoped becomes our forever;
Tomorrow.

Sawyer Lawson

Sawyer smooths her palms over the skirt of her dress. "Okay, how do I look?"

A devilish smirk tugs at my lips. "Freshly fucked. Ravishing like always."

She stomps her heeled foot, her arms braced on her hips. "Which one is it, Maddox?"

I step into her, kissing the corners of her mouth. "Both, little fairy. But you'll hear no complaints from me. That's *my* ring on your finger. Can't blame me for being proud as fuck of how we've celebrated our newly minted engagement."

She rolls her pretty eyes as she flips her hair over her shoulder. "At least I'm not the creep who breaks into people's homes, reading their private poetry, then tattooing it over their chest," she throws back as she pushes through the door of the bar.

Loud music blares as people mill around, some dancing, some huddled up in groups talking animatedly. I wrap my fingers around Sawyer's wrist and spin her until she collapses against me. I grin as I see the fire brewing in her eyes. "But you're the one engaged to that creep, little fairy. No takesies-backsies." I sway with her, my free hand low on her back as I move my hips, following the beat pulsing through the walls. I trace her jawline with my nose, nipping at her earlobe as I whisper, "And it just so happens, the creep is head over heels in love with you."

She scrunches her nose adorably but presses her red lips to mine. "The creep's lucky I love him right back."

The music cuts off abruptly as Violet climbs onto a table and claps loudly. "All right, folks. It's nearly time," she shouts. "TEN! NINE! EIGHT..."

All heads turn toward the bar when a loud crash sounds from that direction. I'm just in time to see Jackson sprawled across the bar top, his palm held against his face, a dozen broken bottles around him. Blake looms over Jake, cradling his fist to his chest, his hair in complete disarray as he rips the bow tie from around his neck.

"YOU SON OF A BITCH! YOU MARRIED EMMA? THAT'S HOW MUCH YOU HATE ME?!"

Curious about what happens next in Lost Hope?

Find out in book four, *Lux Solis, Fumus, et Specula*,

Blake, Jackson, and Emma's story.

Coming soon

Thank you for reading *Atramentum et Telum Pulvis*.
If you enjoyed Sawyer's and Maddox's story,
please consider leaving a review.
Reviews are a great way of showing other readers the book is worth picking
up and a huge help for indie authors like me.

Acknowledgements

To no one's surprise, Maddox is a reformed asshole, so of course his book had to be an asshole to me. I wrote about forty percent of this book in a whopping two weeks. And then nada. No words for Alina, no words for anything. Which is even more frustrating, considering Maddox was YAPPING into my head since January. I honestly felt like I was a two-book wonder and buh-bye.

A whole lot of changes in a short period of time and a surprise shower-idea book that turned me into a three-book wonder later, the asshole of Lost Hope started talking to me again. Apparently, the infuriating dude had to put himself in a timeout. And because misery loves company, he forced me into a timeout, too. But look at him all redeemed and not such a bad-boy anymore. Huh. Who would've thought?

As it always happens in Lost Hope, chosen family sticks together and grows together. Maddox surprised me a lot. But Sawyer surprised me even more. She took my love of poetry, fountain pens, and ink-stained fingers and burrowed so deeply into my heart. I love all my FMCs, but when I plotted the book, Sawyer was the most-different-than-me FMC. I felt like maybe... if we'd met in real life, we'd never be friends. But boy am I wrong. I love Sawyer to bits, and all I want to do is cheer her on while hiding her away to protect that beautiful soul of hers.

One thing other thing Sawyer and I have in common is a solid chosen family. Waving energetically to mine:

The biggest thank you goes to my Mr. Right. I sometimes look at you and can't believe you're mine. And other times I look at you and genuinely wonder how you're still alive, because, SIR, the audacity is strong in you. But mostly, I can't believe you're still here, every day, putting up with me and my book-dramas, listening intently and NOT laughing in my face whenever a book makes me cry, even though you couldn't care less about books in general. Thank you for your support, all the coffees you've made, all the mornings you woke up to find me still awake and writing and not kicking me out of bed, and all the chocolates to keep me sane and going. **PS: You're still doing the dishes. I'm starting a duet and book four.**

Siiri, thank you for the absolutely incredible cover you've created for the first edition of AeTP. You took the essence of Maddox and Sawyer and made them shine. I am beyond thankful and grateful to you, my dearest friend and the best cover designer.

Bella and Jayme, thank you for always being in my corner, cheering me on and kicking my bottom as required. I couldn't have asked for better book besties and support system. You guys are amazing.

Claudia, Abby, and Ashley, thank you for being the best Alpha and Beta readers this writing-cave-woman could have. Your support and advice mean the world to me. You are incredible women, and I am in awe of you.

Laura and In Somnis Publishing, thank you for your support and amazing proofreading and advice. I'm beyond excited about all our future collaborations.

A special thank you goes to my editor Annie, my lovely, you are incredible. I'm in awe of you, your work, and your growth. I'm beyond proud and thankful to know you and to work with you. Thank you for all your work and support in making AeTP the beautiful love story that it is and making Maddox and Sawyer shine.

The biggest thank you goes to my readers. Thank you for continuing to take a chance on my dream with every page you read. I am overwhelmed in all the best ways for all the love and support I've received so far. It goes beyond my wildest dreams. And it's all thanks to you. You fuel me, give me hope, and keep alive this dream of mine that just one year ago seemed so far-fetched. I hope you found little pieces of yourselves in Vanilla et Motricium Oleum, and I hope I've done all of them justice. All my love <3

For the smallest contribution in the grand scheme of things, I need to mention coffee again. Thanks for keeping me awake. I literally couldn't have done it without you. The new coffee machine I've convinced Mr. Right I couldn't live without hits just the right spot.

Lost Hope Series
(small town, contemporary romance)

Lege et Lacrima - Lalah & Cole
Vanilla et Motricium Oleum - Tatum & Maevis
Atramentum et Telum Pulvis - Maddox & Sawyer

To Have and To Hold - a dark romance standalone

For the most up to date list of released books, please visit
my website www.alinacomsaauthor.com

About the author

Alina Comsa is Transylvanian, and her little vampire soul now lives in the UK with her partner, dodging like a pro her turn to do the dishes—and that pesky little star called the Sun. She dabbles in quality assurance by day, writing and reading by night, and lives with little to no sleep.

In high school Alina was voted most likely to... become a lawyer. What a letdown, right? She aced those creative writing tests, though, worry not. Because she's an overachiever, she was also voted most likely to become a journalist. So far, high school votes have been zero out of two.

Eternally exhausted, she believes that "life was meant for reading" and coffees. Loads, and loads of coffee.

She loves everything romance, but has a slight obsession with shifters. They'll win her heart every single time.

If you'd like to poke the vampire and find out more about other novels she's currently writing, please join her private book cave here:

AC's Book Cave

Since procrastination is an effective punishment tool when her characters misbehave, if she's not waiting for a latte to be delivered, she can (sometimes) be found here:

Facebook - Alina Comsa Author

Instagram - @alinacomsaauthor

TikTok – Alina Comsa Author

Sign up to her newsletter here for bonus scenes, character art, and other surprises.

She promises to be on her best behaviour, whatever that means.

For news of upcoming books, trigger warnings, and events, please visit www.alinacomsaauthor.com

www.ingramcontent.com/pod-product-compliance
Lightning Source LLC
Chambersburg PA
CBHW020347220726

48290CB00014B/1303